THE
the Jo

MORTAL FIRE

C. F. Dunn

MONARCH
BOOKS

Oxford, UK & Grand Rapids, Michigan, USA

First published in the UK in 2012 by Monarch Books
(a publishing imprint of Lion Hudson plc)
Wilkinson House, Jordan Hill Road, Oxford OX2 8DR, England
Tel: +44 (0)1865 302750 Fax: +44 (0)1865 302757
Email: monarch@lionhudson.com
www.lionhudson.com

ISBN 978 0 85721 202 3 (print)
ISBN 978 0 85721 313 6 (Kindle)
ISBN 978 0 85721 314 3 (epub)
ISBN 978 0 85721 315 0 (PDF)

Distributed by:
UK: Marston Book Services, PO Box 269, Abingdon, Oxon, OX14 4YN
USA: Kregel Publications, PO Box 2607, Grand Rapids, Michigan 49501

The text paper used in this book has been made from wood independently certified as having come from sustainable forests.

British Library Cataloguing Data
A catalogue record for this book is available from the British Library.

Printed and bound in the UK by MPG Books

For Cinders and my family,
without whom…

Truth is what we make it. We believe what we want to believe, see what we want to see; but when reality is thrust upon us, we are faced with the ultimate dilemma: to acknowledge it – or to run.

Contents

Acknowledgments

Loving thanks to my parents for their unswerving encouragement, and unbounded enthusiasm for punctuation and a good story. For my patient readers – especially Dee Prewer, for honing her editorial skills on my nascent writing, and her delicate candour, which kept me on a literary straight-and-narrow. For Lisa Lewin, who could see the wood for the trees, and Kate who saw them with me in Maine. For Sophie, who kept the home fires burning, and Tim, my erstwhile guide to the Web.

Also in the UK, Chris Pringle of Spencer Thorn Bookshop, Bude, whose support led to a meeting of ways worthy of its own story. Huge thanks to Tony Collins, editor at Monarch, for his patience, guidance and leap of faith in taking on a complete unknown. For author Pen Wilcock, and her twin attributes of keen insight and encouraging voice. For Jenny Ward, also at Monarch, for seeing the process through, and for Swati Gamble, who helped get me started. I also owe much to Mike Chew and MaryAnn Good for their connections and help in Stamford, and to Sherry Kenyon for authenticating detail with such zest.

Special thanks to author Colin Dexter, for his generous gift of time, experience, and wisdom, and to writers Fay Sampson, Taylor Holden, and Mel Starr for taking time out of their busy schedules to endorse this book. Gratitude also, to Dr Kiki O'Neill-Byrne, Consultant Psychiatrist, for her advice on psychopathic disorder, and to numerous people for information along the way.

In the USA, my thanks to Noelle Pederson at Kregel. In Maine, to innkeeper and chef, Keith A. Neubert – our host at the Inn at Long Lake, Naples – and his staff, whose hospitality, delectable Hermit Bars and apple cider kept us warm in a glorious New

England fall. To Norm Forgey, Maine Day Trip, for expanding our horizons up to Rumford in comfort, for his information on black bears and dead skunks (but alas, no moose), and to all who made our stay a home from home.

My appreciation to Warner Bros for *The Last Samurai*, and Hans Zimmer for his soundtrack, that supplied the rhythms behind many of my scenes.

And above all to my husband, Richard, whose unstinting forbearance and military technical advice I plundered at will, and our daughters, who have lived the writing of this book with me every step of the way.

Characters

ACADEMIC & RESEARCH STAFF AT HOWARD'S LAKE COLLEGE, MAINE

Emma D'Eresby, Department of History (Medieval and Early Modern)

Elena Smalova, Department of History (Post-Revolutionary Soviet Society)

Matias Lidström, Faculty of Bio-medicine (Genetics)

Matthew Lynes, surgeon, Faculty of Bio-medicine (Mutagenesis)

Sam Wiesner, Department of Mathematics (Metamathematics)

Madge Makepeace, Faculty of Social Sciences (Anthropology)

Siggie Gerhard, Faculty of Social Sciences (Psychology)

Saul Abrahms, Faculty of Social Sciences (Psychology of Functional Governance)

Colin Eckhart, Department of History (Renaissance and Reformation Art)

Kort Staahl, Department of English (Early Modern Literature)

Megan, research assistant, Bio-medicine

Sung, research assistant, Bio-medicine

The Dean, Stephen Shotter

MA STUDENTS

Holly Stanhope; Josh Feitel; Hannah Graham; Aydin Yilmaz; Leo Hamell

IN CAMBRIDGE

Guy Hilliard, Emma's former tutor

Tom Falconer, Emma's friend

EMMA'S FAMILY

Hugh D'Eresby, her father
Penny D'Eresby, her mother
Beth Marshall, her sister
Rob Marshall, her brother-in-law
Alex & Flora, her twin nephew and niece
Nanna, her grandmother

Mike Taylor, friend of the family

MATTHEW'S FAMILY

Harry Lynes, his nephew
Ellie Lynes, his niece

Chapter I

Of Magic and Monsters

IT MUST HAVE HAPPENED only minutes before.

The startled birds still circling above the tree from which they had risen were the only witnesses to the last moments of the woman's life. The impact tore the door from her car and from the twisted remains her eyes stared sightless, lifeless. Shredded shards of metal pierced the airbag – now a pale deflated bladder onto which her slow blood dripped.

A single uniformed officer bent over and picked up a small card from the edge of a wheel rut already filling with water. He flicked it on his finger, dislodging muddy drops from its plastic surface. He looked up at the sound of the engine and raised his hand.

"Hey, Frank!" My cab driver called to the officer from his rolled-down window as he slowed just yards from the scene. "What's up?"

The policeman ambled towards us. "Hi, Al," he greeted him. "She must've skidded on all this mud hereabouts. Reckon she was using her cell at the time. Lost control."

He toed a shiny black mobile, its blue-lit face more alive than she would ever be. The cab driver grunted morosely.

"Darn technological revolution. Where's she from?"

The officer flipped the card again, then wiped his thumb over the stubborn mud-smeared surface, straining at the tiny print.

"San Diego. She's a long way from home."

He stared at the photo, then at the dead woman, canting his head to get a better look. "Sure is a shame, hey, Al? Bit of a looker too. What a waste."

"Huh, she's from away! Wouldn't you know it; darn foreigner wouldn't be used to our roads." Al sniffed, prepared to hawk out of the window, thought better of it. His eyes slid towards mine in the rear-view mirror. "Not that I got anything 'gainst foreigners, you know?"

"San *Diego*, Al, not San Salvador."

"Yeah – might as well be – she ain't a Mainer, anyhow."

A second car drew up behind the police vehicle, reflecting brief sun and blinding me momentarily as the driver's door opened. Squinting, Frank looked over his shoulder and, seemingly satisfied this newcomer was no random rubbernecker, nodded to the stranger once, then resumed his conversation.

"Where're you off to?"

Al shifted the gear and the car's engine made ready-to-go noises. I urged him silently to leave; the image of the mutilated wreckage lingered, sickened. A figure now bent into the shadowed interior; the wreck slid a fraction.

"I'm taking this lady to Howard's Lake. I'd better be goin'; I've got another fare to pick up at eleven."

The officer let out a low whistle.

"That college place, huh?" He leaned down and shaded his eyes against the light, peering into the back of the cab where I sat. He acknowledged me then looked back at his friend. "You take care on them roads, Al; the bridge is almost under water this side of town." He jerked his thumb over his shoulder. "Don't want to end up like her." He gave me another curious glance as if I had grown two heads in the intervening seconds since he last looked, and patted the roof of the cab.

Distracted by movement, my focus shifted. In the shroud of the car, the man carefully rested the body of the woman against her seat; gently – almost reverently – folding the fabric of her torn skirt over her legs and closing her eyes. As if he cared; as if she mattered. The car suddenly shifted, jerked, metal razoring his bare arm. Before I could react, the man pulled his arm free, shot a look in our direction, and turned his back. But it wasn't the expression on his face as he turned away, nor the almost casual disregard as he covered his arm with his jacket, but my sudden shock of recognition as the sun struck his hair that left me speechless.

As the cab pulled away, leaving the officer to collect the scattered contents of the woman's life, I wondered in a passing thought at the deceptions conjured from a distant past and liberated by an exhausted mind.

Barely an hour before, an expansive sweep of blue sky gave way to thickening cloud as the aircraft made its descent towards rain-blackened tarmac, finally coming to a standstill under a leaden sky. Not so very different from home, really. The slight pang twisting in my throat instantly reminded me that home lay far behind on another continent and that I could still be vulnerable to a bout of homesickness despite the years spent away. I caught sight of my ghosted reflection in the thickened glass of the aircraft's window, then looked beyond to where airport buildings hunched together against the sky. Any regret at this year-long commitment dissolved in a feathering of anticipation; my life in England represented the old world – this was definitely the new.

The cab driver had thrown a question over his shoulder.

"I'm sorry, could you repeat that, please?"

He grinned in the rear-view mirror at me, a man with a crumpled face and rabbit teeth, then repeated it slowly – idiot-fashion.

"You British?"

"Is it that obvious?" I smiled back at his eyes framed in the mirror. He shrugged what I took to be a *yes*, then continued.

"You a student?"

Either that meant I looked particularly scruffy after the long flight, or he was a poor judge of age.

"I wish! Not for a long time. How far is it to the college now?"

He thought for a moment.

"'Bout fifteen miles to town. Then another eleven to Howard's Lake. Won't be long – 'haps..." he screwed his eyes, calculating,

"… thirty-five, forty minutes."

He frowned at an oncoming car as it veered towards us in the centre of the road, muttering under his breath something I wasn't probably meant to hear. I pretended not to notice and looked out of my window at the road gently curving around the edge of a large outcrop of rock, sparsely lined with thin birches, their leaves yellowing against the patchy September sky. The taxi came out of the long curve and the vista suddenly widened. The road ahead traced a line that intermittently disappeared between heavily wooded foothills towards a queue of mountains, some shrouded in cloud, some barefaced except for the darker shadows of trees. I craned forward over the front seat to get a better look.

"Town's 'bout thirty miles from them." The driver nodded in the direction of the range. "Snow'll be covering 'em soon as maybe – last 'til spring. Good hunting, too. A man can lose himself up there…" he trailed off.

"What sort of hunting?" I prompted.

"Most sorts – bear, deer. Got wolves too."

"They're hunted? Are you allowed to?"

I sounded like a conservationist. Not that I had anything against conservationists, but I didn't want to be summed up in a cliché.

"*Su*-re, you have to have a permit." I felt him peering at me in the mirror again. "You one of them anti-gun lobbyists, or something?"

"We don't really have an anti-gun lobby in Britain," I dodged. "So, what other wildlife is there?"

I sat back and leaned my head against the rear head-rest and let him talk about the eagles as jet lag finally set in and I drifted towards sleep.

Framed by a wreath of blonde hair, the woman's eyes stared back at me from the coffin of her car, longing for life. Her extended hand stretched towards mine, her once living colours fading to grey before evaporating like a wisp of smoke in the wind. There had been no time to say goodbye.

At the changing note of the engine, I woke with a start, scrubbing sleep and the lingering image from my eyes, shaken as much by the fact I dreamt at all as by the contents of the dream. Seeing me wake, Al grunted, "This is it," and I craned forward to look. Extravagant wrought-iron gates heralding the threshold of the campus, lay open like arms.

The long drive wove through parkland until – sitting on a broad knoll by a placid lake – the old college appeared. The house might have been built for a nineteenth-century industrialist in any county back home, with its façade of rich burgundy bricks with bacon-stripes of pale yellow, and gleaming eyes of arched windows. Turreted and bespectacled with ivy, it alluded to a variety of styles and in doing so, had none. But looks can be deceiving – as I had once found to my cost.

The cab drew up before the classic columned portico and the taxi driver climbed out while I delved into my handbag to find the letter of introduction with instructions on where to go and whom to see, surprised to find my hands shaking a little. I hadn't been so nervous in a long time, but then this lay beyond my comfort zone in unfamiliar territory where all but the weather seemed new to me. He pulled my two pieces of luggage from the boot and left them on the wide, white steps leading to the entrance and, once I had pressed the unfamiliar currency into his hand, he left me there.

As the car disappeared down the drive, the stillness – the absolute quiet – came as a shock after the persistent hum of the engine. No birdsong carved the air, no wind stirred the tired leaves, and a light rain fell silently against the sodden ground. The creeping doubt returned along with the hollow twisting in my throat, reminiscent of my first day at another university a long time ago. I pushed away the dread, putting it firmly in its place, and slammed the lid shut before it could escape again. I was here out of choice – an opportunity I couldn't afford to miss – my chance of a lifetime. Before I lost my wafer-thin resolve, I took a deep breath, grabbed my bags firmly to prevent my hands from trembling and walked through the doors.

The entrance hall took me by surprise. Far from being as

portentous as the sombre, discordant exterior suggested, the low coffered ceiling of the porch gave way to a room filled with light from a huge glass dome that rose above the inlaid marble floor – an atrium in the Neo-Classical style. Sort of. Diffused by the clouded sky, the light gleamed quietly on the polished wooden surfaces of the panelling around the room, and the faint scent of beeswax hung in the air. I stepped into the pool of light illuminating the intricate stonework of the floor – a Cosmology – the known world replicated beneath my feet; the whole world summed up in complex patterns of blue and green and gold.

"Professor D'Eresby?"

I looked up. A woman in her early twenties, with dark eyes and the healthy glow of youth, stood by a reception desk. Her straight brown hair, drawn into a high ponytail, swung buoyantly as she stepped towards me.

"Professor D'Eresby?" she asked more hesitatingly, carefully pronouncing my unfamiliar name.

"Yes – I'm Emma D'Eresby."

The girl looked relieved and her smile broadened in welcome, showing perfectly even teeth, brilliantly white against her tan. She made me feel pale just looking at her.

"We have been expecting you, ma'am. Did you have a good trip?"

I returned her smile. "Thank you, yes. It's very kind of you to meet me"

She beamed. "Professor Shotter – the Dean – thought you might like someone from the history faculty to meet you; I volunteered. I'm Holly Stanhope – I'm a post-grad and you're my tutor." She smiled shyly. Every sentence ended on a rising note like a question. I remembered her name from the list I received before I left home.

"Hi, Holly – that was brave of you." She looked blankly at me. "To volunteer, I mean."

"Oh!" Holly nodded enthusiastically, "I get it," and she laughed. Her attention switched as she looked at my luggage on the floor, frowning slightly.

"Did the porter get your bags already?"

"No, this is all I brought with me."

Her frown deepened; obviously visiting English academics were expected to arrive with a baggage train.

"I sent most of my books and things on in advance," I explained.

"Oh, sure," she nodded, but that wasn't the sort of luggage she meant, and I wondered if I would find myself short of clothes. "I'll show you your room, Professor."

I followed her, our footsteps echoing through the empty atrium towards the far end of the room where a large, modern glass door filled one of the series of high glassed arches that separated it from what lay beyond. Above them, carved into the stone and gilded so that each letter reflected the subtle light, a Latin inscription teased:

Res ipsa loquitur.

Holly heaved the huge door open with her shoulder and held it for me, forestalling my urge to try and puzzle out the caption.

The damp smell of old stone hit me as we entered an enclosed cloister, the familiar, haunting scent of old buildings everywhere, of the castles and abbeys, hall houses and churches with which I grew up. Ornate windows framed the view onto a large grassed area, surrounded on all sides by buildings and, from every arch, grotesque gargoyles spewed water into stone urns for as long as the rain fell.

Holly led me along the cloister, chattering animatedly as she described the history of the college. It had been conceived as the culmination of a rich man's desire to emulate and recreate all that he admired on his Grand Tour of Europe in the mid-nineteenth century. The bequest of the philanthropic owner led to the formation of a university college in the early part of the twentieth century, establishing a reputation for academic rigor that rivalled its much larger cousins. It felt steeped in its own history and would perhaps have been hidebound but for the addition of the new building enclosing the quadrangle with an altogether different structure. Conceptually brilliant, soft red sandstone enclosed extensive walls of glass. Holly noticed my evident admiration.

"That's the faculty of medicine. It has the med centre and the medical research facility. It's won awards," she added, with evident pride.

"I'm not surprised," I said with feeling; Holly glanced at me appreciatively and I smiled back at her and, even if we hadn't found the same wavelength yet, I felt that we were beginning to tune in.

I scanned the quad out of the cloister windows as we rounded the corner, looking for the reason I came here in the first place. No building within view matched the description I had been given.

"Where's the new library, Holly?"

"The library's beyond the med fac, that way," Holly nodded towards it. "It's awesome; it's got an amazing collection of historic manuscripts and texts. That's what I'm basing my research on." The upward cadence made her sound uncertain, as if she sought reassurance.

"*You and me both*," I thought. The opportunity to indulge my obsession, to follow my desire, lay in that library. Other women of my age were married, had children, at least a boyfriend – a *life*. History was my lover – where its strands of truth led, I followed as slavishly as a mistress.

"What's your area of research, Holly?"

We reached the end of the cloister and she hesitated with one hand on the stone newel of the stairs curving away towards the floor above.

"Yeah, uh – it's 'Religion and Reality in Early Modern Europe'." She cast a brief look at me to gauge my reaction.

"Ah," I said.

"I based it on your dissertation, Professor D'Eresby; it was my..." she struggled for a word, "... inspiration," she finished, reddening.

"Oh!"

I felt at once both flattered and embarrassed by the admiration in the girl's eyes; my students at Cambridge were less reverential and after all, barely six years separated Holly and me in age. I glanced away, seeking something appropriate to say in response.

"Thanks," I ventured lamely. She looked doubtful and I realized that my answer inspired little confidence. As she led the way up the stairs, I fought against the blunting influence of the long journey on my increasingly soggy brain to make more of an effort.

"What particular aspect did you find interesting?"

She looked pleased to be asked her opinion. We reached the second-floor landing and took a left turn down the long corridor to a smaller wooden staircase leading to what would have been the servants' quarters in the past. She shifted the bag she carried to the other hand before replying.

"I really liked your theory on the mystery plays – you know, where you said 'religion is the shadow of reality'. That's where I got my idea from, right?" She stopped outside one of the doors and beamed at me. Had I really said that? Even repeated with such sincerity by this girl, my own words sounded absurdly pompous now that my outlook on things had changed so completely. But that was then, and this was now, and she wouldn't know what I went through to get to this point in my life, so I just murmured, "I'm glad you found it useful," and changed the subject. "Is this my room?"

"Uh huh." Holly unlocked the door to the attic room with a key she fished out of her jeans pocket, holding it out for me and stepping to one side to let me through.

"I hope you like it," she said brightly. "It's not very big but it has the best views."

The view through the window to the mountain range was indeed spectacular and the room considerably bigger than my one in Cambridge.

"This is perfect, it reminds me of home, but the views are so much better – and it's so quiet." That reminded me – I'd hardly seen anyone since I arrived. "Where is everyone?"

She looked surprised. "They're in class; they don't get out yet."

Of course. I forgot that here term began weeks earlier than at home.

"The Dean said for me to show you where the dining room is if you would like some refreshment; or I could show you your tutor room – if you prefer."

I did prefer. The thought of meeting more people whose accents and humour I would have to negotiate with the single brain cell left to me was too much to contemplate at this stage of the day. Food could wait; too tired to eat anyway, the memory of the dead woman's face curbed what appetite I might have summoned.

I deposited my bags on the single bed in the tiny adjoining bedroom and poked my head around the door of the bathroom. With only a cramped shower in one corner and no natural light to brighten the drab tiles, it still contained everything I needed. I left the exploration of the little kitchenette until later.

Holly led me back to the side of the quad where the floors seemed to be divided into faculties, and up a set of stairs. History twinned with English, the long corridor divided by a communal meeting area with a few, low-slung seats upholstered in a coarse fabric the colour of beech leaves in spring. Open staff pigeon-holes, gaping like teeth, lined the back wall. Numbered tutorial rooms lay on either side of the corridor with my room halfway along on the left. The door already proclaimed my name and designation: "Visiting Professor". Holly needed to get back to class and I thanked her profusely and wondered vaguely, watching her ponytail swing as she disappeared down the corridor, what she would report to her fellow students about their new tutor.

Large enough for a modern desk with a half dozen chairs ranged in front of it, the room provided ample space for five students and my books. Two big windows let in plenty of light and an old-fashioned radiator belted out heat; but it was stuffy and felt as if it had been unoccupied for some time, with that musty smell that comes with layers of dust and a lack of fresh air and humanity. I threw open one of the windows and welcomed the clean scent of rain-washed grass and wet brick that accompanied the cool breeze.

Turning my back on the window, I then surveyed the rest of the room. Deep-set bookshelves lined the short wall behind the desk and on them were the boxes of books I sent in advance. I opened the box nearest to me and lifted the book from the top: *Monsters, Magic and the Mediaeval Mind*. I smiled fondly, oddly comforted by the familiar title. A sudden squeal followed by laughter from the quad below reminded me it must be nearly lunchtime. Weaving unsteadily across the wet grass in the rain, students made their way towards the atrium, a boy throwing handfuls of soggy leaves that a girl attempted to dodge. No change there, it seemed. I waited a few moments more until the flurry of student activity in the corridor outside my door subsided, then, tucking my book under my arm, shut the door behind me. The key jammed in the lock and the wretched thing wouldn't budge. I wriggled it in frustration and muttered at it under my breath.

"You have to turn it the *other* way."

I jumped, spinning around in embarrassed confusion, already beginning to apologize for my language, and a willowy dark-haired woman of about my age admonished the lock with mock severity and no malice. Her light, accented voice cut through my protestations.

"Americans," she tutted, her eyes dancing. "It is something about being ex-colonists, I think – they had to put the lock in upside down to make a point."

She held out her long-fingered hand to me, her head tilted to one side so that her dark, short hair formed a glossy curtain that caught the light.

"Elena Smalova, lecturer in Post-Revolutionary Soviet Society, and you must be…" she made a show of reading the name on my door, "… ah yes, Professor D'E-re-sby." She pursed her lips as she struggled with the alien pronunciation. "How do you say that?"

"*Dares-bee*. And it's Emma, by the way; it's good to meet you."

Her name seemed familiar but, too tired to remember why, I took her offered hand instead and we shook with all the dignity our Imperialist past could muster before bursting into giggles at the absurdity of it. Her brown eyes tilted up in the corners, tiny creases emphasizing the laughter that seemed to be on the verge of breaking out at any moment.

"This is my room." She patted the door of the room opposite mine. "I am so glad you are here, we can keep each other company. Have you eaten yet? Everyone can't wait to meet you. If you come now, I can show you the staff dining-room. It was a shock when they found the old professor; nobody knew he had a bad heart, but now it is good to have someone who is young. We did not think you could be here so soon." She rattled through her words and phrases so rapidly that I lost track of what she asked at the beginning, although I thought it might have been something to do with food, so I winged it in the hope I wasn't far off the mark.

"Thanks, that's very... er, kind, but I haven't unpacked yet and I'm bushed, so if you don't mind, I think I'd better get back to my rooms and sort myself out."

Elena pulled her eyebrows into a tight "V". "*Booshed*, is that where you are from? I thought you are English?"

"No. Yes – sorry, my mistake. I'm *tired*; I couldn't sleep on the flight so I won't make much sense at the moment."

"*Da*, I understand now. So, you must have tea. Come with me; I will make you Russian tea and all will be well."

She eyed me with such a look of expectation that it would have been rude to refuse. Linking her arm companionably through mine, we began to walk down the corridor towards the stairs, out of the humanities fac, across the quad, to her rooms the floor below mine.

Bigger than mine and much more homely, the room had cheerful throws covering each chair and, above the sofa, a distinctive needlepoint wall-hanging with stylized roses in reds on a cream-and-black background. Elena saw me looking at it.

"It is an Uzbek Suzani embroidery; do you like it?

It reminded me of the painted barge-ware I had once seen on holiday on the Norfolk Broads.

"Yes, I do – it's very unusual."

I held back a yawn and she pointed wordlessly to an armchair with a sheepskin cushion by the window. I sat gratefully, the high back supporting my aching shoulders into which I locked all the tension of the last forty-eight hours. Elena disappeared through a door; shortly afterwards I heard running water and a kettle being filled. I let my head rest on the back of the chair and closed my eyes.

I woke abruptly. It took me a moment to remember where I was and a second more to locate Elena sitting in the armchair opposite, her legs slung over one arm, reading.

She looked up at my sudden movement.

"Sorry," I mumbled. "I must have been more tired than I thought." I rubbed my eyes and sat up. She didn't seem in the least bit put out by the stranger falling asleep in her chair.

"That's OK; you are tired, I think. You would like some food?"

I shook my head. "No thanks, I'm not hungry."

"Yes – yes, you are hungry; you must eat now."

Before I could reply, she disappeared only to return a minute later with a bowl and a large mug, which she placed on the low coffee table before me. I peered blearily at the food, trying to locate my appetite.

"Soup – chicken soup. I make it," she declared triumphantly, then with a slight note of anxiety, "You are not vegetarian, are you?"

I shook my head.

"No, and not a chance of becoming one with homemade chicken soup on offer."

I picked up the spoon and gingerly sipped at the hot liquid. It tasted very good. A second later the paprika hit my throat and I coughed involuntarily, tears springing to my eyes. Elena looked pleased.

"Good?" she asked.

"Very," I wheezed. The warmth spread through me, my brain becoming more alert. She nodded again and picked up the book she had been reading. A company of demons danced across the front cover in the glaring colours of a fifteenth-century manuscript; I recognized the book I brought with me. I finished the soup and started to drink the hot, black tea thirstily. Elena looked up from the page she read, frowning slightly.

"This is your area of study, no?"

"Yes, sort of."

She narrowed her eyes as if assessing me, and turned back to the page. I finished my tea. Elena sucked air in through her teeth and closed the book with a snap. She gazed at nothing in particular for a moment, then suddenly asked as if in mid conversation: "And do you believe all... *this*?" she indicated the book in front of her with a flick of her hand.

"In what way, '*believe*'?" I asked, taken aback.

"Do you think this is true? All these demons, these monsters; this book... it talks as if they were true."

I couldn't fathom the sudden change in her manner. I thought carefully for a moment, choosing my words.

"It's not so much a question of what we believe, it's what *they* believed that matters."

Thoughtful again, she peered at me, searching for hidden meaning in my words.

"But what if it *is* true?" she whispered, her eyes becoming round.

"I haven't ever considered that," I admitted. "Why?"

"No, it's nothing. I am just being ridiculous." She squirmed upright, swinging her legs around and turning to face me.

"Now," she said, slapping her hands determinedly on the tops of her thighs. "What are you going to wear for your welcome reception?"

I couldn't help the alarm in my voice. "*What* welcome reception?"

"For you, of course. Every new senior member of staff must be introduced; it is the tradition here."

"To the history faculty?" I asked hopefully. "I can handle that."

Elena looked shifty. "Not exactly, no."

I raised an eyebrow.

"To the college staff," she admitted.

"What, *all* of it?"

"No, no – not *everyone*," she backtracked rapidly. "Just the senior members."

I closed my eyes and sighed. I couldn't think of anything I would hate more at this point.

"I suppose it can't be helped," I said, almost to myself.

Elena's face brightened. "*Da* – it will be fun..." She stopped and adjusted her choice of words. "Well, not *fun*, perhaps; but you will meet everyone and then you won't have to see them again."

That was so far from being encouraging, that I laughed. She saw the funny side of it and joined in.

"I thought I'd got away with it – no welcoming committee or anything," I said ruefully.

She obviously thought that highly amusing. "Oh, no! You can't expect to be a highly respected visiting academic from *Cam*-bridge..." she emphasized the word, "and not be... what is the word...?"

"Humiliated?" I suggested.

"No, no!" she laughed again, "*proclaimed* to all the world." She waved her willowy arm with a flourish.

"Well, let's just hope that the world isn't listening."

"Ah, but it *will* be; the college has to celebrate your arrival. The Dean will want to show you off."

"What on earth for?"

"Because..." she hesitated, "because he will think you a great catch for the college."

"Good grief," I muttered.

"Now, what will you wear?" she asked again.

"I haven't a clue," I answered truthfully, considering I hadn't known about it in the first place. I mentally scanned my luggage. "How formal will it be?"

"Quite formal." She looked smug, the humour back in her eyes.

"Not gowns, surely?"

She shook her head. "No, not gowns now. We wear gowns for *other* occasions."

That sounded ominous, but at least a reprieve.

"Will a skirt suit do?"

She looked suddenly very serious. "Yes, that's good, but no *jeans*." She waved a censorious finger at me as a warning. About to protest that it wouldn't have crossed my mind to wear jeans to a formal occasion, I caught her stifled smile before she bent double, tears forming in her eyes.

"Ah, that is a good joke," she howled.

A mobile rang somewhere close by with the theme from *Dr Zhivago*. Elena squeaked and darted to the kitchen. I heard her exclamation and the rapid fire of Russian as she asked a question and then answered another. I picked up my book from where it lay dismissed, turning it over to study the front cover more closely. A devil's face leered at me, one cloven hoof crushing the face of a man underfoot. Behind him, a demonic scene played over a darkly pastoral landscape. I focused on the figures in the background – tiny in comparison, but clear enough to make out. Naked humans sprawled contorted in near-death while thickly furred monsters clawed at their eyes and devoured their intestines. Black-eyed demons worked in pairs, the faces of their victims white with terror as their lives were made void. On their knees, arms raised skywards in supplication, men and women looked for hope. And all the time, reaching down from an idealized Heaven, a hand strained to reach theirs, almost touching – but not quite. I had seen dozens of such images from right across the medieval world; images reflecting the horror of people besieged by war and death, hunger and disease – a reconciliation of hope and fear in a pictorial fantasy, in religious analogy. Little more than that, its relevance lay in what it told me from a cultural as well as historical point of view. I fingered my cross, bringing the chain up over my chin, deep in thought.

Elena skipped back to her vacated chair, flinging her legs over the side again. "That," she proclaimed, "was Matias." She looked very pleased with herself. My face reminded her that I had no idea who she was talking about.

"Matias is my *gor*geous boyfriend."

I waited.

"He is flying back tonight. From Helsinki." She clapped her

hands in glee.

This called for an appropriate response. "That's... um... great. Does he live there?"

"No," she sounded slightly impatient, then took a deep breath. "Matias is *here*, he's a professor too – in genetics. He's absolutely brilliant. He's been to visit his parents in Finland for *weeks*. His mother is not well. Look..." She scrambled up and crossed the room to a series of shelves where she reached for a framed photograph. She brought it over to me. It showed her standing with her arm linked through that of a stocky, broad-shouldered, clean-shaven man in his mid to late thirties. His unruly, pale-brown hair would be inclined to curl if he let it grow any longer. Deep lines of an innate good nature ran from the edge of his nose to the corners of his mouth and he looked at Elena as if she were his most treasured possession in the world. Behind them, the Winter Palace gleamed in pale sunlight.

"Home visit?" I asked.

"*Da.*"

"So it's serious, is it?"

"Mmm," she beamed at me. I looked at the photo again; they looked very happy. A pang of longing for a memory – followed by a stab of jealousy – snagged my contentment, but I didn't want to let it surface to diminish hers.

"I'd better skedaddle, Elena, you'll have lots to do," I said, rising stiffly and stretching taut limbs. She began to protest, but I shushed her.

"Thanks for taking a complete stranger in hand," I smiled. "I think they would have found me in a sorry heap somewhere if you hadn't rescued me."

"It was my pleasure," she replied, and meant it; then spoilt it by adding, "I bet the others that I was to be the first to meet you, and I won."

She was still smirking as I pulled a rueful face at her and left to find my own room.

I enjoyed light duties for the rest of the week, including the opportunity to meet the post-graduates under my supervision.

From the inquisitive looks they gave me on entering my tutor room, Holly must have given them her first impressions. By all accounts the venerable professor who preceded me stuck by the rules to the letter, whereas my interpretation of convention tended to be more *flexible* – as long as I considered it moral, legal, and in the best interests of my students.

I gave the room a thorough clean and what academic gravitas I could muster in a few days. The books helped, but there were too many for the shelves and now they spilled along the window-sill and stood in more or less neat piles at the edge of the room. The walls were otherwise bare and I regretted not bringing some of the prints and posters I used at Cambridge for visual inspiration in dull moments. Nonetheless, my laptop and organized bundles of paper made my desk look fit for purpose and I prepared to begin.

It hadn't taken long to gauge my group. I started by asking them to summarize their dissertations – in writing – in no more than 200 words. Protestations and accusations of cruelty led to a general breakdown of order, followed by their realization that I was pulling their legs. I reminded them that, for the most part, I had been in their shoes less than a decade before. Once they understood I refused to be taken overly seriously, we all relaxed and work began in earnest.

Overseeing the five post-grads came as part of the deal that brought me to the States. In return for unfettered access to the contents of the library and ample time for research, I aimed to guide them through the intricacies of producing a viable MA thesis by the end of the year. Holly took it upon herself to introduce the other four: Josh – clearly recovering from celebrating his birthday the day before – lounged long and lanky in regulation jeans and T-shirt, with tatty green Converses coming apart at the seams. He flicked back dark hair from his eyes to look at me. Someone, somewhere produced students like these to order. Open and friendly – once he decided I didn't bite – he would need keeping an eye on to complete his dissertation to a passing standard.

Hannah, on the other hand, was short, sturdy and resolute.

Her golden-brown hair bubbled around her face and her hazel eyes flashed determinedly. Her overshot jaw made her look stubborn and – although I thought she would require little motivating from me – I envisaged a battle of wills if she needed directing in any way.

Next came Aydin. Sensitive and studious, his Turkish accent made it difficult for the others to understand him at first. In his thirties and as new to America as I, he struggled to adjust. His thesis looked promising, but he wrestled with the written aspect and he knew it. A sense of desperation surrounded him; an insecurity in the way he interacted with the others, as if he expected them to discover his true identity and reject him. Aydin needed special care to graduate successfully.

Leo, however, knew exactly who he was and where he wanted to go. His shock of white-gold hair stood in carefully gelled spikes, the colour matching the cream jacket which emphasized the breadth of his football player's shoulders but which was impractical for student life in its blatant exhibition of wealth. His demeanour shouted confidence and he considered himself handsome and made sure we knew it as well. I couldn't fathom why he put in the effort to complete an MA when it seemed blindingly obvious he would rather be in Hollywood. I wondered if there would be enough space in my room for his ego. Holly dimpled when he spoke, already captivated.

The easy part of the week over and jetlag waning, the Dean invited me to his study for tea. Elena shrugged when I asked her what she knew about him and Matias wasn't much better. "The college is his life," he'd said. "Shotter will do anything to promote it – or protect it, for that matter. Believe it or not, it's difficult to get a position at this place unless you're a heavyweight academically – or you offer something else he wants. So, there it is."

I considered myself a relatively junior lecturer back in the UK. I could think of nothing else that distinguished me from any other person in my position, except, perhaps, for my grandfather's academic standing; but he had died many years ago and his reputation faded as others superseded him.

Professor Shotter rose to greet me as I entered the ground-floor room. Clearly once a principal room in the original house, windows overlooked the grounds to the front. Sunlight fell across polished broad oak boards and the edge of an oriental rug, its fringe frayed and its pile rubbed and worn where hard, leather-soled shoes had taken their toll over the years. The Dean inched around the large desk where he had been sitting, pulling his blazer close to him to prevent the embossed gold buttons from catching on the edge.

"Well, well, Professor D'Eresby." Sharp, pale-blue eyes appraised me from under neatly trimmed eyebrows twitching upwards as he took me in.

I held out my hand automatically. "Professor Shotter. How do you do?"

He looked at it for a moment before taking it. "Yes – of course, my dear, very nice to meet you too." He held my hand a little longer than I expected.

He peered at me again, harder this time; not what he anticipated, perhaps? Whatever his thoughts, he gathered them quickly, ushering me towards a deeply buttoned sofa, glowing ruby in the sun. I sat down feeling awkward and self-conscious, crossing my ankles to one side and hoping he didn't notice me pulling my skirt over my knees. A knock on the door heralded a middle-aged woman bearing a large butler tray complete with burnished silver teapot and bone china. She set the tray down, giving me a fleeting look.

"Mrs Shotter." The Professor indicated without looking at her. "Any sandwiches, my dear?"

I started to rise to my feet to greet her, but she turned and left the room without waiting. She returned a minute later carrying an old-fashioned three-tiered cake stand with a selection of sandwiches and little cakes.

"Thank you, Mrs Shotter." I made a point of looking at her as she placed it at an angle on the table. She nodded in acknowledgment, meeting my eyes properly for the first time.

"You're welcome," she replied, darting a glance at her husband who leaned towards the table to pick up a napkin. He didn't seem to notice and she left without another word.

Behind him, ranged across the wall, a series of photographic portraits of people in academic gowns relieved the monotony of the plain surface. He broke my gaze.

"Will you pour, Professor D'Eresby?"

"Yes, of course, but might I ask that I'm referred to as *Doctor*, rather than *Professor*? It has different connotations in Britain and I have yet to be raised to such an elevated status."

I didn't think it an outrageous request but, although he maintained his smile, the Dean's eyes became decidedly frosty.

"My dear, while at *this* college, I would be obliged if you would adopt the customary title you are entitled to in this country; it is a matter of maintaining standards. You understand, of course."

Well, that told me. Low and soft, his voice might be considered pleasant were it not so smooth. Too smooth – slick like oil – it lacked sincerity, so everything he said came with an unvoiced thought. And his age? I would guess early sixties, but there is a point with some people at which they appear ageless. I judged his wife younger by at least a decade – if not more – and once attractive before a drawn cast replaced the bloom. The Dean, on the other hand, with greying hair thinly covering a head dappled with age, and skin in gentle undulations around his cheeks, reminded me of an iguana. His deep-set eyes, still an arctic blue, followed every move I made. He watched me pour the tea, add milk, and stir. He asked questions about my work, my research, who I knew at Cambridge, whom I had met. He paid particular attention to the status of each individual as if making a mental note for future reference. Finally, he leaned over and very deliberately patted my knee. I flinched and he smiled.

"Make no mistake, my dear; I – and all the college staff – look forward to welcoming you tomorrow at your reception." He emphasized the word "*your*"; I internally shivered. He showed me to the door and I kept one step ahead of him, avoiding the hand that hovered too close to my back.

Chapter

2

The Reception

RAIN CONTINUED TO FALL when I woke on Saturday morning. Elena said they had endured one of the wettest summers for a long while and I told her that I had been in training for this in Britain for the last twenty-nine years or so and a little more rain wouldn't deter me. She then asked me about tea with the Dean.

"You could have warned me, Elena. I was given the third degree by…" I couldn't think of a name more suitable, "Mengele – with hands," I added, grimacing at the memory. I told her what happened. She tutted disapprovingly.

"He didn't! What did you do? Did you hit him?"

It was my turn to be surprised. "No, of course not!"

"Why not?"

Quite frankly, it wasn't the first time I had encountered such behaviour. In the past, I dealt with it by adopting a distinctly icy demeanour with anyone who attempted such overfamiliarity without my express permission, which seemed to do the trick.

"It's not what I do, Elena." She pouted, effectively telling me what she thought of my tactic and I changed the topic to one that was far more terrifying. "OK, then, what's the drill for tonight?"

"Drill?" she queried.

"What happens, what am I expected to do? Will I have to make a speech?" I asked, the thought sticking in my throat.

"*Nyet!*" she said, brightening at the idea of my reception party, and launching into the gory details with more relish than I considered decent. Formal functions at Cambridge were the norm, of course, steeped as most of the colleges were in tradition. Used to a different way of doing things, I derived comfort from the rituals that needed no interpretation, just acceptance – and adherence – to a tried and tested plot. Here, on the other hand, I anticipated a new script in a play with which I was unfamiliar but where I became the principal player. I never liked drama at school.

She bounced onto the sofa in her sitting-room and sat cross-legged looking like a skinny Buddha. "It's really not that bad. You just have to smile and make small chat. They all want to hear your accent, so it doesn't matter what you *say* to them. And anyway, Matias will be there."

I couldn't resist a touch of flippancy. "Oh well, that's all right then, I'm saved. Honestly, Elena, small talk is *agony*."

She refused to accept my idea of torture and instead wanted to see my clothes. With my limited wardrobe, that didn't take long.

That evening, I selected the safe black suit that let me fade into the background, my small gold cross given to me by my father on my sixteenth birthday, and the little pearl studs from my grandmother. Wherever I went they travelled too, my companions, sitting comfortably against my skin, the cool gold warming almost instantly it touched me.

In the mirror of the small bathroom, my eyes stared nervously out of my pale, oval face. Tawny freckles dappled my nose and high cheeks, not so obvious now as during the summer when the sun made a mockery of any attempt to disguise them. I contemplated more make-up but decided against it – a pale and freckled academic being decidedly preferable to a painted maypole.

My long hair, however, needed to be taken in hand. It lay heavy against my back and I pulled my brush through it fiercely, willing it into submission, but it kinked unattractively where I slept on it and I regretted not having washed it again. I gave up and plaited it, turning the untidy end under like the tail of a show horse, and secured it with a velvet scrunchy. In the dim electric light, my hair looked respectable enough and tied back like that, it wouldn't attract so many comments.

Light from the reception room spilled onto the ground of the quad, making pale-green squares in the dark grass. I shivered in the rapidly cooling night, but continued to loiter, not wanting to lose this moment of solitude. Already crowded, illuminated figures travelled in random conversation around the room, stopping briefly before moving on. The gentle murmur of voices became a hubbub then softened again as a door opened and shut with each addition to the guests. Elena clutched Matias's arm for warmth and turned around, beckoning me to join her.

"Emma, come on, it's so *cold*."

In no hurry to face a room of strangers, I dawdled. "Go on in, don't wait for me; I'll join you in a minute."

She dropped Matias's arm and trotted back to me, putting her hand firmly around my shoulders and driving me forward despite my resistance.

"Look, don't worry. It is only for a few hours…"

"… and then it will all be over. Yes, I know. Just what my mother used to say before taking me to the dentist," I interposed. "But it didn't make the experience any more pleasant."

Elena giggled. "I like the dentist," she chirped.

I rolled my eyes skywards and shook my head. "You would."

The chill intensified as cold dew seeped through the fine-stitched soles of my evening shoes. I would have to go in before they were ruined and my new-found friend abandoned me for good as a hopeless case. I ran my eyes along the range of windows, willing myself on. At the far end – furthest from the gathering crowd inside the room – a figure stood silhouetted against the light, intensely still. Although I could not be sure because his eyes were clothed in darkness, I felt certain he watched us – the force of his gaze as palpable as my racing pulse. Elena pulled on my arm, breaking the spell.

"Matias…!" Elena pleaded for help over her shoulder and he strode purposefully towards us.

"We'll have entered the next ice age if you two don't hurry up. I don't believe in brute force, Emma, but if I don't get a drink in the next few minutes, my genes will become extinct shortly after I've extinguished *yours*." He attempted to look threatening, but spoilt it with a grin that just made him endearing and more like a well-loved teddy-bear than ever. We were friends the moment we met. I loved his acerbic wit, which he used freely at every opportunity to tease me, yet not once had he crossed the unspoken divide between humour and offence, and the depths of his kindness, though well disguised, knew no bounds.

I held up my hands in submission. "It's all right, I'm coming; I surrender."

He offered us both an arm to lean on and I glanced around his back as he walked us briskly towards the door, but the figure had gone.

The reception room swam with people. I wavered at the door and peered in at the large, masculine space – all wood panelling and heavy grandeur. Iron candelabra dominated the ceiling as ominous as crows, but lamps stood on oak tables at intervals around the room, throwing welcome warm pools of light in which people gathered.

I recognized several members of the history faculty, but there were more senior academic staff here than I thought existed at the college and their combined voices were an engulfing wall of sound as I entered the room. A hush fell as dozens of curious eyes turned to focus on me. Fleetingly, I considered making my excuses and making a run for it, but Matias blocked my escape and Elena held on to me with a grip of steel. No going back, I would have to make the best of it.

"OK, let's get on with it. Who's first?" I said cheerfully, despite the nerves bouncing around my tummy like a hyperactive ball in a bare room.

Elena squeezed my arm encouragingly as she led me over to a well-dressed woman in her late fifties. Greyed fair hair framing a benign face gave me the distinct impression of being broken in gently, and Elena all but pushed me forward as the woman held out her hand in greeting.

"Siggie Gerhard, Faculty of Psychology and Neurological Science, and you must be Professor D'Eresby. I have so looked forward to meeting you; we have common interests, I believe." Her voice smiled, her northern European accent just apparent through impeccable English.

"Please call me Emma; how do you do? Do we?" I searched for a connection but couldn't think of any off hand.

"We do," she confirmed. "I have read your paper on the use of torture during the Inquisition – there are many similarities with incidences I have recorded with more recent victims; apart from the obvious use of pain, that is. This is Saul Abrahms, he is particularly interested in your theory." She indicated to a slight man with a little beard and a bald head with whom she had been talking a moment before. He nodded, a faint smile on his fleshy lips as he gauged me.

"We were only discussing a case the other day. A little morbid, perhaps, but we would be most interested to explore this further with you." He spoke rapidly but softly and with a strangely soothing, lilting expression like listening to water tumbling over pebbles in a stream. I needed no encouragement. A subject with which I was sadly very comfortable, it enabled me to legitimately indulge my interest at the expense of meeting a room full of strangers.

"What aspect of torture are you looking at? Political, cultural, military...?" I asked.

"Ideological," Professor Abrahms said quietly. I felt my interest quicken.

"I can see the relationship," I replied. "Religious and ideological: different reasons, similar motives. You said that the cases you are investigating are recent; what areas are you looking at in terms of region?"

The unctuous voice of the Dean broke in and I felt a hand on my elbow.

"Professor D'Eresby – welcome, welcome. I see you have met Professors Gerhard and Abrahms already." Siggie Gerhard's smile became fixed. "Professor Abrahms is internationally known for his work on Functional Governance relating to dictatorship and Professor Gerhard is, of course, a leading expert in the field of psychological disorders, as I'm sure you know. I'm afraid I must steal Professor D'Eresby from you, my dear."

His ingratiating smile did not reach his eyes and he didn't

appear in the least bit sorry. It occurred to me that he reserved the endearment for those whom he disliked. The Dean grasped my hand in his. Hot and fleshy, his palms were tacky, and I tried to pull my hand away, but his grip tightened as he manoeuvred me towards a cluster of people in the centre of the room.

"I am so pleased that you have been able to join our little family; I think you will find we have some of the finest minds gathered here. Quite the elite in their fields, as I am sure you are aware."

I fought temptation to look behind him to see if he left a trail of slime, and instead smiled politely, gritting my teeth as I nodded to the unfamiliar faces.

A small figure with close-cropped hair stepped away from a group and placed herself squarely in front of me, looking expectantly at Shotter. He cast an acrid look at her, then, reassuming his veil of civility, introduced us.

"Professor D'Eresby – Professor Makepeace, one of our most illustrious lecturers and holder of the Chair of Anthropology." His voice slid with obvious gratification over her accolades.

"Emma D'Eresby." I removed my hand with alacrity from Shotter's grasp and held it out to the tiny, grizzled woman standing in front of me. She leaned towards me with a conspiratorial air.

"Don't listen to him, he's full of wind," she remarked in a low, husky voice, looking tartly at Shotter who huffed at her.

"Call me Madge," she said, turning to face me finally and shaking my hand. "I'll take it from here, Stephen." She dismissed the Dean without looking at him and he reluctantly acceded and, giving a stiff smile, turned away. "By the way," she whispered audibly in the direction of his retreating back, "don't ever accept an invitation to tea from the old lech." His shoulders flinched noticeably and I grimaced. She caught my expression. "Too late already? Well, you've obviously lived to tell the tale. We've all been expecting you, you know – new blood. Now tell me, what are you doing in this godforsaken place? You're far too young to be buried along with the rest of the forgotten and unloved." She squinted up at me, calculating, deep creases scored in skin leathered from years of sun and smoking. "You didn't come for the climate, so what did you come for?"

Her questions came laced with a sharpness I couldn't quite place; I found her directness disconcerting and became reluctant to open up under her scrutiny. To my relief, we were interrupted. She scowled.

"Hey, Madge, you old crow, you're monopolizing the chief cause of this gathering and that's very bad manners in my books. Well, he-llo there, Professor D'Eresby." Warm brown eyes and an easy, self-assured grin accompanied a tall, very attractive, loose-limbed man, whose casual garb defied the formal dress of the rest of the gathering. He threw his arm around Madge's shoulders and made no attempt to hide his appreciation as he ran his eyes over me. I didn't know where to look, feeling my colour rising.

"Are you the latest in our dear Dean's collection?"

"Collection of what?" I asked, returning his smile without hesitation and forgetting to answer Madge's question.

"Trophies. Been for tea with the Dean yet?" He raised a dark, arched eyebrow.

I nodded, frowning and his eyes gleamed.

"*Su*-re you have. Didn't you see the line of stuffed heads on the wall?"

"Heads?" Was I missing something here?

His grin widened. "Uh huh."

Madge tried to wrench herself free from his arm, but he kept it lying across her shoulders as if she were an old, comfy sofa.

"Stop playing with the girl, Samuel. She doesn't know what you are talking about," Madge admonished him. He ignored her glare and continued looking at me through half-closed eyes. His voice as warm as his eyes, he dripped seduction quite irresistibly, making my limbs weaken.

"He accumulates academics. This college has the greatest concentration of PhDs per student-head of any university in the US. Didn't you see the photographs on the wall? *You know you've made it when you've been framed*," he crooned like a TV advertisement, wrapping his hands around his neck to illustrate a mounted head. I couldn't help laughing – he was irrepressible. Madge grunted.

"Professor Emma D'Eresby – *Professor* Samuel Wiesner – if you can believe he's mature enough to have ever been to school. He has an excess of confidence."

He bowed with pretend formality and I laughed; I couldn't begin to take him seriously. "Don't be taken in by his charm, my dear – it's a honey-trap. He's just divorced his second wife."

"*She* divorced *me*," Samuel corrected. "Don't believe a word the old harridan says, she's just jealous."

"Believe me, you're not my type, Sam."

He feigned disappointment but within a split second bent down with his mouth to her ear. "Sure I'm not, but *she* is," he said, still looking at me. "This one's not for you Madge; *strictly off limits*."

She ignored him and succeeded in freeing herself. "You rudely interrupted my subtle interrogation," she continued archly; Samuel looked interested.

"Can I help?" he eyed me hopefully. Madge returned to her former question.

"So, what does bring you here?"

I concentrated on her, controlling the urge to smile as Samuel's dark-brown eyes danced wickedly at me.

"The college has something I want," I said carefully.

Samuel let out a low whistle. "British, beautiful *and* enigmatic. The Dean has surpassed himself. You're here for the year, right?" I nodded, wondering why it was relevant. "There's plenty of time then." He rubbed his hands together in relish, grinning again. Madge nudged him hard in the ribs and he massaged them ruefully. "Time for a drink. What would you like?" he asked me, shooting a glance at the nearest table covered with half-consumed bottles.

"Nothing, thanks."

"Aw, gee, let me get you something. Wine, beer…?"

"No, thank you, I don't really drink. You get one if you like."

Madge cast a swift look at him. "Take my advice, Emma, my dear, and don't let yourself get distracted. Before you know it, you're a Mrs Nobody with three kids and a mortgage. You'll never know what happened to your career and nobody will care."

Samuel placed a hand over his heart. "I'm mortally wounded by that remark. My wives didn't disappear but they sure sucked the life out of me. Or are you talking from experience, maybe?"

"No, just from observation," she answered dryly. I glanced towards Elena and Matias. She didn't look as if she would fade into obscurity any time soon. I caught her eye and she waved. I waved back.

"I've not found anyone I'd want to marry so far and besides..." I tried to think of something to say that didn't sound fatuous, "I have my work to focus on." I failed: Madge didn't look convinced and Sam rolled his eyes. "I'd better introduce myself to some of the others," I said, not meeting their eyes, grateful when Elena came bouncing up and hooked her arm through mine, saving me from embarrassing myself further.

"I hope Sam's behaving himself – he has a reputation, you know." Elena winked at him. Sam smirked; it was a reputation he obviously enjoyed.

"I wouldn't have guessed," I replied and Elena giggled.

"Come and meet the rest of the history department; I want you to tell them I met you first and won the bet; they do not believe me and I want my pizza."

"Thank you," I whispered when we were out of earshot. "That was getting a little... odd."

"You're welcome." She squeezed my arm. "But I thought you said you couldn't act; I think you should go on the stage."

"I didn't say I *couldn't* act, just that I don't *like* acting; there's a difference."

Elena checked that nobody was within earshot. "What do you think of Sam? He likes you, I can tell."

"He's..." I hesitated, trying to describe him, "... very funny."

She squeaked, only just suppressing laughter. "*Funny?* Do you not think he is good-looking?"

"Mmm – that too," I conceded. "But I didn't come here looking for a man, Elena, so don't go having any ideas about match-making." That was one thing with which I heartily agreed with Madge: I didn't need any complications right now.

Not discouraged, Elena scanned all the faces in the room as we crossed it.

"What about him?" she suggested, indicating a baby-blond man with a cherubic face and a dimpled chin.

"Too blond."

"You don't like blonds?" she exclaimed.

"Shhh," I hushed her. "I'm sure he's very nice, but he just doesn't do anything for me. I prefer darker hair."

"Tall, dark and handsome?" she probed, with an impish smirk.

"Yes, I suppose so..."

"Like Sam?"

She laughed at the look on my face.

"Yes, all right, like Sam," I admitted, not only to her, but to myself as well. He exuded a seductive humour difficult to resist even though I loathed men who thought themselves attractive and used it to trap women. He must be aware of his good looks, but his sexuality wasn't a snare, just how he was and I found his attention quite beguiling even though I should have known better by now.

There ensued what passed for a relatively normal conversation with the senior members of the history faculty, one of whom I knew from a conference in Florence and another two for their formidable reputations in their particular fields. It came as a relief to talk the same language without any further explanation or amplification and I would have happily stayed with them. However, I saw the Dean look towards me and detach himself from an earnest-looking couple with intent.

I tugged urgently on Elena's sleeve, indicating an escape with a slight nod of my head. I made my excuses to my colleagues, already moving away in the opposite direction to the Dean.

"Not that way," she hissed. Puzzled, I stopped short. A man standing to one side of the room made no attempt to disguise the fact that he watched us – his eyes unblinking, his face immobile. He stood between two lights where the shadows fell and, although in a group, he seemed alone. My skin crawled and I felt my face pale under his stare. A slight smile formed across his lipless mouth and I turned quickly away, but I could feel his eyes as clearly as I had seen them. I wanted to get away from them more than anything else at that moment. I didn't need to explain; Elena wriggled nervously next to me.

"I'll go and find Matias." She craned her neck to look for him and saw his back at the far end of the room by the emergency exit, talking to Sam. "I will not be a moment." She began to weave her way towards him.

"No, wait!" I called after her but it was too late: the man slid through the crowd towards me like a wolf through trees. I started to follow her but found my way blocked by a little dumpy woman in a two-piece suit that bulged, talking animatedly to her companion as they made their way towards a table of canapés.

"Professor D'Eresby."

I didn't need to see the man to know who spoke, as his voice cornered me. I froze. To leave now would be unforgivably rude. I forged a mask of courtesy and swivelled slowly on the spot. Middling in height, everything about him appeared grey although he dressed entirely in black, the only point of colour the silver buckle of his belt. Pale eyes – cold as the North Sea – neither blinked nor deviated from my face. Nervously, I pushed a wayward strand of hair back into place.

"Professor D'Eresby," he said again and when he spoke, only the bottom half of his face moved, like the jaw of a skull. "I have waited such a long time to meet you; I believe we are neighbours."

My throat – dry as dust in the stuffy room – strained as I tried not to stutter.

"Neighbours?"

"My name is Kort Staahl." He seemed to think that I should have heard of him. "Faculty of English," he explained when I didn't react.

"Oh."

"There are things that I would like to share with you. The Dean has expressed a desire for me to mentor you – to show you the ropes, so to speak." Hairs rose on the back of my neck. "Such interesting things," he added softly, the air hissing slightly on his "*s*".

That did it. Irrational or not, I did *not* want to talk with this man whose motives were obscured by the mirror of his face. I nearly yelped with relief to see Matias striding towards me with Elena close behind. He raised a hand in greeting.

"Emma, I've been looking for you! Sam's been asking about you and I said that only you would know the answers to his questions. You don't mind do you, Kort, if I borrow Emma?"

Staahl's expression remained rigid.

"No, of course not, there will be plenty of opportunities to meet in the future."

He smiled stiffly but there was an element in his intonation I didn't like, almost as if what he said was not a promise, but a threat. Matias kept his arm in place as he walked me away.

"Now, if you two have finished using and abusing my manly strength by rescuing you from the untold horrors of Professor Staahl, I have to speak to a colleague. Will you be quite safe, Emma, or would you like me to fetch Sam over for you? I'm sure he would be more than willing to step into my shoes…" he trailed off with a suggestive grin.

The thought – although quite appealing – I considered a little too obvious for my taste; besides, an attractive woman had attached herself to Sam and, from what I could see, he enjoyed the attention, although every now and again, his eyes wandered over to where we stood.

"Nope, thanks – I'm in search of a drink. Elena, can I get you one?"

She didn't hear me as she waved vigorously to someone by the table laden with food. The man looked up and waved back.

"I'm just going to see David," she said.

"If you must," Matias grumped, but he shrugged with a degree of resignation as he watched her skip out of hearing, before turning back to me. "Emma, I won't be long; I'll be over there if you need me."

"OK," I nodded. "Thanks."

Staahl seemed to have vanished and I welcomed a bit of thinking space where I didn't have to be archly correct or dance on somebody else's eggshells. But I longed for a drink. I picked up a bottle of water from a nearby table, and shook it, peering through the thick green glass into its empty heart. The juice similarly consumed, only a dribble of white wine remained and I wouldn't touch *that*. I should have accepted the drink from Sam when offered. I pivoted, searching the rest of the room for something more promising. Tucked away in a corner over by the window in the general direction in which Matias disappeared, stood a table where the bottles looked more or less untouched. I made a beeline for it, but a little man in an ill-fitting suit and odd socks stepped in front of me so suddenly that I nearly ran into him.

"Pro... Professor D... D'Eresby," he stammered, his eyes hardly meeting mine before darting away again to a fixed point somewhere behind me. "I... I understand you have come from the University of Cambridge."

He spoke rapidly like a typewriter, his head hunched forwards so that his body made a rough "*s*" shape. The same height as him, his gaze now rested on my clavicles and stayed there.

"Yes, I have..." I said, unsure to whom I spoke and what he wanted. My hand twitched to my neckline protectively.

"Good, good. Per... perhaps you might know Dr Hilliard? He would be in the same faculty as you."

For a moment I thought I misheard him. He glanced at me again and pushed his thick-rimmed glasses up his nose with one finger. "Ah, Dr Hilliard – yes, yes, a leading academic in your own field."

I heard myself reply, surprised by the dispassionate tone in my voice.

"I don't believe he is at the university any more."

The small man blinked rapidly as if this represented a grave piece of news.

"Pity, such a pity, but of course you have heard of him, a man of his standing?"

I smiled stiffly. "Yes, I have heard of him."

I wanted this conversation to end. It had taken me unawares and the resulting knot in my stomach was an all too familiar sensation I didn't expect tonight – not here – not *now*. I caught sight of Matias talking to a man I couldn't quite make out in the dimly lit corner of the room.

"Will you please excuse me?" I said, politely. The jittery academic looked crestfallen. I couldn't help but feel sorry for him as there was no reason why he should have known, but talking to this awkward little man with the strange mannerisms about Guy Hilliard and another life brought me to my limit of endurance for one evening. Besides which, my head began to throb.

"Ye... yes, of course," he stuttered, but he remained rooted to the spot so that I found myself obliged to edge around him to escape.

Matias saw me and smiled an invitation to join him. I wished fervently we were alone so that I didn't have to go through all the introductions again and make "small chat", as Elena put it so succinctly.

"Hi, Emma," he greeted me with a jocularity born of the near-empty glass in his hand. "I see you were cornered by our resident campus eccentric. You're doing well for one evening. You didn't look very happy over there; what did Eckhart say to you and how did you manage to shake him off?"

He meant only to tease but my head ached and I struggled to find my sense of humour. His companion turned away and went to the table nearby.

"He only asked if I knew someone, Matias. I think he finds it difficult to talk to people. He can't help it; he didn't mean anything by it."

Matias sobered for a moment. "I stand corrected; I'm getting crabby in my old age. Now, I'd better go look for Elena and make sure she's behaving herself." He winked at me then suddenly remembered the man who had returned from the drinks table and now stood quietly to one side, waiting.

"I'm sorry," he apologized. "Emma, let me introduce you; this is Dr Lynes."

With some reluctance and a degree of curiosity as to who could get away with being called simply *Doctor* if I couldn't, I turned to the person I scarcely glanced at before. My breath caught as I met the intensely direct gaze of the tall, singularly attractive man in front of me whom I instantly remembered from the scene of the crash.

"How do you do, Professor D'Eresby?"

He made no indication he recognized me as he offered his hand.

"How... how do you do?" I faltered, my eyes leaving the disconcerting familiarity of his fair hair, dropping to his arm where no sign of a bandage interrupted the immaculate line of his sleeve. Instead, his long fingers were strong, and I reacted slightly to his touch as his pulse beat against my palm. He smiled apologetically and withdrew his hand. I gathered my wits.

"Please, I'm just *Dr* D'Eresby – I can't get used to this *Professor* thing everyone insists on here."

I realized with a jolt that I had probably just managed to insult him without trying and a flash of heat rose to my face, but the corner of his mouth almost lifted into a smile.

"Would you care for a drink?" I couldn't place his accent, but it might have come from either side of the Atlantic; a measured voice, resonant and instantly appealing. He offered me the glass he carried, ice suspended in the clear liquid.

"Thank you." I took it without thinking, finding it difficult to look away from eyes the colour of indigo that had remained focused on my face from the moment we met.

"You are most welcome," he replied.

My attention slid to his hair again and this time he questioned it in the slight upward lift of an eyebrow.

"I saw you – the other day – at the crash," I stumbled in way of explanation. "With the dead woman," I clarified, in case he'd forgotten – as if anyone *could* forget.

The merest flicker of reaction in the tightening of his mouth.

"Did you." His response didn't invite further comment and I searched for something to say rather than endure an uncomfortable silence.

"*Lynes* – did your family originate from England?" I asked.

He looked surprised – a slight frown creasing his forehead.

"Scotland, I believe," he replied.

"Oh, yes – well, it's the right island anyway."

I could have kicked myself for being so asinine. He smiled politely. I looked away, embarrassed. Another pause followed.

"I understand you are on secondment from Cambridge." It came as a statement rather than a question. I glanced up at him as he calmly looked down at me, his corn-gold hair contrasting with eyes that now seemed more denim. I deemed this topic safer ground.

"Yes, it's part of a research project. History," I added, although he probably already knew that, given his presence here at the reception. For me. For the first time in my life it occurred to me that my subject might sound dull to someone else.

"What period do you specialize in?" he asked.

"Sixteenth- and seventeenth-century England – persecution of minority groups."

Dull *and* trendy.

His eyes flashed momentarily over my face. "It sounds interesting." His voice didn't reflect the sentiment and I suspected he wanted to be polite, but he continued anyway. "Why are you interested in that era in particular?"

"A number of reasons, I suppose." I thought for a moment, arranging my answers in order of priority, aware that I didn't want to test his limits of boredom.

"First, it's a time of immense change socially, politically and culturally. Secondly – from a practical point of view – it's reasonably well documented compared with earlier periods. And thirdly..." I glanced up to see if I still had his attention. I did, but with an expression now veiled. I found it difficult to articulate my ideas under his scrutiny and I lost my train of thought.

"And thirdly...?" he prompted.

"And thirdly, it's of particular significance to the region I come from."

Dull, trendy *and* pointless. The wisp of hair disengaged itself again and I pushed it impatiently behind my ear. His eyes followed the movement.

"And where is that?"

"Lincolnshire – the East Midlands and East Anglia really." For the briefest moment, his eyes narrowed as he looked at me, and I felt myself blanching beneath his gaze. I shuffled uncomfortably, the ice clinking noisily in my glass. I took a sip – just water; I remembered how thirsty I was and took another.

"I expect you miss your home." His voice held an echo of longing and my reaction to it took me by surprise.

"Don't you?"

I don't know what made me assume him to be far from home, perhaps his name or his accent, or even the colour of his hair, but he reacted immediately. His face became blank as a shutter fell between us.

"This is my home," he said quietly.

I bit my lip; he responded as if I had tried to cross a threshold unbidden and uninvited. I attempted to rescue the situation by answering his original question, although I doubted whether he now wanted to hear the answer.

"I... I haven't had time to miss it yet, but I will – I always do – though there are certain similarities between here and Britain which might make it easier."

"Such as the weather?" he suggested, wry humour breaking through his reserve.

"Definitely the weather," I allowed a smile in return; "and the functions," I appended. We simultaneously looked at the still-crowded room, more as observers than participants. His voice – gently inflective, soothing almost – indicated he seemed to have forgotten my *faux pas*, even if I hadn't.

"Not your choice of an evening's entertainment perhaps?"

"No, not really, but I wasn't given an option. 'Resistance is futile'," I intoned in imitation of a Borg, then thought that if he never watched *Star Trek*, the reference would be lost on him. I reddened again.

He smiled faintly. "Quite."

Someone threw open a window and a stream of fresh air wrapped itself around my shoulders, cooling my flaming cheeks which I knew would be clashing horribly with my hair and freckles. In contrast, he maintained a quiet dignity, which the heat didn't seem to touch. I found it difficult to pinpoint what made him so attractive. I sneaked a look and found him scrutinizing me in return.

"There you are, Ginger! I wondered where you'd got to; I thought I'd lost you." Sam's buoyant voice cut in. He cast a look at my companion, then back at me. "Lynes." He nodded a cool greeting.

"Professor Wiesner," Dr Lynes returned, but Sam barely acknowledged him as he looked at me.

"Matias mentioned you were probably wanting to leave pretty soon, and that you don't want to go on your own; something about Staahl, he said. I told him I'd go with you – see you safely to bed."

His brown eyes were expectant, and his full, sensual mouth twitched suggestively, making me immediately wary. I glanced towards the edge of the room where Staahl had been, but the shadows were still empty; I shook my head.

"No thanks, Sam – I'll go with Elena and Matias; where are they?"

I scanned the rest of the room for them. Despite the thinning crowd, I couldn't see them anywhere.

"They left a few minutes ago. Elena thought you might like some company and I said I'd take you back when you're ready."

He obviously relished the idea and my jaw clenched as I restrained the wave of irritation at Elena's betrayal and Sam's supposition that I agreed to it. Denied a choice, I resented being manipulated. Sam peered at me, "Emma?" His cloak of confidence slipped. I felt suddenly tired.

"Yes, all right, Sam," I responded, a little sharper than I needed to be. "Thanks," I remembered to say with a little more grace, and resigned myself to being escorted back to my room by him. I'd let Elena know exactly what I thought of her when I saw her in the morning. He threw an arm around my shoulder, his unexpected closeness making me flinch away from him. I removed his hand firmly, and gave him a warning look, but Sam's self-assured grin returned and I reddened, embarrassed and annoyed. I caught Dr Lynes watching, his face impassive; he saw me look up and pretended not to have noticed my discomfort.

"Well, I'll say goodnight then – Dr D'Eresby, Professor Wiesner," he inclined his head slightly in an almost antique gesture of courtesy.

"Yup sure, 'night Lynes."

Eager to leave, Sam's manner neared dismissive. I wanted to say something that would let the other man know how I appreciated him listening to me, and asking me about my home, and that Sam made assumptions that I neither welcomed nor shared. But I couldn't and I didn't so I could only say "Goodnight, Dr Lynes," and hope that the tone of my voice said it all.

Chapter

3

The Library

... thou art the book,
The library whereon I look
Though almost blind.

HENRY KING (1592–1669)

Elena's excited knocking on my door woke me next morning, accompanied by her high tones urging me to hurry up. Dragging myself out of bed, I pulled my dressing-gown over my pyjamas, shivering in the cold room. The ancient radiator bravely fought to pull heat from the boiler in the basement but at best it remained tepid and hardly warmed the air. Outside, a freezing mist had risen in the night, obscuring the mountains I greeted every morning, and the frozen fingers of the tree tapped my window impatiently with the lightest breeze.

Elena knocked again, more urgently this time. I remembered to be annoyed with her and arranged my face accordingly. She tripped lightly through the door, wearing fluffy pink pig-slippers with cerise noses and coiled curly tails on the heels.

"Well?" she demanded immediately without stopping to say "Good morning".

"Well what?" I scowled. Oblivious to my chagrin, her face lit in anticipation.

"How did it go with Sam? Did he hit on you?"

Glaring, I took a deep breath. "Don't you ever, *ever* do that again," I fumed. Elena took a step backwards, her mouth dropping open in surprise.

"What did I do?"

"Don't you *ever* put me in a situation like that with Sam – or with anybody else."

Her mouth turned down at the corners, making her look sulky.

"But I thought you liked him; he likes you."

"Don't assume anything with me, Elena. I don't like being manoeuvred into relationships, or anything else for that matter. You said you would wait," I added accusingly. "He's a serial womanizer; I could have been wearing a wig and a tricorn hat and it wouldn't have mattered a jot to him."

Her eyes widened with astonishment. "I'm so sorry, Emma," she whispered. "He didn't try... anything, did he?"

I calmed down slightly.

"No – nothing like that; it's just... well – it was *embarrassing*. He's like an overeager puppy who knows he's adorable and plays on it. It might be more flattering if it wasn't habitual with him. It was like I was expected to roll over and..."

Elena stifled a giggle. I looked sternly at her and she managed to look suitably serious again.

"I am truly sorry, Emma. I didn't think you would mind and I wouldn't have let you go with him if I thought it would upset you or anything..." she trailed off. "It's just that Matias and I – we are so happy, and I thought..."

"That you would like me to be happy too?" I finished; she nodded emphatically.

"You don't know me very well yet, do you?" I said. She shook her head, her expression pleading. "I possibly over-reacted, OK – *probably* over-reacted," I relented. Elena bounced over, flinging her arms around me in a hug and kicking me in the shin accidentally with a piggy snout.

"Just don't do it again, OK?" I warned her.

"OK, OK, I'll be good, I promise. But he *is* very good-looking, isn't he?" She flumped into one of the two armchairs that made my cramped flat a little more homely while I sat in the other, pulling my feet under me to keep them warm. I considered her assertion.

"Ye-es, I suppose so – for a puppy," I said.

She squeaked with laughter, wiggling her feet up and down. Her contagious enthusiasm drew me into the conversation against my better judgment.

"I think the two ex-wives are a little off-putting though, aren't they? He said they left him; do you know why?"

"He's never said and I have not asked, but he used to flirt with me before I met Matias and he was still married then."

"That just about answers the question then, doesn't it? How old is he, by the way?"

Elena thought for a moment. "Thirty-five, thirty-six, something like that. Not old. He is younger than Matias."

"Well, he's older than I am and I haven't even had one marriage to my name. In my experience – not that I've had much," I said rapidly, "multiple relationships become a pattern of behaviour and – like history – are doomed to repeat themselves. I'd rather steer well clear. Anyway, there's no future in someone like Sam – not with his proclivities. I want someone I can trust without question; someone who shares my values – who doesn't lie." I found myself tugging at my dressing-gown cord and stopped before I ripped it.

Elena pulled a face, waving a correcting finger at me.

"You sound like my mother; she is always saying such things to me. You are too young to be thinking like this; it is boring and for the middle-aged. You know, 'Live a little – love a lot' – or is it the other way round?" She shrugged. "Anyway, you could have fun with Sam, no?"

Although this was not the first time I'd been accused of being too old for my years, coming from Elena, whose childlike approach to relationships was becoming increasingly clear, this seemed galling.

"Fun? Yes, possibly – while it lasts; shallow – definitely; but it's not the sort of relationship I'm looking for. I don't… it's not… just let's not go there, Elena; not now."

Her eyes narrowed with curiosity but before she could pursue it, I asked a question that had niggled since the night before.

"Matias introduced me to Dr Lynes yesterday evening." Elena looked up, interested again. "What is he a doctor of, exactly?"

"He's a *doctor*, doctor. But he is also doing research. Matias works with him sometimes." A doctor – of course, how obvious; that explained his presence at the crash.

"He says he is *ve-ry* clever," Elena went on, emphasizing the word with her strangely accented English, "but he doesn't like to talk to people much. That is the first time I have seen him at a party for *ages*. He is strange, *da*?"

I conjured the image of the quietly courteous, almost restrained man who listened to me so patiently, his blue eyes oddly intense. I squirmed unexpectedly at the agreeable memory.

"Strange? In what way?"

She pursed her mouth, fiddling with a curly tail absent-mindedly. "It is difficult to say, I do not know him, but he is not like other people, he is – different."

I frowned. "If by 'different' you mean he's polite and thoughtful, then that's just fine by me – give me 'different' every time."

She inspected me through half-closed eyes. "Do you think *he's* good-looking then?"

"Elena, you are impossible! Is that all you have on your mind at the moment?"

"Mostly," she admitted. "Well – do you?"

"Yes, but he's almost *too* handsome," I qualified, without looking at her directly. "Almost too good to be true; I didn't know what to say to him and when I did, I kept saying the wrong thing." I writhed again, but this time from embarrassment. True, I found him quite unnerving, whereas Sam was a one-man show in his own right: I could just stand back and let him do the entertaining. I shifted in my chair and pulled my dressing-gown closer around me although my face glowed hot.

Elena clapped her hands triumphantly. "You like him! Hah! And he is blond. You are a hypocrite, Emma; you said you do not like blonds."

She was right, as a general rule blond men didn't attract

me, but in his case, I could make an exception. A quiet strength surrounded him, an attraction that went beyond his good looks. Steady, honourable perhaps – I found it hard to describe – and he made me feel *safe*. But he also made me self-conscious, almost as if he searched for something in me and I didn't like that – I didn't like not knowing what he saw. Elena jiggled with excitement.

"I will tell Matias and he can arrange a date for you. It will make him very happy; he likes Dr Lynes."

I clamped my mouth shut to prevent me from saying something I might regret and rose abruptly from my chair before answering. I decided to make some tea in the little kitchen barely separated from the sitting area by a low breakfast bar. I let water flow noisily into the kettle, drops splashing my hands and escaping in silvered rivulets down the sink, taking a little of my frustration with them. I placed the jug on its stand and turned slowly to face Elena.

"You – will – not – say – *anything* – to Matias, or anyone else, do you understand? You *promised*, Elena." I looked fiercely at her to make sure that the message went home. I didn't want to risk her gossiping at my – or his – expense. Her face fell but she didn't argue because she knew she trod dodgy ground.

"I won't, not a word," she agreed and zipped her lips with thumb and forefinger.

I gave her strong black tea with lemon, and sipped my weaker version, feeling it calm me. I briefly wondered why I reacted defensively over something so insignificant, and then remembered what else I wanted to ask her before the distraction posed by Dr Lynes.

"Elena..."

"Yes, Emma?" She did her best to appear contrite.

"What do you know of Professor Staahl?"

"Staahl? Not much. I don't know him, but I've seen him around. He is from Holland, I think. He always makes me feel..." she hesitated, searching for a description, "... naked. The way he looks through you." And she shuddered, remembering.

"He said he's a lecturer."

"Oh yes, he is quite senior, I think. But we don't have much to do with that department. At least, *I* don't." She sounded relieved. I sincerely hoped I wouldn't either. I stretched, feeling warmer and more awake.

"I'm going to shower and get dressed and then explore the library. I have to prepare my lecture."

Elena took the hint. "And I am going to do some marking and then find Matias. We are supposed to be going out for lunch today, but I bet he will be in that lab of his and he will forget." She didn't sound overly peeved, so this probably represented a normal state of affairs.

I closed the door behind her, sampling the sudden silence that fell on the room. I liked Elena – we were already good friends – but she could be an unpredictable sprite at times and her good-natured meddling had already led to one tricky situation I could have done without. And, quite honestly, I didn't need any help in that quarter; I was quite capable of messing things up on my own.

The frost had melted by the time I crossed the deserted quad on my way to the new library, but the mist lingered, weakening the sun's attempts to burn the last of it away. Standing alone in its role as protector of the past, the library lay beyond the medical building in an area of parkland. Broad and squat in the shape of a drum, its linear windows swept from ground to rooftop in narrow stripes of dark glass, framed by pale fins of smooth concrete. Tracing the pathway, my heart beat a little faster with each step I took until – breathless – I stood before its doors. I had resisted the urge to visit the library until this moment as an incentive for surviving the reception party, like saving the best bit of a meal for last. This was it – I came to claim my reward.

The doors swung open like the release of an airlock, liberating the scent of new oak and old books – a shrine to the written word. I had the same sense of emotional uplift every time I visited a church. The centre of the building lay open to the glass roof which softly illuminated the area below. Three floors encircled the central space and each held rack upon rack of shelving radiating from the centre outwards. The building appeared empty of students and only the gentle hum of a humidity-control system filled the void.

"Can I help you, ma'am?"

I jumped, startled by the sound of a voice that was little more than a dry whisper; I hadn't seen the woman at the low desk almost behind me. Dressed in greens and browns, her dark skin as thin and lined around her narrow eyes as a dying leaf, she was so inconspicuous that she looked as if she grew there.

"I'm sorry, I didn't see you." I hoped she didn't take that the wrong way, but she smiled, her face crinkling into a series of deep lines like contours on a map.

"It is beautiful, isn't it? Do you have your card?"

Returning her smile, from my pocket I fished the photo card sent with the other documentation.

"Professor D'Eresby," she read then looked up to check the photo before handing it back.

"Thank you." I took it from her, already eager to begin my search.

"You're welcome," she said, her voice like the dry pages of a book in the hush of the building. "Which section are you looking for?"

I wavered. I knew what I wanted, I knew what I came for, yet once I held it in my hands – my long search over – I would not relinquish it until I devoured it entirely, or it consumed me. I took a mental step back; it would have to wait a little while longer until I earned my keep.

"History – Medieval and Early Modern, please."

I rode in one of the glass lifts, rising silently to the second floor, the door sighing open to expel me onto the carpeted deck. I quickly found the section and became totally absorbed in the task, my fingers running over the spines of the books, stopping now and again to pull one from the shelves. Mouth-wateringly extensive – like sweets ranged in jars on the shelves of an old-fashioned confectioner – there was almost too much to choose from. Time drifted and the occasional soft breath from the doors below was the only indication that others used the building.

I heaped a number of books in a wobbly pile on the nearest

desk while I found my library card. I should have brought a bag – I always came away with more than I intended – but I never learned. Gripping my card between my teeth, and brushing my hair back from my face, I balanced the books as best I could. Gingerly, I turned around and nearly leapt out of my skin as I almost collided with a figure I had neither seen nor heard approach. The unsteady pile began to slide from my arms and swift hands reached out and took them.

"I'm sorry, I didn't mean to startle you. Good morning, by the way." Dr Lynes held out the books for me. Quite unexpectedly, he smiled, the corners lifting into a compelling curve that had me nearly dropping them again.

"Good morning, Dr Lynes," I managed, as I struggled to take the rebellious load, grateful for something to do that explained my confusion.

He frowned at them. "They're not going to co-operate, are they? Please, allow me." And he took the pile, balancing them with little effort against his body.

I skipped a glance at him from under my eyelashes. "Thank you."

"Not at all," he replied, glancing down at the books he held. He raised an eyebrow; I felt I needed to explain.

"They're for my lecture next week – for my research."

He held up the first book in the stack, examining it.

"A truly enlightening subject for your inaugural lecture," he said, dryly. He turned it towards me so that I could see the book to which he referred. The dust-cover showed a German woodcut depicting a man burning at the stake, flames licking around his legs, his agonized eyes towards Heaven.

"I suppose it does look a bit suspect," I admitted. "But I can justify it on academic grounds – if that makes it any better?"

"Better – no – acceptable, perhaps. I hope your audience has strong stomachs."

"Oh, that's not going to be a problem; I don't suppose many will be there," I replied with certainty. He looked down at me curiously, his eyes a lighter, richer blue than they appeared last night. My heart did a little flip. "Anyway, I'm not planning on cheap thrills; if I were, probably more would turn up."

"Probably," he agreed.

I shot a look, prepared to be taken aback, but no undercurrent of sarcasm soured his tone and his face remained amiable. Last night and every moment that passed since leaving the reception, I persuaded myself that even if I did meet him again, he wouldn't want to speak to me, my faults amplified in my memory.

"I need to get back with these," I indicated the books, "if I'm to get this lecture finished in time." I held out my arms expectantly but he continued to hold them and I let my arms drop, uncertain.

"Where are you heading?"

"I'm taking them to the history faculty – my tutor room. It's bigger than my flat and there's more space to spread out..." I could hear myself beginning to prattle and curbed my tongue. Without relinquishing any of the books, he headed for the lift, standing aside so that I could enter first.

We left the library and headed for the main college complex. The mist had disappeared, but high milk-white cloud still obscured the sun. In the distance, the tips of the mountains hid their heads in cloud. He paced his stride so that I could walk comfortably next to him and it was he who broke the silence first.

"Forgive me if I say that you don't seem to have much confidence in attracting an audience for your lecture." He watched me with the same expression of veiled curiosity he wore the night before.

Surprised he had noticed, I asked, "Don't I? Is that how it comes across?" I thought for a moment, considering. "I suppose it's because, although *I* can see its relevance, I'm not always sure other people can. I think that most people are so busy with the present and planning for the future, that they have little time for the past." An unlooked-for wistful note crept into my tone. "And besides, relevant or not, I'm not sure how useful my work is in the grand scheme of things."

Who was I kidding? It wasn't useful at *all*. We walked on a few paces and he looked thoughtful. "Is being 'useful' a prerequisite for living?"

"That probably depends on your perspective on life generally – I mean, whether you view yourself as a random element or conceived as part of a wider plan."

He stared straight ahead and I took the opportunity to peek at him. His strong profile might have been dominated by any one feature, yet it held a perfect balance between forehead, nose, mouth and chin. He looked down at me and I rapidly looked away.

"And which do you see yourself as?" he asked.

Eyeing the doctor and giggling, two girls headed down the path towards us, tossing their hair as they passed. He appeared unaware of them, waiting for my answer so that I felt his interest genuine in what it might be. Such intense attention to what I did or thought was unfamiliar, yet he gave the impression of being a good listener and easy to talk to – as long as I didn't look at him.

"I think I have a purpose here, I'm just not sure what that purpose is yet. Nor am I certain that what I do as a historian is going to help me much in finding it."

If I tussled with working out the meaning of my life, I wasn't making it any easier for him to understand my take on it. The sun finally made an appearance. He stared directly at it for a moment without blinking, considering what I said, before looking away.

"But you said yourself that you could see the relevance in your work."

"Yes, I can, but is it enough to justify an existence spent studying it?" I meant it as a rhetorical question, but he dug further.

"So what does make your work relevant to you?"

I might have been flattered by his attention except that I couldn't see the reason for his interest, and there was no balance to our conversation – it all revolved around me. I attempted to redress the equilibrium a little. We crossed the ground between the library and the back of the medical faculty, following the dark ribbon of path. I stopped and turned to look up at him to gauge his reaction.

"Well, given what you do in comparison – as a doctor, I mean

– probably nothing. Why are you a doctor?"

He shifted the books to his other side so that he could open the door to the faculty building. Weak sunlight gleamed dully off something on his hand as he held the door ajar. He wore two rings: one – an indistinct band of gold on his little finger and the other – clearly a wedding ring. It shouldn't have mattered and I don't know why I felt surprise, but the momentary flutter of regret flared uninvited. Quelling the reaction, I led the way, waiting for his response, but he wouldn't be diverted, which I thought unfair of him, and he returned to the original point.

"You haven't answered my question. I do what I do because I can. Equally, you choose to do what *you* do because that is your area of strength. That doesn't make it any less relevant – just different."

The hall remained deserted but for the silence clinging to the walls, our echoing voices making me more self-conscious than ever. I lowered my voice.

"But what I do is not in the least bit practical; I don't save lives, I can't research diseases… or whatever else you do." I realized that I didn't know what he did. "What do you do, precisely?"

"I'm a doctor."

I couldn't help but smile. "Now who's being evasive!"

He let me lead the way up the stairs to the first-floor landing; I was already a little out of breath from walking and talking, but he breathed as regularly as if sitting in a chair at rest. I envied his level of fitness.

"I provide medical cover at the med centre infirmary, and occasionally at the hospital in town – if they're short staffed."

I suspected he sold himself short. "And your area of research? Elena said Matias works with you sometimes." It sounded as if we talked about him.

"Molecular mechanisms of mutagenesis," he said shortly. "And you still haven't answered my question."

I wasn't sure if I wanted to, considering what he did for a living: he saved the world while I made a note of it for posterity.

"What makes my work relevant – to me at least – is that it helps me understand the motives behind the decisions that people make and it is those decisions that are often the drivers behind events that change history."

He spoke quietly. "And do you? Understand people's motives?"

I realized how absurdly big-headed my claim must sound and I thought for a moment, probing the depth of my belief in what I said.

"Yes," I nodded slowly, "I think I do, at least some of the time and in a historical context."

It was his turn to look reflective. He walked to the end of the corridor and looked out of the window towards the medical faculty mulling over what I said, his eyebrows drawn together as he waited for me to find my key. The lock chose that moment to stick again and I chastised it almost silently under my breath, feeling clumsy.

"I doubt that it understands Anglo-Saxon; can I help you, perhaps?"

"Sorry," I said, wondering how come a doctor would understand such an obscure language. I tried the lock again and this time it rotated smoothly.

"Don't be," he said, waiting for me to go in first, then placing the books on my already crowded desk. He scanned the room, noting the growing mountain of texts accumulating under the window.

"I know, it's a tip; I need some more shelves," I said, stating the obvious and feeling disgraced by the organized clutter. He tilted his head on one side and read down the spines, his lips moving silently as he examined them. Astonishingly handsome, he might have been intimidating if aware of it. I realized I was staring and started to sort out the recently acquired books, allowing my cheeks to cool.

"There they are!" I exclaimed more to myself than to him, as my iPod earphones became visible when I shifted a book to one side. Dr Lynes looked up, seeing me brandish the lead, untangling as it dangled from my fingers.

"What do you listen to?" he asked, straightening.

"Oh, anything. Lots of things – Classical mostly, though I hate string quartets. I love choral works. Some sixties and seventies classics as well. And modern film scores." I tried to refine my dubious eclectic musical taste but I knew it appeared a real mish-mash that lacked cultural cohesion. "Do you like music?"

"Yes, I do," he said but, frustratingly, didn't elaborate.

My stomach rumbled quietly. I hoped he hadn't noticed, but he smiled and said, "Hungry?"

"Am I? Yes, I suppose I am." Lunch must have passed some time ago and my tummy murmured again to confirm it. I poked it unenthusiastically. "I'd better feed you before you shout at me," I addressed it. The doctor smiled more broadly than before, exposing even teeth. I would have placed him in his early thirties, but it was hard to tell; he combined the restrained refinement and quiet confidence of a much older man.

"I will let the two of you get better acquainted. May I borrow this?" he asked, holding up one of my favourite texts. He would have to return it one day, and that thought was very appealing.

"Yes, by all means."

"Enjoy your lunch," he said as he left the room, book in hand. I frowned after him, wishing he could have joined me. Wishing he had asked me to join him.

Waiting for me outside my flat when I returned, Sam attempted to look nonchalant as if passing by, but his grin became anxious, and his eyes troubled as he saw me. He unfolded his arms and straightened as I approached.

"Hi, Sam."

If my greeting was unenthusiastic, it was more to do with hunger than not wanting to see him; until that moment, I had all but forgotten to be annoyed with him.

"Emma, I'm sorry – really sorry; I had no idea and I didn't mean to presume anything. Elena said we – *I* – upset you." He saw the expression on my face. "Not that we were talking about you or anything. Well, we were, but nothing you wouldn't like." His words came out in a rush. "Emma, please – can I come in?"

I wavered for a second, my hand on the door, before acceding.

I sensed his relief as he followed me into my flat. I went straight to the little fridge, retrieved the bread and slammed two slices into the toaster. Sam wisely kept quiet, watching as I moved around my flat, and seemingly content now that he believed himself forgiven.

Four slices of toast later – two for me, two for Sam – I was more or less human again. He avoided the subject of the previous evening while I ate, but I guessed that he hadn't done with it yet. I finished the last crust of toast and picked up my mug of milkless tea before prompting him.

"Get on with it, Sam."

He eyed me cautiously, before resuming the topic.

"Hey, I wasn't *that* pushy last night, was I?" he began.

I looked into the bottom of my mug where the rich tawny colour of the tea was the exact colour of his eyes.

"Yes," I said, "you were."

"It wasn't intentional. Look, I know I messed up and came on pretty strong and I'm sorry. Can I take you out for lunch or something to make up for it? No strings," he added, looking at me through his long, black lashes. When he put it like that – when he wasn't trying so hard – he made it sound like a relatively safe and reasonable proposal. Despite my reservations of the previous night, Sam was very likeable, and I wanted us to be friends. He waited for my answer.

"OK, lunch is acceptable; there's just one thing I think you ought to know," and I paused to make my point.

"What's that?"

"I came to the States to complete some research, Sam, and I'm not looking for any complications. You're not thinking of becoming a complication, are you?" I went on before he could answer: "Because if so… it's not what I want."

He pursed his mouth and regarded me thoughtfully. I suddenly realized that I might have entirely the wrong end of the stick and he had no designs on me other than purely platonic ones. I could feel myself begin to squirm at my inept attempt to put the record straight.

"Sure, I get it, that's OK," he said slowly. "I like a challenge," and his full-lipped mouth flicked up in a seditious grin.

Nope, I had been right all along. "Well, don't see *me* as one, Sam; I'm not that sort of girl; you are so exasperating!"

"Infuriating – yeah, that's what my ex-wife told me." He leaned back in the armchair, folding his hands behind his head, looking comfortable and somewhat smug as he continued to examine me through half-closed eyes.

"Which one?" I asked, mopping up residual crumbs from my plate with my finger.

"Ouch." His attempt to appear hurt failed and he changed tack, shifting forward in the chair as he did so. "What did you think of your reception? Still glad you came to the States or did we make you want to turn tail and run for home?"

The disturbing image of Staahl imposed itself as he moved towards me through the crowded room, lifeless eyes seeking to penetrate the protective cloak within which I perpetually wrapped myself. I mentally retreated and instead found myself ensnared by the doctor's cool gaze.

"It was interesting meeting everyone, Sam, but I don't like being in the limelight much."

"You might not like it, but it sure likes you."

I pulled a face and he rubbed his chin, trying not to laugh.

"You said last night that the college has something you want. You drove Madge mad with curiosity and you don't want to get on the wrong side of the old witch; if you don't tell her, she'll make it up. Now, what exactly did you mean?"

I hadn't wanted to explain last night – and a part of me didn't want to now. So personal a subject had it become that revealing it seemed tantamount to a full-frontal confession, and I didn't know Sam well enough for that; I settled for a shortened version of the truth.

"It's a bit difficult to know where to begin, but the college holds a manuscript that I am particularly interested in researching."

"Go on," he urged, leaning forwards a tad more until his knee-cap touched mine. I drew my legs under me and he shifted away, apparently unaware.

"Well, that's it really. I need it for part of my research and it's here. And so am I."

He looked puzzled. "So what's the big deal? Why didn't you just tell us that last night?" He threw himself back against the chair, his turn to sound frustrated.

"I said it's difficult to explain," I said flatly. "But it must be the same for you, if you are so deep into an area of research that it completely takes over your life and you become consumed by it."

Sam chewed his lip. "Sure, I can see that, and I suppose my wives couldn't, which is why I've ended up paying two sets of alimony. Yeah, it makes some sort of sense. But you can still tell me more, can't you?"

I conceded that point. I risked stretching my legs so that the blood could flow through them again, conscious of him examining me although he tried to disguise his interest.

"It's a seventeenth-century diary kept by an Englishman who emigrated to America with his family. It covers about twenty years of his life and it's unique from my point of view. Anyway, I'm here because I've only had excerpts from it before. The man who built this house – Ebenezer Howard – acquired it and it's his handwritten extracts that brought me to where I am now."

"So what does this diary look like?"

I hoped he wouldn't ask me that. "I – I haven't seen it."

"You're kidding me! You mean you've come all this way and you haven't even seen it yet! Why not?" His incredulity stung and I scowled because I knew that it wouldn't make much sense to anyone but me, but I felt more sheepish at my own perfidy than cross with him for mentioning it.

"I know it doesn't make much sense, but I've wanted this for so long and, well…" I couldn't find an alternative phrase, "I look at it almost as delayed gratification."

He raised his dark eyebrows enquiringly and a bemused smirk crossed his lips. I found a safer analogy instead.

"Oh, you know, it's like when you buy a bar of chocolate and instead of eating it straight away, you put it at the back of the cupboard for later. And every time you pass that cupboard you know it's there, waiting, and that makes it somehow even more enjoyable when you do eat it." Sam looked mystified. "It's a woman thing – you wouldn't understand. Anyway, I have to get this inaugural lecture completed first and get my post-grad supervision under way properly before I allow myself to even see the journal – it'll be too much of a temptation otherwise." Sam still hadn't said a word. "Well, you did ask," I said defensively.

"I had no *idea*..." he began slowly, "that research could be such an emotionally charged issue, and as for bringing sex into it..." He grinned playfully.

"That's taking it out of context and you know it!" I said, alarmed at the way his thought processes were going.

"Sure – but *you* brought it up, Freckles."

I grimaced at his use of my old nickname, but I wanted to make things clear on the relationship front as a matter of urgency, so it would have to wait.

"And I'm putting it right back down, so don't even go there," I replied fiercely. "Anyway, I must get on with my lecture, so beat it – I have work to do."

He leaned forward again, trying to engage my eyes. "I love it when you talk rough."

"Now!" I avoided looking at him to stop myself from laughing.

He drew himself to his feet reluctantly and paused. "Lunch then – Friday? As friends?" he asked.

I collected the plates and mugs and put them on the kitchen counter.

"As friends and *only* as friends. Possibly," I replied without looking up; I didn't need to – I could sense his grin of triumph as he left the flat.

Chapter

Trial by Ordeal

RESEARCHING HISTORY IS, for the most part, a mundane task. It involves cross-referencing, note-taking, remembering and – more often than not – forgetting. The moments of inspiration can be few and you are fortunate indeed if your work leads to an earth-shattering revelation. Slow, painstaking and pedantic it may be, but research has its moments of tension. You can work on your particular subject for a lifetime either to be pipped at the post by an upstart undergrad, or see your pet theory disintegrate under the weight of the latest scientific advances. Either way, the life of a historian is fraught with unexpected dangers, not least of which, they might lose their touch, or their path, or their reason for being.

Devoid at last of all distraction, I returned to my tutor room that afternoon to settle down to some serious amounts of work. The delivery of an inaugural lecture was a time-honoured custom in some of the more traditional universities; almost a rite of passage, it entitled you to full-blown membership. Giving a lecture provided one area in which I could feel reasonably confident; I followed a set pattern, a format, which proved successful in the past. At least it *had*, but then previously I always ensured that I came well prepared.

My laptop slumbered on my desk, and the pile of books accumulated from the library in the morning sat still untouched. Every time I made ready to start work, I found my mind wandering down uncertain paths of half-remembered conversations, images of faces, eyes, hands. It didn't help that the books in front of me brought some of those pictures sharply into focus and compellingly lingered with the touch of a voice. But the voice belonged to someone who was married, and I didn't date married men; I didn't even give them a second look, let alone allow them to gain a foothold on the first rung of the ladder to my affections.

Been there, done that, burned the T-shirt.

The sun broke free of the high cloud and now shone weakly on the quad. Poorly insulated as it was, my room grew stuffy from the radiated heat. I struggled with the unfamiliar window catch and it pinged open, letting a rush of fresher air invade the room. I breathed deeply, smelling the earthy mix of warm, recently damp grass mingled with the scent of drying brick and stone. A scattering of students – mostly in pairs – basked in the late September sun. It looked much more inviting than sitting in my room waiting for inspiration. The light breeze which helped dispel the cloud caught the sounds of their voices and carried them towards me and I felt a sudden hunger for the exuberance of youth. I closed my eyes and remembered lifting my face to a warming sun, felt cool turf beneath my back, a hand holding mine, but briefly, before I eliminated the memory.

A smack of sound brought me back, as one of the books catapulted into the air and belly-flopped on the floor as the window blew shut. I picked it up, turning it over, its front cover immediately recognizable as the one Elena reacted so strongly to that first day. That reminded me.

I went over to my laptop and typed in an email address. My friend at Cambridge responded almost immediately with a cutting witticism that reprimanded me for not being in touch since I'd arrived. I returned the message with some general remarks and asked her to send me the roll of posters and prints I left behind. We exchanged a few more barbed comments – the sort that only good friends can – before I made my excuses and signed off.

The room was cooler now, and the sounds from the quad stilled. I typed in a search and came up with a list of specialist suppliers of unusual and historic prints. A few minutes later and several new posters were ordered to add to my collection. The room would not feel so spartan now, and I felt in the mood to focus on my work. I allowed myself to become fully engrossed, blotting out all other thoughts, sounds and images from my mind with my iPod and a wall of melody.

Darkness encroached as I finally finished the first draft of the lecture. I switched off the light, and closed and locked my door. The corridor lay silent and dark; I was alone.

I could see enough using the emergency lighting not to bother finding the light switch, and made my way carefully towards the communal seating area. Here, the staircase linked it with the other floors of the building.

T-chck.

A soft *click* of a door closing somewhere in the dark corridor beyond. I stopped, holding my breath, straining for the telltale footfall of another person.

Nothing.

Somehow, the absence seemed worse than the presence of another human and I waited a moment longer, but no other sound came from the English department. Acutely conscious of every noise I made, I continued through the lobby and down the stairs, each step lengthening as the desire to reach my flat overcame my caution and my own footsteps echoed in the void. As I neared my door, a whisper of air brushed my cheek, a movement so slight it might have been nothing more than the beating of a moth's wing. Heart pounding, I fumbled in my bag for the key to my door, half-expecting, any moment, to feel a hand on my shoulder. I almost fell into my flat, slamming the door shut behind me and throwing the bolts. I stood in the dark waiting for my crashing heart to calm.

I had seen nothing, heard less, but every ounce of me screamed that someone had been watching, waiting, killing time.

By morning, I succeeded in putting the non-events of the night before into perspective. Tiredness and shadows were a perfect recipe for an active imagination and besides, there remained too much to do before Wednesday to allow a little night terror to come between me and the lecture. So I spent Monday morning with my students discussing research strategy before launching them at the library and on the internet. The afternoon sped by as I refined my presentation, although I made sure that I managed to leave my room before the last of my fellow academics left theirs. I devoted Tuesday to polishing off phrases as well as chocolate, and preparing visuals to support the lecture. Fellow historians would find plenty to get their teeth into and I ensured enough to tantalize the less initiated. Although satisfied enough with the content, I felt less certain about my performance. It didn't help that a number of people said that they were coming to hear me; a scattering of individuals I could cope with, a crowd was less welcome.

The lecture hall occupied the central part of its wing. It resembled a theatre, with the plush-seats rising in crescent rows towards the back. Not big, but large enough to be intimidating if full.

And it was.

With growing dismay I watched as the rows filled one by one with mostly unfamiliar faces. I recognized several: Elena and Matias bagged seats near the front. Professor Gerhard sat next to Saul Abrahms and Sam was right at the front where I couldn't miss him. He gave me an encouraging grin that made me all the more nervous because he thought I needed it. The Dean sat nearby, his hands folded, neither encouraging nor dismissive, but with the air of a judge presiding over his court. Members of my tutor group formed a cluster: Joshua next to Hannah, and Holly near Leo, his arm around a girl I didn't recognize. I searched quickly, and found Aydin sitting two rows behind.

I began to phase out as the room filled, and the familiar dryness of first-night nerves desiccated my mouth. Lights dimmed, the theatre falling into darkness leaving spotlights to illuminate the podium. Shuffling from the seats and clearing of throats ensued and then the room hushed expectantly.

I breathed slowly, raised my eyes and...

"We are all familiar with the concept of torture as a method of extracting information..." I began. "We also presume it to have been used in ritualized execution and as a form of punishment, and we have evidence for its use in Europe pre-dating the Roman occupation." Picture number one: a garrotted disembodied head, nicely preserved, looking like a pickled walnut; a satisfying groan rose from my audience. I liked to start with a punch.

"Equally familiar will be the perception that torture was used as a form of punishment in medieval courts of justice and as a way of discriminating between the guilty and the righteous." Cue picture number two: colourful fourteenth-century court scene, man and red-hot poker. A shudder from the serried ranks reassured me that I had their full attention, and allowed me to launch into the rest of my discourse. I leaned forward slightly.

"What is less well understood, however, is the use of torture for the benefit and salvation of the recipient, and it is this which concerns us today." I began to get into the swing of things, and the hazy mass in front of me resolved into individual faces as I grew accustomed to the darkness. I looked into my audience, preparing them to engage with me – and straight at the rigid face of Staahl. Sitting directly in front of me about eight rows back, devoid of colour, he watched, and the blood drained from my face as the room momentarily spun and blurred. He registered my reaction and a look of slow satisfaction spread across his face. I hesitated, words frozen, caught in the web of his stare. A soft murmur rose from my audience and a few shuffled uneasily. Elena sat forwards on the edge of her seat, willing me on and Sam looked puzzled, glancing over his shoulder to see what caught my eye. I remembered to breathe and looked anywhere but at Staahl, struggling to regain my composure and to refocus. As my eyes scanned the obscurity at the back of the auditorium where the shadows were deepest, Dr Lynes stood; even in the darkness, his fair hair set him apart from those around him. His eyes locked on mine and he nodded imperceptibly. My heart thumped back into life, Staahl's spell broken; the pause had been only seconds, but it seemed like an eternity. I took a deep breath and, injecting strength into my voice, continued.

"Our... understanding of the medieval and early modern mind is largely based upon our interpretation of history through our own experience. It is almost inconceivable to us, that the purposeful infliction of pain by one person on another, was done with the intention of saving their soul."

I progressed from the Albigensian Crusade through the evidence of the trials during the period of inquest and inquisition in the Spanish kingdoms, and then into the witch hunts of seventeenth-century England and the new colonies in America. Finally, I drew the lecture together on a theme that had haunted me all my adult life.

"As our knowledge ever increases with the discovery and interpretation of new historical material, and in our search for greater understanding through scientific advance and cultural cross-reference, we are at risk of ignoring the *motivations* that lie behind the actions of individuals, and in so doing, forgetting that within each monster, lies a man."

To illustrate my conclusion, I chose a fantastical scene captured in a photograph of a fifteenth-century Doom wall-painting from a church in the Swiss Alps. On the screen high above my head, the standard fare of medieval monsters preying on the sinful was displayed in all its polychromatic glory. But in the right-hand corner, a lone creature gazed balefully as from his torn body – from chest to belly – stepped a new-born man. As a depiction, it begged as many questions as it answered.

It was over. Not a murmur came from the crowded seats before me. Heat from the spotlights bore down on the top of my head and the overhead screen went blank as I switched off the power to the display and waited for a reaction. A sudden *whoop* emanated from the front row, followed by a wave of sound as the audience stood, breaking into a wall of applause. Abashed, I barely remembered to smile in response and needed saving by Elena joining me on stage and giving me a big hug.

"You did so *great!*" She squeezed me again, beaming, with Matias behind her, laconic as usual.

"Not bad for a newcomer, despite the content," he drawled.

"I kept it simple for you," I shot back, recovering rapidly. Then Professors Gerhard and Abrahms were shaking my hand, congratulating me, and Aydin, smiling shyly.

"I'm sure glad I didn't have much breakfast," Sam called over Elena's shoulder. "It might've been embarrassing, not to say messy!"

I grinned back at him. "It wasn't that graphic – you should have seen what I left out!"

Relief ran through me and I began to gather my things, thanking strangers as they came up to congratulate me on a riveting lecture. The Dean made comments to a small, dark-haired man next to him, who nodded in agreement and, to my relief, neither looked disappointed.

Beyond the smiles and handshakes I kept raking the back of the auditorium, now awash with light, looking for the figure of the doctor; but the theatre was already nearly empty and he had clearly gone. Regret flickered briefly, then Sam asked a question.

"What happened, Ginger? I thought you'd forgotten your lines or something. What were you looking at?"

I didn't want to talk about it.

"Nothing – I just lost my place, that's all." I concentrated on finishing putting my things away in my briefcase.

"Looked like you were staring at something," he insisted. "I thought you looked scared there for a moment."

"Sam, is it usual for the Dean to appoint a mentor to new staff – or visiting lecturers?"

He shrugged. "Not that I know of. Why – would you like me to offer, maybe?" He grinned hopefully. I shook my head and picked up my bag.

"Time for food," Elena interjected, giving me a swift look. "Come on, I'm starving. You are paying, Matias."

"*Your* generosity is overwhelming, Elena," Matias replied caustically. "Coming, Sam?" Sam slewed a grin in my direction.

"Naw, I'll wait 'til our date on Friday, thanks." His raised eyebrow promised more than he said, and Matias and Elena glanced at me, a look I studiously ignored.

"Well, we'd better go then," I said briskly, making my way towards the exit. "Bye, Sam," I said over my shoulder.

"Yup," he replied.

Elena caught up with me. "Staahl?" she whispered and I nodded in reply.

The college maintained several places to eat, depending on your status, your preference and your pocket. Elena had indeed been most generous with Matias's wallet and we ended up in the senior lecturers' dining-room. Although considerably smaller than the staff dining-hall, the dark oak panelled room was much quieter, and we found a table to ourselves.

Matias ordered a bottle of red wine to share.

"Is that going to be enough for you?" he asked doubtfully, eyeing my small portion of pasta salad when it appeared in front of me.

Elena answered before I could. "Emma doesn't eat much; I am always telling her 'eat more', but she just picks, picks, picks." She stabbed at bits of rice on her plate to illustrate.

"I'm not used to American-sized portions; give me time and I'll be wolfing a herd of cattle before breakfast."

Matias laughed. "Don't take any notice of Elena; she eats for Russia."

She wrinkled her nose at him, chewing a piece of beef.

"Talking of eating," I said, spearing a cherry tomato and watching it explode in a mass of seeds and juice, "Did you really find the lecture too violent?"

"No, I was only kidding," he replied. "Why do you ask?"

"Oh, I just wondered, that's all."

His knife hovered over his plate. "If it's one thing I have learned about you, Emma, it is that there is always a question behind the question; so I repeat, why do you ask?" He fixed me with his dark-grey, shrewd eyes so that I writhed and felt obliged to answer.

"It's only something Dr Lynes said the other day in the library about it not being too gruesome for the audience. I didn't think it would be so well attended," I muttered, as if that excused it.

"A little bit of gore is just fine before lunch; it gets the appetite going."

Matias purposefully cut into the near-rare lump of beef on his plate and bloody meat juice oozed faintly red and pooled around the dauphinois potatoes. "And anyway," he continued, "Matthew should be used to it – he is a surgeon, after all."

Something jangled in my memory, "Matthew?" I said. "*Matthew* Lynes? Is that his name?"

Both he and Elena looked up at the tone of my voice.

"Yes – Matthew. Why?" he asked.

I couldn't say what it was that tugged at my memory, but somewhere deep down inside the acres of unimportant facts I stored away over the years, I knew it to be significant.

"It reminds me of something I've heard before, but I can't remember where – or what." I ate a piece of pasta thoughtfully then shook my head as the memory refused to be retrieved. "I suppose it's a common enough combination or it sounds like another name perhaps; I don't know."

Idly, I tried to see how many pieces of pasta I could get on the tines of the fork and managed four, the last one falling off and rolling towards the edge of the plate. Elena sipped at her wine, a mischievous glint in her eyes.

"Matias, you work with Dr Lynes sometimes – what do you think of him?" She winked at me and I frowned at her in return.

Matias dissected his steak with precision. He stopped, giving greater consideration to the question than either I or Elena anticipated.

"Matthew's a very quiet man, intensely private, dedicated and quite brilliant; I've never met anyone like him. He does a lot to help out at the hospital and the med centre, but you wouldn't know it; he's very modest."

He sounded in awe of him although he must have been older by some years. Elena seemed just as intrigued.

"Don't you find him cold? *Nyet*, not cold... ah!" And she waved her fork in the air as she grappled with the language before rattling off a word in Russian to Matias.

"Aloof?" he said.

"Yes, yes, a-loof," she repeated. "Do you not find him a-loof?"

Matias leaned forward, and picked up his glass. He swirled the contents around the bowl, examining the glowing colour in the light, thinking, then shook his head, slowly.

"Not aloof, no. Sad – remote, even – but not aloof. He's always very polite and correct, and I'd say that he's self-contained, but I don't find him arrogant or anything like that. But sad, yes."

I stopped eating. What he said chimed with something I had been mulling over since I first met him.

"Yes," I said. "But why?"

Matias paused, uncertain whether he should continue then, seeming to make up his mind, he put his glass down on the table with deliberate care.

"Matthew has every reason; he lost his wife a few years ago – a car accident, I think."

My skin ran cold.

"I didn't know," Elena murmured.

"No, not many people do – he doesn't talk about it. It's only because you asked, Emma, that I'm telling you now. And it's not for public knowledge, either." He fixed a stern eye on Elena, and she nodded wordlessly. I found my voice.

"When did it happen?"

"It must be five – maybe six – years ago, I'm not certain; he's never said and I've never asked. Before he moved here with his family, anyway."

"Family?" The cold was replaced by a flash of heat to my face. I realized how little I knew about him but, in that instant, how much it seemed to matter that I did. I grabbed my glass and gulped wine in sudden confusion, and the discordant roar of voices in my head became a muted murmur once again.

"Emma? Did you hear what I said?" Matias asked.

"What's that? No, sorry."

"I said, Matthew lives with his family, from what I can gather. I've met his father and his niece briefly – and one of his nephews; they help out with the research sometimes."

I didn't give him a chance to finish; the wine did a good job of loosening my grip as well as my tongue.

"He's a widower?"

"Shhh, you're shouting!" Elena shushed me. Several other diners turned to look in our direction.

"A widower? He's not old enough," I repeated in hushed tones, leaning forwards over the table. "He can't be much more than thirty."

"About that, I think," Matias confirmed; "but I didn't think there was an age limit on dying. And – if you would let me finish...?"

"Sorry."

"I was going to say that he doesn't have any kids, that's all. I've known him some time but I don't know much else. As I said, he's a very private man – keeps himself to himself." Matias sat back, running his hands through his unruly hair, making it stick up in erratic tussocks. He looked from me to Elena and back again. "Why are you two so interested, anyhow?"

"No reason," we both said at the same time and for once Elena did me a favour and let the matter drop. We continued to eat in the silence of our own thoughts and Matias ordered coffee as Elena consumed a wedge of cheesecake with gusto.

"Did you finish that already?" she said, eyeing my barely touched food a few minutes later.

"You have it." I pushed it towards her, my appetite evaporated, to be replaced by an unpleasant gnawing sensation. Matias said something to Elena, but I stopped listening. I couldn't get my head round what I had heard and why it should bother me so much. I drank half the coffee to offset the effects of the wine and the hollow feeling inside intensified. My head buzzed and my ears hummed with the air-conditioning. Something nagged away just out of reach and, hard as I tried, it eluded me. Conversations tables away sharpened, intruded, then Elena shook my arm.

"Em, what do you think you will wear?" I gathered my mind and brought it back to the table.

"Wear to what?"

"The All Saints annual dinner, of course, at the end of October. You were not listening again, were you?" She rolled her eyes impatiently.

"No, sorry. I haven't thought about it yet. Look, I'm getting a headache, do you mind if I get off now before it gets any worse?"

"Would you like us to take you back?" Matias looked concerned, already on his feet.

I needed space to think.

"Thanks, but I'll be fine once I've had a couple of paracetamol." I grabbed my jacket and briefcase, pushing the chair away from the table. "And thanks for lunch – it was just what I needed."

"See you later?" Elena called after me.

"OK," I said over my shoulder as I left the room.

I reached the seclusion of my flat, shutting the door on the world. My head ached from the unaccustomed intake of alcohol, but the source of real discomfort lay elsewhere. Tossing bag and coat on a chair, I went through to my bedroom and flung myself on the bed. I lay there for a few moments, letting my head settle, then kicked off my shoes and wrapped myself in the duvet, not bothering to rescue my suit from the inevitable creasing to which I subjected it. I stared at nothing in particular and tried to analyse my reaction.

Learning that the man was no longer married but a widower might have been little in itself; what took me by surprise was the strength of my reaction. Who was I kidding? Matthew Lynes had a quality about him hard to ignore – let alone forget – and not just his looks, although he must be one of the most attractive men I ever laid eyes on. His manner, his voice, the way he spoke, the inflections he used, the way he carved through the muddle in my mind to the very heart of me. My gut flipped and churned and I went to put the kettle on. I retreated to my bed with a mug of tea, feeling the waves of nausea subside. I must have drunk more than I thought; either that or it was the first time I felt sick because of a man. Stupid.

Stupid, stupid, *stupid*. And he probably wouldn't speak to me again after today's blood-soaked lecture. I dreaded to guess what he thought of it, given my undertaking that I wouldn't rely on cheap thrills to sell my theories. That is, if he thought of me at all. I moaned, rolling myself into a tight ball. What was worse:

him seeing me as a purveyor of cheap academia or not thinking of me at all? I wrapped my arms around my legs, squeezing against the intense current of nerves that rolled inside me, the legacy of too much wine.

But if he didn't think of me, he wouldn't have been at the lecture, would he. Would he? Why not, since a rash of other people turned up unexpected and, in one case, unwanted. At the thought of Staahl, I pulled my cross around my chin and toyed with it, the metallic tinge familiar and comforting, and my mind slid back to where it felt safe.

If I identified just one thing that made Matthew Lynes stand out, it would be his consideration: his quiet, understated courtesy that offered me a drink when thirsty, took the heavy books from me, gave me unspoken and unlooked-for reassurance when I faltered in my lecture, who exuded a rare integrity – qualities I looked for in a man, qualities that mattered. And he was no longer off-limits. Now I understood his reaction to the mention of the crash the evening of my reception, and felt mortified at my unintentional blunder.

And Sam. Edgy, funny, interesting – and interested. Sam – taking me out on a non-date-lunch-date on Friday. Who broadcast his interest more obviously than a neon sign. Sam – whose two failed marriages should be a warning to any vulnerable female he pursued. I usually went by my instinct and everything about him shouted "No!" I sensed no common ground with Sam but a quicksand on which I could not rely. And without the shared bedrock in which I believed, there could be no way forward. I had lived that lie; I would not do so again.

I breathed out, determined and resolute once more; I did not – *did not* – seek any form of relationship while in the States; it made life too complicated when all I wanted to do was work and study and tread water for as long as it took to complete my research. And then I would go home: back to Cambridge, my family and my mundane, predictable and ultimately safe existence that made no demands on me, nor I on it.

The nausea began to ease and I rolled onto my back, stretching my arms and legs as I did so and pushing the constricting duvet into a tubby, rumpled heap at the end of the bed. I shouldn't drink; it was a lesson I learned a long time ago to my lasting regret; it made me reckless.

It must have been after one-thirty because, despite the fact my rooms were on the top floor, I could hear the babble and scuffle of student voices making their way to afternoon classes. I followed their example; the only way to suppress unwelcome thoughts of any kind lay in work.

I passed through the joint faculty lobby on my way to my room, checking my pigeon-hole as a matter of course. A note from the porters' lodge waited in the open slot, informing me of a parcel to collect. I stuffed the note in my pocket; it would keep until later.

Holly surpassed herself, having turned in her synopsis and study plan early, and it waited for me on my desk. The lengthy paper proved her to be a bright student, but I had seen the hopeful glances she threw at Leo, and the way she looked when he put his arm around the girl in the lecture hall. I had seen it before; I experienced it first-hand. "The call of the wild", I termed it, because once you felt it, it became almost impossible to ignore.

I made notes for her on separate paper, detailing areas she might find useful in her research, and left it on my desk ready for our next tutorial. A sudden clamour of slamming doors and voices and footsteps outside in the corridor, ended afternoon classes. I had no intention of staying any later by myself; I stuffed the iPod in my bag, and picked up the note from my desk as a reminder to collect my parcel.

Students crowded the corridor as I left. The few I recognized said "Hi" as I wound my way through them to get to the lobby. A huddle of students blocked my path; there were times when my distinctive English accent came in handy.

"Excuse me, please."

They looked around and all but one stepped aside.

I tried again. "Please excuse me?"

The man turned slowly and a feeling of disgust welled up as Staahl's hooded eyes licked over me.

"*Excuse* me!" I repeated more sharply, and this time he

stepped to one side. Several students snickered but a palpable tension ran between them, like a telegraph sent along a wire. I walked rapidly to the staircase, feeling his eyes on my back even when out of sight, even as I ran down the stairs and across the quad without looking behind me. The gentle rain became torrential, soaking my jumper in seconds.

Breathless, soggy and cold, I reached the sanctuary of the cloister. Less intrusive here, I could still smell the rain in the solid, damp walls that rose protectively into the arcaded ceiling. The door from the quad crashed open against the wall and I half-expected to see Staahl's leer in front of me; instead, a group of students tumbled laughing out of the rain. They disappeared down the cloister hall, voices bouncing off the walls, growing fainter and then fading into silence as they went through the stair door one by one. My heart began to beat less ferociously and my breathing steadied.

I went through the heavy glass door to the atrium where the porters' lodge stood to one side. Above, the rain lashed the great dome. No one sat at the waist-high reception desk, so I leaned over the polished wood surface to see if my parcel had been left there. Only a telephone sat on the empty desk behind it.

"Can I help you, ma'am?" The slow, cracked voice of the elderly porter made me jump, and I handed him the note. He shuffled over to a room to the right of the desk, returning a moment later with a long cardboard poster tube that rattled promisingly as he handed it over. "Excellent! Thanks," I said and retraced my steps to the cloister.

It was clear that he waited for me by the way he watched the door as I pushed through it. Staahl must have known I would come to pick up the parcel. He must have known that I had a parcel *to* collect. I swore silently to myself, cursing the open pigeon-holes at the history fac. The door closed heavily behind me with a conclusive *clunk*, preventing retreat. I didn't acknowledge him, barely hesitating as I began to walk hurriedly, hugging the right-hand wall of the broad stone passage and looking straight ahead to avoid making eye contact. Matching my pace for a few yards, he suddenly stepped in front of me, forcing me to stop abruptly to prevent a collision. Although not tall, he dominated the space around him. His voice coiled.

"Professor D'Eresby, how good it is to see you again. I must apologize for the confusion earlier, it was my mistake; I have so looked forward to meeting you *properly*."

He hardly opened his mouth when he spoke and deep vertical creases between his eyes gave him the look of a wolf – unblinking, ever vigilant. His smooth-shaven face was oddly unlined; it dawned on me that there were no creases at the corners of his eyes or mouth, no smile lines, no laughter at all in his face. Damaged.

He took a step closer and I involuntarily backed away, glancing nervously over my shoulder. We were alone in the cloister and the porter couldn't see us from the reception desk where he stood. In the distance, so faint that I could only just make it out although there were barely a dozen yards between us, the empty bell of a telephone rang. No escape.

He stood close – too close; I could feel the heat of his body.

"I found your lecture fascinating this morning, very much along the lines of my own research, especially with regard to the *monster within* – a subject close to my heart. We really must get together sometime."

He spoke excellent English with only a hint of his Dutch origins. Had I not known, he would be difficult to place. I said nothing; there was nothing *to* say and I don't think he expected an answer. What did he want? The lines between his eyes deepened as he peered closely at me in the weak light of the corridor. I flinched back and he smiled the same way he had this morning as he enjoyed watching me squirm. The smile didn't touch his eyes, nor did it register in the history of his face.

"I was telling my students about your theory relating to torture and the Inquisition. Ties in so nicely with the literature of the period, don't you think? I'm sure you are familiar with it. It has been a deep interest of mine for many years, an interest you share, I believe."

A faint, stale odour hung about him, not helped by the wet, dead-dog smell of the wool coat he wore. It hung in my throat, making me queasy. I wanted to run, but he placed himself so that whichever way I went, he had only to move an inch and he would touch me.

The sound of a door opening at the far end of the cloister brought fresher air, and I felt a flash of relief. Footsteps and two low male voices came rapidly closer; Staahl's head jerked up and his eyes narrowed as he registered the newcomers.

"Dr D'Eresby, good afternoon."

A newly familiar and very welcome voice greeted me. I spun around to find Matthew Lynes standing behind me, looking over my head directly at Staahl.

"Staahl." He acknowledged him with no warmth in his tone and a gaze that could cut ice. Staahl stared rigidly back for a moment before his lip lifted in a sneer, his eyes sliding towards me once again.

"I'll catch you later, Professor D'Eresby – it's a *promise*." He emphasized the last word, his voice creeping down my spine. I shuddered. Matthew took a quick step forward and Staahl baulked. Turning abruptly, he left through the door to the quad without another word. Matthew watched him until he was out of sight, and then calmly looked down at me.

"Hello," he said, and he smiled so that the warmth of it drove away any lingering fear.

"Hi," I replied, shakily, although nothing tangible had happened to warrant the shiver that went through me now. His eyes cast over me and he frowned.

"You're soaked, you must be cold, here…" He took off his dark-blue coat, wrapping it around my shoulders before I could protest about getting it wet.

"Thanks," I murmured, and I meant it doubly because he seemed to understand, although he made no reference to what just happened, instead turning to the young man standing behind him in the diffused light. I barely noticed him until that moment.

"I would like to introduce you to Harry. Harry, this is Dr D'Eresby."

The boy took a pace towards me, close enough for me to see him clearly for the first time. He must be his nephew – he was the right sort of age. Good-looking and startlingly like his uncle, he extended his hand, his smile open and friendly.

"Dr D'Eresby, it's good to meet you."

"Harry's been helping me with a research project this afternoon," Matthew explained, indicating the box the boy carried under one arm. I looked shyly at the pair of them, not at all sure what to say next.

"Perhaps, Harry, you would kindly take the box to my car."

Harry looked swiftly at his uncle then back at me, and took the set of car keys from Matthew's hand.

"Sure," he said. "Dr D'Eresby, please excuse me; it was a pleasure to meet you."

"Are you on your way back to your room?" Matthew asked as the door closed behind his nephew. I nodded.

"Might I walk with you?"

I nodded again. I didn't want to ask him if it was out of his way because I knew that it must be and then what excuse would I have for his company? The rain eased but a light wind drove it periodically against the glass. We walked slowly along the cloister. Although fair, even under the yellow light his complexion had the look of someone who enjoyed robust good health. Not yet recovered from the first smile, I swallowed, pulling his coat closer around me. I tucked the poster tube under my arm.

"Your lecture was very interesting this morning – thought-provoking – and well attended. I believe your audience coped well with the subject matter." A smile ghosted and I couldn't tell if he teased or not. I remembered his abrupt absence.

"Did you think it gratuitous? I know that I said that it wouldn't be and I really thought that it wasn't, and all of the material was entirely relevant." I gabbled self-consciously, not letting him answer. "I'm sorry if you were offended – I really didn't mean to… I mean, it wasn't *that* bad, was it?"

He looked at me in surprise. "Why do you think I found it offensive?"

"You left suddenly; I thought that perhaps… um, well… some of the references *were* quite gory…" I couldn't finish, and I felt my face flare scarlet; facing Staahl had been less awkward than this.

He shook his head slowly. "I had to get back to a departmental meeting. I'm sorry if you thought I left because of anything you said. You were very good, you know – despite the graphic detail," he added, now definitely suppressing a smile. I stopped and buried my head in my hands. "What's the matter?" He sounded concerned, which made me feel even worse. I took my hands away from my face, but couldn't look up at him.

"I feel a complete *idiot*," I muttered.

"Hardly," he said. "By the way," he continued, helping me out, "I've finished the book you kindly lent me. Can I return it sometime this week?"

Grateful for the diversion, my skin cooled and I felt my high colour gradually fade to normal. I recovered enough to smile at him.

"Yes, of course. I'm in tomorrow and Friday morning, if they are any good?"

"Fine – I'll bring it around."

I wanted to ask him what he made of it, but I didn't trust myself not to put my foot in it again, so thought it better to keep quiet.

We reached the end of the cloister and stood at the foot of the stairs to the first floor, waiting to let the person pass, whose rapid steps came hurrying down the stairs towards us.

Elena's flushed face came into view. "Emma! I've been searching for you everywhere!" She stopped suddenly as she caught sight of Matthew, looking from him to me and back again, uncertainly.

"What's the matter?" I asked, apprehension rising.

Her Russian accent choked her English as she panted, "You have a telephone call from England; it is urgent. I have looked for you but I could not find you."

"Who was it from? What's happened? Did they say anything?"

"I do not know – the porter came to find you but you had gone. I have been looking for many minutes now. Why don't you have a cell phone? Come on, I will take you and you can phone them." She tugged at my arm urgently.

Turning to Matthew, I hesitated, my mind in turmoil.

"I'm sorry, I have to go. Thanks... for earlier. Thank you so much." I started to take off his coat, but he stopped me.

"No, keep it; give it back when I next see you. I hope everything is all right... at home." He looked directly at me, and for a moment I saw a depth of compassion in the sadness that haunted his eyes, and I remembered that he might have been through something similar before.

"Thanks," I said again.

"Emma, come *on*," Elena said as she looked again at Matthew before pulling me back in the direction of the porters' lodge and the telephone call home.

It was so brief I thought I had dreamt it. Woken to a night still black and heavy with sleep, I strained to listen through the darkness, only hearing the rapid thump of my startled heart. I reached out and found my alarm clock: just past four in the morning. My eyes closed, ready to sleep, when I heard it again – distinctly this time – a scream – muffled then silenced – but definitely a scream. I sat bolt upright, listening. The clock ticked in the empty space the sound left.

Climbing out of bed, I padded barefoot across the cold floor to the dormer window and, opening it, leaned out as far as I could. It took a minute for my eyes to adjust to the inky night. A thin crescent moon ghosted behind the patchy cloud, giving a little more light now and again to the darkened world. I made out the shape of the trees but little else and no sound other than the faint *shhhhh* of the wind in the pines. I listened to the silence for a moment or two longer then stiffened as something moved quick and sly against the ground beyond the tree. A fox. Relieved but awake now, I went back to bed to churn over the previous day's events.

My father had phoned from England; my grandmother – my dear, dotty Nanna who sang me songs from our favourite musicals in the sunshine of our summer garden – had suffered a stroke. She wasn't dead, but it could only be a question of time.

"Mum must be devastated; I'll come home straight away."

His reply was instantaneous so he must have been expecting my response.

"No, she doesn't want you to leave; there's nothing you can do, and besides..." he quickly intercepted my next argument, "Nanna isn't aware of anything or anyone at the moment. Stay there; I'll let you know if there's any change."

I pressed my lips together; Dad didn't cope with tears very well.

"Tell Mum I'm so sorry and please... tell Nanna that I love her, even if she can't hear you."

"I'll do that," he assured me gruffly. "And you, are you all right, Em – at the college? Is all in order?"

He didn't quite ask me if I behaved myself and worked hard, but it was there in his tone.

"It's brilliant, Dad, everything's fine. Work's going well. No problems." *Except the weirdo, perhaps.* "And everyone's very welcoming."

It's what he wanted to hear. "That's good. Take care. Work hard. Everyone sends their love." *Over and out.* The phone went dead. I placed it back on the receiver, aware of the curious gaze of the few visitors who waited in the atrium and wishing I had replaced my lost mobile. Elena put her arm around my back and looked questioningly.

"It's OK," I reassured her and explained. She nodded and took me back to her apartment to make tea while I dried off in front of her fan-heater clutching Matthew's coat to me. She noticed, but unusually didn't say anything until at last, she could restrain her curiosity no longer.

"That is Dr Lynes' coat, no?"

"Yes," I confirmed, not wishing to be drawn into man-talk at this juncture.

"He lent you his coat; I think he must like you. You like him – this is a good sign."

I tucked his coat to one side of me so that it wasn't so obvious.

"Not now, Elena, I'm not in the mood this minute."

"OK, OK, I understand. But we must talk, yes? We have a

girls' night together and we talk about Sam and Matthew and we drink wine and eat chocolate. It will be good fun."

I smiled at her, at the effort she made to cheer me up and her deep desire for gossip.

"The chocolate sounds good."

"Then it is a promise, *da*? Sometime soon."

"Yes, all right, it's a promise; we'll have to set a date later. I'll drop you a note in your pigeon-hole."

The clock ticked, steadily beating out the seconds of the night and I continued to lie restlessly awake. What of Staahl? His unfortunate manner and appearance might just be that, and no more. Could his sudden manifestation in the cloister be coincidental, because I felt certain I had not imagined that his words were laced with menace.

But why?

It was all very well understanding the motives of others in a historical context, but in everyday life? Historical sources often revealed motives unwittingly and, reading between the lines, they usually fell into four categories: the Mad, the Bad, the Hopeful and the Resourceful. The Mad were self-explanatory and they dotted history as the syphilitic pox marked out the faces of the infected. The Bad were less easy to identify and were more subjective – a mixture of expediency and ambition without the restraining hand of conscience. The Hopeful financed the building of churches, commissioned masses and altar-pieces; they built almshouses, wrote love poems and nursed the dying: they looked to nurture their souls. Then there were the Resourceful – opportunists who might or might not tread upon the backs of others to get what they wanted, and who walked hand in hand with the other three.

Staahl, I thought, belonged to one of the first two categories – or perhaps both. That he posed a threat I felt almost without doubt. What he might do about it was another matter. Almost certainly Matthew had picked up on it; he warned Staahl off in the look he gave him and in the tone of his voice. I turned over, unable to sleep, the image of the doctor and his nephew bright in my mind.

And Matthew Lynes? What could I make of him and where –
in my panoply of motives – would I place him? Whereas I thought
it crystal clear why Sam sought my company, I couldn't fathom
Matthew and, while he was neither mad nor bad and didn't seem
to be an opportunist, of what could he be so hopeful as to want
to talk to me?

5

Maelstrom

I DEVELOPED A STONKING HEADACHE by the next morning.

"But you had only *one* glass of wine," Elena said sceptically when I opened the door to her, shielding my eyes from the sun. Her voice rattled around my empty head and, outside, the birds yelled from the branches of the cedar tree.

"Yes, but I hardly ever drink so when I do, it really counts." I put my aching head in my hands; they felt cooler than my banging skull. "Anyway, what brings you here so bright and early?"

"It's not early, it is nearly 8.45 and have you heard the news?" She hardly contained herself, but I couldn't cope with that level of excitement at this time of the morning.

"Good grief, is that the time? I'm late." I grabbed a towel and made for the bathroom. "What news?" I said, stopping at the door and looking round as her words filtered through the alcohol-induced fug.

"About the attack last night – on a girl – a student," she said breathlessly.

"What – here, on campus?" Instantly alert, my headache forgotten, I came back in the room and sat on the edge of the armchair, my shower now irrelevant. Only then did I see she wasn't excited at all, she was frightened.

"Yes. In the student accommodation – in her room. Matias heard it from one of the researchers – Megan – at the science fac. She is a friend of this girl and it was in the early morning, I think."

The student block lay out of sight from my windows, around

the corner of the next wing, but in the numb darkness of the night, a scream might have carried that far if anyone had been there to hear it. With a stab of remorse, I looked at her, horrified.

"Yes – it was. Something woke me but I thought it was just a fox. Elena, I could have done something to help! Is... is she all right?"

She looked peaky and her eyes stared fearfully at me. "Not really." Her voiced dropped to a whisper and I strained to hear. "She's not dead, but... well, she's *damaged*."

"What happened?"

She described what little she knew and even that made my skin crawl. I remembered the feeling of being watched; I felt the breath of stirred air against my cheek, the rush to lock my door to keep the unknown darkness out, and I shrivelled inside because mine seemed a baseless fear in the face of what this girl suffered.

"You did not know," Elena said quietly, reading my silence. I looked up and saw her close to tears.

"What is it?" I asked.

"The g... girl." Brown eyes stared out of her elfin face and her lower lip trembled.

"Yes, it's awful, but..."

"No, you do not understand; it happened to me." She lifted her hands to her face, collapsing into sobs that shook the whole of her slim body. I put my arms around her and held her until the sobs became whimpers, whimpers mere tears, finally stopping altogether. I found a clean tissue up my sleeve.

"What happened?"

She caught another sob and sniffled and blew her nose, drying pink-rimmed eyes on the back of her hand.

"It was so long ago..." she hesitated.

"But it feels like it happened yesterday?" I encouraged.

She smiled a small, thin smile. "*Da*, like yesterday. I was fourteen years old and I lived in St Petersburg." Her voice wobbled and she retrieved the tissue from her sleeve and blew her nose again. "I came back from school; it was winter, and very cold." She shivered as she remembered. "I heard noise coming from behind me, but I saw nothing. I was first home and it was dark – I remember the darkness. I opened the door and I thought I was safe, but… but – there was a man behind me and he pushed me inside…" Elena bit her lip. "It was horrible. I don't want to say any more."

"Does Matias know?" I asked.

"Yes, he does. That is why he told me about the girl himself this morning. He didn't want me to find out on the… how do you say it?"

"Grapevine?" I suggested.

"*Da*, grapevine. He said he will find out more if he can."

"Perhaps they'll get whoever did this quickly, and then you won't need to be afraid."

Elena pulled away and gave me a pitying look.

"Emma, they will catch him but there will be another like him, and another. There will always be men like this one and the one who attacked me – *predators*." She sneered the word out. "Who will hunt them, eh? Who will be *their* predator?"

There ran a seam of truth in what she said, but predators came in many guises.

"Did they get the man who attacked you?"

She looked away and then down at her hands and mumbled something I didn't catch.

"Elena?"

She shrugged. "I said nothing. I told no one. I was ashamed."

I covered her hand with mine and we sat without speaking because there seemed little either of us could say, until someone knocked on my door, breaking our solitary thoughts; it was Matias.

"There you are," he said, as he entered the room, obviously relieved when he saw Elena. "I thought you might be here." He kissed the top of her head then inspected her face.

"You've been crying, baby; are you all right?" he asked tenderly. She nodded.

"I'm OK now; Emma has been looking after me. Have you heard anything else?"

He balanced on the arm of the chair and stroked her hair.

"The girl is stable – I know that much. Whoever attacked her was interrupted before any lasting harm could be done. She's going to be fine"

"How do you know that – I mean, where did you find out?" I asked as I rose to fill the kettle.

"Matthew treated her in the med centre; she came round and she told him what happened, as far as I can tell."

Elena's face became pinched again. "What *did* happen?"

Matias looked doubtfully at her, before deciding she would be better hearing the most accurate account from him, than find out a mangled version from someone else.

"I don't know much, but it looks like someone – a man – climbed in through her window. Her room's on the ground floor. She woke up and screamed but he had a knife. She managed to fight him off but he was too strong, got her around the throat and... well... she doesn't remember much after that. Only... well, she *thinks* that he spoke with an accent."

"So do about a third of the students here," I said, "and staff," I muttered as an afterthought, grey eyes in a grey face prominent in my unspoken thoughts. "But she didn't see who it was? How old? How he dressed? Anything?"

He shook his head. "No, whoever it was took a great deal of care not to leave anything behind – no prints, no DNA, nothing. And she couldn't say for sure if he did have an accent, just that's the impression she gained from the little he said." We were all quiet for a moment. "You must take care – both of you – no taking risks and stick together until they get this guy, OK?" I recalled again the click of a door, silence on the stairs, someone who wasn't there. We both nodded. "Are you going over to the history block?" he asked.

"Once I've phoned the police," I confirmed.

"I'll take you when you're ready," he said.

We were both glad to have Matias' company for different reasons. I kept a sharp eye open for any signs of Staahl, checking my pigeon-hole briefly as we passed. I remembered to bring my poster roll and had already emailed my thanks to my friend in Cambridge. She replied reminding me that I neglected to give her any real news, but what was there to tell? I filled her in on the inaugural lecture, leaving out the bit about Staahl. I told her about the library and the facilities of the college, but nothing of Sam or Matthew. And I told her about the mountains that beckoned to me every morning as I drew the curtains and saw their grey caps turn gradually to white.

Clouds were beating a retreat ahead of a strengthening sun, and my room was stuffy when I went in. I made sure to secure the door before opening a window. A ladybird had found its way into my room, looking for a place to overwinter in the cracked stonework of the window. This desire to hide away from the world, to bury its head: I knew how it felt. The morning's events put me out of sync and I hoped Matthew hadn't called earlier and found me gone as, despite my clumsy conversation, I felt safe around him.

A quiet knock sounded on my door and I was halfway to opening it before I remembered to check.

"Who is it?"

"Aydin."

I opened the door just wide enough to see, before letting him in.

"You weren't expecting to see me, were you?" I asked, thinking I must have forgotten to put it in my diary.

"No, but I must see you, Professor – do you mind?"

He seemed agitated and he shifted restlessly, avoiding my eyes. Day-old hair roughened his face and dark circles under his eyes made him look more haunted than ever. I pointed to a chair but he didn't sit down. He paced away from me, then sharply back again, his fists clenched around an envelope, creasing the smooth manila surface into ridges. He made me nervous just watching him.

"I cannot do this thing. I have tried but my English – it is not good enough."

He began to twist the envelope, throttling the life out of it.

"Aydin, I haven't a clue what you are talking about."

"This," he said and flung the envelope down, my own papers shifting in the sudden current of air. I drew them back into a neat pile again and picked it up. He stood facing the window, scowling at the sun. He had written the first part of his thesis. Page after page of type with scribbled notes in Turkish, and words, sentences and paragraphs crossed out with livid slashes of pen tearing the heart out of the paper.

"I don't understand, Aydin – what's the problem with this?"

"Read it!" he almost hissed, his eyes wide and angry.

"All right, but calm down – and sit down," I ordered him. "You're making me nervous."

He slumped into the chair opposite, and bit his knuckle, watching intently for my reaction through eyes bloodshot from lack of sleep. I read the first page, then put it down.

"Ah."

"You see now? Rubbish, trash, garbage." Invective spilled.

"No, that's not what *I* meant, but I can see what you mean. Aydin, your grammar is all over the place; what happened to you?"

He glared at me, chewing viciously at his thumb. "I cheat."

"What are you talking about?"

"You read my synopsis, yes?"

"Yes – you know I did; it was very good."

"Well, now you know truth."

"No, not really. Are you saying that you didn't write it – it isn't your own work?"

"My work – yes, of course – but not my words. I have help to make it better English. You have to tell the authority now, and I leave here and go back to Turkey."

"Is that what you want, Aydin?" I asked quietly.

His voice cracked in agony.

"No, no, *no*! But I am *Çok fena* – how do you say? – *very bad!*"

"But all the research you showed me – that is yours; and your interpretation – that is your own work?"

"*Evet* – yes, all of it."

"Then I can't see a problem – not one that's insurmountable, anyway – not if you don't give up, that is. The problem is your ability to record your ideas in standard English, not in the ideas themselves. You have one of the most original approaches to the subject I have ever seen. I won't give up on you, if you don't."

The deep creases crossing his forehead lessened slightly; he looked almost hopeful.

"You will help me?"

"Yes – of course."

I flipped through the rest of the pages.

"I think the best thing here would be to start again..." his face fell, "in Turkish, and then have it translated. I will check each section for linguistic errors and, as long as the translation remains true to your original research, I think it will pass muster." He frowned. "Be acceptable," I explained. "Who helped you with the synopsis? Can they help again?" He looked a little shifty. "Who was it?"

He smiled shyly. "I have a friend; she might help me again."

"Well, I hope she's a *good* friend because this will need a lot of work."

He beamed unexpectedly. "Yes, she is a *very* good friend."

I laughed. "Thank goodness for that; now get some rest – you look awful."

He shrugged. "I could not sleep last night; I tell the others I was so angry with myself but they do not understand. Now, I can sleep." He grinned again and, as I held out the manuscript to him, he took my hand in both of his and shook it.

"Thank you – you have saved my life."

Normally, I would have made some comment about him being melodramatic, but he looked so sincere that I kept quiet.

I locked the door again once he left, and pulled the contents from the poster tube, letting them uncoil in my hands. Some were old associates that kept me company through all my early days at Cambridge – and some very dark nights – and some were new posters my friend sent as an early Christmas present. By the time I arranged them on the walls, the first signs of hunger crept up on me. I glanced at my watch, regretting not making a firmer time with Matthew. His coat lay on the chair where I left it. I picked it up, feeling its softness, and brought it towards my face. It smelled of clean air – a fresh outdoor smell of mountains and forests and streams. It reminded me of him.

By 2.30 he still hadn't arrived and all I managed to achieve was summed up in the posters on the wall and some sorting out of the piles of books into chronological order. Not good. An hour later, and I began to reconcile myself to the fact that he wouldn't show, which was probably more important to me than I liked to admit. At home, I would have buried myself in my work, but here, my ability to focus diminished at a rate directly proportionate to my increasing interest in a man whom I had met less than half a dozen times. I threw myself into my desk chair and rammed the iPod earphones in my ears, letting the music run through me, then at last settled down to write the outline for my next piece of research.

It was some time later when a rapid succession of knocks at the door jolted me back to reality; a familiar voice called out.

"Emma – are you ready?"

It took me a moment to remember that Matias had offered to escort me back to my flat. I stilled the brief flurry of disappointment, grabbed my bag and Matthew's coat, and left, hugging it close to me.

"This is ludicrous, you know that, don't you?"

We navigated hordes of students on our way to the staff dining-hall – a much less formal affair than the dining-room and therefore decidedly preferable in my view. I shot a look at Matias and Elena as I dodged two hefty post-grads who would have done equally well on the rugby pitch. "I mean you having to escort us around campus, Matias."

Elena looked sombrely at him; she had been uncharacteristically quiet all morning. He tucked his arm around her waist.

"Hey, I can't think of anything I'd rather be doing than escorting two gorgeous women around campus. It's not doing my reputation as a legendary lover much harm either; if I'm not mistaken, Megan made a pass at me the other day. Anyhow, it's no problem, and I'd rather you *both* felt safe."

He looked at me meaningfully. I mentally kicked myself; Matias wasn't doing this so much for us, but for Elena, except that he didn't want her to know in case she realized how fragile he thought her at the moment. With Staahl around, I should be grateful for small mercies. I slowed down and kept pace with them.

"Well, it's still good of you, and Elena and I will stick together, won't we? And by the way, whoever *Megan* is, Matias – isn't she more a case of wishful thinking on your part, or do you think she's looking for a father-figure?"

I skipped out of the way as he aimed a finger at my ribs, and Elena let out a squeal of protest at my comments, followed by a laugh. Matias stole a quick kiss and she beamed at him. I felt a wash of spinsterly jealousy at their relationship, not that I begrudged Elena one bit, only there was a bond between them I had never experienced. I had a sudden image of the Maiden Aunts – the lost generation from the First World War – sitting benign and distant around our dining-room table at Christmas like plump, barren hens, clinging to their furs and jewels as to the remnants of their hopes and youth lost to the trenches and fevers of a bygone age. Glumly, I wondered if I would become one of them in years to come.

Elena broke through my reverie. "You could ask Sam to go with you, Emma; he would like that, I'm sure."

I thought that probably he would.

"Thanks, but I bet he has better things to do with his time." And, besides, I didn't want to encourage him. Elena refused to be put off that easily and she regained some of her sparkle.

"You and Sam have a date tomorrow, don't you?" she said innocently, her dark eyes dancing with mirth. We had entered the staff dining-hall and her clear voice carried further in the relative quiet.

"Elena!" I hissed, checking out the other diners, but no one paid us any attention. We began to circle the central food bar like sharks eyeing their prey. The selection was always less varied by late lunch; it looked like leftovers, as appealing as day-old curry after a heavy night out.

"It's not a date; I'm just letting him take me out for lunch to make up for last week. There's a difference. And no, I won't be asking him to conduct me around campus either; it might give him the wrong idea."

I selected a pile of lettuce leaves from a large bowl of red and green salad and concentrated on keeping the frilly bits from falling off the edge of my plate.

Elena peered at my plate, temporarily distracted from the prospect of fresh gossip by the opportunity to apply her peculiar form of nurturing.

"Is that all you are having?"

"And tomato. And possibly mayonnaise." I heard myself being unnecessarily defensive. "I'm not that hungry."

"You are *never* hungry; I think I will tell your mother. There must be something wrong with you." She sounded genuinely cross as she slammed some wrinkled lasagne onto her own plate and piled boiled potatoes next to it. Matias reached across the bar to help himself.

"Leave Emma alone; she's old enough to starve herself if she wants to. Anyway, Sam will force feed her tomorrow, so I wouldn't worry."

He cast a sideways grin in my direction as he ladled the remains of what looked like a meat stew onto his plate followed by a mountain of steamed vegetables, the smell completely unappetizing.

I narrowed my eyes suspiciously. "Has Sam said anything to you about tomorrow?" They shook their heads simultaneously, which I took to mean that he had but that they weren't going to admit it.

"This feels remarkably like a set-up," I griped.

"You'll have fun," Elena promised, smirking as we sat down at the end of one of the long, polished refectory tables that looked as if they originated in a monastery. Dotted along their length, a few other staff members sat in small groups or alone. One of the women looked up and smiled. I recognized her as Professor Siggie Gerhard, head of the faculty of psychology.

"Hi," I smiled back. She said something to the other women with whom she sat and shuffled on her ample bottom along the bench towards me.

"Hello," she replied. "I've been meaning to come and see you since your lecture – since we met, actually."

"That seems ages ago," I admitted.

"You have been busy, no doubt." Her skin, arranged in soft lines, reflected years of good humour. Her eyes were the only feature in her benign face – ageing and plump – that betrayed the pin-sharp mind that lay behind them.

"Busy, yes," I agreed. "Thanks for coming to the lecture, by the way – for making the time."

"That was my pleasure; you have to remember my special interest in your subject. In my world, we tend to concentrate on the victims of torture. Your perspective is quite unique, you know; few are willing to recognize the... *needs* of the perpetrator as you do." She screwed up her eyes as she studied me.

"Put like that, it makes it sound as if I'm making excuses for their behaviour, but that's really not the point."

Her slight Teutonic accent gently interrogated. "No? What is the point then?"

"It isn't a question of right or wrong – not in historical terms – just what *is* – or *was*. I don't sit in judgment on historical figures; I attempt to understand their actions."

"Why?"

"You are the second person to ask me that," I mused, remembering the interest in the shifting colours of the doctor's eyes. I saw she wanted an answer. "I don't really know," I confessed, and it was possibly the first time I hadn't come up with a cogent reason for what I did on demand.

"What did you tell this other person?"

I paused. "That I sometimes wonder whether there *is* any point in what I do."

"And what did he say?"

I looked up sharply. I hadn't mentioned anything about it being a man. The Professor waited, her hands folded neatly on the table in front of her.

"He said that I do what I do because I can."

"Well then, hmmm." She thought about it. "That was a clever answer – astute. Do I know this man?"

"I don't know – probably not." I found myself reluctant to bring Matthew under her scrutiny.

Elena leaned over conspiratorially.

"It's Sam Wiesner from the maths fac," she giggled. Matias gave her a censorial look and she pouted at him. I didn't realize they were listening.

"No – it's *not*," I almost snapped back. All three of them looked at me in surprise. "It isn't," I said more reasonably; "it… it's Dr Lynes." I hoped that by using his title they wouldn't notice the effect even mentioning his name had on me. I could feel the tell-tale warmth spreading around my neck.

"Matthew Lynes? You have met him? He normally keeps himself to himself. I have only met him what… twice, in the last few years. I have *heard* about him, yes, but he tends to stay out of sight except for official occasions like the All Saints' dinner or Thanksgiving, you know? And even then he sometimes doesn't show. But you have met him – talked with him. Well, well…" she trailed off.

Elena pushed her plate away from her, seemingly intrigued by my latest revelation. "Emma, you are a black pony; you did not say you met him again!"

It took me a second to fathom her strange use of the language.

"There's nothing *to* tell, Elena, and it's 'dark horse', not 'black pony'."

By the time Siggie and Matias stopped laughing and Elena ceased pretending to mind, I hoped attention had been diverted from the subject of Matthew Lynes; but Siggie wasn't the sort to let the matter drop.

"Emma, you are very interesting; perhaps I should make a study of you?" She saw my look of horror. "Just kidding! Everyone gets evasive when I'm around; it makes a great game." She chuckled again.

"I'm glad I amuse," I said dryly and concentrated on gluing

lettuce and tomato together with some mayonnaise before attempting to eat it. Matias and Elena began talking about something else in Russian interspersed with what sounded like Finnish.

Siggie bent towards me, "I'm sorry, I didn't mean to embarrass you in front of your friends, but you surprised me. Dr Lynes has a formidable reputation as a surgeon, but people are wary of him on campus."

"Why?" My curiosity engaged, it was difficult not to let it show.

She motioned with her hands. "What people do not understand they destroy, eh? Like Luddites from your history – like witches – you know that as well as anyone. If you do not belong to the tribe, the collective – if you are different in any way – you are hunted down and eliminated, physically or culturally. Either way, Dr Lynes has a reputation."

"For what?"

"For being *different*."

That was exactly how Elena had described him. "Is that all?"

She inspected me closely. "Does it matter?"

I didn't even try to hide my interest from her any more. "Yes, it does – to me." My hand found his coat beside me on the bench, and I wound my fingers into the fabric.

"Look, Emma, as far as I'm aware, he has never put a foot wrong. He is a fine surgeon and he is a dedicated scientist with a mind as sharp as one of his scalpels. He even endowed the faculty of medicine and science – he had the centre built, for goodness' sake! I have never heard one bad thing said about him, but..." and she paused, looking at me cautiously, "but people do not *know* him, they cannot work him out, and they don't like that."

I followed the grain of the table with my finger, like a train of thought.

"But I do," I said softly.

"Ah, then there's no hope for you, is there?" She smiled kindly.

I shook my head, trying not to laugh out of embarrassment. "Probably not," I agreed.

Elena and Matias finished eating and were making ready-to-move noises. I stood up and started to gather my things. Siggie Gerhard suddenly put a hand out as I bent to get Matthew's coat.

"Just take care, won't you?" she urged.

I was about to reply, but something at the other end of the table caught my eye. I turned my head.

"Matthew Lynes isn't what I'm afraid of," I choked. Siggie looked in the direction of my stare. Staahl moved down the room with another man, looking for a space; he hadn't noticed me yet. I turned my back on him. She raised her eyebrows. "Problem?" she asked.

"Oh yes," I replied.

"Now he has a reputation for 'putting it about', I think you might say. A crude term, but you understand my meaning, I think."

"*Him!*" I couldn't keep the incredulity out of my voice.

"You think that surprising?" she asked.

"Do they have to be dead first?"

It was her turn to look surprised and she glanced back at Staahl, puzzled by my vehemence.

"I must go," I said hurriedly. Elena had just seen Staahl and indicated in his direction to Matias. "But it was good to talk with you – you've given me things to think about. Thanks." I stepped out of the confines of the bench and turned to go.

"No, not at all; I find it very interesting talking to you. I will see you again soon." She all but winked. I smiled in reply, holding the coat against my chest as I followed my friends from the dining-hall.

I wanted to be alone to try and piece together the disparate fragments of information I had gathered so far about Matthew. Seemingly, like the rest of humanity, I too needed to understand him. But unlike them, part of his fascination for me lay in the not knowing. More than that, an indefinable element drew me to him and, like a whirlpool, the more I struggled against the current, the closer it pulled me in. *Maelstrom*, the Norwegians call it, and I headed straight for the centre.

Sleeping Dogs

THE MOUNTAINS LOOKED WHITER than I remembered from the day before. Snow that once capped their heads, now bleached their shoulders and, even from this distance, the air flowing from them smelled different – sharper, cleaner, inviting. I yearned to be among them, the natural result of living a life on the edge of the vast Fens where the tallest thing in the immediate landscape was a solitary tree.

After breakfast, I showered and washed my hair, watching as the pink-hued copper emerged through the bristles of my brush and gradually dried in a glossy sheet. As a child, I endured the endless snide remarks of my peers because of the colour of my hair, but adults tended to know better than to comment and only stared when they thought I wasn't looking. It drew less attention if I wore it up so that the light couldn't shine through it. I pulled it back from my face into a ponytail and then flipped it through itself so that it looked almost pleated at the back.

The air was much fresher today on the way to the history fac and I wished I wore Matthew's coat rather than carrying it. Deep in thought as we approached our rooms, I came to only when Elena caught my sleeve before I went in.

"Have you eaten breakfast, Em?" she asked with all the severity of a mother speaking to a teenage girl, "and drunk your tea?"

"Of course." I didn't add that it included the consumption of a small bar of chocolate as well, just for good measure. She inspected me with the thoroughness of a professional dresser, rotating me like a top so that she could check out my rear view, before nodding approvingly.

"I like your hair done that way and also the colours." She waved at my russet shirt and jumper the colour of cob nuts. "Yes, you will do, I think."

"Emma, you look great; have a good time." Matias kissed me on the cheek as he left me at the door of my tutor room.

I smiled absently at him, still miles away. "Mm, thanks."

"Be good, then," Elena twittered meaningfully. She seemed to be waiting for something and I wondered what I missed, but it escaped me, so I simply said, "See you later," and with a pert expression she went into her room to find her waiting cohort of fledgling academics.

I emailed my sister before doing anything else. She had taken my card and flowers – freesias, Nanna's favourites – to the hospital, and placed them by her bed. Stable, if no better, at least our grandmother survived. Nanna could prepare herself for what lay ahead, and not everyone had that. Without warning, the image of the woman's broken body imposed itself, and that of Matthew bending over her – maintaining her dignity even in death. As if she mattered. As if he cared. It made sense now, a story complete; but the image haunted, and I welcomed the opportunity to push the unsettling thoughts from my mind when my students arrived and we focused on work.

Lunchtime soon beckoned. My group dispersed to the various corners of the campus and I remained, ruminating on the topic recently discussed. As background information for their research, we continued to explore the attitudes of clergy from the mainstream denominations towards anomalous religious groups during the seventeenth century. As I contemplated the posters on my wall, I considered the role of the outcast in society, the way each century had its persecuted pariahs – from the twelfth-century Jews of York to the Marsh Arabs and Kurds of more recent times. That led me to thinking about Aydin and how difficult he found it to be accepted by the other students in the group, and then to Matthew, whom both Elena and Siggie

Gerhard described as being *different*.

I closed my eyes and turned down the volume on the iPod. I understood what it was like to feel the odd one out. Even in a county where there was a marked genetic predominance of reddish-coloured hair, mine stood out. And then there had been the issue of my obsession with the past. All-consuming even in primary school (although I very quickly learned to keep it to myself), my peers sensed my singularity and found me an easy target.

So Siggie thought Matthew different – was that because of his striking colouring or because he remained little known? And had he become solitary because of the violent death of his wife, or because something else set him apart? I visualized a car against a tree – wheels still spinning, engine screaming, the sightless eyes of the woman still at the wheel – and I imagined his face when the police told him, his disbelief before the numbing horror of what happened dawned on him. I wish I hadn't seen the wreckage of the car that first day in the States; I wish I hadn't looked; I wish I didn't *know*.

A half-heard sound broke through the music. I yanked the earphones from my ears and sat up, listening. The sound repeated itself and I went to open the door. Matthew Lynes looked down at me, with his half-smile that barely touched his eyes. My pulse danced.

"Good morning, I hope I'm not disturbing you." He glanced behind me at the piles of paperwork on my desk. "My apologies – I think that I must be."

Although I had been expecting – *hoping* – he would visit today, my heart thumped unevenly and not for the first time I wondered if he could sense the effect he had on me.

"No, not at all; I'm not working nearly hard enough, I'm afraid. Please, come in." I stood to one side to let him pass, but he didn't move.

"I have brought your book back." He held it out to me and I took it, turning away from him to put it on my desk and expecting him to follow. He didn't.

"Did you find it interesting?" I asked.

"It is thoroughly researched."

I glanced at him. "By that I take it you mean it is pretty gruesome?"

"It was certainly… enlightening."

I didn't want him thinking me a head-case. I must have become inured through overexposure over the years.

"Ah yes, sorry, it is a bit graphic in places, isn't it? But as you say, it's well researched. Won't you come in?" I asked again, this time a little anxiously. He half-turned back into the corridor.

"I also have something for you; I hope you don't mind."

He motioned towards a bookcase standing in the middle of the corridor outside my room. "Might this be of any use to you?"

The large bookcase looked incongruous there, standing by itself. I stuck my head around the door expecting to see whoever helped him carry it, but he was now alone. I didn't know whether to be thrilled because at last I would have somewhere to put all my books, or because he thought enough about me to have bothered.

"It's great! Thanks!"

He smiled at my unbounded enthusiasm. I couldn't be the calm, cool and collected type, could I?

"Look at it first before you decide."

I ran my hand over the smooth, polished surface of its top. Carved acanthus leaves decorated the faces of the two uprights and in the subdued light of the corridor, the bookcase gleamed a dark, rich mahogany. It stood almost as high as I did with five shelves ranging in height. It looked solid and very heavy.

"No, it really is *just* what I need. It's very kind of you; can I help bring it in?"

"Thank you, but I can manage. I'm glad you like it; where would you like it to go?"

Books in heaps lined most of the spare wall surfaces, but the best place lay between the two windows. I moved a couple of piles to one side as quickly as I could, hoping I didn't look as inelegant as I felt as I bent double.

"I can't *possibly* guess why you thought I needed somewhere to put my books..." I began, turning around to help him, but he was already behind me, waiting.

"It's not as heavy as it looks," he said in answer to my baffled expression, sliding it easily into place.

"Thank you *so* much," I breathed in admiration, feeling the crisp edge to the finely wrought façade.

"I'm having more shelves built, and it looked as if you could give it a good home," he paused, and a slight note of hesitation crept into his voice. "But I wasn't sure if you like antiques – not everyone does."

The muted grey-blue of his jumper made his eyes particularly vivid this morning, but they weren't the arctic blue of the Dean's; these incorporated different shades that gave his eyes warmth and depth. I realized he had said something and I needed to answer.

"Oh – antiques, yes... I love antiques. I would collect them if I had more room. I think it goes with liking history, or anything old for that matter." It seemed a clumsy, inadequate response to such generosity, but I was stumped for anything else to say and I could feel colour rising in my cheeks. He seemed to find that amusing. Even when serious, I noted, his mouth turned up at the corners as if used to smiling, and my blood melted in response.

"Good, well then..." he turned at that point and saw my collection of prints and posters. He stopped, mid sentence, scanning the walls and taking in the detail.

"These weren't here last time," he said, almost under his breath.

"Ah, the gory-ness," I said glumly. "I'm sorry, I should have remembered."

"No, not at all; surgeons are generally a pretty tough bunch. This is a fascinating collection – horrific, of course – but interesting nonetheless."

I frowned at his use of the word *horrific*, because that is not what I had intended to evoke by displaying them on my walls.

"Not all of them are terrible – look," and I went to one of my favourites; "this one's about hope and salvation; see..." and I pointed to the main figure in the centre of the picture, "he's turning away from the sins of temptation and is seeking redemption. It's quite unusual for this period because it shows him succeeding. There – Christ has him by the hand, he won't let him go. Most illustrations from this date show the *trying*, but rarely the *succeeding*, and this pre-dates the Reformation, so it's doubly remarkable."

He spoke quietly as he continued to study the poster.

"Is that why you like it – the fact that his soul is saved?"

I peered at it with him, taking in the details I never grew tired of seeing.

"I think it's probably a good enough reason, don't you? Possibly the best?"

He didn't answer. "And what about this one?" He looked at one of my new posters – the picture Elena disliked so much.

"Well this one is quite different – the opposite, in fact. I chose this because it says everything about the sum of human fears, the reasons behind the actions that make history. I don't like it, as such, but it serves the purpose for which it was made."

"Which was?"

I framed my answer with care to avoid coming across as preachy.

"To remind people of what lies at the end of the road of life – if they choose the wrong path in this case. But it doesn't allow for God's compassion; salvation is portrayed out of reach," and I showed him the man's fingers straining towards God's hand, close but not touching; "which is why I prefer the other one."

Looking at the pictures like this made it less awkward being close to him and gave me something relevant to talk about. I hoped I didn't waffle. From this angle I could study him without appearing to stare; he turned and faced me again and I reluctantly dropped my eyes in case he could read them.

"And which path are you treading?"

Briefly stunned by the directness of his question, I lifted my eyes to meet his and was shocked to see acres of loneliness. I took a step towards him without thinking – almost too close – but he didn't move away.

"Is not faith being sure of what we hope for and certain of

what we do not see? I want... no, I *believe* that I'm on the right path. I made a choice many years ago to follow Christ and I see no point to this life if I don't abide by it."

He considered me solemnly for a moment, then sighed.

"That's a good path to follow, even if it's not easy to do, or even if it's impossible."

"No! It's not impossible." My vehemence took us both by surprise. "I mean, it can't be impossible; it's what we have been promised. There is hope of salvation every second we are alive, right up to our last dying breath..." I stopped suddenly, my eyes widening in horror at my crass insensitivity, then remembered that he wasn't aware that I knew of his wife's death.

"Is something the matter?" He looked alarmed, but not angry, nor upset.

"Nothing – sorry, it's nothing. It just means a lot to me. I didn't mean to be so melodramatic." I recovered and fiddled with the edge of one of the prints trying to un-stick itself from the wall.

"Having faith is nothing to apologize for." He cast his eyes over the posters again, and not for the first time I had the impression that he was taking in every detail printed on them. "It is worth living for," he said softly and then, as if gathering himself, "I have a book that you might find interesting; I'll bring it over if you wish?"

"When?" I said, a little quickly and mentally kicked myself for being too eager. If he noticed, he didn't let it show.

"Would Monday be convenient, at the same sort of time?"

I didn't need to check my diary; whatever I had on, I would cancel it.

"Monday's fine."

He looked me straight in the eyes and I felt it like a rod of lightning. "I look forward to it, Dr D'Eresby." He inclined his head towards the door for a second as if listening, then back at me. "Until Monday, then."

By the time I drew breath he had gone, leaving only the sense of him behind.

I sank onto a chair, not entirely certain if I imagined the last half hour, but the empty bookcase standing solidly between the windows persuaded me that, however dreamlike the conversation, it had been real. He seemed easy to talk to – perhaps too easy – because his questions were direct, searching, and when he looked at me, although not an entirely comfortable feeling, it couldn't be ignored. Perhaps that is what Siggie referred to when she said people found him different; he was, but I liked it. I liked the way he went straight to the heart of the matter. I liked the fact that he showed interest in what I had to say. I liked the way he made me feel when he looked at me. Yes – it was strange, but strange was *good*.

Barely a minute passed before another knock shook the door. I leapt up in the hope that Matthew remembered his coat – but it was Sam. He read my surprise all too clearly as he came into the room.

"You forgot we had a lunch date, didn't you?"

"No, of course not," I pretended, rearranging my expression so that it didn't register disappointment. "I just didn't expect you so early."

I gave him the best smile I could muster and turned around to pick up my bag. Sam consulted his watch.

"It's not that early, Freckles. Hey, nice bookcase, though I'm more of a minimalist myself; is it new?" He wandered over and patted it like a dog. I kept a straight face.

"No, it's an antique, actually."

He shook his head, his mouth readily curving into a smile. "You'll kill me with that English sense of humour. You ready?"

"Yup. Where are we going for our non-date lunch date?" I asked, reminding him that I didn't forget the status of our rendezvous even if I had forgotten the arrangement itself.

He raised an eyebrow mysteriously. "Not far; sure glad to see you have a jacket though, just in case."

I glanced down at Matthew's coat on my chair, and picked it up.

"Just in case of *what*?" I asked, more curious now – the looks Matias and Elena exchanged as they left me this morning suddenly making ominous sense. He grinned and didn't answer, but opened the door, standing in such a way that I had to pass under his raised arm.

At first, I thought we were going to his car, but when we crossed the staff car park, making our way through the trees that framed it, then along a path until we came to a rise overlooking the lake, all became clear. Once only a large, natural pond when Ebenezer Howard bought the land, he lengthened and landscaped it until it covered several acres and disappeared beyond a man-made islet towards one end. Reed-beds along the near-side shore provided cover for the ducks, and privacy from the casual passer-by. Beneath the canopy of a small tree alive with sparkling orange berries, Sam had spread a heather-coloured blanket on which he proceeded to lay the contents of a large picnic basket. He invited me to sit.

"Wow, Sam – this is great," I said, alarmed by the flash of expectation in his eyes. I sat down and curled my legs to one side, glad I wore trousers. He sat down beside me, his rangy body appearing longer now that it stretched across the rug as he settled himself into a position where he continued unloading the basket.

"Hungry?" he asked.

"Uh huh."

I looked around us. We were in a sheltered spot where the wind was filtered by the reeds on one side, and the trees and shrubs on the other. Sunlight danced uncertainly through the shivering leaves, casting restless shadows on the ground. Despite the sun, the air still carried the promise of the winter to come.

He handed me a small china plate, a fork and a long-stemmed glass. He delved into the basket again and brought out some covered bowls and proceeded to take off the lids.

"Saw Lynes leaving the humanities building this morning," he said casually, offering me a selection of tiny canapés.

"Thanks. Did you?" I said, taking one and balancing it on my plate then taking the bowl and holding it for him while he took several. He licked his fingers.

"Don't often see him out of his own department," he observed, picking up a bowl of pasta and putting a short-handled spoon in it for me to help myself.

"Really?" I feigned indifference. "This is a marvellous spread, Sam, for a *non*-date. You didn't make it, did you?"

"Sure, OK – I've got the message. Gee, you sure make it hard for a guy to impress you and yeah, I did, as a matter of fact."

I was genuinely surprised to hear that. "Do I?"

He rolled his eyes. "Yeah, you *do*."

I hurriedly changed the subject onto safer ground.

"You know, I've still no idea what you do at the college."

He reached into the basket, but stopped, his hand on the neck of a bottle. "You mean you didn't ask Elena or Matias yet?"

Blow, should I have done? I suppose I should; after all, I asked Elena about Matthew and it's one of those basic questions considered to be courteous in academic circles, especially if you're supposed to be interested in a person on *any* level.

"I wanted you to tell me, Sam."

He appeared mollified and lifted a long-necked bottle from the basket. It looked like champagne. *Why* did it have to be champagne? By now I had a small pile of food on my plate that looked as if it had taken a long time and much effort to prepare; this looked more and more like a date to me. He sat up and began to uncork the bottle, oblivious to my increasing unease.

"Well, I'm a mathematician," he began. "Ever heard of metamathematics?" He took one look at my face and grinned. The cork popped and he grabbed my glass before the bubbles exploded all over me and I could refuse.

"Right, better drink that before I explain – it'll make more sense."

He waited for the foam to subside so that he could fill my glass to the top but I took it from him, pretending to admire the bubbles as they fizzed and popped at the surface, and balanced it on the rug behind me when I thought he wasn't looking. I began to eat my food.

"Go on," I prompted, "you were saying?"

He topped up his glass and drank a quarter of it before answering.

"Metamathematics, put simply, is the study of mathematics for the sake of it, using mathematical methods."

I must have looked nonplussed because he shook his head, his brown eyes laughing at me.

"Now, this study of mathematics produces metatheories – in other words, mathematical theories *about* mathematical theories."

I bit into the canapé. "Why?"

Sam finished a mouthful of salad with bits of something interesting in it.

"Why what?"

"Why study the study of mathematics?"

He looked at me sideways. "It's immensely sexy, for one thing."

A wave of hair had fallen into my eyes and I brushed it back without thinking.

"No, it isn't."

"It sure is from where I'm sitting." His eyes took on a languid appearance and I noticed he had stopped eating. Picking up a bowl, I offered him some more canapés as a distraction; he took three and ate them without looking.

"You know, you're looking... mmm, *de*-lec-*table*," he hummed almost to himself. "There's this thing about you I can't describe. When you smile you've got all this *life* about you – you fizz with it – you get under my skin." His hand caressed a fold of the rug uncomfortably close to my thigh. It was precisely what I didn't want to hear. I curled my legs further out of reach.

"You were telling me about maths, Sam, but I'm still none the wiser. Can't you give me an example or something?"

He sighed, and stretched out along the full length of the rug with his hands behind his head, emphasizing the breadth of his shoulders in his dark leather jacket.

"It's related to mathematical logic – *intimately* related," he emphasized. "It's like Gödel's 'incompleteness theorem' which says that, given any finite number of axioms for Peano arithmetic, there will be true statements about that arithmetic that cannot be proved from those axioms," he grinned again. "See, I told you

– numbers are pure sex. Strawberry?" he offered, managing to make it sound salacious without trying.

I took one without meeting his eyes and stared towards the lake instead.

"I'm sure you're right," I said primly.

"I can prove it," he suggested, sitting upright and lifting a wisp of my hair and holding it up so that the sunlight could tease the colour from it. "So beautiful," he murmured.

I took possession of my hair. "Sam…" I warned, "this is just lunch, remember?"

He fell back onto his side, propping himself up on one elbow as he surveyed me.

"What are you afraid of, Emma?"

Wind stirred the bulrushes, hissing through the tall stems, causing some of the cotton-white seed-heads to briefly take flight before skimming the ink-blue surface of the lake, where they floated like marooned clouds.

"I told you, I only came to the States to work. I don't do casual relationships, Sam."

I heard him readjust his posture but didn't look around.

"Who said anything about *casual*?"

I glanced at him sharply; he was sitting up now, one arm draped around his knees, the other hand plucking at a long piece of grass by the edge of the rug.

"Any relationship, then. I'm not here for *any* relationship – casual or not."

He decapitated the head of the grass and picked the individual seeds off it before giving it to the wind.

"What happens if you meet someone you like?"

That was a good question and one I continually asked myself, no more so than now. An ant explored the blanket edge tentatively.

"I won't."

"You sound very sure about that."

The ant climbed onto the rug, struggling over the long fibres of wool, intent on a crumb four times its size.

"Emma?"

"What?"

"You didn't say."

"No, I didn't." The ant managed to heave the crumb of food onto its back, but the fibres made its progress painfully slow. I picked a broad, flat leaf from the sward and placed it in front of the creature. It investigated the leaf with its antennae flicking backwards and forwards over the surface and carefully climbed on.

"Emma, c'mon, give me a break here!"

I looked at him over my shoulder, his brooding, smoky-brown eyes sincere and genuinely interested. Gingerly, I lifted the leaf and put it on the grass. The ant climbed off with its precious cargo and disappeared into the green jungle.

"Once bitten, twice shy, Sam."

He nodded slowly. "Yeah, thought it might be something like that. You gonna tell me or do I have to guess? No? Well, don't let it put you off; look at me – *twice* bitten, still not shy."

The engaging grin was back. He had a knack of being intimate without touching and sexuality flowed as naturally from him as water from a tap, that he could no more switch off than I could forget my past.

"Yes, exactly – look at you, Sam."

He considered me for a moment and, for a second, I thought he took offence, but his sensual mouth lifted into a smile and his eyes opened wide.

"Well, you'll forgive me if I don't take *no* for an answer."

"I wouldn't hold out much hope, if I were you," I said. "I can't say it any clearer than that. I'm sorry if I gave you any other impression, Sam, but I didn't mean to and I only want to be friends, nothing more."

He drained his glass and lay on his back again, squinting at the sun as it fell towards the lake. "Sure, Freckles, but you know the saying: 'Where there's life...' And I *always* live in hope." For a fleeting moment I remembered another conversation not so very long ago in an entirely different context, and I wondered whether, if *he* were here instead of Sam, would I prove to be so resistant?

It became cooler; the breeze stiffening and the dark water matting in tiny waves that lapped against the reed beds in little *slap-slapping* sounds. I hugged my arms around my legs to keep warm. Sam picked up Matthew's jacket and put it around my shoulders, leaving his hand resting lightly against my neck.

"Thanks," I said, and drew the collar of the coat up around my chin, displacing his hand.

"Blue suits you," he said. "You should wear it more often."

I didn't reply so he began to pack the basket and I swivelled around to help him. After a minute, he peered up curiously.

"By the way, what happened to the dog?"

I had forgotten my reference to being bitten.

"The dog...? Oh, the *dog*. What happens to all dogs that bite, I suppose; he was muzzled."

He raised his dark eyebrows but didn't ask for an explanation and I didn't offer him one. In this case I thought it better to let sleeping dogs lie.

Chapter

7

Besieged

IWELCOMED A LIE-IN ON SATURDAY, and again on Sunday because, while awake, the conversations in which I had engaged echoed eternally around my waking mind until they whipped into a frenzy of anxiety. While I slept, I did not dream, and found some respite from them.

On Friday evening, I contrived a headache as an excuse not to discuss the lunch, and Elena reluctantly left me to sleep it off, promising – or threatening – to be back in the morning.

On Saturday, I pretended to be out and buried my head under my pillow until she stopped knocking, and I lay fretting at my deceit. I then spent the rest of the day exhuming my old notes on the journal as an attempt to distract myself until it was so late, and I was so tired, that I fell asleep at the little table that served as a desk.

By the time Elena tried again on Sunday, I succeeded in gathering my thoughts into something resembling order and could face the inevitable interrogation.

"So, what happened?" she asked, before even stepping through the door.

I kept it brief.

"We had lunch; Sam made a very great effort; the food was lovely; I came back."

"Alone?"

I pulled a face, askance at the suggestion. "Yes, *alone.*"

"Oh." Her face fell a little. Then she perked up again. "Did he kiss you at least?"

"Elena…" I drew my hand tiredly over my eyes; "no, he didn't kiss me."

"He didn't want to kiss you?"

"Look, I don't know; probably, but I didn't want to kiss him. I didn't go there for any other reason than to have lunch; I thought I made that clear."

She jiggled up and down like a small child wanting the lavatory.

"Yes, you did, but Sam said…"

I groaned. "You've spoken to Sam?"

"Yes, of course. Sam said that it went well."

"Did he now. What else did he say?"

She pulled her brow into a series of tight little furrows.

"Nothing. He said nothing more. Emma, was something wrong with the lunch?"

"No, Elena, nothing; but I don't want either you or Sam to think that anything else will happen – because it *won't*."

She pulled a disappointed face. "Oh, *da*, OK." She sucked her teeth, clearly toying with a question. I waited patiently until she looked up earnestly. "Sam said you had a bad relationship once and it is why you will not go out with him."

"It is part of the reason, yes." It was her turn to wait. "But it's more than that. I don't want to get involved with anyone unless there is serious commitment – on both sides – and Sam, well, with Sam I get the feeling that his attachment is temporary."

She took her time thinking over what I said before finally giving a little sigh and saying, "But don't forget you promised a girl-date because I will not and there is much to talk about, no?" Well, quite honestly, I didn't think there was, but *girl-talk*, as Elena put it, was for her like pollen to a bee: both a necessity and a delight. She suddenly clapped her hands to her mouth.

"I am an *idiot*; I forgot to tell you, Matias said the police are questioning a foreign man about the attack on the girl."

I hardly dared hope. "Staahl?"

"No, not him – I do not know who it is. If it helps, I happen to know that Staahl's taking his group to a play in Portland tomorrow; he will not be back until late."

Knowing there would be at least a few hours when I didn't have to avoid his deadening presence was enough to lighten my mood perceptibly. I spent the rest of the day between the library and my tutor room, dividing my time between continuing to work on my legitimate research project, and gathering and annotating notes on the journal. I stayed longer in the library than strictly necessary because, I told myself, I wished to trace a particular book I needed for my work; but I wasn't being entirely honest, because every time the library doors sighed open, I looked up, only to feel a waver of disappointment as an unfamiliar face filed through.

I welcomed the distraction Monday brought, not least because of the visit Matthew promised to pay me. It was warmer again, and the sun played hide and seek with the clouds all morning until it ventured through my window at an angle that told me it neared lunchtime, and youthful voices rose up from the quad. I opened the window wide to catch the fragrant air from the nearby woods and leaned outside, feeling the sun on my face, and saw Matias strolling across the grass towards the faculty with something in his hand. He looked up, saw me and waved the object in the air, pointing first to it, then me: my newest posters from England.

The posters sprang open when released from the confines of the tube and, once in place next to the others, they told their own story. Still early, I didn't feel hungry enough to accept the invitation to join my friends for lunch. Besides, I felt like a spare wheel in their relationship when I saw the possibility of having one of my own. I adjusted the volume of my music, and continued selecting books for the shelves. Over the weekend, I found myself constantly thinking about Matthew, visualizing him as we talked, wondering what he thought of me, what impression I gave: whether I came across as too gauche, retiring, too boring or trite. His self-possession made me self-conscious. Other than lunch with Sam on Friday, I hadn't been out alone with a man for a very long time, so I felt socially awkward and clumsy and unattractive, and I guessed it probably showed.

By the time I answered his distinctive knock, I had all but

persuaded myself Matthew only visited because he said he would; so when I opened the door to him, I barely met his eyes and the fluttering in my stomach related more to an agony of nerves than delightful anticipation.

He saw my reticence at once and hesitated on the threshold of the room.

"Dr D'Eresby, if this is inconvenient…"

He must think I didn't want him there.

"No – no, not at all, please come in…" I rushed and then stopped and took a breath and tried to pace my words more intelligibly. "Please come in, I've been sorting out books for the case."

He followed me into the room, softly closing the door behind him. I sensed his eyes on my back and turned around, surprised instead to see he had a quizzical look on his face.

"The Flute and Harp concerto?" he asked. It took me a moment to realize he must be able to hear my iPod left playing on top of the bookcase; I couldn't hear a thing.

"Oh golly, I have it switched up too high again, haven't I? I won't have any eardrums left at this rate." I picked up one of the earphones and put it to my ear.

"Yes, Mozart," I confirmed. I didn't think it at all loud.

I began to settle under his steadying influence and risked a glance at him; he looked startlingly handsome today. Although his clothes were tailored, modest, unadorned and expensive, on his wrist he wore an old gold-cased watch, its dial scratched and worn. He might have inherited it because it looked pre-war, and its shabby persona seemed at odds with its owner and I liked him even more for it. There appeared nothing obvious about this man – his cultured urbanity not assumed but natural.

"I thought you might like to see this." He held out a small, leather-bound volume – very old – the cover stained and worn by time. I took it, opening it respectfully because of its age.

"It's an early seventeenth-century Italian treatise on the treatment of heretics by religious courts – including their torture and subsequent death or recantation. I believe it will appeal to you." I detected humour in his voice, then saw the first illustration and my introversion was instantly forgotten.

"Wow! This is *amazing* – I've never seen anything like this before!"

With great care, I opened the book at a woodcut picture of a torture scene, then another, then squinted at a page filled with tight, early, printed type. I instantly regretted dropping Italian in my first year as an undergraduate; it felt like being given a bar of fine chocolate and then being told you can't eat it, but so much worse.

"I can't read medieval Italian," I said in despair.

A smile flashed across his face as he looked at mine. "But I can," he answered. "Would you like me to translate it for you?"

The chocolate came within reach again. "You can? Yes please! But only when – or if – you have time."

His smile faded. "I have plenty of *that*," he said, only a shade off bitter.

I looked down at the book in my hands and realized that – now a widower – he probably had more than enough time.

"Do you mind if I keep it for a few days to have a look first?" I asked. His face softened and he looked pleased.

"Yes, of course, it won't take me long to translate."

"Where did you get it?" I turned it over. "It must be very rare."

"I've had it some time; I can't remember exactly where or when I bought it – and I've never heard of another edition."

It was not something I would be likely to forget in a hurry, but then he wasn't a historian, so perhaps it didn't mean so much to him. To have a treasure like this and not remember the exact date and time of its acquisition, nonetheless seemed remarkable.

"Perhaps you would like to bring it over to me at my office or to the med faculty, when you're ready?" he suggested. I made the mistake of looking up at him and found myself caught in his direct gaze. "Dr D'Eresby?"

"Mmm?" I had been distracted again. I blinked.

"Emma – please, I'm Emma, Dr Lynes."

"Thank you, Emma, will you do that? Bring it over to me – or would you like me to collect it from you? And my name's

Matthew, by the way."

The floor swayed for a second.

"I'll... I'm not sure. No, I'll bring it over to you – save you a journey."

"Yes, it's a mighty way to go," he said with good-humoured irony. I blushed; we stood so close, he must have seen it, but he looked away and caught sight of my newest purchases on the wall. He laughed softly, the first time I heard him laugh since we met. I followed his gaze.

"These are intriguing additions: Andrew Marvell and a photograph of a *cabbage*? Is there a connection?"

I coloured under his scrutiny; intending the visual joke to be mine alone, I hadn't anticipated anyone else noticing it.

"Um... well, yes. Sort of." He would think me bizarre. "Er, it's a play on words based on one of his lines: 'My vegetable Love should grow, vaster than Empires...'"

"'... and more slow,'" he finished and laughed again. "Very good. Do you like metaphysical poetry?"

Astounded that he knew the line, I nodded.

"Yes, I love it – well, much of it; it depends on the poet, of course, and the poems."

"So do you like Marvell in particular?" He studied the black-and-white print of the portrait of the young and serious-looking seventeenth-century English poet, whose receding hairline made him look older. I put my head on one side and considered it with him.

"I like some of his work and the way he handles verse, especially the way he combines objectivity with passion; but I prefer Donne and Herbert overall."

"Why?"

"Because... well, I like Donne's struggle with humanity and Herbert's piety, but Marvell makes me laugh, and there were no prints available of the others, so..."

"Here he is in juxtaposition with a brassica. How very apt; he would like that – it would appeal to his wit."

He made it sound as if he knew a great deal more about the poet than I did.

"So you like metaphysical poetry, too?" I ventured.

Matthew continued to look at the picture for a minute longer, fingering the ring on his little finger next to the wedding band; then he breathed out and turned away.

"Yes, I do."

If ever his own portrait were painted, I imagined it would be in varying shades of dark blue reflecting his calm exterior and the depth of loneliness that pervaded the air around him. And something else – something with which he wrestled, perhaps; something beyond the grief. He seemed to be listening again.

"I don't recognize this piece; it's very poignant, what is it?"

I shook my head, marvelling at his acute hearing, and picked up the earphone, smiling in recognition of one of my favourite pieces of music.

"It's from *The Last Samurai*; have you seen it?"

"It's a film? No I haven't. What is it about?"

I tried to think of a way of summing it up, made more difficult because I hadn't seen it for ages.

"Well, from what I can remember, it's about a lonely, jaded man who's seen too much death, and about his rehabilitation despite the betrayal of time in the face of a changing world, or along those lines."

I might as well have slapped him across the face; he blanched and turned away.

What on earth had I said?

"I'm s... sorry," I stammered. He swivelled back to face me as if nothing happened.

"It's the music; it's surprisingly... touching." He smiled, but a tight line formed around his mouth that hadn't been there earlier.

A sudden, expectant rap broke through the lapse in our conversation, but I wasn't glad of the intrusion; I didn't want our meeting to end this way.

"Who...?" I started to say.

"You were expecting someone?"

"No, not unless I forgot," I said, with undeserved irritation for whoever was on the other side of the door. It shook as someone rattled on it impatiently.

Matthew looked quickly at me. "Would you like me to answer that?"

I grimaced and shook my head, making for the door. I opened it and Sam nearly fell in, hand raised to knock again. A grin lit up his face when he saw me.

"Hello, Freckles, I thought I would look in on you after our date."

He was halfway in the room when he saw Matthew standing by the window, one arm resting on the bookcase, very still. The grin dropped off Sam's face. He looked at me and back at Matthew who didn't move a muscle in the awkward silence that followed. Matthew broke it first.

"I must be getting back; I'm sure you have a lot to do."

He moved smoothly across the room – lithely, like an athlete. I held the door for him.

"Thank you for the book. Oh, and..." I reached over to the chair where it lay, "... for lending me your coat."

I handed it to him, acutely aware that Sam picked up on every nuance of interest I attempted to hide, but at the same time silently calling, *"Don't go, don't go, don't go."* Matthew took the coat, his hand accidentally brushing my arm as he did so. My pulse stampeded. He looked towards Sam shifting morosely from foot to foot, then at me, his eyes darker and more compelling than before, so I couldn't drag my gaze away.

"I will see you again soon, Emma."

It sounded like a promise and, if I didn't know better, if I were less level-headed and more romantically inclined, I would swear that he staked his claim.

The door shut quietly behind him and I turned reluctantly to face Sam. Hands shoved deep in his pockets, his shoulders hunched, he stood in front of the same window where Matthew had been minutes before. An undercurrent of resentment ran through him I had never seen before and it took me aback.

"I'm sorry, Sam..." I began but he didn't let me continue my attempt to placate.

"Sorry – why? Because you've already forgotten about our

date or because you would rather be with Lynes and I interrupted you?"

His accurate supposition rankled, but I fought to control my irritation.

"I haven't forgotten about Friday, of course not, but I didn't expect to see you today."

"That's obvious," he said, rising tension in the set of his shoulders.

"Sam, I'm sorry, Matthew…"

"*Matthew*," he almost spat and I felt a glow of anger; I reined it in, trying to keep calm. There was no reason why I should have to explain myself to him, but the part of me that wanted to tell him to mind his own business and get lost, vied with the part that wanted to keep the peace and, at the moment, peace and reason prevailed.

"Yes, *Matthew* – he dropped in to see me and…"

He cut short my explanation as if my mentioning his name unleashed something in him.

"Right, sure, he just dropped in on the off chance, did he? Well, that's all very nice and dandy but what was he *doing* here?" His venom tipped the balance of the conversation. Simmering anger boiled out of me. I rounded on him.

"That's none of your business."

If he had harboured any illusions about my preference, he didn't now.

"It's like that, is it?"

"Like what?" I glared at him. "Like *what*, Sam, what do you think happened?"

"Don't tell me there's nothing going on between you – it's obvious," he said, flatly.

Was it? I knew how I felt but I thought there was still plenty of room for doubt on Matthew's side. Wasn't there? My heart sang, anger held in suspension for a brief moment.

"There's nothing going on. He brought me a bookcase, and a book he thought might be useful. That's all."

"And a coat," he added sulkily.

"It was raining – he lent it to me," I said reasonably.

"Either you are blind, Emma, or very, *very* stupid if you can't see what's happening here." His incriminations stung and blood rushed to my face.

"That's not fair. It's not as if there was – is – anything between us."

He didn't miss my slip and his expression soured.

"Isn't there? Not for you, obviously."

We scowled at each other across the room.

"I told you the first time we met not to make assumptions about me. I warned you not to take me for granted, didn't I, Sam? I thought I made it clear I want nothing more than to be friends. Anything else is entirely down to your imagination."

He looked at me as if something just occurred to him.

"How could I be so *dumb?*" He hit the heel of his hand hard against his forehead as if trying to beat some sense into it. "That first night – at the reception party – I should have known then when I saw you with him; you'd already fallen for him, hadn't you?"

"Don't be ridiculous." I tried to sound scathing but I wasn't so sure. I slumped into the chair behind my desk, misery clouding my judgment. Sam found another chair and pulled it under him, sitting heavily into the fabric upholstery. It sighed in complaint.

"I suppose I should have known," he repeated. I didn't reply, thinking over what he said a moment before. "I just thought that since we'd gotten on so well…" he raised his hands in defeat and let them drop onto the arms of the chair. I didn't like his vitriol, but I liked his self-pity even less.

I cast a brief look at him; he looked utterly miserable. "Sam, you don't even *know* me…"

"Oh, and Lynes does?"

I ignored the comment. "You assumed something that wasn't there; it was too much, too fast. Anyway, I told you on Friday: I didn't come to the US looking for a relationship." I knew I should have chosen my words more carefully, because a sneer crossed his face.

"So you say. But you fancy you've got one with Lynes, is that right? Hey, Emma – you and half the women on this campus.

Don't think you're the only one mooning over him, or hadn't you noticed *that*?"

No, I hadn't. I felt my face drain of colour. A look of triumph entered his eyes and he went in for the kill.

"You didn't know, did you? Lynes' Kittens – all mewling for his attention, all wanting a little of what he's got. And now you too…"

"Shut up! Stop it, Sam! I don't believe you." All the fight went out of me and Sam saw he'd hit his mark. He chewed at his thumbnail ferociously then whacked the arm of his chair and stood up, coming over to my desk.

"Look, Emma…" he began, but I didn't let him continue.

"You've made your point, Sam, just go." Inside I became a hollow ball, devoid of feeling; I couldn't look at him. He leaned over and put his hand on mine as it lay on the desk. There was a note of regret in his voice.

"Emma, I didn't mean…"

I tried to pull my hand away, but he held it tighter, desperate to make peace. I yanked my arm back, taking him by surprise and he let go. I rubbed my wrist where his fingers gripped too hard for a second too long. His eyes became round with remorse.

"I'm so sorry if I've hurt you – in any way." He reached out again, trying to make amends but I flinched back.

"I'm sorry," he whispered again, his shoulders sagging. I didn't dare look at him or I would cry, but whether for him or for me, I didn't know.

"Please, just leave."

He didn't say anything and, when I looked up again, there was nothing left in the room but the overwhelming feeling of loss for a friendship barely begun.

The sun came out from behind cloud and shone slanting across my desk. The slim brown leather volume Matthew lent me lay in its path, and I automatically moved it out of the bleaching light. Touching it, holding it, threatened to set off another wave of bewildering emotions, and I clutched it tightly to me until they subsided.

At last I calmed enough to be able to assess the situation and, whichever way I looked at it, it was bad. First, through no real fault of my own – whatever Sam might think – I managed to hurt him and lose a friend in one fell swoop. Secondly – and for this I felt less inclined to forgive him, Sam sowed seeds of doubt on fertile ground: why would Matthew look at me with a campus of young, apparently willing women to choose from? And worse, he called into question the one thing I never doubted – Matthew's integrity. I don't know why it never occurred to me before that I wouldn't be the only one to find him attractive. Would it be so very strange if he responded to other women in the way I wanted him to respond to me? But then that didn't tally with what I knew, or at least, what I *thought* I knew of him. Both Siggie Gerhard and Matias referred to him as a loner – polite, but distant – and he rarely appeared with anyone else, let alone hordes of women. Then I recalled the times he helped me – none earth-shattering in itself – but there nonetheless when I needed him. Lastly, I considered his wife and the grief he all but hid from the world.

In my heart of hearts, I knew Sam was playing mind games and I understood he did so out of jealousy rather than malice. There seemed something incomplete about him, a desire to control I had not detected before except in his persistent pursuit of me. I wondered if his wives felt suffocated by his attention, as I did. By now he probably regretted ever saying anything about Matthew, but the damage was done and I would have to find a way to mend it.

There seemed little point in hanging around; the books still stood in their stacks on the floor and they would stay there until I had a mind to arrange them in the bookcase – whenever that might be. Taking the direct route back to my flat, I didn't bother with caution as I passed Staahl's department; with him out of the way for the day, there seemed little need and, given the mood I was in, he would regret running into me even if he did.

My north-facing flat felt bare, boring and cold. I ate a handful of nuts and dried fruit looking out towards the mountains. Lit by the afternoon sun, the range rolled away in all the blazing glory of a New England fall; I longed to escape my dismal room and flee into untamed space and the mellow air of the late September day, like a lizard onto a sun-warmed rock. I took just a coat and the little book with me and headed towards the back of the college where the arboretum lay.

Initially the path wound through a dense planting of trees interspersed with large shrubs. The further away from the college I walked, the less tamed the grounds became until they resembled the wilderness they replaced a hundred years before. The trees were taller here and more of one type – American conifers of some sort – and it was from these the night breezes sometimes carried the pine-laden scent to my room. The forest floor – thick with brown needles – formed a dense, yielding carpet, and the last warmth of the season bled the lingering fragrance of summer into the air.

The path disappeared and I found the land rising steadily towards what I assumed would be a viewpoint. It might have been once, but the clearing on top of the hill had long since been overshadowed by trees, and the view now looked onto the softly swaying crowns with huge cones glowing like russet baubles in the rich light of the sun.

I found a fallen trunk to rest my back and settled comfortably against it, balling my coat into a cushion and feeling the sun warm through me until it reached the cold centre of my wretchedness. I closed my eyes against the light and focused on the sounds of the woods. Although completely alone, I felt no fear, relishing the sense of liberation brought by the news of the recent arrest and Staahl's absence. Over the years from early childhood, I found company in my own thoughts, and peace in a solitary existence. The gentle hiss of the wind through branches became a melody punctuated by the *snap* and rattle of pine-cones opening and ejecting their seed. Finches chipped and whistled in the tops, an occasional *whirr* of wings telling me they were in flight from one tree to the next. Out here, the ache of the day faded. Out here where distractions were few, I could pause, I could voice my doubts and my fears and know that they would be listened to – be answered.

I took out Matthew's book and let myself become engrossed. The illustrations were fairly self-explanatory – some similar to pictures in other texts; others quite new to me and it was in interpreting these that I needed his translation. But the tenet of the text became clear in the illustrations accompanying it. This represented no treatise on horror; the common misconception that torture was used solely to extract information and to punish the indicted belied the fact that in some circumstances, it had been used to temper justice with mercy in the belief that the heretic might be cured. Still, it was difficult to believe when faced with pictures such as these, but if you looked beyond the obvious, the faces of the torturers did not display pleasure or anger, but *concern*.

Humanity was perverse. Humanity *is* perverse. There could be no excuse for what we did to each other, but part of reconciliation is in the understanding of what impels people to behave in such a way, and that is what I sought to understand. Because in understanding the causes of behaviour, it is easier to predict the actions of the future, for ignorance breeds fear; fear breeds loathing; loathing breeds persecution, and persecution is what I stared at in this little book of learning from 400 years before.

People sometimes ask why I chose to study what I do; was I not corrupted by what I read? Did it not make me question the validity of my faith if those who used such methods also shared it? And I patiently explain that I am not interested in the modes of torture so much as what prompted those who used it. It did not contaminate me because I did not – dared not – let it touch my soul, and I continued to follow Christ as surely as those who went before me. The issue lay not in the cure but in the disease of fear that led society to think it justified in its use of torture at all.

A *crack* followed by a rustle close by reminded me of my solitude. A squirrel leapt between trees, the tips swaying under its fragile weight, and disappeared into the shadow of the woods. The descending sun sapped warmth from the day, the air cooling rapidly, and I shivered into my coat, carefully closed the book, and began to retrace my steps down the slope. Darkness falls early amid the forests and woods of the world and I picked my way gingerly through the trunks, searching for the beginnings of the path that would lead me back. The wind died; silence lay among the branches and I became conscious of my breathing – shallow rasps made louder in the overwhelming hush as I raced against the setting sun.

The automatic lights were glowing into life when I reached the covered passage that served as a short-cut between the med fac and the quad. I reached the end as the last of the lights came on, and stopped to catch my breath. The air stirred and I glanced up to catch the slightest movement at the end of the passage from which I emerged, so slight it might not have been there at all. I peered into the darkness that escaped the lights, but whatever hadn't been there, was gone. I made my flat in record time, slamming the door shut on the darkness of the day.

Chapter

8

Cause and Effect

I SHOULD HAVE KNOWN BETTER than to expect Elena to keep out of it.

"I have seen Sam, and he is very upset. What did you say to him?"

I took a deep breath. "Elena, I'm trying to have breakfast. It's too early to do this; can't it wait?"

"No, it cannot and it is Tuesday and you must work. Tell me about Sam; I won't go until you do." She folded her arms across her chest, her mouth set and determined. My cornflakes were getting soggy.

"Was Stalin a relative, by any chance?"

"Not funny, Emma – I'm waiting."

"For goodness' sake, Elena, it's…" I glanced at my watch "… a quarter past seven and anyway, I thought you were supposed to be my friend," I said, sounding a little peevish.

"Sam is my friend too – you are *both* my friends and I do not like to see my friends unhappy."

I plonked my spoon into the bowl, sending ripples through the milk, and resigned myself to as brief a description of Monday's encounter as I could get away with.

"What did Sam say this time?" I asked.

"He didn't say; he would not talk about it and he was so… down."

At least he hadn't made any scurrilous remarks I would have to explain.

"Elena, yesterday Sam made some assumptions – jumped to

conclusions – that made things… difficult."

"Uh? You are not making sense." She looked bemused.

"Sam got the wrong end of the stick about something."

"Yes, yes, you said that already, but why did he make conclusions, about what? I don't understand." She shook her head, her thick, dark hair swishing from side to side.

"Well, for one thing, that we were on a date, with all the assumptions that go with it, when I thought I had made it clear that it was not. And… and that I like Matthew."

Which I do, I thought. I waited for the reaction. Elena chewed her lip for a moment, her eyes mere slits through which she contemplated me. When she answered, it was not what I expected.

"Has Matthew asked you out on a date yet?"

"Not exactly," I admitted.

"And do you think he will?"

I didn't answer.

"Why do you push people away, Emma?"

"I don't!" I said, astonished.

"Yes, you do, you keep them… how do you say… at arm's length. Sam likes you and you don't give him a chance. But Matthew – what has he done? He hasn't even asked you on a date but you throw yourself at him. And he is strange – he is not *here* – he is like a ghost. I think he will make you unhappy."

I heard every word she said, I understood what she meant, but how could I begin to explain how he made me feel? How did I tell her that all her misgivings fell on deaf ears and that, even if I wanted to, I no longer had the willpower to resist the distraction he posed and all the complications that would, no doubt, come with it.

I stood up and went over and gave her a hug. She eyed me suspiciously at first before returning it when she recognized my unguarded sincerity.

"Thanks for minding enough to care about me – and Sam – but it's too late; I know what I want and it's not Sam, and I don't think it ever was or ever could be. He has too much history for me to deal with, too many hang-ups, Elena; too many skeletons rattling around his closet."

I said it with such finality that I hoped she would accept my decision. From my point of view the matter was closed. Elena shrugged, nodded her head in resignation and with that, seemed to think so too.

I was five minutes late for class and my group lounged against the walls outside the door to my room.

"Sorry, everyone; morning's not my best time of the day – nor for you either, Josh, by the look of it. Heavy night last night?" He grinned blearily and pushed himself away from the wall as I unlocked my door. "Come on in and let's get started: it's kill or cure time."

Josh sidled in past me and went straight to one of the chairs and sat down, slumping inelegantly with his eyes closed. A faint sheen covered his forehead and his skin appeared grey under his olive tones. Hannah followed and started taking a folder from her bag. Leo and Holly hung back in the corridor, heads close together. Things were looking more promising there. "When you're ready, you two."

Holly smiled self-consciously and they came in holding hands. I went to open the window for Josh. Only four chairs were occupied.

"Where's Aydin? Has anyone seen him?"

Leo shrugged his big shoulders "Cops took him downtown for questioning," he said, as if it were an everyday occurrence on the campus.

As shocked by his indifference as by what he said, I stopped latching the window open and returned to stand in front of them. "The police, why?"

"Something to do with that attack last week, I guess."

"You don't think that Aydin had anything to do with that, do you?" I looked from face to face. They all avoided my eyes.

"Why not? It isn't as if he belongs here, is it?" Leo looked at Holly with a self-satisfied smirk and she sniggered.

"What is *that* supposed to mean?" I snapped. They all looked up at my change in tone.

Leo put his hands behind his head and leaned back in his chair, regarding me indolently.

"Well, he's different, isn't he? Where he comes from, they don't treat women in the same way as we do, right? It's their *religion*," he sneered, his lip rising unattractively in his derision.

I looked at them aghast. "And do you all think that?"

Holly stared at the floor while Hannah busily arranged the papers in her folder. A violent sneeze punctuated the uncomfortable silence.

"Sorry," Josh apologized, sniffing. "Doesn't bother me one way or the other. Aydin seems OK to me; I've got nothing against the guy."

"I didn't get to talk to him much," Hannah acknowledged.

"What about you, Holly – do you think Aydin is capable of that?" I turned to her.

She glanced at Leo, who still looked smug; I was rapidly growing to dislike him.

"I don't know – he is foreign, I guess," she ventured.

"Well, so am I; what difference does that make?"

"Yeah, but you're different," she defended herself; "you're English."

"I'm British," I corrected her. "I'm part Scottish. And as historians – let alone humans – you should have learned by now that it is precisely this sort of bigoted attitude that allowed the National Socialists to gain a foothold in Germany," I fumed. They looked at me blankly. "Hitler?" I reminded them.

Josh grunted and nodded. "I'm Jewish." He sneezed again.

"You're Jewish, I'm British and you three are... whatever you are. I don't know and frankly I don't care. But don't *ever* come to a tutorial with me again with that attitude." I glared at Leo.

"OK, OK, I get it, Professor, *co-ol* it." From the leer on his face he obviously didn't *get it*.

"And don't tell me to 'cool it' either; I'd like to remind you that you are this far..." and I pinched the air between my forefinger and thumb, "from me failing you. Got *that*?" The self-satisfied complacency dropped from his face. I breathed deeply, controlling my temper. "Now, to work. What have you brought me?"

They each produced varying amounts of paper for me to pull apart. I gave Holly the work I had assessed the week before. My praise for it gave me a bridge to allow us to re-establish a more positive working relationship and she smiled gratefully as I handed it back with my comments. I had little to say to Leo, who was sulking – almost as little as the amount of effort he obviously hadn't made in producing the few pages of type he'd given in. Josh, on the other hand, surprised me with brief but succinct notes that showed a thorough grasp of the subject. Hannah's work, too, was competent – nothing startling but well thought out and precise. It turned out to be a good morning's work after all, despite the shaky start.

After they left, I contemplated the bombsite of a room. Matias was due to collect some books Elena loaned me and I wanted to ask him how to get to the police station. I didn't know if there was anything I could do to help Aydin, but at least I could try.

I started to sort the books out on the shelves, the smallest at the top. Every time I moved, my watch rubbed against my sore wrist where Sam had grabbed it, so I took it off and put it on top of the bookcase while I worked. The shelves easily absorbed the books, revealing the floor under the windows for the first time in weeks. I began to feel better. I reached up for the last book on the top, my hand sweeping the polished surface for it, and brushed against something that slid off and down the back of the case. My watch. "Blow," I said under my breath. I squinted behind the bookcase; it lay there towards the centre and just out of reach. I searched around for something to hook it with, but the days of metal coat-hangers were long gone. "Bother." The shelves were too heavy for me to move while loaded with books, which left me with but one option. "*Blast!*" I said none too quietly this time.

Unloading the shelves didn't take as long as I expected. Once empty, I took hold of the front to slide it away from the wall. It didn't budge. I tried again, lower down. It stayed stubbornly put. About to give up, I heard a knock at the door. I knew it would be Matias but that didn't stop me hoping. He must have seen the disappointment on my face.

"Everything OK?" he asked.

"No – I've dropped my watch behind the bookcase," I said, petulantly.

He went over to examine the offending piece of furniture. "Whew! Very nice. I don't remember this being here." He stroked the lustrous surface and carved edges of the acanthus leaves. "Been shopping?"

"No, Matthew brought it over to tidy me up."

"That's very generous. I didn't know you'd seen him again." I detected hidden meaning behind the raised eyebrows.

"It was spare," I muttered.

Matias didn't answer, but the sardonic look he adopted said it all. He peered behind the bookcase, but even his long arm couldn't reach that far. "It looks heavy," he said almost to himself and put his shoulder against it, taking care not to damage the carved edges. He heaved. It barely moved. He tried again.

"It slid into place easily enough," I offered unhelpfully.

"Well, it certainly doesn't want to move now," he said, his face a brighter shade of pink. "Give me a hand?"

"Yes of course, sorry."

We both took one side and on the count of three managed to move it away from the wall.

"It must have taken a least three men to get this up here," he panted.

"No, just Matthew – there wasn't anyone with him." I remembered how easily he moved it and it dawned on me what that implied. "He must have had help, though. Thanks," I added as Matias handed my watch to me.

He glared at the bookcase. "Perhaps you'd better wait until Matthew can help next time."

"I could always ask, I suppose," I said, thoughtfully stroking the silky wood. Matias' eyebrows shot skywards again and he grinned roguishly at me.

"Want me to drop it behind again for you?"

I pulled a face and turned away. "Matias, could you do me another favour?"

"What, *another* one?"

"It's one of my students – Aydin, he's been arrested or something and he's down at the police station in town. I need to see if there's anything I can do."

"You want me to take you there?"

"Yes, please; would you mind?"

He scratched the back of his head. "Let me get Elena's books back to her before she scalps me – and then I'll take you."

"Thanks..." I hesitated.

"C'm on, Em, what else?" He sounded like an older brother trying not to sound impatient in a sort of indulgent, brotherly way.

"You know where Matthew works, don't you?" I asked. He nodded. "I have something to give him. I was wondering if..."

"Do you want me to take it?" he interrupted.

"No, no!" I said far too quickly.

"Ah, you want me to take you there – I understand entirely." The suggestive eyebrow rose again, for which I thwacked him on the arm and he pretended it hurt; he would have made a good brother. He dashed off and I finished tidying my room before I remembered the note I meant to give him for Elena. From my desk I plucked the lilac Post-It arranging a time for our long-overdue 'girl-talk', and stuck it in her pigeon-hole as Matias reappeared panting and out of breath.

It didn't take long to find the police station; the garish red-brick building dominated the street in which it sat. What would I say in Aydin's defence? What *could* I say? And one thing worried me as I sat in the car next to Matias: when he came to see me the morning after the attack, Aydin told me he had not slept the previous night.

The entrance hall smelled of institutional cleaner and it stung my throat – a dubious preference to the odours it supposedly suppressed. In a side room, the officer looked down at the notes already taken.

"So you're saying, ma'am, that you didn't see or hear anyone that night other than the screams?"

I was already regretting this. "Yes."

"But you know this guy – who you've met, like what – four times..."

"No, more than that – five," I corrected him.

"Yeah, *five* times and you think he is innocent, like... why?"

"I just don't think he's capable of attacking someone," I said lamely.

"Oh yeah, sure." He had stopped bothering to write down anything I said some time back but I didn't want to leave without making the only point I could think of.

"Can I ask, Officer, why you suspected Aydin in the first place – just out of curiosity?"

The policeman scratched behind his ear with his pen. He wasn't giving much away.

"We had a tip-off, a phone call."

"Is that all? I mean, no physical evidence or anything?"

"Now look, ma'am, I don't mean to be rude, but..."

"It's just that, what's Aydin's motive?"

"A guy like that doesn't need a motive."

"A guy like what? And why did someone give you a tip-off? What motivated *them*? I bet it wasn't for the public good."

"Ma'am, we're not country hicks here and this isn't Oxford and you sure ain't Miss Marple, so you leave the detecting to us and we'll let you get back to teaching." He must have been a fan of British detective series. He was on his feet, impatient to see the back of me. I stayed where I was.

"Of course, you are quite right – I know absolutely nothing about the process and you are the professional; but in my line of work I always have to look for the reason behind the action and, you see, Aydin doesn't have anyone to look out for him, and then there's the prejudice..."

"I hope you ain't saying we're prejudiced..."

"No, not in the least, but what about the person who made the call? Not everyone is as fair-minded as you. I know I haven't given you anything to go on, but did they?"

I realized I trod a very fine line but the officer stopped and scribbled a few words on the pad. "Is it possible for me to see him, just for a few minutes?"

"No can do."

I wanted Aydin to know that someone thought about him, had taken the time to ask about him.

"Can you give him these, then? It's just some work – he mustn't get behind in his studies." The policeman flicked through the pair of textbooks I hastily grabbed as I left college; he winced, but didn't give them back.

"Yeah, sure – is this what he's studying?" He held up one of the books showing an illustration of a gutting. I saw the direction of his thoughts and smiled sweetly.

"No, those are mine, but Aydin has to write a paper on it. You will make sure he gets them, won't you?"

"Sure, sure," he said again, eyes fixed on another page; he was taking a far too unhealthy interest in the material.

Matias waited in the car outside, thrumming his fingers on the steering-wheel as he listened to some plaintive wailing on the car radio.

"How did that go?" he asked as I climbed in beside him.

I shook my head. "I don't think it's going to be much use and they wouldn't let me see him, and I don't think they have any evidence either, but apparently I'm not Miss Marple or Morse, for which I think I should be grateful."

Matias laughed. "OK – so where next, Inspector?"

I made my voice all gravelly and dropped it an octave. "The medical faculty, Lewis, and step on it."

He grinned and to my relief, switched off the music.

I had never been in the science and medical faculty before. Siggie Gerhard said that Matthew endowed it but what I hadn't appreciated was the extent of that endowment. The medical centre took up the whole of the ground floor, and the medical science and research facilities the two floors above that.

The glass-and-steel doors swung open and I followed Matias into the foyer, a little nervous now that I came to it; but I wasn't prepared for what I saw, nor for the strength of my reaction to it. The frosted-glass sign hanging over the reception area declared in big, clear letters back-lit in blue: *The Ellen Lynes Memorial Centre*.

My heart lurched and I stood transfixed staring up at it. From somewhere close by, a tittered comment closely followed by a shriek of laughter rang out as if they could read my thoughts and mocked my shame. I shouldn't have reacted – it shouldn't have mattered – but somehow seeing her name up there came as a slap in the face, a reminder that I couldn't compete with a dead wife so obviously revered, and so clearly mourned. I should have known when I saw the wedding ring he still wore.

"Emma?" Matias called from the lift door. "You don't look too good; do you need to see a doctor?" he chuckled, but I didn't feel like laughing. I gave him a tight smile and he looked puzzled for a second; then the lift arrived and he entered its glass box and I followed because, despite my apprehension, it intrigued me to see what so much love for one woman inspired.

The first floor made up the medical research laboratories. On the east face of the building the double-decked windows were tinted to take the glare of the morning sun.

"What are these for?" I pointed to rolls of metal above each of the windows in Matias' own laboratory in the department of genetics.

"Those are UV shutters; they operate automatically and close when sensors detect a certain level of sunlight; they prevent damage being done to light-sensitive experiments. Brilliant, aren't they? Matthew had them specially made for all the windows on this side of the building." I heard the admiration in his voice.

"*Matthew* designed them?"

"Yup – with the input of someone else in his family – his older brother, I believe. Everything you can see and most of what you can't – custom designed and made for the scientists who use it. It's seventh heaven for people like me." He stared around his lab as if admiring it for the first time. He patted a table. "C'm on, I'll show you where Matthew works."

We walked out of his lab and along the corridor towards the far end of the building and through a set of automatic doors. My head spun with the influx of new information and I found it hard not to be beleaguered by it all. Matthew not only had the facility built but he designed it as well. Money, brains *and* looks – and a dead wife; this was getting too much to cope with. I traipsed after Matias with ever decreasing enthusiasm, past rooms where intriguing apparatus engaged the attention of the occupants, until we neared the end of the long corridor. Talk about cold feet, mine were rapidly becoming blocks of ice.

He stopped outside a laboratory where large sheets of glass separated us from the people within. They all wore identical lab coats making them a homogenous group of white, heads bent over microscopes and tables and computers, like long-legged shore birds on a beach searching for molluscs in the sand.

I saw Matthew at one end of the room, his flax-coloured hair starkly contrasting with the blue-black mop of the young man with whom he spoke. His white coat should have made his fair skin look wan; instead he managed to look devastating. I clutched the small book in my hands and my mouth went dry; I didn't know whether I wanted to see him or not; I didn't know what I would say or whether he would read the doubt in my face.

A young woman came up to them, a printout of some sort ready in her hands. Matthew took it from her, scanning it. The girl didn't take her eyes off his face. She stood as close to him as was decent and even at that distance, I could feel her pulse. She looked Norse with white-blonde hair loose below her shoulders and large, baby-blue eyes fringed with long lashes. She wasn't wearing make-up because she didn't need to and her natural rose-blush highlighted perfect skin without a freckle in sight. Had he been blind he still couldn't fail to notice such flawless beauty. He said something to her, still reading the stats. She replied, flicking her hair over her shoulder as he looked up from the paper with a slight frown. I'd seen enough; perhaps Sam had a point after all – this was one kitten who obviously wanted to play.

"I have to go," I said hoarsely. With a hand on the door handle, Matias paused.

"What's the matter? Don't you want to see Matthew?"

But I had already walked away.

"Emma!"

The urgency in Matthew's tone stopped me in my tracks. I looked over my shoulder, surprised to hear his voice. He stood next to Matias.

"Don't go," he said, when he saw me hesitate. I wanted desperately to believe he wanted me to stay. I took a faltering step towards him.

"I… I've brought your book back," I stammered, because I thought he needed to know that I had a legitimate reason for being there. I still clasped it in both hands and didn't move any further. A few long strides brought him to my side.

"I know," he said. "Thank you."

I looked away, suddenly shy. "I said I would."

"Yes."

I looked up at him then and he smiled, his mouth turning up in an unguarded gesture of real pleasure, and I couldn't remember why I wanted to leave. I held the book out to him like an offering. He reached out to take it, but a shadow passed across his face. I glanced down to see what he was looking at; faint darkening smudges where Sam had held onto my hand coloured my wrist under my watch.

"Sam did this?" His voice held an edge to it.

I yanked my sleeve down to cover it. "He didn't mean to – it was an accident. It doesn't hurt or anything."

Matthew regarded me, his now denim eyes seeking out the truth; then his forehead smoothed and he smiled again and the tension lifted. He took his book from me.

"So, what did you think of it?"

"It's amazing – I've never seen some of the methods depicted before. I tried to work out what some of them were from the text, but it's *so* frustrating not being able to read it." Bubbles of enthusiasm threatened to burst my composure.

"Well now, we can't have you in a state of frustration over not being able to decipher methods of torture, can we? That would do terrible things for your blood pressure. I'd better get this translated before any permanent damage is done." His tone gently teased and I realized I must sound like a complete geek.

"Sorry," I murmured.

"What for?"

"I get a bit overenthusiastic about my work."

"I'm glad someone does and anyway, you come alive when you talk about it; it makes your eyes spark."

A dozen sprites tap-danced inside me. I shot him a quick look to see if he still teased, but saw no mockery in his eyes. Good grief, was he *flirting* with me? I looked away, not sure how to react, searching for something to say.

"How come you can read medieval Italian; it's not on most school curricula in the US, is it?"

"Not that I'm aware, no, but it's closely related to Latin, which comes in useful now and again. Don't you need to have an understanding of Latin in your line of research?"

"Um, well, you see – how can I put this..." I chewed my lip then decided honesty was the best policy. "I'm utterly *useless* at languages. I spent twelve years failing to learn French, I ditched Anglo-Saxon after two weeks and I only scraped Italian at university because I passed the history and culture units with almost full marks. I did want to learn Latin at school though, but I was the only one, so they didn't run the course. Probably a good thing, come to think of it; I would have failed."

I risked a glance at him and found that he was looking at me with a distinctly humorous expression. His eyes seemed a brighter shade of cobalt than they had moments before, as if they reflected the sun.

"Mmm, is there anything else you would like to confess while you're at it?" He smiled broadly, and at that moment, there wasn't anything I wouldn't confess if that was what he wanted. I reined in my heart which threatened to stampede again, and thought of a more sober topic.

"Talking of Latin, I don't suppose you know what the inscription over the door in the atrium means, do you? The *res ipsa...* something or other."

"Hoy, you two – my arm's getting tired holding this door; are you coming in or not?"

I had totally forgotten Matias waited for us and reluctantly looked away from Matthew's eyes – an action requiring conscious effort, like pulling two magnets apart. We started walking towards Matias and the open door.

"Would you like to see the lab?" he asked, not assuming – just hoping – and I nodded, not trusting my voice. "The inscription, roughly translated, means 'The thing speaks for itself.' Does it, do you think?"

I managed a laugh. "Things are rarely what they seem!"

"Quite," he murmured, his hand barely skimming the small of my back as he showed me through the door. I started, and he murmured an apology, but for once, I hoped it was on purpose.

The half-dozen people in the large room looked up as we entered. The young man with the raven hair stood nearest, and Matthew introduced him first.

"Emma, this is Sung, one of the best researchers I've ever had the pleasure to work with. Sung, this is Dr D'Eresby."

Sung thrust out his hand and shook mine enthusiastically, his face puckering with delight to such an extent that his eyes almost disappeared behind folds of skin.

"Dr Matthew is very generous with his praise – I wouldn't be here if it were not for him."

I looked enquiringly at Matthew, who seemed a little embarrassed.

"You overestimate my role, Sung."

"Don't listen to him; he got me out of Korea – *North* Korea – and do you know how difficult that is? Nearly impossible!"

"It was worth the effort to secure him for the department," Matthew explained evenly. I sensed more to this story than he let on but Matthew adopted a blank expression and I thought it better not to ask.

"What are you researching?" I asked Sung out of politeness, not being scientifically minded. Sung looked at Matthew, who nodded for him to go ahead.

"Most of our work focuses on corpuscular mutation in mammalian species resulting in cellular restructuring and sub-species transmutation and metamorphosis."

I must have looked particularly dense, because he broke into a broad beam that transformed his face again.

I shook my head. "I'm no good at foreign languages, so roughly translated, that means…?"

"Put simply, changes to the structure of blood that directly affect the evolution of species."

"Surely that would involve changes to DNA? Is that where you come in?" I addressed Matias.

"Uh huh, I'm looking at the fundamental changes that re-write DNA."

I could see the endless avenues for research, the implications behind the possible outcomes. "Wow, that's fascinating!"

Matias and Sung looked pleased at my enthusiasm, but Matthew's face became a mask. I shot him a quick, puzzled look and he caught my glance and his expression changed instantly to incorporate a smile.

Sung was talking again. "Megan's got the best bit – she gets to extract the *samples*." He grinned in the direction of the blonde girl who came to stand on the outside of the circle; she pulled a face at him and then stared at me inquisitively with startlingly blue eyes that were decidedly frosty. So this was the girl who supposedly made a pass at Matias. It must have been a total fabrication on his part because she could barely take her eyes off Matthew as he introduced her.

"Megan joined our team from another university last year."

The girl came forward, continuing to hold the stats in her hand. Close up, she was even more attractively nubile, and probably in her mid-twenties – she just looked younger.

"Dr Matthew headhunted her from Europe; Shotter was well pleased," Sung butted in. *I bet he was,* I thought. Megan simpered and Matthew paid no attention to the looks they exchanged, which were more akin to the sniping of siblings than mature researchers. Instead he turned to the girl.

"Megan, would you like to explain your role in the research?"

She flicked her long, thick, silky hair back from her face. Whereas the movement had been intended to disarm Matthew earlier, it was more a dismissive gesture for me. Taller in her high-heeled shoes than me by several inches, she stared down with an imperious look I guessed she reserved for inferior mortals such as myself. Her sing-song voice would have been melodious had she not been chewing pins.

"I specialize in atypical bio-morphological chromographic abnormalities indicating structural mutation in the blood samples. It's very complicated."

There was a tinge of smugness in her explanation. I adjusted the expression on my face to look suitably impressed.

"It sounds it; I'm not sure if I followed that. Let me see, so you chart unexpected colour changes in the chemistry of blood samples that point to an alteration in the cellular structure – is that correct? Is that at a sub-cellular level?" I asked innocently.

There was a pause. "Yes," she said, almost surly.

"Thank you, you explained it very clearly."

Sung guffawed. "Nice try, Megan." She glowered furiously at him. Matthew cleared his throat or it might have been a laugh.

"Everyone else here is at various stages of completing doctoral work."

"Where does your area of research fit in?" I asked, looking up at him.

"Most of my time is spent in supervision; it doesn't leave me much for my own research."

The corners of his mouth had tightened imperceptibly, as if he kept something back from me – or perhaps he thought I wouldn't be interested. He moved to the side of the room and I followed him.

"And this is where we analyse the data," he said, showing me a bank of computers along one side of the wall; an awesome amount of brain-power must be locked inside those machines.

"I wonder what a suitable software package could do to *my* subject," I said wistfully. He came back to stand by me.

"I think that you probably already have the best tool available, don't you?"

I must have looked mystified because his mouth twitched in amusement.

"There's no programme on earth that will understand the

intricacies of the human condition as you can."

"Oh."

Was that a compliment or merely a statement? Matias wandered up to us, hands in his pockets.

"Did Miss Marple, here, tell you where we were this afternoon?"

Matthew raised an eyebrow enquiringly and I clarified the situation before Matias said something I might regret.

"One of my students is being questioned over the attack on the girl; but I'm sure he didn't do it and, from what I gathered from the police, I don't think they have any real evidence to implicate him anyway."

"Who is it?" he asked.

"Aydin Yilmaz – he's Turkish and I bet that isn't helping."

"What do you mean?" Matthew said sharply.

"Well, someone tipped off the police and from reading between the lines, I'm guessing his religion came into it. There's an element of prejudice, I'd bet on it."

He regarded me shrewdly. "You're quite good at that, aren't you – reading between the lines?"

Am I? I thought. No mistaking it this time: that was a compliment.

"Oh, I don't know about that, but I *do* know Aydin is in a vulnerable position and, well…"

"You thought you would try and help," he completed for me.

"If I can, yes."

Without warning, a slight click and whirr from above my head made me look up as the automated UV shutters were activated by a faint gleam of sun. They rolled down the length of the window, locking securely in place. The room was cast into semi-darkness, almost instantly replaced by artificial daylight as the light-sensors came into play. I remembered to stop myself from gaping unattractively.

"See – I told you he's clever," Matias gloated. He didn't need to tell me, but I liked to hear it all the same. "But I have a bone to pick with you, before you get complacent," he added in

Matthew's direction. "That bookcase is darned heavy." He rubbed his shoulder ruefully. "How did you shift it by yourself?"

"There's a knack to it," Matthew answered. "Did you hurt yourself?"

"Not really, only my manly pride; I had to get help from a *girl* to move it an inch." He directed a look towards me.

"Are you all right?" Matthew asked me, overlooking Matias' faked self-pity.

"I'm fine; Matias did all the heavy work."

Matias leaned between us. "Emma, thanks but I was really after some sympathy from the doctor here."

"You have it," Matthew grinned.

"Lunch would do as compensation?" Matias suggested.

"Sympathy is all you'll get, I'm afraid; I've some work to finish up here."

"Sympathy won't fill my belly, but if that is all that's on offer, it'll have to do. Lunch, Emma?"

I would rather have stayed, but felt guilty at keeping him from his work, and I didn't want to outstay my welcome.

"I'm coming," I said, then more shyly to Matthew, "Thanks for showing me around."

"I'll bring the translation over when I've finished, if you wish."

"Yes, please," I said, trying not to let my eagerness show, and he smiled the way he did when it touched his eyes.

When I glanced through the big glass window as Matias shut the door behind us, Matthew was saying something quietly to Megan before moving on to speak to one of the students. She pouted and pulled her hair back from her face, securing it with a band.

9

The Diner

"**L**ET'S GET OUT OF HERE FOR A BIT; I'm going stir-crazy in this place." I stared gloomily out of Elena's window. "And the weather doesn't help."

I waited for Elena to finish some work after the last class of the day. She hadn't turned up for our girls' night in the day before and she denied getting my lilac Post-It note. Cryptic though it might have been, I thought it clear enough to warrant a reply at least. As she had also been pretty preoccupied with Matias of late, she agreed we must spend some time together.

It had been a week of unprecedented amounts of sunshine for the time of year and I itched to get outside. More to the point, I hadn't seen Matthew since going to the lab, and I began to think something was wrong. As usual, I analysed every word I said and every look he made, but couldn't identify any one thing in particular. As my neurosis accumulated over the course of the week I became increasingly grouchy with everyone around me until I decided that I would either have to lock myself away out of compassion for my friends, or do something to divert myself.

My group found it difficult to concentrate as well and I couldn't blame them. Aydin joined us again after being released from custody without being charged. He remained quiet, but not as subdued as the others, who had cause to feel chastened. He returned my books after the tutorial.

"Thank you for your help for getting me out," he said in his heavily accented English.

"I didn't do anything, Aydin," I said, surprised.

"You came to the police station. You brought me the books and you said something to make the doctor come and see me."

Now I felt totally confused. "What do you mean? What doctor?"

"The doctor from here – from the medical centre."

An inkling of suspicion grew rapidly. "Do you mean Dr *Lynes*, Aydin?"

"*Evet* – yes, the *çoc güzel* – very handsome one. He came and he talked to me, and then he left and I was set go."

"Set free," I corrected his English automatically, without paying attention to what I said. What on earth did Matthew know that swayed the police, except, of course, that he treated the girl immediately after the attack? "Did Dr Lynes say anything to you?"

"No, he just asked me questions."

"What about?"

"My studies, my home, my family. Things such as this."

"Nothing else – the college, the attack, people you know?"

He shook his head. "No, he listened and he watch me, that's all."

What had he been up to? There must have been a purpose to it.

"Well, I'm so glad they let you go; you can concentrate on getting your work done now, can't you?" I didn't mean to sound patronising, but I wanted to put a positive spin on it. Aydin grimaced but didn't comment; the whole episode must have stuck in his craw and there was little anyone could do or say to make it any better.

"People make mistakes, Aydin, I'm sorry," I apologized, perhaps because I thought someone ought to and it may as well be me.

"Thank you," he said, but our conversation did nothing to lighten my mood.

Infused in late-afternoon light, the wooded slopes rose beyond the college parkland, wild and free; I yearned to be among them and my bones burned with impatience.

"Well – shall we go out? Escape? Break free? Make a *run* for it?" I opened and closed a book left on the window-sill without looking at it.

"*Da,*" Elena said, snapping the folder she was reading decisively shut. "We will make it a women's night out – man-free. Where shall we go? Not the woods – or mountains," she added rapidly as I threw a wistful look towards them.

I hadn't been further than the campus shop so considered myself hardly in a position to make an informed choice.

"Somewhere no one will recognize us – nothing flashy and *definitely* not a dive. And no clubs – I don't do clubs. Or singles' bars."

Elena put her head on one side, as she always did when considering something. "OK, OK, I know where to go. I drive."

"You do?"

"Of course – you do not?"

"Well, I *can*, but I don't – there's not much need in Cambridge."

Elena tutted. "Here you have to drive or you are…" and she cupped her hands in a cage, keeping the air trapped inside, "… like so."

The "All American Diner" encompassed everything I considered a diner should, given my diet of films from an early age. There were no red-checked tablecloths, and cigarette smoke didn't hang over the occupants, but banquettes and booths ran along the length of one wall, and low-slung glass shades hung over each table, lending an air of comforting familiarity.

I shuffled along my satisfyingly red-upholstered bench opposite Elena, and plonked my bag next to me. She was already devouring the menu and before long she folded it and placed it back on the table.

"You haven't made your choice yet?" she asked.

"I have," I contended.

She held her menu out to me. "But you must look at the menu."

"No need, I know what I'm having. I'm embracing American

culture and going for a burger and chips." I felt pretty hungry this evening in an odd, hollow sort of way. Elena pulled a face. "What? Don't tell me they don't do burgers?" I asked.

"Burger and *fries*," she corrected. "Of course they do, but you have to say *fries* or you will get..." she looked around the diner, and pointed to another table, "... chips."

I applied my best cut-glass English accent with a dash of plumy-ness for good measure.

"Oh, *crisps* – I keep forgetting; these cultural differences are very confusing."

Elena giggled. "They will think you very strange if you talk like that."

"I can't help it if English has moved on since we *colonized* the place." I grinned at her horrified expression, but her eyes laughed.

"Shhh, they will hear you."

The waitress came over to our table. "What can I get you guys?" She sounded bored. I recognized her as a student from our campus; she must be working her way through college.

Elena started to place the order. "I'll have the extra-large Hawaiian and diet soda and Emma will have the house burger and...?" She waited for me to complete the order.

"Chips. Ow!" I exclaimed as she kicked me under the table. "Fries," I amended as Elena reprimanded me with a frown, every bit the mother to her recalcitrant child.

The waitress gave me a funny look before going back to the kitchen with our order.

"Behave yourself!" Elena hissed.

"But I don't *want* to; I'm always behaving myself and it's my night off. Just because I'm British everyone expects me to act all *proper*." I sounded suitably peeved. "And anyway, you can't talk; where else on this planet would someone openly declare that they're wearing an item of underwear?"

"Huh?"

"*Pants.* You'd get an odd look in Britain for that. Honestly, pants/trousers, trousers/pants; cultural differences are rife and very confusing – but also immensely entertaining."

"Are you going to be difficult tonight?" she asked with a degree of gravity although her cheeks dimpled as she tried not to smile.

"I certainly hope so – it's been a while since I had the chance. What about you – when were you last naughty?"

"Matias says I am *always* naughty." She simpered deliciously and we both burst into giggles. I felt strangely light-headed at my freedom. I dibbled the straw in my drink, making the ice-cubes dance up and down in the water.

"So tell me, you and Matias are pretty serious, aren't you? You've been together for some time."

"Mmn." She drank thirstily through her red-striped straw. "Three years."

"He's older than you, isn't he? Has he been married before?"

"He's thirty-eight and no, he hasn't been married before – not like Sam." She eyed me slyly, seeking a reaction, but I wasn't thinking about Sam.

"What about you, Emma? If the most *amazing* man walked through that door right now and wanted to take you away from here, what would you do?"

"I would..." I rattled my fingers on the edge of the table, thinking it through. "I would ask him to wait a bit until I'd finished my latest research."

Elena flipped her hands in the air and sat back with a look of exasperation.

"I give up – you are hopeless. You love your history so much that you would give up your life for it!"

"*No-oo* – not at all. I *love* chocolate and music, but I could almost do without them – almost. But I couldn't live without my work – it *is* my life. There's the difference. Isn't it the same for you?"

"*Nyet*, it is not. History is my work, but if Matias asked me to marry him tomorrow, I would give it all up for him."

"Why would you do that?" I asked, remembering what Madge said about losing one's identity when you married. "You can work *and* be married; times have moved on a bit since our parents' day. Surely Matias wouldn't want you to give up your job and I can't honestly see you baking cupcakes all day."

"It is not what Matias wants, it is what *I* want, Emma. I want to make a home for him, to have children. Why would I want to work if I could have all of that instead? Have you never wanted this with a man?"

I pushed some stray grains of salt around the wooden table-top before answering.

"No, not really; not recently, at least." I gathered the grains in a little heap and sub-divided it into four equal piles. I could feel her eyes on me and a little gasp escaped her lips.

"But there *was* someone, wasn't there! Sam did say – go on – tell me; I won't tell anyone else, I promise."

I rapidly weighed up the wisdom of telling her anything, but it was bound to come out sooner or later so I might as well broach the subject now when we were alone, rather than risk her asking me in front of someone who might matter – someone like Matthew.

"That includes Matias," I warned.

She gave a little pout. "Oh, OK, not even Matias." She leaned forward eagerly, her eyes sparkling.

"It's not *that* interesting," I said, dryly. She waved her finger at me.

"Don't underestimate your ability to entertain; hurry up, I want to know *all* the details."

I sighed and delved deep to find the right words before launching on a subject that I had rendered taboo for nigh on a decade.

"Well, he was older than me for a start – a lecturer when I was an undergrad – totally off limits, you understand, which made it all the worse – and all the more exciting." Elena nodded her head in agreement. "I should have known better, but I hadn't been away from home before and he was very attentive, and attractive – in an odd sort of way – and confident; he made me feel… wanted." I usually avoided talking about my past to anyone and, doing so now, raked memories like hot coals.

A pucker crossed Elena's brow. "What do you mean, 'sort of attractive' – was he or wasn't he? Or was he *ugly*?" She enunciated the word with relish.

"No, certainly not that. He was half French and half English, and he had that Gallic look about him – you know, all dark hair and slightly olive-skinned, brown eyes – very attractive in a somewhat superior way, but not handsome as such..."

Elena giggled, "Not like Sam, you mean?"

I could see her point. "Sam's much better looking, but then his looks are not the issue... Anyway, Guy had this way about him: he could look at me and make me feel as if I were the only person that mattered – or at least the only person he *wanted* – and that made him quite... irresistible, I suppose you'd call it. Well, at the time anyway."

The candle guttered as the door opened and someone came into the diner. I pulled it in front of me and began to pick at the wax dribbles around the sides of it.

"Go on, what did he do?" Elena urged, almost drooling with curiosity.

"He was my supervisor – my tutor – in my second year at uni, and he specialized in the English Civil War – also my specific period of history, so..."

"Your *personal* tutor," she grinned, wallowing in the delicious anticipation of salacious details.

"Ye-es, thank you for your delicate observation, Elena," I drawled. "He was also a Royalist by inclination and I think he fancied himself in the role of Cavalier and courtier. He made it very clear what he wanted, which made it both embarrassing and flattering." My face grew hot as I remembered the expressions on the faces of the other students in my group as he virtually ignored them, while he plied me with questions and praise. He liked to see me blush.

I broke off a thin piece of wax and began to melt it in the flame.

"Don't stop, Emma! Then what?"

"He did a lot of wining and dining, took me to the theatre, made me feel more adult than I was..."

"And you fell into his arms and made passionate love." Elena faked swooning like the heroine in a silent movie. I flicked a piece of wax at her, which she managed to dodge, nearly knocking over her glass in the process.

"Not quite, no. I held out for eight months – which I found pretty hard going, given his persistence – and..."

"Why?"

"Why what?"

"Why did you take so long to sleep with him?"

"I had my morality to consider, Elena, and it was my first proper relationship. I wasn't into casual affairs then and less so now; if there's no future in them, I can't see the point of getting involved in the first place."

"Not even for the fun of it? Emma, you are so old-fashioned!"

It wasn't the first time someone told me that and no doubt it wouldn't be the last.

"I know, but I can't see the *fun* in getting hurt and if it's not a serious relationship – not leading to the commitment of marriage – then that's all you're going to get out of it, isn't it? Yes, I know Elena, apart from the sex," I said rapidly as she opened her mouth to interject. "Still, I would have held out for longer, except he managed to get me drunk one afternoon and by that time my resistance was wearing very thin and so..."

She clapped her hands together in glee. "He made passionate love to you!"

I stopped fiddling with the candle and the hole I made in the side filmed over as the molten wax oozing from it congealed. I shook my head at my friend.

"You're a hopeless romantic, Elena Smalova; you've been watching too many soppy films, haven't you?"

"I *love* romantic films. So, did he?"

"Yes, he did, well – it might have been passionate but I was pretty far gone, so I don't remember that much. Nor the *love* bit, come to think of it."

"Ugh – that is not at all romantic for your first time. Did he leave you once he had his wicked way with you? That would be so like a man – use you and then throw you away like a piece of trash." She flung out her arms dramatically, nearly knocking the plates out of the waitress' hand.

"Thanks," we both said once she had placed our order on the table and Elena had apologized.

"And...?" Elena said as the girl left.

"Well, no, actually. After that it became very serious – scarily so, in fact. I reached a point where I had to make a decision."

"So...?" she squeaked.

"So, another tutor – my *bona fide* personal tutor – called me in for a chat one day, about eighteen months after I'd met Guy, and she made one or two things very clear to me..."

"The cow!"

"No, not at all, she was very decent – like Siggie Gerhard in many ways – quite maternal – no, not maternal – kindly, well-meaning, benign, that sort of thing. She said that my work had gone downhill – 'gone to the dogs, Emma,' I think she actually said, and that she thought me at grave risk of being sent down if I didn't sort myself out. She also said one other thing..." I took a long drink to ease my dry throat. Elena took the opportunity to sip hers.

"She told me – she asked – if I was aware that Guy was married."

Elena clapped her hands to her mouth, her eyes quite round.

"I hadn't been." I leaned to one side to pick up a menu and used it to fan myself, feeling hot in our airless corner.

"What did you do?"

"I confronted him and he told me all the same old rubbish: how his marriage was failing, how he would leave her and get a place of his own – you know the sort of thing." Elena nodded sympathetically. "But being Catholic, he wasn't going to divorce her – not on your nelly."

"What's 'nelly'?"

"Oh, uh – 'not for anything', I suppose. So, I had to make a decision: it was either him or my degree – and I had worked very hard to get to Cambridge."

"But you were in love with him?"

"Possibly – I thought so at the time, but anyway, he did

something I couldn't forgive."

Elena's eyes almost popped; she hadn't touched her food. I picked up a chip, examining it thoughtfully.

"Emma!"

"What? Oh yes, sorry. Mmn." I nibbled on the chip. "The fact that he made me into an adulterer."

Dumbfounded, she said, "That's all? You gave him up for *that*? Lots of people have affairs – it's normal."

"Not for me, it isn't – it's wrong. Besides, I don't like being lied to, Elena. What he did was enough – I can't forgive that level of betrayal. I told you – and Sam, for that matter – never make assumptions about me, do you remember?" She nodded. "He assumed I wouldn't care about his marriage. He thought I could live with him – and myself – after that. He thought wrong. Anyway, I made my choice," I said with finality.

"Do you regret it?" she whispered.

"Sometimes I think I do – or I did – but not any more. I made the right decision for me at the time; I won't make the same mistake again." I flung the half-eaten chip back on the plate. "I felt bad about his wife – I mean really, *really* bad. There were some days I didn't leave my room; I couldn't face the world knowing what I'd done – I couldn't face myself; it was like being eaten up inside." All too sharply I recalled the torment of each sleepless night, shame and hurt gnawing away at my conscience. I became aware of Elena, waiting. "I wanted to make things right. I thought that breaking up with Guy would somehow be enough, but it wasn't; if anything, the guilt intensified; I was a real mess." A shadow of the past must have shown on my face because she put a hand over mine and asked gravely, "But you are OK now?"

"Yes," I smiled softly, "now I am. A friend of mine – Tom – spent a lot of time with me..."

"Ah," she said with a knowing look, before I could finish.

"No – not 'Ah' at all," I laughed. "Tom sat with me, talked, listened; he helped me make sense of it all."

"How?"

"By showing me that I didn't have to cope with it by myself. I spent my life being independent. I relied on no one for anything – or so I thought. When I split up from Guy I thought the answer lay in throwing myself into work, but it wasn't enough to fill the hole inside me."

"Because you loved him so much?"

"No, because I didn't love him enough. And, more than that, I didn't love me. I didn't even like me very much. I felt unloved and unlovable. I achieved academically, was good at sport and all the rest of it – but at the most basic level, I didn't respect myself."

"But this Tom did?"

"Yes, he did – although I didn't deserve it after what I did to him." I felt a stab of remorse, recalling the disappointment on his face. "Anyway, one night – about two in the morning – I sat on my bed wondering if I could ever escape this *darkness* that surrounded me all the time, this endless, endless night inside me. And then Tom turned up. I hadn't called him, I didn't know why he came – but there he stood at my door."

Elena wrinkled her nose and pinched a chip. "He sounds creepy."

I shook my head, smiling. "Far from it, he came across with an inner... goodness, I suppose you could call it..." *Like Matthew*, I wanted to say, but didn't, as she looked sceptical enough as it was. "Something he said that night struck a chord in me – perhaps I reached a state where I could listen after years of being walled up in myself. He quoted Matthew 11 – you know the one? 'Come to me, all you who are weary and burdened, and I will give you rest.' I felt as if a weight had been lifted from me, as if a light had been switched on, and all the darkness disappeared." I peeled my jumper over my head, welcoming the temporary chill that followed. Her eyes dropped to my cross hanging in the "V" of my T-shirt.

"So, is that when you became a Christian?"

"It started then but I didn't have a sudden conversion experience or anything, more of a gradual process as things made sense whereas before they were just words. My life took on a different purpose and everything I do – or don't do – is with that in mind. It's hard, though, and I get things wrong. History is still my addiction but I see things from a different perspective now. In that respect it made what happened with Guy worthwhile – life-changing – in the best possible sense." I coughed to clear a tickle and drank again. "I hadn't understood Donne's lines from his *Holy Sonnets* until then:

> *Batter my heart, three-personed God; for you*
> *As yet but knock, breathe, shine, and seek to mend;*
> *That I may rise, and stand, o'erthrow me, and bend*
> *Your force, to break, blow, burn, and make me new…*

Elena's serious countenance swam back into focus and I smiled. "As I said, I see things differently now."

Elena disengaged a piece of pineapple from her pizza thoughtfully.

"So, no fun – no *sex*."

"Hang on, I didn't say anything about not having fun – or sex – it just has to be within the context of marriage; *my* marriage," I clarified, thinking of Guy's loose interpretation. "If ever I get married," I tagged on glumly, thinking now about Matthew.

"Did you go out with Tom?"

"No, I missed the boat on that one – missed the opportunity," I explained as her face puckered with a question. "We remained friends but he went his way, and I mine. I think he's married, though. There, now you have the sorry little tale of my life – or that part of it, at least; exciting, isn't it?"

Elena could tut more expressively than anyone else I knew.

"I still think you love history more than this man, more than *any* man," she declared, as she picked at the strands of melted cheese at the edges of her pizza; "but you can't make a life with history – you can't make *love* with history. You will be very lonely – a sad, lonely old woman." She shook her head sorrowfully.

I selected a chip and laid it carefully at right angles to another one, not as hungry now as I thought when I ordered.

"Oh, I don't know; it has its advantages."

She raised a quizzical eyebrow and huffed impatiently as I

tried to balance one chip on another like the beginnings of a log-cabin wall.

"History's more predictable than a man – it's a done deal – no surprises, and it'll never take you for granted. It's a good enough bedfellow." The wall collapsed and I gave up and consumed the upper third of it.

Elena's eyes glowed with indignation. "Yes, and it will never take you out or buy you presents or… or marry you either."

"That's very true. But I didn't say I wouldn't contemplate getting married, it's just that there are certain parameters I wish to stick to." I dipped another chip in mayonnaise before eating down its length. It crunched satisfyingly. "Such as, he must not make assumptions, of course, and not be much older than me: there was a generational issue with Guy – his cultural references were the same as my parents'. And he mustn't be married – except to me; that's inviolable. Married men are a definite no-no: it's wrong. Besides which, like Sam, they come with too much baggage."

I recognized I came close to playing double standards on that score; I seemed to be making a fine distinction between married, divorced and *widowed* men. The last I saw as an exception to my golden rule even if it meant stretching the point a little. Matthew might very well come with loads of baggage, but through no fault of his own, and perhaps it might be something I could help him carry. I peeled the bun off my burger and piled on the side salad until it bulged, found the area of least resistance and bit into it. The mayonnaise gratifyingly cooled my hot throat.

Elena wore the sort of expression I thought reserved for eighteenth-century statues of the Madonna and martyrs.

"Did you break Guy's heart?"

After everything I said, she still worried for Guy – but then she didn't know him.

"Whose side are you on?" I accused. "You don't think it was an easy choice, do you? Nor am I heartless, before you say anything."

Elena shut her mouth, then cast a swift look at me before asking, "Is he why you hide from people – no, not people, from *men*?"

"I don't!"

"Yes you do. Why do you not wear your hair down so it can be seen?"

"What's my hair got to do with anything?"

My head protested as the room suddenly reverberated with the sound of an old Elvis number from the juke-box; Elena rapped her fingers to it, waiting for an answer. I pulled a face at her persistence.

"This was supposed to be a girls' night out and all we do is talk about men. Can we change the subject? For instance, you promised to show me those sources from Stalingrad – remember? The ghouls and ghosts?"

"I would rather talk about men," she hinted heavily. For that matter so would I, but the lack of Matthew made me morose, and I didn't want Elena to know how I felt about him – not yet, anyway, not until there was certainty on *both* sides. So Stalingrad it would have to be, then.

"I don't want to discuss it now – you will put me off my food." She tried to evade the subject again, but the remains of the enormous pizza lay on her plate and, as I considered her to be in no danger of starvation, I persisted.

"It is better for you to see the sources yourself, but..." she raised a hand as I began to protest, "I can tell you something. These documents were among papers left to me by one of my professors when he died. He served in the army as a... what do you call it?... a secret soldier, no, an intelligence officer, *da*. His job was to prevent certain information destroying the happiness of the army."

"Morale?" I suggested, trying to get the story straight in my head as she told it.

"Yes, that is what I said. There were rumours – many rumours – that people were dying in ways that were not normal, not natural."

"How come? Surely people were dying all the time – there must have been a very high mortality rate among civilians as well as combatants; in all the chaos of the siege, who would know?"

"The doctors knew who died who were not starving, or

wounded or ill. They could see the *marks*."

I shivered, my skin running cold even though my head began to burn. Elena evidently enjoyed the reaction her tale evoked.

"Marks?"

"*Da*, marks of the *Fiend*," she said in hushed tones.

I ignored the reference to a cultural superstition. "But people don't die of marks, so what killed them?"

"The medical reports only said that it was 'a stopping of the heart'."

"So, they had no idea what caused the deaths, then." I sat back and folded my arms, not impressed.

"They were not allowed to say because of the morale, no, but the professor said that he was told in secret that all the victims had fear in their eyes and that they had been *touched*."

"By what?"

"The Fiend. Or at least by a creature of some kind, but they could not say what exactly."

"Because it was secret?"

"*Nyet*, because they did not *know*." She leaned back to gauge my reaction, looking very satisfied with herself. I thought about what she said.

"What did they do with the bodies?"

She anticipated where I headed with that question.

"All the bodies were burned immediately – no more evidence, no autopsy, nothing."

"Because of the threat of disease or... or to keep it secret, or what?"

"My professor said that it was to stop the dead from walking."

The hairs on the back of my neck tingled; I ran my hand over them, soothing the nerves and the ache that was developing at the base of my skull.

"Go on."

"He said that they make sure the bodies were *really* dead, not just a little dead."

"Did your professor say what he thought that meant?"

Elena didn't answer immediately. She fingered the last

quadrant of pizza before putting it down again.

"He said that people talked about the Fiend walking the streets and feeding on men's souls." She spoke so softly that I strained forward to hear. "And that the dead would rise and fight for Germany."

I tried not to laugh. "What – like *zombies?*"

She looked crossly at me. "Shhh – not so loud. He said so, yes. But he didn't believe it; the Soviet Government banned all superstition, all religion, so it could not be so."

"It sounds like something the German propaganda machine dreamt up to scare the natives," I muttered.

"That is so. But still people believed; they were very superstitious, and the rumours spread and soon neighbours did not trust one another. People took to the streets to search for those who had these marks – any marks – and they killed them and burned their bodies. And then it was not enough just to kill the marked ones, but they hunted down their families in case they were infected also. It was a very terrible time."

"Why hasn't more been made of it? I've never heard any of this before."

"Because it was forbidden to talk about it. The deaths were put down to 'enemy action', but after the war, my professor made it his study. It was very difficult for him because of the regime; he went all over the Soviet Union when it was much bigger than Russia is now, and he made a study of people's beliefs – the Government did not ban anthropological research – and he came to believe that these rumours were true in some part, and the very fact that people believed them *made* them true."

"That the Fiend is dormant inside every man, ready to be awakened, do you mean? What, *literally?*"

"He was not very clear about that, but I think he thought that, yes."

"Um," was all I could think of to say; all that I missed was a log fire on a beach, a group of wide-eyed and credulous students and some marshmallows.

"You do not believe me," Elena challenged, folding her arms defensively.

"Hey, I'm not in any position to say one way or another, not without evidence – and that was burned," I reminded her. "Do *you* believe it?"

"I don't know, but..." She looked up from beneath her eyelashes and something told me I'd just fallen for an almighty con.

"It makes a good scary story," I completed for her.

"Hah! Yes it does; did you like it?"

"It was great; you done good, girl."

The waitress came back to see if we had finished. Elena didn't hesitate.

"I *always* have ice-cream – it's so much better here than in Russia. Do you want some?"

"No, I won't have anything else, thanks. Where's the rest-room, please?" I asked the waitress, remembering the correct word. She pointed to a sign hanging over a door on the other side of the diner. "I'll be back in a minute," I said to Elena as I left the table.

I ran water over my wrists and splashed my face to cool it, and then stood by the open window, letting the cold air soothe my burning temples while the juke-box music slammed away inside my head. I didn't feel great.

By the time I washed and dried my hands, Elena had almost finished extracting the remnants of pale-pink ice-cream from the tall, narrow glass with an extra-long spoon. She licked it with an expertise that comes only with years of practice and deposited it in the glass with a clatter.

"OK, I'm good; now I go too." And she slid out of her seat and disappeared the way I came. I unzipped my bag and rummaged for my purse and the cash I'd taken out for the meal. Elena slid back into her seat, breathing heavily.

"That was quick!" I exclaimed, without looking up.

A colourless voice answered. "I'm glad you think so."

My head shot up in alarm and I froze, my hand half-way in my bag. Staahl sat opposite, his pupils small, black pits like olive stones in the centre of his eyes as he stared.

"It's so good to see you again, Emma. You don't mind if I call you by your first name, do you? It is so much more friendly, and I do so want us to be friends." His mouth made a slit when he spoke, words sliding out between his too-thin lips.

I found what must have been my voice. "What do you *want*?"

"Now, now – that's not very friendly, is it? I just wanted to have a little chat to get to know you better. I did promise I'd catch up with you and I always keep my word."

My head spun beneath the dazzling lights; I wanted to shade my eyes but kept my hands still.

"Did you follow me here?" I asked in a voice hoarse with a mixture of fear and defiance. He leaned forwards over the table; if anyone else in the diner looked our way, they would just have seen two people talking.

"Now, why would I do a thing like that?" He spoke very quietly, tonelessly and I could smell his breath. "Unless that is what you wanted. Did you *want* me to follow you, Emma? Do you enjoy the thought that I might be watching you? Have you been waiting for me as I have waited for you?"

The need to get away from him became overwhelming and I made a grab for my bag, struggling to get out of my seat at the same time, but it slid sideways, tipping onto the floor, a few of the contents scattering in an assorted jumble under the table. I scrambled to pick them up, but he bent down and scooped up my bag even as I tried to snatch it from him. He held it close to his body, the blood-red leather the only colour against the grey of his clothes and his skin. Breathing through his teeth, a faint *hiss* as he pulled air through them, with deliberate slowness he held out my bag to me, watching my face, anticipating my reaction, tasting my fear.

I was blowed if I would let him intimidate me with his games. Anger began to seep through me as his non-smile turned into a leer. I seized the strap of my bag but he wouldn't relinquish it.

"Give it back!" I snarled and tugged, but instead of releasing it, Staahl pulled back sharply, jerking my arm towards him, surprisingly strong. Now within inches of his body, I wouldn't give up; I wouldn't let go.

I glared at him. "Let… *go!*" I demanded, my teeth clenched to stop my voice from betraying my alarm.

"Why are you in such a hurry? I have plenty of time. You know, there is much I can help you with; we have so much in common. *Monsters and Magic* – now, there's a title to conjure with. Why did you choose a subject so full of darkness, so much pain, so much *fear*? But thrilling also, don't you think?" He savoured every second and, still clasping the strap, extended a finger towards my hand and stroked the back of it. Hackles stood on the back of my neck.

"Don't you *dare* touch me," I hissed, more furious now than scared. Staahl hesitated then laughed, a dry, humourless rasp, running his tongue over his lips.

"I see you have a little fight in you, I *like* that." He let go of my bag and I fell back against the bench.

I simultaneously stuffed my things back in it as I skimmed along the padded bench to escape, but Staahl's arm shot out, blocking my exit. He suddenly withdrew it at the same time I became aware that someone stood next to us. I looked up. My heart jumped and I didn't attempt to hide my relief at the unexpected sight of Matthew's nephew. "Harry!"

"Hey, Dr D'Eresby. I'm sorry – I hope I'm not disturbing you, but I saw you were here and I couldn't pass by without saying 'Hello'."

"I'm so *very* glad to see you, Harry."

I didn't know what this boy could do, but he seemed to sense the sum of my fear and turned towards Staahl.

"Professor Staahl, right? I believe we've met once before, when I was with my uncle." He spoke politely but there was an undercurrent to his voice I couldn't quite place. Eyes fixed on the boy, Staahl didn't answer at first, and Harry deliberately perched on the edge of the table, forcing him to move back. Although not heavily built, his shoulders were broad in comparison to Staahl's, and the way he held himself spoke of a self-assurance that belied his youth.

"My uncle will be disappointed to have missed you this evening, Dr D'Eresby."

I scanned the room behind him, looking for Matthew.

"He's not here?" But it was obvious he wasn't. In a flash of disappointment, I realized how deeply I missed him that week, never more so than now.

"Nope, I'm afraid he's been kept busy at the hospital; there's been an outbreak of seasonal 'flu, and they need all the staff they can get."

Staahl looked sullenly at Harry and when he finally spoke, sounded resentful.

"Emma and I were discussing a subject of mutual interest before you interrupted."

I cringed at his use of my name but felt more terrified that Harry would leave. A knot of panic in the pit of my gut echoed the ligature rapidly tightening around my skull. Staahl showed no signs of moving, but the boy made it clear he wasn't going anywhere.

"That was inconsiderate of me, Professor," Harry replied conversationally, turning towards him again and not sounding particularly contrite. As he moved, his hand brushed the rim of my glass, sending water flooding over the varnished surface of the table. Harry smiled apologetically as Staahl leapt to his feet, glaring at him.

"That was so clumsy of me; how very stupid. You must let me pay for the dry-cleaning."

Staahl spat a few words, grabbing a paper napkin and scrubbing at the wet area on his clothes. He flung the shredded napkin on the floor and a foul look at us, before pushing roughly past the waitress who had come up to see if she could help.

Harry shook his head, watching Staahl's retreating back.

"That's too bad – just as I was getting to know the guy. Sorry if I spoiled your fun, Dr D'Eresby," he grinned, his naturally good-humoured face alive with suppressed mirth; then he became suddenly serious. "Are you all right, ma'am? He's gone now; I reckon he'll not be back to bother you tonight."

"Harry, thank you, I… I'm fine." It all happened so quickly it seemed quite surreal, almost as if I imagined it, but as Staahl's words sank in, my fumbling brain registered what he said. My flesh itched and crawled and I rubbed my hand roughly against my jeans until it was so red and sore I could no longer remember the sensation of his finger on my skin.

"What's happening? Why was Staahl here?"

"Where have you *been*, Elena?" My voice shook, my scratchy throat tight with tension.

"I… was just at the checkout," she stuttered, pointing behind her. "Why was Staahl here?" she repeated.

"He followed us; I think Harry scared him off." Despite my confusion I remembered my manners and introduced them. Harry bent down to pick up something from under the table.

"I think this must be yours, unless Professor Staahl secretly wears make-up." He held it up. "Nope, definitely not his colour."

He handed me my lipstick. "Harry, thank you so much; I didn't know what to do. Staahl must have followed us here and waited until… 'til… he saw me alone." My words tumbled over themselves as the implication dawned on me. Harry put out a hand to guide me as I sat rapidly.

Elena's eyes were round. "Why would he do that?"

I shook my head. "I don't know; he didn't say much and it wasn't what he said, but the *way* he said it." I shuddered as a wave of cold hit me. I shivered again.

Harry frowned, "I think we'd better get you back to campus. Can I take you?" he offered.

"No, thanks, we came in Elena's car." I unzipped my bag to find my purse, forcing myself to handle it after Staahl touched it, but it felt different, lighter. Stuffing my hand inside, I searched for the familiar metallic jumble of keys.

"My keys – I can't find my keys!" I tipped my bag upside down on the table; checked the inside again; shook it. The keys to my flat, my tutor room – everything – gone.

"He's taken them – Staahl *took* them." A flash of heat coursed through my veins, making me dizzy again.

Elena's eyes widened. "Why did he take them?" We looked at each other, already knowing the answer.

"Do we call the police?" she ventured.

"And tell them what? I can't prove he took them," I said,

feeling more and more that I'd been manoeuvred into a trap. "If he has all my keys, Elena..."

Harry walked a few paces away, talking rapidly on his mobile, but I could hear neither to whom he spoke, nor what he said. Elena bit her nails, her forehead knitted in consternation.

"But he must know we would suspect him; surely he would not be so stupid as to think you wouldn't notice."

I shook my head, regretting the movement as it pounded and I became queasy.

"I think that's just the point, though; he wants me to know."

"Why?"

"Something he said about me enjoying being watched. I don't know – it's as if he likes the thought of me being frightened." I picked up her half-empty glass from the table and held the cool surface to my head. The ache in the back of my head threatened to drill its way through my eye socket.

She eyed me with a degree of concern. "I think you will come and stay with me tonight, yes?"

Harry finished speaking and clicked the mobile shut.

"There should be no need. It won't take long to get the locks changed – they're on to it now. It'll be done by the time you get back. Can I show you both to your car?"

Too drained to be surprised by his efficiency, I followed him to the door. Harry stood aside to let us go first.

"Thank you," I said, automatically, then, "Harry, how did you know we were here?"

"I saw you."

"How?"

He looked puzzled by my persistence, and I hoped I didn't sound rude.

"A couple came out as I was passing; I saw you when the door opened."

"Oh, I see," I said, not convinced.

We crossed the road to Elena's car. "Another thing..." I said, and he flashed me a sideways look. "Staahl said something when he left, but I couldn't quite hear what it was. Did you hear it?"

"It was Dutch and nothing worth repeating," he said with

a conclusiveness that told me he wouldn't say even if it had been. His mouth tightened at the corners, and in that instant his resemblance to Matthew appeared so marked that momentarily, the ache I felt was in my heart and not my head.

Elena drove back to campus as fast as the speed limit allowed. I wrapped my thin coat around me, cold to my core, and she put the heating on full blast to no effect. We were not alone on the journey; every time I looked in the rear mirror, headlights gleamed low on the road, keeping a steady pace behind us. Elena saw them too, but said nothing, keeping her foot on the accelerator all the way.

By the time we reached campus I was roasting. My skin burned and I took my coat off, letting the cold air envelop me. It wasn't enough and I pulled off my jumper to get some relief and breathed lungfuls of air over my stinging throat, which left me giddy.

"You don't look too good," Elena peered anxiously.

"I'm fine, I'm just reacting, that's all." I leaned on the cold bodywork of the car and waited while she fetched her bag. The shadowing car had dematerialized into the night at a junction several miles before we turned off the highway ourselves, allowing my fanciful mind to settle. Nonetheless, I raked the area for any signs of life. The car park was still – even the chill air didn't move – and the first signs of frost lined the longer blades of grass by the kerb. Nearly eleven, most staff were ensconced in their rooms, and only a few students braved the cold and the wrath of college security.

My legs aching with the effort, yards became miles between the car park and our block, every step like walking through porridge.

"I will come and help you get your things if your lock is not changed yet," Elena offered as we approached our stairs, but Harry already stood by my door, waiting, new keys dangling from a finger.

"How...?" I began.

"Students lose their keys all the time; maintenance keep

a supply of locks in stock so there's no problem getting them changed." He dropped the keys into my hand. "I had a spare set cut, just in case you needed one. Oh, and I checked your rooms out to make sure they're clear."

"Thank you, Harry; I don't know what I'd have done without you." Staahl's lupine eyes bore into my memory; I extinguished them. "Thank you *so* much."

He peered at me. "Are you feeling unwell, ma'am?"

My T-shirt clung to my lower back as sweat soaked through it.

"I'm fine – just a little warm, thanks."

As soon as my door closed I dropped my bag on the floor and went straight to the window in my bedroom without bothering to put on the light, and flung it open, drawing the night air over me. The tightness in my throat had been replaced by molten sand. I stumbled into the kitchenette, filling a glass with icy water, spilling it down my front in my haste to put out the fire. The heat returned in seconds.

Making my way towards the bedroom again, the room swayed like the deck of a ship and I lurched forwards, trying to steady myself with the edge of the doorframe. I missed, yelping as my shoulder caught on the corner. I managed to get as far as the foot of my bed before the room twisted momentarily, then the floor rose in waves and I collapsed onto it gratefully.

The room rotated, spinning like a roundabout every time I tried to open my eyes until I felt sick. Someone else moved in the room, leaned over me. *Staahl*. He must have been waiting – watching and waiting until I was alone. I attempted to call for help but he stole my voice and the strange, strangled sound came from so far away it might not have been mine at all. His face loomed, closer and closer until it merged with mine. I lashed out as he lifted me, and I struggled against him, but he was too strong and I had nothing left to fight with. I gave in to the fear and the pain and the heat, and sank below the surface of consciousness into the welcoming void.

Cold came from within like the fire before it. Lead weighted my eyelids and I fought to open them, but they remained stubbornly in place. Where was Staahl? Where was I?

A rasping came from close by; I held my breath and the sound stopped, and I became invisible. Triumphant lights danced behind my eyes, a display of colours so beautiful, so free that I wanted to follow where they led; but ice moulded around my neck like a collar and I gasped, and the jagged breath was all around me again, but louder now, and unrelenting, and each breath echoed the grinding beats of my heart.

I whimpered, waiting for his touch but the dark moved, rocking me to unconsciousness although I wrestled against it until it covered my mind as well as my eyes once more.

Time passed, the fire returned and I burned under a fierce sun. I thrashed out trying to find some relief but my body felt so heavy in the heat. I called out in despair, and coldness pressed against me, chasing away the sun. The cold raised me up, became cool hands, a glass against my lips, a bitter, icy liquid that tamed the fire. I coughed and pushed it away, but it came back, insistent and softly murmuring, making me drink. The coolness spread, dissolving the terror and the flames, and I slept.

Time passed in wave upon wave of heat followed by cold so intense that I would have cried with the pain of it if I could have found my voice. Strange, waking dreams haunted every moment between the dim depths of sleep. Time passed unmeasured. Time was the dripping tap, the ticking clock, the whispering in the night.

The darkness lifted.

I strained my eyes open and caught the first, faint grey of dawn filtering around the edges of the curtains. I wasn't alone and stiffened, listening to the shallow breathing in the room, trying to establish how close. Minutes ticked by before I recognized it as my own, roughened by the sand in my throat; but it no longer burned. I slowly located my limbs – identifying each one by the piercing ache that ran in every joint. My back ached and my head pounded but anything was better than the fire.

I listened for the tell-tale movements that indicated Staahl's presence. Why hadn't he hurt me? Or had he, and I just didn't know it yet? Nothing made sense in my cotton wool brain and I tossed my head from side to side to clear it.

"Keep still – it'll make it worse." A voice – unnaturally loud in the silence of my room. I held my breath, my heart rattling against my chest, until my lungs strained. "And breathe," the voice commanded again. I gulped air. A movement in the lightening darkness by the window sent a wave of panic through me as a shape came towards the bed.

"Get away from me!" My voice grated. I tried to roll over and escape but my body wouldn't obey and I succeeded only in flinging my arm against the sharp edge of my bedside cupboard. I cried out in pain and alarm and struggled, but too late, and a hand grabbed my wrist before I could lash out again. The voice spoke, cool and soothing like sorbet on a hot day.

"Emma, stay still; you are quite safe – go to sleep."

How could I be safe? How could I sleep? But the voice beguiled and, as hard as I tried, I couldn't fight the lethargy that lay on every limb, and I drifted again, afloat on a sea of silvered waves.

Thirst woke me before I remembered to be scared. A slight movement at the side of the room rattled my consciousness; my eyes shot open.

"Good morning," Matthew said, as if I should expect him to be there. I tried to locate his voice and he rose as if in answer from the deep chair in the corner, and came to stand by my bed. I swallowed, trying to ease the arid waste in my mouth.

"Where's Staahl?" I rasped, struggling to sit up. The room danced and my head with it. I fell back against the pillows, exhausted.

"Staahl's not here, Emma."

"But he was – I *saw* him." I had to make Matthew understand, my voice shaking with the effort.

"No, he has never been in your room – you are quite safe. You have influenza and have been delirious." His voice sounded very gentle, plausible and I wanted to believe him. Muted light of day barely reached my bed but even so, the calm pools of his eyes stood out against his fair skin as he observed me.

"Thirsty?" he asked.

"Yes," I whispered. On my bedside table, a glass sat dripping condensation on a saucer, but I shook so much I couldn't take it and he put his arm under my shoulders and held the glass to my lips. I drank thirstily.

"Thank you."

He looked at his watch, the metal gleaming dull gold in the half-light.

"You'll need some more medication to keep your temperature down. Do you think you can manage a capsule or would you rather have it in suspension? Or a shot?" he added as an afterthought. I must have looked horrified because he smiled slightly and produced a packet of capsules, popping two and supporting me again while I swallowed them, his arm cool against the heat of my skin.

"What time is it?" I asked as he laid me down. The fog in my head began to clear a little. He replaced the glass on the saucer.

"Nearly seven – in the morning, that is."

I wanted to ask him something, but it was all a little hazy and the question that formed was not the one I intended.

"What are you doing here?"

He looked surprised. "You have 'flu and I *am* a doctor. Harry said you didn't look well last night, so I thought I would check on you. Good thing I did, too."

I could just about muster enough truncated sentences to ask him, "I mean, *how* are you here? How did you get in?" He took my wrist in his right hand, feeling my pulse, counting silently before answering.

"The spare set of keys you gave Harry just in case, remember? I knocked on your door but when you didn't answer I had to make sure you were all right. I let myself in."

He gently laid my arm under the cool, light sheet that covered me, and tucked the edge under. He crossed to the bathroom and I heard a running tap and the sound of something wet being wrung out. I searched my disjointed memories of the night before, looking for one in which I gave Harry a set of keys to my flat. I found none, but I did recall him dropping both sets of new keys into my hand.

Too weak to argue the point, I asked instead, "How long have you been here?" Long enough to give me medication at least twice in the night, I thought. I let my eyes close.

"Some time." His voice came close by. I opened my eyes again as he laid a cool flannel over my forehead.

"That was a very late house call," I muttered sleepily.

"I'm a very dedicated doctor," he replied.

Chapter

10

In Translation

"**D**O YOU THINK YOU MIGHT BE UP TO reading this?" Matthew held up an A5 notebook before offering it to me. "It's your punishment for complaining of being bored." His grin made me forget to be ill for a second.

"What is it?" I began to struggle pathetically into a more upright position and he helped raise me enough to slip another pillow behind my back. I trembled with the meagre effort and the effect of his unexpected touch. He put the slim book in my hand. Opening it on the first page, I squeaked as loudly as my throat would allow.

"You've finished it already?"

"I promised you I would; I'm only sorry I took so long getting it to you."

I remembered the week that seemed an eternity. He drew the original book from the pocket of his jacket and opened it, laying it side by side with the copy he made. I scanned the frontispiece and first page, revelling in the detail. Matthew smiled wryly, reminding me I was being fanatical.

"Harry said you were busy at the hospital, but it's still only taken you, what... less than two weeks? That's amazing!"

"Something like that. Anyway, you'll need to read it in conjunction with the original. I've tried to match it page to page so you can keep track of the illustrations; it doesn't make much sense otherwise. Look..." and he sat on the side of my bed to show me, close enough to feel the pressure of his body through the duvet that replaced the sheet. I swallowed, making my throat sting.

"I've taken liberties with some phrases where there isn't a direct translation, but I don't think it's altered the meaning as such – it's just made it easier to read."

Transfixed, I scanned each page covered in exquisitely even, handwritten script. Flowing letters in dark ink looked as if they belonged to another era. I closed my eyes fleetingly.

"Emma, are you feeling unwell?" Concern coloured his voice and I opened them to find him observing me closely. I wished I were well enough to make something of it, but I felt so lousy that I couldn't even be self-conscious under his attentive gaze. I managed to rustle up enough enthusiasm to show my appreciation for the book, although it took every grain of effort to do so.

"You're amazing," I croaked. "This would have taken most academics months to translate. Even reading an English text from this date can take ages. How did you do it?"

"It's not so difficult if you're familiar with the original and the language isn't a problem."

I hummed sceptically. "Hmm, well, not for you, maybe, but for the rest of us mere mortals…" I caught the edge of a frown out of the corner of my eye. "I'm just so useless at languages that I can't ever imagine somebody else finding it easy," I explained. I turned the pages of his leather-bound book, searching for an illustration that intrigued me. Matthew flipped through the translated text to find the corresponding page. I couldn't resist raising something I had been dying to ask.

"Did you find the book interesting to translate – as a subject – or is it too close to reality because you have to deal with it on a day-to-day basis?" I twisted to look up at him while he wasn't looking at me, the expression on his face one of intelligent consideration.

"This?" he tapped his long, fine fingers on the book, thoughtfully. "Yes, interesting to a degree, but I hope that I don't torture my patients – not intentionally, anyway."

I almost laughed but it turned into a cough instead. "Sorry, no, I didn't mean that *you* inflict pain – except for the threat of injections maybe – I meant that you have to cope with what has been imposed on your patients by other people, like the student who was attacked. The difference between treating someone with 'flu or someone with a black eye because her husband didn't like the brand of beer she bought. I suppose what I'm getting at is, how do you cope with man's purposeful inhumanity?" I lay back on my pillows, controlling my breathing; it was the most I had managed to say since becoming ill. He became quiet, his face blank, then he looked down at me with a strange – almost curious – expression.

"You come at things from a different angle to most people, do you realize that?"

"Are you implying I'm obscure?"

His mouth twitched upward. "No, but possibly oblique. I could ask you the same question, since you have chosen to study a subject bathed in centuries of human blood: how do you cope with *that*?"

"That's easy," I said and he looked surprised. "No, it is, really, because it's all safely tucked away in the past. I don't have to face the reality of it like you do every day. Whoever wrote this book presumably had a conscience he had to square with what he witnessed. But *my* conscience doesn't come into it. And you haven't answered my question, by the way."

"Ah, I thought that in your weakened state you might have forgotten what you asked."

"Not likely; it's taken me a long time to get around to asking you."

"Why?" he asked.

"You're doing it again," I warned. "Stop prevaricating."

"It's probably because I don't have an answer to give you right away; I'll have to give it due consideration. Can you wait, do you think?" When he smiled at me like that – his eyes lifted at the corners, emphasizing tiny creases that echoed the ones at the rising bow of his mouth – despite myself, warmth trickled into my veins.

"That means you'll have to come back then, doesn't it?" I said hopefully, all too aware of his closeness at that moment.

"Well, I don't know; you're making an excellent recovery and we are short-staffed at the moment..." His smile widened at the look on my face and my breath caught in my throat, engulfing me in a fit of coughing that shook my whole body, making it difficult to breathe. He supported my weight as I fought to control my wheezing and reached for the water by my bed, holding the glass until I had managed to sip enough to calm my throat. Gradually, the coughing stopped and I lay against him, utterly exhausted. He put the glass down and placed his hand on my forehead, cool on my searing skin.

"That's enough for one day," he chided gently, his voice close to my ear. "Your temperature's up again and you know what that means, don't you?" I shook my head, not daring to speak in case it set me coughing again. "It means that I'll have to keep checking on you until I'm convinced you're fully recovered."

The sprites in my stomach squirmed feebly. "What about your other patients?" I managed to ask, not wanting to move in case he took his arm away.

"Well, as a doctor I'm obliged to prioritize my casualties and, in my qualified medical opinion, you require frequent medical supervision."

As a doctor, he should have known better than to tell a sick and vulnerable patient what she wanted to hear.

"You shouldn't get too close," I whispered.

"Why not?" he said, suddenly cautious.

"Because I'm contagious."

He smiled, clearly relieved. "You're certainly that." And he pulled me closer than strictly necessary for him to support me.

"No, I mean I don't want you to catch 'flu." I thought my self-sacrifice admirable, considering I wanted him to be as close to me as possible for as long as feasible.

"Oh – well, there's not much chance of that; I'm immune to pretty well most things."

Not to me, I begged silently. "Except to you, of course," he added.

One of the worst things about having 'flu was being totally dependent on others having to look after me in those first few days when I couldn't even lift my head off the pillow without it threatening to shatter. Being dependent also meant doing as I was told, which I hadn't needed to do since puberty, and didn't come naturally. After the initial forty-eight hours when my temperature moderated, I became desperate to get back to work, and began to dissect the treatise in earnest, much to Elena's disgust. However, moving beyond the confines of my bed was entirely another matter.

Thankfully, the only people who could walk into my flat without me having to let them in were the two I looked forward to seeing. Matthew kept the spare set of keys, and I didn't ask him about them again because seeing him every day was more important to me than the truth at the moment. Elena, on the other hand, took the other set so she could pop in. That meant I could ask her to help me with the necessities of life.

I could manage to get to the bathroom in stages but had to improvise to wash, so Elena stuffed the drainer in the shower base with a flannel and ran the water until it filled the base with enough warm water to bathe in. She helped me to the bathroom door, and dignity and modesty gave me the wherewithal to do the rest – albeit with the elegance of a beached seal. At least I could brush my teeth sitting on the chair.

The other disadvantage – or advantage, depending upon how you viewed it – was that I might not be awake when I had a visit.

I surfaced to the sound of worried voices.

"Matthew, what's the matter?"

"Sorry, we didn't mean to wake you," he apologized. "There's been another attack on a woman – not here, but in town. Harry's just been updating me."

A chill finger ran the length of my spine. "When?"

Harry moved into my line of sight. "The same night you were there – about one-thirty – though they didn't find her until later the following day and they can't be sure until…"

"Harry," Matthew cautioned him.

"Until… what?" I looked from Harry to Matthew.

"They have to do an autopsy," Matthew said, soberly.

So she was *dead*. Nothing connected this ill-fated stranger with me except that Matthew and his nephew discussed her as if they saw a link, and that unnerved me. I stared at my hands, not seeing them but dead eyes empty of life. "And… you think it's the same man who attacked the girl here, don't you?"

"Possibly."

"*Don't* you?" I persisted, looking at them both.

"Yes, it seems that way but we'll wait until the report's completed; we can't jump to conclusions." But it was clear to me they already had.

"And you think Staahl might have something to do with it?" Matthew put his hand over mine, prying my fingers from my tortured duvet cover before I tore a hole in it. "What makes you think these attacks were by the same person? If the autopsy's not yet been done, what's the connection? And how do you know?" He frowned at the rising note in my voice and his own dropped correspondingly.

"Emma, it's not difficult getting information; I carry out some of the autopsies for the police department and have contacts there – and I cared for the student initially so I know what her injuries were like. The correlation between the two attacks lies in how they were carried out and the nature of the injuries. And before you ask…" he said, raising a hand to stop me as I opened my mouth, "I cannot say any more in case it jeopardizes the investigation." His face wore a look that told me there would be little point pressing the issue. "And no," he said, anticipating my next question. "There's no chance Aydin is involved, and I don't know if the police have any suspects; and as for whether there is any association with Staahl, that, I'm afraid, remains to be seen."

"Oh." I thought about the dead woman. "Did she have a family?"

"A little girl."

"Poor little mite." I closed my eyes, squeezing tears back

before they escaped.

"Yes."

Later, in the absolute dark, I wrapped my arms around my knees, unable to sleep as I tried to rationalize the latest information. Matthew saw a link between the attack on the girl on campus and the murder of the woman in town. What appeared to have been a random assault now related to a murder, representing a much more sinister trend. More to the point where I was concerned, did it implicate Staahl?

Neither of us commented on the frequency of Matthew's visits, nor did I enquire whether they were strictly necessary; but I felt safe when near him and lost when not. Now, when I closed my eyes, I no longer saw Staahl, but Matthew; I saw the aquiline plane of his face, the balanced breadth of his jaw; I heard the sonorous timbre of his voice and replayed the graceful movement of his walk. Yet his attraction went far beyond his looks to something intangible I had yet to decipher and the depth of his attraction worried me. I knew I risked losing myself in him, but what really frightened me was that I didn't care.

Chapter

II

Almost Human

By day four, I achieved a degree of self-sufficiency. I didn't wait for Elena, but shuffled to the bathroom using the wall to lean on when the room threatened to turn upside down. Blissful hot water ran in streams through my hair and over my still aching body, washing away remnants of 'flu and leaving me almost human again. I managed to drag on some clothes but the effort left me completely drained and I lay on my bed with my arm draped across my eyes recovering, my wet hair spread messily around me.

A loud knock on the door followed by the sound of the key in the lock announced Elena's morning call. She had been in every morning and each afternoon on return from tutorials. She took her visits as an opportunity to boss me in her attempt to nurture, forcing me to eat as soon as she thought me able and keeping me up to date on campus gossip. I was touched by her kindness, although she refused to be thanked.

"Emma, are you decent?" The door to my flat opened and her cheerful voice preceded her into the room.

"Sort of," I croaked, my eyes still covered because my arm was too heavy to lift.

There was a giggle in her voice. "Good, because there's someone here to see you."

I thought about sitting up but the notion of it made the room rock, so it seemed easier just to lie there.

"Hello, Freckles."

I shot into an upright position.

"Sam... hi..."

He stood in the doorway to my bedroom in his dark leather jacket, hands stuffed in his jeans pockets, and everything about him looked awkward and uncomfortable.

"I heard you have 'flu; are you OK now?" He could barely meet my eyes and showed none of his customary bravado.

"I'm much better, thanks." I decided on a direct approach. "Does that mean that I'm forgiven, Sam?" I cleared my throat, still husky from the infection. He scuffled his feet and shrugged.

"Yeah, well, that depends..."

"On what?"

In the kitchen, Elena hummed while making toast; I heard the scraping of a knifc on the rough surface before I smelled it wafting through the flat.

Sam looked up under his lashes "On whether you can forgive *me*. I'm sorry for the way I reacted the other day – I had no right to."

It was all so long ago, and so much had happened in between that it no longer seemed relevant, but Sam obviously didn't think so; he acted as if it was all he had thought about since then.

"Sam – it's forgotten; forget it – life's too short, and I'm sorry too, for the misunderstanding." My hair dripped down my back, soaking my top. I searched around for the towel, but it had slipped off the bed and onto the floor. I leaned sideways to pick it up, but Sam was there first, holding it out to me, his eyes pining. I took it from him, taking care not to touch him in case he thought it meant more than it did.

"Elena says Lynes – Matthew..." he quickly corrected himself, "comes here every day to check on you? That's uh... very dedicated of him."

His attempt at nonchalance wouldn't fool anybody. Elena appeared in the doorway, plate in one hand, a steaming mug of tea in the other. She stopped, waiting to see the direction of the conversation. I wrapped the towel around the dripping tail of my hair and squeezed water from it.

"Yes, Matthew's been very kind; Elena too," I said evenly, making sure I included her even though it wasn't what Sam meant, and I knew it and so did she. Elena rolled her eyes behind his back. Sam rubbed a hand over day-old beard. He still managed to look very attractive with it and I wished for his sake he would find someone else to smoulder at so effectively.

"Does it mean you and he are, you know... that I don't... that you wouldn't consider us getting together... at all," he fumbled, trying to find something appropriate to say for which I wouldn't snap at him. I sighed; I thought that we were beyond all that and, after our last encounter, that the situation had been made perfectly clear. Elena walked quietly past him and put my breakfast on my bedside table, looking at me meaningfully as she did so.

"Thanks," I said automatically, but any hunger fled, pursued by his question.

"Well? You know what I mean, Emma, don't make me spell it out, *please.*"

He looked so pathetic that I couldn't help but feel sorry for him, and I struggled to find a way of telling him I wasn't interested that didn't sound harsh because, so far, anything I said failed to make an impression.

"Good morning! You're looking better."

I hadn't heard Matthew come in and my heart jumped wildly at the sound of his voice. He walked purposefully over, kissing me lightly on the top of my head as if this level of intimacy were ritual. My pulse nearly exploded and I flushed crimson. He turned to the other two.

"Good morning, Elena, Sam," he said pleasantly as I struggled to regain my composure. Sam's shoulders hunched forward, his hands back in his pockets.

"Yeah, sure, and I guess that answers *that* question." He conceded defeat. "Well, I expect I'll see you around campus, Emma. Glad you're feeling better, anyhow."

"Thanks for coming to see me, Sam." I offered him a smile as a token of peace and he half-heartedly returned it.

"Yeah; I'll see you soon – sometime."

As soon as he left the room, with Elena seeing him to the door, I faced Matthew, who had watched Sam's retreating figure with narrowed eyes.

"You did that on purpose!" I accused him.

He looked at me innocently. "What?"

"You didn't have to rub it in like that."

Matthew defended himself with a grin. "I was only answering his question."

"You heard that?"

"Well, you didn't say anything, so I thought I'd better make the situation clear for him – it's only fair."

"Matthew, *I* don't know what the situation is, let alone being in a position to be able to tell anyone else."

"Don't you?" he asked, his teasing eyes suddenly soft, leaning over me so I could feel his warmth on my skin. I kept completely still, my face raised.

"I'm not sure," I breathed, my heart tumbling over itself to keep up. He leaned in closer, his mouth grazing my ear. "Mmm, you smell good." He inhaled deeply, raising his right hand and running it under my wet hair. "Poor Sam," he murmured wickedly, "he doesn't know what he's missing."

I turned my face and his lips were millimetres from mine, denim eyes burning with an intensity that melted my blood.

"Still not sure?" he whispered. "Do I need to persuade you?"

"Oh! Sorry!" Elena came into the room unannounced. I jerked away from Matthew, reddening. He drew upright more slowly, eyes still on my face.

"It's OK, Elena," I managed to say, feeling like a teenager caught behind the bike shed.

"I... I just wanted to make sure you were eating," she stuttered, avoiding looking at us.

Matthew recovered his poise. "Quite right, and you've reminded me what I wanted to tell you this morning..." We looked at him expectantly. "I bumped into the bursar and he has allocated you another apartment; you can move today – now, in fact."

"Why, what's wrong with this one?" I asked, looking around my cramped room to the dormer window between the eves, and the view to the mountains in the distance I loved so much.

"There's nothing wrong except that these rooms are small, damp and cold and are not the best place to be in when recovering from 'flu. I don't want you developing any secondary infections; besides, they need redecorating – and they can't do that if you're in them. The new ones are closer to Elena – and you're moving today so we'd better get you packed." He made for my wardrobe but I began to feel uprooted and obstinate.

"So, don't I get any say in the matter?"

"No."

"But… but I might not want to move."

"Tough."

"I think it is good," Elena piped. "You argue too much."

I started to get up.

"Stay there and eat your breakfast; this won't take long," Matthew said as he opened the wardrobe door. I flopped back on my bed, still too weak to argue or do anything other than comply, however unwillingly.

"Elena!" I hissed. She came over so I could whisper to her. "Please, don't let him pack; there's girl's stuff – knickers, you know – in there." I looked at her imploringly. She nodded, but Matthew had turned away from the wardrobe and chest of drawers.

"On second thoughts, I'd better concentrate on heavy items." He cast a sideways glance at me, with a half-smile which made me wonder if he'd heard me.

I didn't have much so it didn't take long to get everything packed; Matthew had the bags tucked under his arm and disappeared before Elena could offer to help. She sat on the edge of my bed as I puffed getting my shoes on.

"So you and Matthew…?" she queried.

"It looks like it, doesn't it?" I couldn't help breaking into a jubilant grin, then coloured as I remembered the unexpected kiss, laden with meaning no matter how chastely he had placed it.

She laughed, her eyes merry. "It certainly did from where I was standing!"

"Poor Sam, though," I said, recalling the look of deep disappointment on his face.

She flapped a hand dismissively. "Ah, he'll get over it."

"You've changed your tune a bit, haven't you?" Elena looked puzzled. "You were on Sam's side if I remember correctly."

She giggled, evading the question. "But you should have seen the look on Matthew's face when I came in; I don't think he liked being disturbed. I think he only has eyes for you; it is *very* romantic. I am sorry for Sam, but Matthew is..." she trailed off, staring dreamily out of the window.

"Matthew's *what*, Elena? You can't stop now – it's cruel. Come on – tell me."

"I was not sure about Matthew, you know that, and I still say he is different. He is very handsome, of course – like his nephew," she mused, "but, he is also a strong person; *inside* he is strong like iron, not like Sam. I have seen how he has looked after you and I think he cares for you *very* much. Has Matthew said anything about his wife?"

"No, and I don't want to ask until he is ready," I said firmly. I didn't add that her memory still petrified me; that I felt convinced that Matthew would one day turn around and see me for who I was and that I wouldn't be enough. I played with my cross absentmindedly. I brought the conversation back to the ordinary. "Talking of gorgeous – where's Matias? I haven't seen him for days."

Elena shook her head mournfully "He's in Oslo for a conference until Thursday. He takes his work too seriously." She pouted; then her face lit. "We can go out as a foursome when he's back! What fun we will have!"

"Um, well, perhaps," I said, doubtfully; I couldn't honestly see Matthew as the sort who would relish the prospect. "I tell you what; let's see how things go before we arrange anything; it's early days yet."

"OK," she said lightly.

Matthew returned from my new apartment.

"Are you ready to go?" he asked. I nodded and took one more look out of my window at my favourite view. He held out his hand to me, and I slid off the bed towards him, but he slipped his arm around my waist to support me, catching me by surprise.

"I can carry you if you would prefer?" he ventured. He wore a shirt in a crisp, fine fabric in a muted tone complementing his colouring. Classic without being stuffy or overly conservative, he wore it open at the neck, revealing an area of skin at the base of his throat where his collar-bone spread strongly under the cloth. If he carried me, I would be closer to him than at any other time, closer to that enticing triangle, and I could legitimately inhale his clean-air scent without him knowing. Sorely tempted, I nonetheless shook my head.

"I don't want your wrecked back on my conscience, thanks."

He grinned in reply and took my weight with his arm around my waist instead, almost lifting me off the ground.

Compared with my attic rooms, my new apartment seemed huge. On the floor below Elena's, it must have been a principal room once. A full-height wall separated the kitchen from the living area, and the bedroom spanned an area at least three times the size of my previous one, with an en-suite bathroom with a bath *and* a shower, which didn't drip incessantly. Much to my delight – and Elena's envy – a working fireplace took up one wall of my bedroom; I promised her plenty of pizza and girl-talk in front of it as recompense.

Elena started to unpack my bags for me, despite my protestations that I could manage. She sent me back into the sitting-room where I could admire the best feature of all, for the windows filled the entire outside wall in Gothic arches, letting light flood into the room. Heavy velvet curtains fell as far as the deep window-seat that ran the length of the windows, and a matching box cushion softened the hard bench-top. In the distance, I could still make out the summits of the mountains, but the foreground was filled with the smouldering colours of autumn. I didn't realize how much the trees had transformed over the few days of my illness. A fine, aged cedar stood nearest, the same one whose branches whispered against my attic windows at night. Its dark, blue-green branches provided the perfect contrast to the pulsating colours beyond.

"Acceptable?" Matthew stood close to me as I took it all in.

"Very," I acknowledged.

"I can hear a 'but' in there. I know that it needs something to make it more homely, and…"

"No, it's fine as it is; it's lovely – but I'm not used to somebody making decisions for me; I'm not used to anybody… caring." I bit my lip, thinking how limp that sounded and added more resolutely, "And I can still see my mountains from here." I turned around to look at him, to be immediately taken aback by the vibrancy of his eyes in the northern light from the windows. He used them to full effect, and I needed to remember to breathe.

"Let me take you up into them when you're fully recovered," he offered.

I could think of nothing I would like better. "Promise?" I asked a little shyly.

"Promise."

"I think that would be very acceptable," I assented; "and I love this apartment; 'flat' is nowhere near grand enough a word to describe it."

He reached out to catch a stray strand of my hair that curled as it dried, twisting it between his thumb and forefinger before tucking it back behind my ear in a simple, unconscious gesture, making my blood sing.

"There's one thing I'd better mention; I'm going to be away for a day – perhaps two" – I crashed back down to reality – "and it is going to take you at least another week before you are up to tackling any mountains. So…" and he reached into one of his pockets, "… take this in case you need me." He held out a slim, black mobile. "Elena said you lost yours. Take it, Emma – it's for you." He smiled at my hesitancy. I took it from him.

"Thanks," I said, bashful again.

"I've put my number in the memory; you just press this button," he said, showing me, "and I'll be there."

"Thanks," I said again. "Are you going far?" It mattered, somehow.

"Some distance."

I wanted to ask him where and why and what, but he would have told me if he wanted me to know, so I just said, "Well, I have a lot of work to catch up; that'll keep me busy."

If I said it enough times, perhaps I would begin to believe it. The image of the dead woman in the mutilated car flared in my memory and a sudden wave of anxiety hit me at the thought of him leaving.

"Matthew, you will take care, won't you?"

He shook his head, trying not to laugh. "Emma, I'm not the one who's had 'flu. *You* take care."

"Doctor's orders?" I muttered, sitting down in a big armchair, my stamina all used up.

"Something like that," he agreed.

Elena came in from my bedroom at that point, checking first to make sure she didn't interrupt something.

"I've finished unpacking, Emma; you do not have enough clothes. What are you going to wear for All Saints?"

I peered through my fingers at her wearily. "All Saints what?"

Disbelieving, she stood with her hands on her hips, and I tried to remember something that either she had told me already or was deemed so important that I should have known about it anyway.

"If this discussion involves clothes, I think I will depart and do something more useful," Matthew said rapidly.

I looked imploringly at him. "Please don't leave me alone with this strange woman; she's a dreadful bully."

They laughed simultaneously and I pulled a face at them.

"Elena's probably the only one who can get you to eat, so I'm leaving you to her tender mercies."

"You're all heart," I grouched. He stepped forward and quickly kissed the top of my head again. "You don't know the half of it," he said softly. "I'll see you again soon."

"What is that supposed to mean?" I called after his disappearing back, but he just chuckled as he left.

Chapter

12

The Journal

TIME WOVE ITS INEXORABLE PASSAGE through the following days and, now that we had come to some sort of understanding, every moment without Matthew ached. I kept the mobile fully charged and on at all times and he called me once; he sounded very far away and I heard a remoteness in his voice that seemed less to do with distance and more to do with his state of mind. I worried then, that our time apart diminished the fragile bond we had formed, unravelling like twine under the stress of separation, and I began to wonder whether his tender concern derived more from my imagination than from his making. But almost as if he sensed my apprehension, he sent me a text that had me spinning into his vortex once more.

Just a few simple lines:

> *All this fair, and soft, and sweet,*
> *Which scatteringly doth shine,*
> *Shall within one Beauty meet,*
> *And she be only thine.*

And perhaps, had it been anyone else, I would view this as mere flirtation, an attempt to seduce, but because it was him and I wanted it to be true, I read the lines with a hope of future fulfilment he neither stated nor promised, but which nonetheless lay in the colour of the words.

I recognized the lines vaguely, and wasn't sure how to respond, so I merely texted him back with the word "Marvell?", then racked my brain for some appropriate rejoinder, but each that nearly hit the mark spoke of love, or death, or God – and nothing quite seemed to say what I wanted without saying too much or not enough. In the end, I settled for a horribly misappropriated verse from Henry Vaughan, because it was the nearest I could get to saying I missed him without resorting to cloying sentimentality:

> *He is all gone into the world of light!*
> *And I alone sit lingering here;*
> *His very memory is fair and bright,*
> *And my sad thoughts doth linger here.*

I sent the text with a silent apology to the poet for mutilating his verse and a hope that Matthew wouldn't turn out to be a purist who resented liberties being taken with the lines.

He replied almost immediately: "Vaughan?!"

And I sent back: "Sort of."

That was the last I heard from him and, to prevent my descent into anxiety-ridden brooding, I spent my time buried in work, which is what I should have been doing in the first place.

Matthew had been right, I didn't even have the strength to get to the history department, so I invited my group over to my apartment for tutorials. The sessions benefited from the addition of coffee and donuts for the group, so they went particularly well, and the tension of the previous meetings dissolved. Whatever prejudices Leo might have held, he wisely kept them to himself. Aydin brought the first part of his thesis, translated and ready for my scrutiny. It was impressive; the additional time spent with his girlfriend had greatly benefited his English. I complimented him on both his work and his grammar, and he beamed hugely.

Working with my group again helped me get back on track with my own research. Elena and Matias ferried my laptop and some books from my tutor room, and I made a section of my new living area by a window into a temporary study.

As soon as I could, I emailed my parents to ask about my grandmother. Still no change; she might continue to exist in the limbo that represented life for the next five years, or have another stroke and die tomorrow. We agreed we didn't know which would be preferable for her at the moment.

"Your mother needs a situation report, Emma. How are you getting on over there?" Dad asked, using my sister's computer. I gave him a positive spin on all my work and told him I'd had 'flu but was much better now. My mother wanted to know if I was eating properly and taking the vitamins and minerals she gave me before I left the country to make up for my inadequate diet. I winced guiltily, glancing over to the kitchen where an impressive array of bottles sat unopened. I confirmed I could see them right now but neglected to say anything else; she wasn't fooled.

We were blessed with another series of days of blazing colour as the sun ripped through the multi-hued canopy, throwing the ground beneath into a constantly moving glow. I sat outside on one of the benches under the trees, wrapped against the cold, although I could tell that my British coat would be no match for a winter in Maine. Students and lecturers kept up a steady flow along the path in front of me and, although alone, I could not fear Staahl out here in the colours of the sun, as he was a creature of the shadows – as washed-out and formless as a half-remembered nightmare.

I kept Matthew's books with me for company, bit by bit unravelling the workings of the Italian cleric's mind as revealed by his detailed descriptions of the interrogation techniques he used. His humility and compassion would have been touching were he writing a treatise on the care of the sick, but his singular objective was the healing of the soul, and nothing could be more pressing in this life or the next. I could take only so much at any one time, despite the beauty of Matthew's flowing script, and I laid the books down, and raised my face to the sun.

"Ah, we are all come to worship the sun."

I opened one eye. Siggie sat down and picked the Italian treatise off my knee. She raised her eyebrows as she took in the graphic illustrations.

"A little light reading for your convalescence, no?"

I smiled cheerfully at her. "It keeps me focused. How do you know about the 'flu?"

She tapped my leg jovially. "It's a small campus, Emma, and a little gossip goes a long way when there is nothing else to talk about."

I failed to see how, even given a dearth of anything else to discuss, my catching 'flu could be remotely interesting to anyone else.

"'Flu?"

She smiled. "Not perhaps the 'flu, no, but then there is a certain young man who seems to have taken a fancy to you, much to the disappointment of one or two of his students, I presume."

I looked at her sharply; I had no idea Matthew and I were linked in any way unless Elena had been talking. I didn't like my private life being the subject of gossip; I'd seen the results of lies and tittle-tattle scattered throughout history too many times to pretend they meant anything other than trouble. I attempted to appear entertained by the thought.

"What are they saying – these campus crows?"

"That he didn't get as far as he would like with you, and he is not used to being thwarted. I must say, he wasn't looking his normal jubilant self this morning."

A sudden intake of breath caught my throat and I coughed hard to stop the resulting tickle. "You've seen him *today*?" I choked out eventually.

She patted my back, looking surprised. "Is that so strange? He gave a lecture to my students on an aspect of statistics I never understood; I don't know why we have to include so much math in psychology; I think I will rewrite the course."

"Maths, statistics…? You mean *Sam*?"

"Yes, of course, who else would I be referring to?" Her eyes twinkled from their deep-set sockets. She took Matthew's translation from where it still lay on my lap and opened it. Her greying eyebrows twitched when she saw the fine script. "How is the elusive Dr Lynes, by the way?"

I retrieved the pocketbook from her hands and closed it.

"As far as I'm aware he is his usual self; I haven't heard otherwise, have you?"

She laughed unexpectedly, a deep, good-natured laugh. "Ah, I know when I am being told to mind my own business," she chortled. "But you know, Emma, *this* is my business." She tapped the little leather treatise once with a finger. "Saul and I have a draft paper we would like you to look over if you have the time; we have made reference to some historical texts you will probably know, but we need them validated. Saul would ask Kort Staahl, but I think we need a more... let's say, *balanced* view, if you understand me." She looked sideways at me but all I could do was stare.

"Staahl is *not* a historian; why ask *him*?"

Momentarily taken aback, Siggie placed a placating hand on my arm. "There's no need to take offence; Saul wanted to get this checked out quickly and you had 'flu and Kort is an authority on such texts from a literary point of view, so he..." She peered at me. "Emma, is something the matter?"

I didn't know whether to laugh at my sheer stupidity or at my blind presumption that Staahl had been following me, and I reflected ruefully on the rapidity with which I had condemned him. Few academics specialized in our specific area, and to find two of them within the same university pushed the boundaries of coincidence. In that light, did it seem so peculiar he wanted to discuss the subject with me? The keys must have fallen from my bag in the diner after all. Was my ego so very inflated that I assumed his attention must be for some purpose other than academia? I might not like the man, but that didn't make him a *monster*.

I shook my head slowly as I came to the reluctant conclusion that I must have been wrong about him.

"No, nothing's the matter, I just realized something and yes, of course, I'll be delighted to help out if I can." I rubbed a hand tiredly over my eyes.

Siggie beamed. "That is very good, thank you; and now I have worn you out and you must go inside before you get cold."

It was indeed getting cold although the late-afternoon sun warmed the sky with colours of fire. I stood up and, as I did so, Matthew's transcription dropped to the ground. Siggie bent to pick it up before I could. She handed it back to me, her eyes on my face.

"Beautiful, quite beautiful; I don't know anybody who writes like that any more."

I smiled down at the little notebook, but didn't answer her unvoiced question.

At night, the temperature dropped below freezing, the sky revealing a richness of stars in an intensity and detail not seen in the light-polluted sky of my urban home. I leaned out of my window as far as I could, my duvet the only protection against the frost, and gazed at the sky until my neck ached and I felt compelled to retreat into the warmth of my room. I lay awake, my thoughts drifting listlessly between the journal and the man that endangered its pole-position in my affections, and decided I could put it off no longer.

The first fall of leaves lay scattered across the path on my way towards the library, my legs still unsteady from a lack of exercise. The foliage scrunched satisfyingly underfoot and, were it not for my fragile state, I would have been tempted to kick them into eddies of colour. As it was, I entered the library out of breath and shaking.

The librarian sat where I left her last, and it wouldn't have surprised me to find she grew roots where her legs should have been. Her thin, shrivelled face peered up as I wheezed to her desk, using it as support until I could breathe more easily.

"How are you, Professor? I haven't seen you for a long time; I wondered when you would be back." Her thin, dry voice rattled but her eyes were as sharp and bright as the first time we met.

"Thank you for remembering. I was wondering if you could help me locate the Richardson journal?"

The woman's face lit. "Yes, of course!" she said, as if she had been waiting for this moment as much as I. She unfolded herself from the chair, her thin body cracking as she straightened, and led the way to the lift.

Instead of rising to the floor containing the history section, we descended into the basement.

"This is where we keep our most precious manuscripts," she said, her voice an awed whisper. We approached a glass door in a wall of concrete and she tapped in a four-digit code on the entry box. The door slid silently into the wall; immediately the air changed, becoming filtered and without taint.

"The vault is kept at a constant temperature and humidity to protect the contents – some of them date back two thousand years," she announced like a tour guide. She stopped at a series of long, head-high shelves on which archive boxes stood guard, shielding their contents.

"This is what you are looking for." She pulled a plain box forward and took it to a reading table, lifting the tight lid and revealing a shabby, brown, leather bag with a fold-over flap secured with a simple horn toggle, like the sort you find on a duffle coat. She slid the book from its cover.

"It was kept in this – that's why it's so well preserved." She indicated the crumpled bag, just big enough to fit the book in.

"Has anyone else ever read it, to your knowledge?" I asked, without taking my eyes from the book.

"Not in all the years I have been here, no. Do you want to hold it?" she offered.

I nodded wordlessly, swallowing hard against the core of desire that threatened to have me reach out and possess the journal at once. She placed it carefully in my hands. It was the first time I had seen the original and, as far as I knew, the hand-written copy of a section of it that I possessed was the only one in existence. The black leather volume – little bigger than A5 in size – felt heavy and thick, its cover creased and cracked with extreme age. A long, black, leather strap had once wrapped around the book, tying it shut; now truncated, it remained hanging redundantly from the back cover. The edges of the journal were chewed and rubbed through long years of use but, remarkably, the interior survived intact. Holding it after such an eternity, I could imagine the impact of seeing your new-born child for the first time: waiting, imagining, dreaming until it finally lies in your arms, an entity so entirely unknown but already beloved.

"I have waited so long to see this," I almost choked, pressing my lips together to suppress the wave of emotion.

She indicated a chair with a hand. "Take as long as you like."

I felt her eyes on my back as I sat down and placed the ancient volume on the book supports that protected the spine from splitting; then I opened the cover, and forgot she was even there.

Nathaniel Richardson had been an early settler in the American Colonies. He left England in the 1650s or thereabouts, taking his family with him to start a life in the New World, recording, in some detail, the trials and tribulations his family endured. But before he left, he acted as steward to a family in the tiny county of Rutland, and the early part of his journal charted the day-to-day account of his management of the land they owned. The segment of the account my grandfather bequeathed to me represented the only section transcribed by Ebenezer Howard after he purchased the journal from a private collection in the 1880s. He started his transcription part of the way through – from Richardson's arrival in the Colonies – and concentrated on the American years; but he died before he completed it.

On his death, some of the contents of the house were auctioned to provide funds for the new college, and a young visiting academic from Cambridge – with no money and an insatiable desire for knowledge – bought the transcribed version in a box of assorted papers, and took them back to England with him. The original journal lay undiscovered in the library until the academic – now a professor of history – began asking questions, and a series of telegraphic messages led to the rediscovery of the journal among the forgotten books of Howard's old library.

The professor intended returning to America to transcribe the rest of the journal, but war intervened, and the shrapnel lodged in his left lung prevented him from travelling. Largely unknown outside academic circles, the journal lay undisturbed. It might have remained so but for the moment when my grandfather recognized the same fire in my eyes that had driven him all his life and, when he died, he left me a box of postcards, some academic memoirs, and a wedge of old, hand-written papers to remember him by.

The book lay open on the reading table in front of me – my holy grail – as my grandfather's before me. I had delayed seeing it, touching it, reading it, because I knew it would totally dominate my life to the detriment of all my other academic duties. It had been my obsession and my desire for as long as I recalled.

Except now, the book had a rival.

The tight, taut style unfamiliar – the words cramped to save space and paper – letters split where the quill gave out, or smudged where the ink failed to dry before his hand touched it: it was everything I lived for in my work. I closed my eyes and let out a long breath as if held for all those years. But before me in my mind's eye, instead of the image of the small black book, warm blue eyes explored mine, reaching inside to read me. My eyes blinked open and I looked down. Minutes passed, then slowly and with deliberate care, I reached out to pick up the journal and gently slid it back into its bag, positioned it in the box, and softly replaced the lid.

The librarian looked startled as I emerged from the lift. She opened her mouth to say something, but closed it when she saw the look on my face. I said nothing as I left the building and headed back to my apartment, my ambition as unfulfilled as my desire.

Chapter

13

A Waiting Game

I CONSIDERED MYSELF TO BE SELF-SUFFICIENT and had been most of my adult life. Barely out of my teens when I met Guy, the emotional transition between home and university had been bridged by a man nearly twenty years older than me. Since I made the decision to exorcise him from my life and my degree, I resisted all efforts to engage in any other relationship. There were several Sam-like individuals at Cambridge, their attempts at courtship predictable, blatant and ultimately resistible, but I had never met anyone like Matthew.

Still convalescent and with plenty to do, I managed the first two days without him with little difficulty. Matthew said he would only be gone for a few days at the most, but by the third day the waiting was wearing at my nerves. By the fourth day, the empty sensation at the very heart of me grew to a hole, which I eventually recognized for what it was: a sense of loss.

I found myself waking before dawn after a restless night and, unable to sleep, lay mulling over our conversations, reliving every touch, every look. As the hours passed, I began to doubt what happened, reducing his words and actions to mere semblances of friendship. By morning, he became the doctor and I the patient, and nothing more.

I dragged myself out of bed and showered and brushed my teeth automatically. I consumed breakfast mechanically, sitting cross-legged on the deep window-seat, staring without seeing past the flickering trees, leaves dancing frantically against the stiffening breeze. I contemplated doing some work and prodded the laptop into life. Its face glowed expectantly, but the iridescent fish swam irritatingly across the screen and I closed the lid a little too emphatically. I slouched upstairs to Elena's room in the hope she might be there. She recognized the symptoms at once and offered a cure.

"C'mon, Emma, you are thinking too much, you are..." She looked across to Matias who was reading the morning newspaper and wasn't paying attention. "Matias? Emma is... what is the word...?" She located it in Russian.

"Moping, pining," Matias translated without looking up. He folded the broadsheet in half, the paper rustling noisily.

"I'm not," I said grumpily, "I'm just bored and I've come to inflict it on you."

"You're too kind," Matias muttered acerbically from behind the paper. Elena ignored him.

"The best thing is not to think about him; you must keep busy and then the time will go quickly."

"That's easier said than done. He said he would only be away for a few days; where *is* he?" I groaned, hollow despite breakfast. Matias emerged from reading, folding the paper and thwacking it on the low table in front of him.

"Why don't you two go shopping; that usually works, doesn't it? Men versus clothes? No contest. I've got to collect something from town so I'll take you, if you like."

"Excellent!" Elena whooped, clapping her hands, her eyes gleaming. "Now we can get clothes for All Saints – I *love* shopping."

I felt my throat itch and coughed a little too enthusiastically for it to be real.

She folded her arms. "That was pathetic, Emma, you can't get out of it that easily. Anyway, you want to look nice for Matthew, don't you?"

"If he's there," I said, petulant.

"Of course he will be." She poked my arm. "Get your things and we will go now. Matias, hurry up, you are keeping us waiting."

Replacing the colour supplement on the table, Matias sighed, hauled himself to his feet and reached into his pocket for his car keys.

The town offered a better range of shops than I anticipated and Elena's boundless enthusiasm for shopping proved contagious. Despite myself, I found I enjoyed mooching around the clothes shops more than I had ever done in England. And best of all, Elena wanted to talk about Matthew.

"*My* doctor never kissed me," she said. "Not that I ever wanted her to..." she added, with a bubble of laughter. She held up an orange dress in taffeta, cut short above the knee and puffed out at the hem with layers of netting. I pulled a face at the concoction.

"Good grief; I'd look like a pumpkin in that!" She crumpled up with laughter and I had to rescue the dress before she dropped it on the floor. "Yes, but he only kissed the top of my head – does that *really* count?" I selected a soft, blue-green, shot-silk two-piece, holding it against me for her to see. Elena looked me up and down approvingly, and I put it to one side with the others to try on.

"Of *course* it counts – that is why he did it, silly." I found her absolute certainty comforting. I picked out a long, figure-hugging, teal-green dress.

"This is your colour, Elena; what do you think?"

Holding it up to her shoulders, she examined herself in the long mirror.

"*Da*, I like this one – Matias will approve," she said.

"Yes, but do you? You're the one who'll be wearing it."

"I *love* it." She swirled the dress around herself, pirouetting on the spot. "And Matthew did give you the cell phone." She gathered an armful of clothes to try on. "You could always call him and say you're feeling ill again," she suggested slyly, disappearing into a cubicle to change. I went into the one next to her.

"I could *not*! That would be deceitful." Tempting – but deceitful. "Anyway, that would be crying wolf and I wouldn't want to tempt fate." I imagined her silently shrugging her shoulders next to me. She rattled the curtain of my changing cubicle for my attention.

"Emma, what do you think of this one?"

The sugar-pink confection clashed horribly with her skin. I didn't need to say anything; she took one look at the expression on my face and vanished to try the next one on.

I rejected the dark-gold brocade suit almost the second I put it on. It made me feel depressingly old, like a worn-out sofa – once glamorous and treasured, now faded and ready for the skip. On the other hand, the blue-green ensemble the colour of a kingfisher's wing fitted the bill perfectly. We paraded in front of the long mirror, critically assessing our reflections.

"I like this," she said, tugging at the peplum of my jacket; "it reminds me of Tsarina Alexandra's riding jacket – but in silk."

"It looks Edwardian; I always like that style." I half-turned so that I could see my profile and then twisted a little more to see my back. The jacket flared over my hips, longer at the back than the front. Silk-covered buttons started just above my bust, and continued down, pulling the jacket in tight and emphasizing my waist. A broad revere revealed my collar-bone, rising to a high collar which framed my face and offset the copper of my hair. The long, plain skirt gently followed my curves, making me feel flattered and feminine; the outfit was eminently suitable for what was deemed to be one of *the* college events of the year; I just wished Matthew would be there for me to enjoy it.

"I hope they have shoes to go with this – matching the colour will be a nightmare otherwise," I mused.

"They do," Elena assured me from her cubicle. "It is a pity we have to wear our gowns as well."

"You're joking! I thought I'd left all that behind in England."

"No, no. The Dean is very particular; we all have to wear gowns." She poked her head out from behind the curtain. "Didn't I tell you before?"

"No, you neglected to tell me that part," I said dryly.

"Oh, *da…*" there were sounds of a struggle with clothes as she pulled a jumper over her head. "You know that Shotter takes this very seriously." The struggle ended and she reappeared looking slightly dishevelled but happy. A horrific thought suddenly occurred to me.

"Staahl will be there, won't he?"

Elena shrugged apologetically, "He has to be – we all do, it is expected. And Sam."

"I'm not *afraid* of Sam."

"Staahl can't do anything, Emma – not with everyone there."

"He doesn't have to do anything; he just has to sit there and... *loom*." And make me feel guilty, I thought glumly.

Elena stifled a snicker.

"Glad you find it funny," I glowered.

"Sorry, it sounds odd – *loooom*. Shoes next, yes?"

"Shoes," I agreed.

By the time we were fully equipped, Matias was halfway through his second cup of coffee when we joined him in the deli.

"Successful?" he called, eyeing our bulging bags as we bumped our way to the table by the window.

"*Da.*" Elena dumped her bags on the floor.

"What are you going to wear?" I asked him as I sat down, gratefully flexing my throbbing feet to ease them. He scratched the back of his neck.

"Tux, evening suit, that sort of thing – it's pretty formal. Are you two eating?"

We plumped for two of the house specials, for which I paid, reminding Elena that I owed her from the diner. When I thought they weren't looking, I took out the slim mobile from my pocket and checked it surreptitiously.

"She does that a lot," Elena smirked. "Emma's in *lo*-ve," she taunted. I shot her a withering glance.

"I am *not*. I just miss his company, that's all." Annoyingly, they both laughed.

I wrinkled my nose as the tang of Matias' coffee wafted in my direction and ordered tea instead and then concentrated on consuming the squidgy part of the burger while my friends discussed All Saints and I didn't, my thoughts elsewhere. Elena suddenly prodded me.

"He looks like Matthew."

My head shot up. "Who does? Where?" I asked, trying to see who had caught her eye.

She pointed and my heart leapt. A young man of about twenty or so, leaned against a lamp-post while he talked on his mobile, his bright-gold hair severely cropped until no more than wheat-stubble through which he habitually ran his hand as he talked.

Elena grabbed my arm. "Don't you think?" she whispered eagerly.

Similar in colouring, the boy's face had the same well-defined features, with a balance between beauty and strength for which models went under the knife. And when he laughed, his mouth turned up in just the same way as Matthew's, so in that instant, I could almost believe it was him. But his shoulders were heavier-set, and his movements not as graceful.

"I see what you mean," I conceded. "But he's not. Are you *sure* you don't know why he's not back yet, Matias? He doesn't seem the sort to break his word." And I sighed without realizing I did so until Elena puffed her cheeks, looking like she had caught mumps. I became so engrossed gazing at the boy as I tried to picture Matthew that I hardly noticed him flipping his phone shut, looking up towards the deli, and right at me. For a brief second I could have been looking at Matthew's eyes, then, just as quickly, he turned his back and walked away towards the end of the street, where he turned the corner and was gone.

Chapter

14

All Saints

The guilty Serpents, and obscener Beasts
Creep conscious to their secret rests...

ABRAHAM COWLEY (1618–67)

ALL SAINTS' DAY MARKED THE EVE OF the new season, the precipice on which balanced the end of summer and the beginning of winter – the season of sleep and the long death. In Cambridge, while children trick or treated their way around the town under the watchful eyes of their parents, several of the colleges marked the last day of October with a service in one of the chapels – Christian light against pagan dark – where those of us so inclined sang hymns in celebration of life. The college at Howard's Lake had long upheld the tradition of celebrating All Saints, and the Dean determined to perpetuate the ritual with all the nuances of class and status he could contrive.

Preparations were well under way, and still with no word from Matthew. The mobile lay mute next to my bed, and night after night I fell asleep watching it, willing it to ring. To fill empty waking hours, I spent time making my bare apartment into more of a home with a few soft furnishings bought while in town. There was part of me – long dormant – that hungered for a home and not just a place to sleep. It had not bothered me until now when I saw what Elena achieved and understood the investment she made in terms of her relationship with Matias; a solidity surrounded them, a permanency which I neither had now, nor attained in the past. Improving my apartment helped a bit, but the empty hole returned and nothing I did filled it.

I rarely dreamt, my sleep deep and restful for as long as I remained unconscious; but that night I woke gasping with my heart racing and a film of sweat across my brow. I sat up and bent over trying to catch my breath, my head blazing with half-seen images, words and phrases that spun in the whirlpool of my sleep-drenched brain.

Lynes.

I knew I had seen the name before in a memory lodged on a long-forgotten shelf at the back of my mind.

The air bit my bare feet as I crossed the cold floor to find the transcription of the Richardson journal I brought to the States with me – back to where it originated over a hundred years before. I had spent so long studying it over so many years that I hadn't needed to refer to it in a long while. Now, there was only one word I wanted to find and, more importantly, the context within which it was written.

Laid out on single sheets of paper, the transcription had been bound with thin, red ribbon. Now faded, it passed through two holes in the margin like an antique version of a treasury tag. I pulled the sheaf of papers out of my portfolio and took it back to bed. The heating switched off, cold night air penetrated the room, and I huddled into my coat to keep warm.

Ebenezer Howard's familiar scratchy handwriting scrawled across the pages in front of me like an old friend. His transcription began when Nathaniel Richardson reached the embryonic colony with his family. Page after page recorded their daily life: the search for land, planting of crops, near starvation, animal attacks and the death of his daughter. Somewhere in all that life, Richardson mentioned his former employer and the family which his had served for several generations.

The sun had risen behind a dense layer of cloud when I found it. Half obscured by a smudge and with part of the "L" missing where one of the margin holes punctured the paper, the name "Lynes" leapt out. Its context unremarkable, insignificant – the bland reference to when "Master Lynes lived" was nonetheless enough.

I didn't bother with breakfast. I almost ran along the tree-lined path to the library, welcoming the warmth generated by exercise after the cold night's labour. Thawed frost glazed each leaf as they lay dying on the branches. Without a persistent wind, they would linger there, a remnant of autumn, until the weight of winter snow overwhelmed them, and they fell.

I held a part-formed idea in my mind as I entered the hush of the building. The librarian's desk stood empty, although the lights were on and the doors unlocked. I didn't wait, but immediately made for the lift, impatiently pressing the button for the lower floor in which the archives were kept, willing the lift to hurry.

The quiet hum of the climate-control system welcomed me into the vault as I punched in the four digits of the code I recalled from my first visit. Feeling like an intruder, I made straight for the shelves, located the only one that interested me, and pulled out the box. Then I did something I had never done before, something I abhorred in others and would no doubt loathe in myself: I picked up the journal in its bag and, without hesitation, tucked it into the inside pocket of my coat.

I left the library feeling the eyes of every book on my back and, holding my usually well-developed conscience in abeyance, slipped back into my room before most of the college woke.

Black and accusing, the journal faced me on my desk, yet the shame I should have felt failed to materialize. I did not intend keeping the book, only borrowing it for as long as it took to transcribe the rest of the volume; for although not mine, the information locked inside it belonged to me: my inheritance, my life – and I wanted to release it. I searched around the room for somewhere to keep it until ready – somewhere secret, somewhere safe.

The long bench-cushion ran innocently beneath the length of the arcaded windows. I located the end, examining the seams. The top of the pad had a rolled and reinforced edge. I picked at the bottom seam with my nail, loosening the stitches, gradually working them until I could wriggle a finger through the hole I made, and I could open a gap wide enough to slip the journal through.

Only when the journal was securely hidden in the bench-pad, with the edge of the curtain falling in folds over the end of the cushion, did I sit back and feel the reality of my crime, adrenalin seeping from my veins allowing the guilt to flow in its place. The hiding place looked innocuous enough, except that it screamed "thief" every time I glanced at it. By this one act I had made a stranger of myself and of my conscience.

I went through to my bedroom and lay on the bed, shutting my eyes against the world, and I must have slept for a while because – when I woke – the sun bronzed the snow-capped summits with evening light. I tried to sleep again, but there could be no respite from the remorse creeping in around the edges of my defences. Eventually I gave up and went into the kitchen to find something to eat.

I half-heartedly munched on an apple while I tried to reconcile my conscience, wondering how Matthew would react if he knew what I had done, when Elena rattled at my door wanting help with make-up.

"Aren't you getting ready yet?" she queried, as she came through the door wearing only a very short dressing-gown and looking like a long-legged colt, her new dress over one arm.

"Why, what time is it?"

"It's five-thirty and we have to be there at seven for drinks."

"It can't be!" I gasped, checking her watch and finding her right. "Give me a minute to have a shower and then we can do our make-up together."

"Matias is not going to know what's hit him when he sees you," I complimented her when I emerged some time later from the bathroom to find her dressed and ready.

She smiled impishly. "I have it all planned; he won't escape."

"Poor man, I ought to warn him."

"Don't you dare, it'll spoil my fun," she giggled. She tilted her head on one side, "You look... amazing!"

I looked down at what I could see of myself. "Is that 'amazing' good or 'amazing' bad?"

Elena ruined the elegant pose previously adopted by putting both hands on her hips like a fishwife. "You are so silly sometimes, Emma. If only you could see yourself as other people see you..." She flapped her hands, for once lost for words.

"That's what I'm afraid they might do," I said sombrely, thinking about this morning and wondering if people would see the guilt I felt written all over my face, which no amount of make-up could hide.

"I give up on you," she said with a little more drama than strictly necessary. "Are you not wearing your cross? You look sort of... naked... without it."

My hand flew to my throat and in a moment's panic, I thought it lost. But it lay where I left it.

"Forgive me," I whispered, and put it on where it belonged, and where it would stand sentinel to my soul.

It was already dark by the time we made our way to the reception room to meet for drinks before proceeding to the Great Hall where the dinner would be held. We went the long way rather than risk the open ground of the quad. The first of the Halloween revellers were just getting started and the students considered academic staff fair game. From the safety of the cloister, we watched a pumpkin run past, pursued by Dracula waving a string of firecrackers at the fruit's waggling posterior. From all around the quad, figures in varying degrees of costume emerged, and their voices – intent on mayhem – echoed within the confines of the college walls. We quickened our pace.

We arrived earlier than anticipated to a nearly empty room. I scanned it immediately, hoping to see Matthew; he was not there, but then – to my great relief – neither were Staahl nor Sam. I swung my gown around my shoulders.

"Do I have to wear this *all* night? I'll boil, and lobster clashes terribly with freckles."

Matias chortled as he helped Elena with her gown, managing to steal a quick kiss on her nape as payment in kind for his efforts as he straightened the edge of her robe.

"I usually manage to lose mine by the time we sit down and Shotter's generally too far gone by then to notice much. You do as well, don't you, kitten?" he said to Elena, who looked just about ready to curl up in his lap, almost purring; Matias would be in for a lively night if the languid glances she gave him through half-closed eyes were anything to go by. She nodded in agreement although I didn't think she was listening. I cheered up somewhat and looked to see if I recognized anybody.

"Having a drink tonight, Emma?" Matias asked.

"Just mineral water, thanks," I answered, not taking my eyes from the door.

"Smile, Shotter alert!" Elena warned, and I turned around just in time to greet him with what I hoped looked like a genuine smile. He had a small dark man with him who barely reached my eye level, his hair swept back and glistening, revealing a receding hairline.

"Good evening, ladies, you both look quite stunning. What remarkably red facings to your gown, Professor D'Eresby. I had no idea Cambridge was so... colourful; you will certainly stand out tonight."

In full ooze-mode, Shotter obviously enjoyed the concept of his latest acquisition standing out. His gaze wandered between Elena and me, finally settling on Elena's bust, and she fidgeted with the bodice, pulling it up as far as she could.

"Have you met the bursar, Professor Smalova, Professor D'Eresby?"

We shook our heads politely. The small man extended his hand to us in turn, a firmer handshake than expected, and he fixed me with small, sharp, but not unkind eyes. I recognized him as the man who sat next to the Dean at my inaugural lecture.

"Professor D'Eresby I heard you were quite unwell; this outbreak of 'flu has certainly taken its toll this year. I hope your new apartment is more suitable and that you are now fully recovered?"

"Yes, thank you; it is – and I am – much better," I replied, wondering how he knew about my illness.

He continued, "I must say that Dr Lynes can be very

persuasive – very *insistent* – when he wants to be, and when it's in his patient's best interests, of course."

His voice held an unasked question. All became suddenly clear and heat shot to my face. The Dean missed the point entirely, his eyes still buried somewhere in Elena's cleavage. He caught Matthew's name but no more.

"Yes, yes, make no mistake, Dr Lynes is one of the finest surgeons, one of our greatest academics – quite brilliant."

I coloured even more on hearing Matthew praised so fulsomely and the bursar's face relaxed into a smile, his question answered.

"Well, I hope that you'll have a good evening – and let me know if there is anything else I can do for you."

I thanked him, as there wasn't much else I could say. As soon as they walked away, I turned to Elena who was peering down at her bust with a slight frown.

"Am I showing too much, do you think?" She patted her breasts as if that would make them less conspicuous.

"No, you're perfectly decent; you could be wearing a shroud and it wouldn't make any difference to Shotter; just ignore him. Look, did you know anything about this?" I demanded, but she seemed as bemused as I felt.

"Know anything about what?" Matias asked as he arrived, gingerly balancing three glasses between his fingertips.

"The bursar's just told me that Matthew *persuaded* him to give me the new apartment. That's not what Matthew told me," I said indignantly.

"It's very romantic," Elena said, taking a glass and handing me one.

"What did Matthew tell you?" Matias asked, wiping condensation on his gown.

"Well, he did say something about me moving on health grounds, but I thought the *real* reason was that the rooms had to be redecorated and they needed me out of there because I would be in the way, or something like that."

Matias choked into his drink, spilling it over his hand.

"That's a good one!"

"Why didn't he just tell me the truth?"

"He did, but you weren't listening. Aw, come on Emma, would you have gone if he said it was just for your benefit?"

He had a point there. "No, probably not," I admitted.

"It sounds to me as if Matthew has the measure of you." He grinned and I pulled a face, realizing the reality behind the uncomfortable truth. "Where is he, anyway?"

He swivelled around to scan the room but I could have told him he wasn't there; I could sense his absence as clearly as I could feel my own body. I sipped at my water, wishing for once that I'd chosen something with greater anaesthetic qualities in which I could escape the evening. A tap on my shoulder interrupted my self-absorption. Diminutive Madge squinted up at me with gimlets, wearing a black velvet trouser suit as severe as her haircut and as masculine.

"What have you girls been up to, or shouldn't I ask?" She licked her scrawny lips suggestively as she eyed us.

"We're all fine, thanks for your concern," Matias answered abruptly, and I sensed he wasn't overly fond of her.

"You've made quite an impact, from what I hear," she addressed me, turning her back on him.

"Why, what have you heard?" I asked, noting the sly element to her tone.

"Nothing, nothing – except Sam has been looking a little down lately. Is that anything to do with you?"

"Should it be?"

"You know what they say: 'No smoke without fire', and Sam looks as if his has been extinguished. I'm just looking out for my friends." She pulled a knowing face, answering a question that had been bothering me since my conversation with Siggie about "campus crows". My instinct had been right; nothing said in front of Madge would be safe from gossip. I took a deep breath, annoyance rising to the surface like a bubble. I popped it before it had a chance to break, but Matias barely contained his irritation.

"That's none of your business, Madge; Sam's a big boy, he can look after himself."

221

"I was only asking, Matias; there's no need to get so defensive – is there, Emma, my dear?"

Siggie Gerhard spotted us and came over. She wore the same gold suit I had seen at the boutique, but with a plump elegance I couldn't hope to match, making her look like a regal dowager, completely at ease with herself.

"Hi, you guys." She smiled benignly and leaned forward to give me a kiss on the cheek. "You're looking better than when I last saw you and I like the outfit – good call," she said, managing to look beyond the glaring red and black of the gown that caught my eye every time I looked down. "Have you had a chance to look over the paper I gave you?"

I had, much to Elena's annoyance, since I'd cancelled a trip to the cinema to get it finished.

"Uh huh, and it's fine from the historical context. If you don't mind, I've made a couple of suggestions about some sources you might find useful. I really liked some of the comparisons you made, especially the reference to cultural genocide. It has interesting parallels to… to…" I was going to say that there were some remarkable similarities to several lesser-known events in the Early Modern period of history, but instead I paused, distracted by Madge who tapped her foot impatiently beside me, like a small dog yapping for attention. "Look, Siggie, would you like to meet up to discuss this? I have some extracts you might find illuminating."

Siggie beamed. "Excellent; I'll let Saul know when I see him later. We were hoping you might join us for dinner sometime, perhaps next week? You would be most welcome to bring someone with you, if you'd like."

I noticed she left the choice of who that might be entirely up to me, and she mentioned no names.

Madge stopped tapping and assumed an air of immense curiosity I had no intention of assuaging. Elena's mouth opened as she was about to make a suggestion, then it shut just as abruptly as she remembered who listened.

"Siggie – I would love to, but I will be alone, I'm afraid; but I might bring over a couple of books that you might find good company instead."

I cast a sideways glance at Madge who could barely hide her frustration. Siggie smiled again, this time with a humorous twinkle that suggested she understood precisely what just occurred.

"Then next week will be good; I'll talk to Saul first before we fix a date, OK?"

"Fine," I agreed.

The room steadily filled, burgeoning with academics whose gowned figures converged then fanned out as they worked their way around, stopping, chatting, drinking, then moving on like a slow dance. As the door opened again, a flurry of hope breathed life into me, flooding me with a warmth instantly reflected in my face. Madge followed my gaze.

"Ah, the Ice-Man cometh. Well, well – twice in one semester; this must be a record. I wonder what *he's* after."

Matthew had been intercepted by Shotter as he entered the room, but he looked beyond the Dean, searching among the faces until he found what he sought and our eyes engaged, sending a jolt through me as physically as if I touched an exposed wire. He said something quietly to Shotter, extricating himself, moving between the heaving mass of bodies and crossing the space between us without taking his eyes from mine. Then he was by me, absorbing every detail of my face, and I, his. He looked just the same, except his irises appeared darker, almost navy pools of blue, and there seemed a tension in the set of his mouth that should have cautioned the rapid beat of my pulse. Yet, he appeared exquisite in formal evening wear, the breadth of his shoulders accentuated by the black silk cummerbund, and his smile – once he had greeted the others with his restrained courtesy – was for me alone.

"Dr D'Eresby," he murmured.

"Dr Lynes," I breathed, and as far as I was concerned, from that moment no one else existed.

"How are you?" he asked.

"Surviving – and you?"

"The same." He paused, his eyes travelling over me, saying

more than he wanted to put in words. "You look... well," he said and his smile ate into my heart.

Madge watched us with eyes that were mere slits. She *harrumphed*, sounding like a cat coughing up a fur-ball.

"How come you never usually grace us with your presence, Matthew? Where have you been?"

"Unfortunately, influenza is very contagious," he said, clearing his throat without really answering her question.

"Caught it off one of your patients, maybe?" she said, eyes sliding in my direction. He regarded her coolly and without replying led me to the side of the room by one of the windows where it was relatively quiet. I ignored the whispers and the dozens of eyes that followed us and I realized that what Sam had referred to in anger might partially be true: half the women on campus might indeed lust after Matthew; but Sam was entirely wrong if he thought it reciprocated.

"I missed you," I burst out when beyond earshot and instantly regretted saying anything, as his face became unreadable.

"I'm sorry; I didn't mean to be away for so long. It was... unavoidable."

I didn't want him to think me the clingy sort; I didn't want him thinking I assumed a relationship at all. I took a deep breath.

"No, I'm sorry, I didn't... I shouldn't have said anything; it just seemed a long time, that's all."

We stood close enough to touch, for him to hear the desperate call of my heart, but he kept his hands rigid by his sides and I clutched my glass with both of mine in case the tremor running throughout my body betrayed me.

"Have you been busy?" he asked, his tone even, but his voice taut with an unspoken stress I couldn't fathom. What did he want me to say? How did he expect me to answer such a bland question when there were so many I wanted to ask him? *Oh yes, ever so busy, thanks; I bought some cushions from town, stole a priceless manuscript from the library, oh, and by the way – I love you.* The moment I thought it, I realized the truth of it.

I love you, Matthew.

I felt the colour leave my face. When had curiosity become

fascination? At what point did fascination become love? How could I have let it happen after everything I had been through, after all the promises I made to myself? After all the years spent reined in so tight that I hadn't let my guard down – not once, not ever – and now this – stealthily and without declaration and without any shadow of doubt. I swayed slightly as I struggled to regain sovereignty over my thoughts.

"Emma, are you all right?"

I opened my eyes; I must have closed them in an effort to distil some sense out of the confusion. He frowned again, but this time with concern. It was as much as I could do to look at him without my face revealing how I felt, or speak to him without my voice giving me away.

"Yes, I'm fine; I have been quite busy."

I jumped as a scream and a ricochet of firecrackers from just outside in the quad were followed by a tumble of bodies as students upped the tempo. Two faces, distorted by the uneven milling of the glass, pressed against the window. I recognized Josh and Hannah despite her witch's costume and his horrendous wig flapping around his unshaven chin. Josh grinned at me, his face warped into a demonic sneer, and Hannah's face whipped away from the glass as he grabbed her around the waist, and they both fell backwards into the darkness, laughing. I turned back to find Matthew gazing at me with a strange expression.

"Would you like to be out there with them?"

I allowed myself to be distracted because, at this moment, I still reeled in shock from my self-revelation.

"No, not at all. I'm not into Halloween or anything like that – quite the opposite."

He allowed the faintest smile to reach his eyes. "Despite your choice of subject matter?"

"*Because* of my subject matter; witches, monsters, demons – they scare me."

His eyes lost their humour. "Ah, so you think they do exist, then?" His voice had a remoteness to it that hadn't been there before he went away and it frightened me more than I could let him see.

"I think – I think I'm more scared of the monster in the man, than anything else."

He unexpectedly laughed – a short, harsh sound so unlike him. I trembled.

"Are you cold?" he asked.

"No..." I wavered; "Matthew, what's the matter? You seem different – you – your eyes..."

"What about my eyes?" he interrupted, staring straight into mine, almost challenging. I blanched and looked away, baffled by the sudden change.

"Emma, I'm so sorry." He drew a hand across his face. "I'm tired, it's been a long week. I didn't mean to take it out on you." I heard pain in his voice and, without thinking, put my hand on his arm; but he flinched and I withdrew it instantly, conscious that I had crossed an undefined boundary.

"No!" he said, louder than he meant, and several faces turned to look at us. "No, don't take your hand away," he said more gently, and took my hand and placed it where it had been. "Please, Emma, it isn't you. I shouldn't have come here this evening – not like this. But... but I needed to see you; Heaven forgive me, I missed you."

I didn't know to what he referred; I didn't understand what could have happened that placed an invisible barrier between us. I only heard those few words that showed he had missed me as much as I did him. I took a pace closer, wanting to comfort him and needing his reassurance in return but he stood stock still, his arm rigid under my hand.

"I'll be all right tomorrow," he said, and he smiled a remote smile, taking a step away from me.

I tried not to look hurt; I thought I probably wasn't the cause of whatever seemed to be eating him from inside but – despite what he had said and until I knew otherwise – there was nothing or no one else I could blame.

A discordant metallic clamour issued from somewhere in the outer hall.

"Dinner time," Matthew said, and his smile twisted a little. I became suddenly nervous at being separated from him again as people began to converge on the door.

"Will I be able to sit with you?"

He shook his head, and it gladdened me to note that he appeared as disappointed as I felt.

"We all have set places to sit."

"You don't like this very much, do you?" I said softly.

"I play my part – but I don't find it easy, no." He looked down at me. "But then neither do you."

"No," I whispered.

He straightened. "Let's get it over with," he said, almost to himself, and he walked me towards the door and the line of people parading through it.

It reminded me of the darkened ribs of a tide-washed hull.

Like its medieval antecedents, the Great Hall's barrel-vaulted ceiling yawned high above our heads to the full height of the old building. As with much of the college, here Ebenezer Howard had imitated the features of the antiquity he so admired without really understanding the rhythm of the architecture they sang to. There was something endearing about his attempts though, like a child's version of Van Gogh's *Sunflowers* – all gaudy pattern and no substance – but recognizable all the same. At one end of the hall, a raised dais bore a baronial chair of throne-like proportions, by which the Dean already waited.

Almost a third of the way along the series of tables which stretched almost the length of the room, Elena waved, pointing to the chair on the opposite side from her. Matthew took me over and I saw my name in gilded letters on the heavy parchment place-card.

"Where will you be?" I asked.

"Up there, somewhere," he said, looking towards where Shotter presided with several senior members of the academic staff. They all looked so much older than Matthew. "I'd better go," he said with regret. "I'll see you later."

I missed him the moment he left, the gulf widening between us as he moved towards the end of the table. I felt at a loss now that I recognized the void inside me for what it was; it hurt knowing that I loved him, but so much more thinking he might not feel the same way about me. In the past week we both had changed. I had become something I did not recognize: a thief – but a thief in love – and one whose prime motivation in life had been replaced by nothing more than a man; not a dream to better the world or a greater aspiration to study its past, but a man – lonely and fallible.

And Matthew?

In that time the reserve had returned but also something else, a secrecy – perhaps frustration – something I couldn't quite pin down or put a name to. But he said he had missed me; he made the effort to come tonight because he wanted to see *me*; I meant enough to him for that at least, if nothing more.

I had all but forgotten the dinner until I heard my name being called urgently.

"Emma!" Elena leaned as far forward over the broad table as she dared without exposing too much to the male guests who took an intense interest in her posture. I looked up. "Staahl – he's not here, he's ill."

"*Yes!*" One thing less to worry about.

"He's got 'flu!" she whispered loudly. I raised my eyes to Heaven and mouthed "Thank you." She grinned back at me.

"But you have me instead." Matias said over my shoulder right by my ear, making me start.

"You, Matias, I can deal with – you're just a pussy cat really, aren't you?"

He lowered his voice to the level of a lewd proposal. "Does that mean that if I roll over on my back you'll scratch my belly?" he smirked suggestively, but without any real intent. Elena squeaked at him from across the table in protest. I wrinkled my nose and poked a finger at his chest.

"No, it means that if you misbehave I'll put you out with all the other mangy mogs and you can exchange fleas."

Matias sucked in air over his teeth, pretending to be mortified.

"Ow, vicious! I'm glad I'm not your pet."

"So am I," I said, feeling better for having him around. Elena made warning faces as a general shuffling preceded the gong in the hall and everyone stood to attention behind their chairs. The chatter faded into an expectant hush. Adopting his most pompous voice for the task, the Dean intoned a prayer in Latin. I looked up from under my eyelashes to make sure I followed the correct etiquette and found Matthew watching me from near the end of the table. I smiled briefly, hopefully, as the Dean pronounced "Amen" and the room filled with a wave of sound in response. Matias pulled the heavy chair out for me. The chair to my left chafed as it moved and someone sat next to me.

"Hello, Emma." A familiar, edgy voice cut through the noise as the room broke into chatter once more; I hadn't seen his name on the card.

"Hi, Sam." He was the second person I least wanted to see tonight and my voice echoed my lack of enthusiasm.

"Well, this *is* going to be fun," Matias said, rubbing his hands together in anticipation. "Hey, Sam, you were leaving it a bit late."

"I'm not going to make trouble, Emma," Sam said, ignoring him. "I got the message last time, don't worry."

"OK," I said slowly. "But tell me, why – of all the places we could be sitting – I end up with you three reprobates for company? What have I done to deserve such a fate?" I couldn't help glancing towards Matthew further up the table. Sam followed my gaze.

"Huh, yeah, didn't he tell you? Shotter's so crazy about keeping it traditional, he's got us all sitting according to our 'academic status'." He drew two quote marks in the air with his fingers.

"So the four of us are roughly equal – academically – that is?" I asked.

"Yeah, and anyone at *that* end..." and he jabbed his finger in Matthew's direction, "is 'top table', the 'elite' of the university, Shotter's blue-eyed..."

Matias coughed loudly, interrupting him before he said something he shouldn't and which I wouldn't have been able to ignore.

"Matthew's considered to be one of the best minds here, Emma."

I felt a glow of pride for him. I turned towards Matias so that I couldn't see the barely disguised sneer on Sam's face.

"I know he's supposed to be good – Shotter said he's *brilliant* – but I thought that was a bit of hyperbole, you know, reflected glory and all that."

Matias raised an eyebrow "No, for once Shotter's right. You see Matthew doesn't wear a gown like the rest of us?" I nodded, though in truth I hadn't noticed. "That's because he doesn't have to." I drew my eyebrows together in a question. "Matthew has more qualifications than the rest of that top table put together. It's pointless trying to represent them on one gown; not wearing one is a mark of his status."

"Oh. He never said."

Matias gave me a sort of told-you-so look. "Well, that's typical of Matthew – he wouldn't say, would he?"

Sam's gown caught his fork as he moved; he put out a hand and straightened it.

"You wouldn't have thought he'd want to stick around here with the rest of us klutzes when he could've gone to any place he wanted," he said, sourly, then leaned back again and flicked his glass, making it *ting*. Matias shot a look at Sam then up the table to Matthew.

"Well, Sam, not everyone's seeking fame and fortune; some have less selfish motives."

"Good old Matthew," Sam muttered on the other side of me.

"Sam, you said you were going to behave so I expect you to," I said sternly. He unexpectedly smiled and saluted.

"Yes, ma'am."

"That's better," I acknowledged.

A bevy of uniformed staff served the first of the six courses; that meant six glasses of wine I wouldn't be drinking tonight. Delicate hors d'oeuvres involving salmon in a lime sauce with a sprinkling of caviar appeared in front of me, and the first of the wineglasses filled. I looked for the customary water carafe, and selected the largest wine glass.

"That's for *wine*," Sam said, still slightly caustic.

"Thanks for educating me," I replied, dripping sarcasm in return.

"Yeah, OK – sorry; so, there's more for me." He pulled my full wine glass in front of him.

I managed half of the first course before I felt full.

Sam mellowed with the wine; his shoulders gradually relaxed and he even remembered to let a smile break through once or twice.

"I reckon you're used to this sort of thing – coming from Cambridge and all that, right?"

I put my knife and fork down, glad to talk rather than eat.

"The colleges have their traditions, certainly, but this is trying to be more English than we are. And no, I'll never get used to this amount of food – it's like a marathon in terms of eating and I'm not up to running it."

He grinned, a little of the Sam I first knew shining through.

"Saves cooking, anyhow."

"That's true," I agreed, leaning back to allow my plate to be removed and the second course to be served.

"So, what are you doing for the winter break?" he said, making an effort to be conversational.

"I don't know, I haven't thought about it yet; I suppose I'll go home." I peeked discreetly at Matthew so as not to wind up Sam. Christmas in England with my family as usual I considered normal; but Christmas without Matthew? That would need thinking about. I eyed a piece of asparagus draped with a rich butter sauce that would be the undoing of my suit if it spattered.

"What will you do, Sam?" I said, as I remembered he was not long divorced.

He shrugged, the grin sliding away to nothing.

"Don't know – might stay here, might go see my kids – don't know." He looked utterly despondent and I recognized his loneliness. It was my turn to make an effort to introduce some conviviality.

"I didn't know you have children. How old are they?"

Sam drank the remnants of his second glass of wine. "My boy's seven and I have two girls: one's five and the youngest is three. I get to see them sometimes over the holidays or on vacation but they live a-ways from here with their moms."

How little I knew about him, but then even that was more than I knew about Matthew. I scraped most of the sauce to one side, and risked the asparagus successfully, then speared a single petit pois on the end of my fork, thoughtfully. Elena caught my eye, and raised her eyebrows at me, then looked at Sam. I couldn't reach to kick her under the table, so I dragged my brow into a furrow instead until she got the message.

The second course had been and gone without me eating more than a quarter of it. By the third, the food looked less and less appetizing, although a cursory glance at other diners told me I was just about alone in that. Elena tucked in with as much gusto as she had the first course. I ate a French bean slowly and looked to see how Matthew fared at the end of the table. He wore a polite expression of interest as the distinguished woman of at least forty years' seniority talked animatedly between mouthfuls. Although he held a fork in one hand, it never went near the food in front of him nor touched his mouth. I wondered what he thought about and why he didn't eat.

"Are you drinking that?" Sam asked, hand already around the third glass of wine I'd rejected. I shook my head and he took it, taking a swig before putting it down in front of him.

"You look really great tonight, Em," he said, without looking at me.

"Thanks," I said, automatically, still watching Matthew as closely as I dared. He picked up his full wineglass and put it to his lips but drew it away again without drinking as he answered a question from the Dean. Shrieks from the quad interrupted the polite conversations around the table; several people laughed and Shotter looked annoyed.

"At least *they're* enjoying themselves," Sam said into my glass of wine. He hadn't attempted to talk to his other neighbour, who looked bored. I internalized a sigh; there were another three courses and five glasses of wine for Sam to drink before we could leave, and there were bound to be speeches. This was excruciating. Matthew seemed to be faring better at the other end of the table, his composed, aquiline face never betraying a moment of boredom. As I watched, he reached swiftly into the inside pocket of his jacket and withdrew a small mobile, or it might have been a pager, apologizing to his neighbour as he read a text. His eyes flickered towards me and it took only a few seconds before he snapped it shut and leaned towards the Dean, saying something quietly. The Dean nodded and Matthew left the table without looking in my direction again. The brief flurry of interest at his departure died almost as soon as he left the hall, but I felt bereft.

By the fifth course I gave up any pretence at eating, ready to fall on my sword if one had been to hand. I inspected every aspect of the room's architecture, guessed from which universities the other academics graduated, and tried to engage an elderly professor in conversation, rendered futile by failing batteries in his old-fashioned hearing aid. To cap it all, Sam wallowed in self-pity as he drowned his sorrows, and Elena busily entertained both men either side of her. Matias and I kept up the banter, in between him doing his duty with the woman to his right, whom he obviously found hard going.

My gown hung heavy and itchy and hot, and I longed to take it off, but Shotter was being uncharacteristically restrained in his intake of alcohol and would notice if I slipped the vivid cloth from my shoulders. I thought about eating the fragile chocolate basket surrounding the strawberries, but became distracted when one of the porters from the front desk entered the room and went straight to the Dean, his solid-heeled shoes clumping noisily against the raised chorus of voices in the room. Matias sensed my despair and offered me another glass of water.

"No thanks. Is it always like this?" I groaned.

"Pretty much, but the best bit comes later – well worth waiting for."

"Best bit? What's that?"

"The speeches – they last just over an hour."

"*Please*, Matias, I can't take much more of this; end my

suffering *now*," I begged him.

He was about to reply when the porter leaned between us, bringing with him the smell of old stone and spent fireworks.

"There's a call for you, ma'am – it's urgent."

My heart lost step. "Who's it from?"

"I'm sorry, ma'am, I'm just told that it's a call from England." His gentle Maine accent couldn't soften the impact of the long-anticipated call, and I felt my world implode.

"Do you want me to come with you?" Matias asked.

"No... thanks, I'll be fine," I said, aware of the other diners straining towards us inquisitively, and pulling myself together. He helped draw my chair out for me, but my gown snagged under one of the chair legs and I tugged to free it.

"Never mind about that," he said, helping me undo the clasp that held the gown in place. I let it fall, and left it on the chair, acutely conscious of my curious audience. Restrained by my tight skirt, my shortened footsteps were the only noise to be heard in the ensuing silence as I followed the porter from the hall and down the cold cloister towards the porters' lodge. Screams and cordite punctuated the stillness of the dark passage and outside, shadows scurried and tumbled, partially lit by torches and the burst of yellow flame from firecrackers. It looked as if all hell had broken loose, intent on inflicting maximum damage on the world beyond the windows. The porter muttered something that sounded like he intended "Sortin' them young'ns aut," although I couldn't be certain above the racket. He held the heavy door open for me. "Through there, ma'am, and on the desk." He indicated with his head towards the reception desk. I went through, but he didn't follow, and the door closed with finality behind me.

I was alone.

Almost total darkness covered the atrium except for the faint glow filtering from the great glass dome lighting the immediate floor beneath. Subdued light escaped from the porters' lodge to one side through the partially open door.

A telephone handset lay beside its cradle, a light indicating it was in use – a red, glowing eye in the dark. I hurried to pick up the phone, my footsteps echoing eerily in the insulated hush as I tried to keep my high heels from slipping on the smooth marble floor. My heart thumped unevenly; this was the call I had been dreading from my father. I took a deep breath and picked up the handset.

"Hello?"

I expected to hear his voice, but instead, an empty buzz like a trapped insect issued from the earpiece.

"Hello?" I repeated and shook the handset in case of a loose connection. I tried again, a mixture of foreboding and anxiety competing to dominate.

"Hello? Dad?"

An insignificant movement – nothing more than the ghost of a shadow against the pale stone floor – caught my eye. I stared intently at it, trying to work out what caused it, the barren telephone now redundant in my hand. I quietly replaced the handset, aware of the oppressive silence that bore down around me, senses stretched taut to catch the least sound.

A slight hiss, an exhalation of air directly behind me, so close it raised the hairs on the back of my neck. I whirled around. Staahl's grey face materialized out of the darkness. My mouth opened instinctively to scream but he placed a finger to his lipless mouth in warning and I closed it soundlessly. I stared at him, a surge of cold fear gluing me to the floor.

"That's better," he said softly. "Thank you for coming to meet me, I didn't know if you would be able to get away." He made it sound like an invitation.

He was supposed to be ill; he wasn't supposed to be here.

"What are you doing here?" My voice trembled even as my legs began to move and I backed away from him, but he mirrored my movement step by step in a sinister dance. I shot a look behind me; the door to the cloister was too far away across the slippery floor to reach without the risk of being caught like a calf brought down by a wolf. He watched me with amusement.

"So eager to leave when you've only just arrived. No, no that *won't* do." He moved quickly to my right, forestalling any hope of flight in that direction.

I thought rapidly; the front door would be locked, as would

the doors to the offices either side of the atrium. There was only one way out and Staahl blocked it.

"What do you *want* from me?" I demanded. He didn't like that.

"I told you the other evening, but you were obviously *not – paying – attention*." He slapped his open hand hard against his thigh as he spoke the final words and I flinched back. His eyes opened wide momentarily and then narrowed again as he ran his tongue over his lips, leaving a trail of spittle trapped in the crease of his mouth. His voice became a careful monotone as if soothing a scared child. He closed the gap between us by a step.

"I know you, Emma, I *understand* the way you think. We have so much to offer each other; is it so much to ask that we spend this little time together?"

My gut instinct had been right all along: this man was dangerous and I needed to get away from him *now*. I flexed my fingers and curved them into fixed weapons, holding them at my sides in readiness. I placed as much strength and authority in my voice as I could and glared stonily at his hooded eyes.

"I want *nothing* to do with you. I'm leaving."

I managed to get as far as the outer circle of the delicate marble cosmology before he caught me, his hand clenching my left wrist. Instinctively I lashed out, panic rendering the effort futile as he caught my other arm. He brought his face so close that the stale stench of his breath made me want to retch, his colourless eyes boring into mine.

"*Get off me!*" My terrified voice caught in my throat, no more than a harsh whisper. In one swift movement he moved behind me, encasing the upper part of my body in a vice formed by his arm. I opened my mouth to cry out, but Staahl shifted his arm around my neck, cutting me short.

"Not a sound now... no, no *shhh* – don't struggle," his acid articulation cautioned me as I gasped for air, my mind in chaos. He pulled me back against him, the length of his body hard against mine. He moved his hips insidiously. "That's *nice*," he breathed. "I've so looked forward to meeting you like this, but I never dreamt that you would *invite* me."

Rigid with fright, I fought the instinct to pull away from him, forcing my body to relax and go limp. His arm loosened slightly in response and I wrenched forwards, kicking back with my heel at the same time, trying to connect with his shin. Much stronger than he looked, his arm constricted sharply, choking the air out of me.

"*Don't* do that again," he reprimanded, and a sharp sting in the side of my throat made me gasp and stop. From the corner of my eye, a silver gleam reflected off a blade.

"Now, Emma – be a good girl. Easy, back this way. I don't want to cut you, not yet." He dragged me back towards the half-open door of the porters' lodge, nudging it wide as we passed through. The door collided with wooden racking inside the room with a burst of sound, the contents of the shelves rattling unsteadily.

"What do you want?" I choked. His breath came in short, foul bursts near my ear as he concentrated on pulling me back further into the dim room lit only by a single bulb.

"There, that's better," he said companionably, the rough cloth grazing my skin as he moved his arm, partially crushing my throat. He adjusted his grip on the knife, pressing it against the thin skin of my neck. Where his hand compressed my left wrist, his nails dug deeply.

"Now we can have the little chat I always promised without interruption from your friends." He tightened his grip a little more and I struggled for air, my breath rasping painfully against the constriction. I tried to remember the basic self-defence learned at school, but the little I could recall was overpowered by revulsion and terror.

"Emma, Emma, Emma, mmm." He ran the tip of his finger down my exposed throat. "We have so much in common, you and I, so much suffering to enjoy, so much darkness to explore." I felt a warm wetness on my neck as he drew his tongue slowly up past the blade of the knife. I gagged, pulling away involuntarily. The point of the knife went into my throat and the saliva was replaced by a thin, wet trickle of blood.

"You – of all people – should enjoy this and appreciate the historical *relevance*." He braced his knee against my leg, bending me back, making it more difficult to inhale.

"Little Emma, didn't you ever stop to consider whether all those stories of monsters might be true? I've watched you so carefully ever since you were sent to me and I've seen what you *dream*. I've seen all those pictures, all those demons you keep on your wall, in your shelves." He laughed – a low, humourless laugh. "Don't you just *wish* it were true? After all these years of study, the sewage must have crept into your soul. Can you not feel how it wants to take you, to consume you completely? And yet you persist in wearing this... *talisman*..." He hooked his little finger under my cross, raising it so that light bounced off its surface as it hung on its chain. "This sentimental symbol, this institutionalized relic of a superstitious age; what do you think He would do in your place, eh? The sacrificial Lamb – do you think He would give His own life to save you – to save *me*?"

"*Especially* you," I choked against his tightening arm.

"Then where is He now – your omniscient God?" Triumph crowed in his jibing voice, riding the currents of my fear. "You see? Nothing – you are *alone*." His breath became more urgent against my throat. "Well, let us put it to the test."

I felt sick as the lack of oxygen threatened my consciousness. Time was running out. With extreme effort I forced the full weight of my body back against his, kicking wildly with my heel, hearing the fabric of my skirt rip as he momentarily lost balance, dropping the knife. With the sudden intake of air I lunged forward to escape, but he was too quick for me. Grabbing my right arm, he cracked it back against the edge of the open door. I heard it snap at the same time as a scream tore from my throat.

Re-securing my left wrist in a quick movement, he picked up the knife. My arm hung limp and useless and I began to pass out from the pain.

"No, no – not yet, Emma, not yet; you must be awake to get the most from this experience." And he hauled me upright as my legs gave way under me. "Now, you can either do this my way and enjoy it, or..." I screamed a denial in his face. "Your choice," he remarked with the merest touch of regret. He wrenched my wrist back, partially exposing the veins. I cried out as his fingers dug into my already bruised skin and his right arm trapped me again, the raw edges of the broken bones grating sickeningly. The long curved blade had a finely worked point – a gutting knife – and he placed it at the top of my wrist where it met the jacket and with a swift, sure movement cut downwards, severing the fabric. The rich, frayed edges of the silk framed my pale skin. Exhaling in satisfaction, he replaced the knife, the tip of the blade making an indentation in my flesh – steel against the blueness of my veins – and pressed a little harder; a thin squeal broke from my lips.

"Mm, I *like* that," he breathed and pushed the blade further.

A low, guttural roar of anger ripped the air, shredding the silence. Staahl's head whipped up, eyes fixed at a point beyond the door.

"Let go of her!" From the depth of the shadows, Matthew's voice cut through my haze. Staahl brought his mouth close to my ear.

"Well, well, it looks like someone's come to join in the fun after all," he mocked. He jabbed the blade suddenly, breaking my skin, blood oozing in rivulets, staining the border of fabric deepest purple. I pressed my lips together to stop from crying out.

Matthew moved into the doorway where the light reflected off the black glass of his eyes.

"*Let – go – of – her*," he repeated with supreme control.

Breath escaped Staahl's grill of teeth. "Stay back! She's mine; you'll just have to wait your turn, *doctor*." He forced my wrist back at an angle, the sudden pressure pulling blood from my veins. Rage echoing around the room, Matthew leapt as simultaneously Staahl sliced down my exposed wrist, my skin parting in a crimson chasm from which blood flowed. The impact of bodies flung me against the wall of shelves, and I fell breathless, broken and bleeding to the floor like a discarded rag doll. A muffled sound, struggling, then high against the back wall, Staahl – suspended off the ground like a puppet, his arms and legs futile as he flailed against the air – and Matthew, his eyes glazed with fury, squeezing the life out of him with one hand.

"*No!* Matthew, *no!* You'll kill him," I heard myself scream through the encroaching darkness, as the room began to fade almost as rapidly as the blood seeping from my arm in an endless cherry flow across the wooden floor.

From a long way away, I heard a thump – like a half-empty sack dropped onto the ground – and then Matthew's low, urgent voice calling my name over and over again. I opened my eyes but saw nothing but an indistinct shape in the gathering night, ice enveloping me from the inside out until all I could think about was the cold and the dark. I could hear him controlling the alarm in his voice.

"Emma – Emma, stay with me."

I felt pressure in my wrist as something clamped it and I whimpered, thinking Staahl was back, but Matthew spoke again and dread dissolved in the warmth of his voice.

"Cold..."

"I know, hang on."

A confused mass of voices erupted in the hall outside, rising and falling and – rising above them – Elena's voice, shrill and small and frightened. Something tightened around my arm, but there was so much pain that its addition made no difference.

Voices came closer, shuffling for space, crowding in around us until I couldn't breathe, suffocating me. I began to struggle for breath, kicking out, legs writhing to escape, break free.

"Keep back!" Matthew told them sharply, and then I felt his arms around me, lifting me, and his steady, calm voice commanding, "Stay with me, Emma... Emma..."

But I couldn't hold back the dark – the peaceful dark – the welcoming blackness which called me, and where he could not follow.

Chapter

15

From Darkness

COLD AIR LASHED AGAINST MY FACE, jolting me to semi-consciousness and the excruciating agony in my right arm, as with each movement the bones jarred. I hauled jagged breaths into my lungs, vaguely aware of being held against his chest as he ran, of doors crashing open and running, running and then the metallic hardness of a hospital bed beneath my back, and faces talking in broken, disjointed sentences, leaning over me.

"Dr Lynes..."

"Don't let anyone in, nurse."

Overhead, lights as hard as arc lights forced through my eyelids and I attempted to turn my head from their glare, but it wouldn't obey. The world stopped moving and I ached to say his name; but no words formed and, with each beat of my weakening heart, I felt my life pulse away, drop by steady drop.

"Emma..." Matthew called to me from nearby.

Sudden voices filled the air, pushing through the doors into the room, humming and buzzing like a swarm, intruding and demanding.

"Keep them *out!*" Matthew sounded angry with them – or was it with me?

Don't be angry with me, I tried to tell him, but it came out as a whimper. The voices had gone, but I couldn't tell whether it was because the room had emptied or because I had left it further and further behind, and Matthew with it.

His agonized voice drifted through the gathering darkness.

"Emma, I have to control the bleeding; I'm sorry, this will hurt."

Pain again – searing as it tore at my arm – and I wanted it to stop, but it went on and on and on until the blackness fell again and through it, I heard him calling me.

"Emma, don't do this, don't go – I can't do this again." But there was nothing I could do to reach him as all the pain concentrated to within a single point located somewhere between my lungs where my failing heart struggled to beat a ragged rhythm in my chest. From behind my eyelids – as if through the window of my life – open shutters began to close, one by one. I wanted to stay but the shutters were nearly all closed and it was time to go. Through the sweet peace of death I heard a howl of misery – but it wasn't mine.

Piercing light flooded in, blinding.

Close the shutters, I wanted to tell them but all I could do was moan. The light went out; then again like a searchlight in my other eye.

Cool hands formed a frame around my face. "Emma?"

"Is she gonna be all right?" another voice asked – one I didn't recognize. Matthew didn't answer. I felt fingers on my neck, feeling my pulse.

"Yes," he sounded relieved. "Emma, open your eyes."

No, I don't want to; let me sleep – there's no pain in sleep.

"Open your eyes," he ordered, and I tried really hard but I lacked the control to obey.

"Is she coming round, Doc?" The other man's voice grated roughly; he didn't care that it hurt – I could hear the impatience in it.

"I'll call you when she does; she needs rest now." Matthew didn't want him near me, I could tell.

The rough-voiced man sniffed loudly. "Yeah, OK, give me a call – you've got my cell number." A door opened and closed behind him and it became quiet again.

"Open your eyes for me, Emma."

They wouldn't open and everything ached, or stabbed, or burned.

"It hurts, Matthew."

"I know it does – it won't soon."

A spreading numbness trickled from my arm, winding its way through my body. My eyes struggled to open, thin lines of light seeping through.

"Matthew?" My voice sounded like a stranger's. My eyes opened; he was so close, his face troubled, and I wanted to touch it.

"What's the matt'r?" I asked him, words blurring.

A haunting smile barely touched his lips. "Nothing now," he said softly, leaning over and kissing me gently. His white shirt was carmine, badged in blood, and I thought I should be frightened but I couldn't remember why.

"Your arm's broken; I'm going to set it."

I vaguely remembered but it didn't seem very relevant. "Yes," I mumbled, but I wanted to sleep so I couldn't do anything to help; I couldn't keep my eyes open any longer.

"Go to sleep, Emma."

"She should be moved to the hospital in Portland." The coarse-voiced man had returned.

"Dr D'Eresby can't be moved. There's nothing they can do for her there that we can't do here." Matthew sounded calm but I recognized the undercurrent in his voice. My eyes flickered open; the two men stood by the window through which full daylight fell. The man argued, "They've got all the medical facilities there." He wore a uniform from the police department; a heavy-set man with thick, black hair crudely cut, and a bullish face – used to getting his own way.

Matthew regarded him dispassionately. "She stays."

Unreasoning panic welled in my foggy brain. "Don't let them take me away."

He left the man and came to me, taking in the fear in my face, hearing it in my voice. "Nobody's taking you anywhere – you're staying here."

The officer peered over Matthew's shoulder at me. He chewed gum in the same way cattle chew cud, his jaw churning.

"I need to ask her some questions, Doc."

Matthew's jaw set in a stubborn line. "I cannot allow that. Dr D'Eresby is in no fit state to be questioned; come back later."

The officer stopped chewing, on the brink of arguing again, but Matthew looked at him without speaking and the man thought better of it, shrugging.

"OK, you're the doc, but we gotta' talk to her sometime."

"Granted, but it will be when I say so." Matthew turned back, assessing me with a slight frown.

"Sure, OK, but you let me know, huh, Doc?"

He declined to answer and the officer hesitated, wondering whether to press for an acknowledgment, but Matthew appeared to have forgotten him, and he gave up.

The door closed behind him and Matthew straightened. He smiled.

"How are you feeling?"

I thought I hurt less, but it was debatable, my body and my mind all jumbled up so that discomfort and fear and anxiety wallowed in the same miasma.

"Foggy," I mumbled indistinctly.

"That's the morphine. Can you tell me where the pain is worst?"

The ache in my right arm balanced out the tight burning in my left. My throat felt painful all over and I found it difficult to breathe, each shallow breath sending arrows of fire through my chest.

"I don't know," I said, confused by the different messages my body sent me. "My throat hurts." I didn't dare swallow.

"It's badly bruised, but nothing more," he said, putting his hand gently around it as if to draw the discomfort. The burning ache began to diminish a little. "Is that any better?"

"A bit – mmm." My eyes closed again as the sting distinctly subsided and I let the medication take over, slipping back into unconsciousness.

Smiling, mouth whip-thin, Staahl stood over me, his colourless lips as curved as the tip of the blade he used to slowly carve my heart from my chest. I opened my mouth to scream at the same time as a wave of pain hit me unawares and I gasped, drawing air through my burning throat. My eyes flew open and Staahl vanished, but Matthew sat beside me as if he had never been away.

"Tell me where it hurts," he asked, concern colouring his voice.

I shook my head although it hurt to do so. "Everywhere."

He frowned, and in that instant it seemed that he reached inside me to locate its source; but another surge hit me, and his eyes widened momentarily as if he felt it. He leaned to adjust something attached to my arm. The slow spread of morphine brought sweet relief and, as the scorching subsided, I had a brief period of clarity in which I remembered my terror.

"Staahl…" I choked out.

"He's in custody, Emma, he can't get to you." He brushed a piece of hair away from where it tickled my cheek, his fingers briefly resting in its place.

"He's alive?" I croaked as I pulled the memory of the room back where I could see it, Staahl dangling limp, high off the floor.

He looked puzzled. "Yes – but the police have him locked up – you're safe."

"No, I mean, you… Staahl… you were going to… *kill* him."

Matthew's face grew still. "No, Emma, I just needed to get him away from you."

My brain began to blur and the memory dulled as the morphine numbed it. I fought against the stupor for as long as I could.

"I saw – you had him up against the wall; you – you were going to… *throttle* him."

His eyes became black coals as the morphine took full effect and I couldn't tell whether the veil that fell over his face was an attempt at concealment or a figment of the medication.

"I wish you had," I murmured, regretfully.

I had no sense of passing time but when I awoke again, late sunlight streamed in corrugated regularity through the blinds of the west windows, striking white lines like lasers across the floor and walls. Everyday college noises filtered through the insulated glass but, in the room in which I lay, all was quiet – too quiet. A noise came from behind me.

"Matthew?"

A woman's voice answered. "He isn't here at the moment." She appeared around the head of the bed where I could see her clearly; she seemed familiar.

"Where's Matthew?" I tried to sit up, groggy and confused, but a spasm coursed through me and I could no more than lift my head from the pillow.

"He won't be long. Are you in discomfort?"

"Always."

She had long, treacle-coloured hair held back from her face so it flowed in a line down her back.

"Can you tell me where it hurts?" the young woman asked; she could be no more than nineteen, perhaps twenty, but serious and unsmiling, and that made her seem much older. She checked a fine, clear tube running into my left arm above where bandages encased my wrist. Replacing lost fluids, a transparent liquid from a suspended bag fed the tube with the regularity of a ticking clock.

"You sound like a doctor," I said, trying to breathe shallowly in case the stabbing returned. She suddenly smiled, her face changing and taking on a humorous aspect.

"That's because I am."

"Sorry," I muttered, thinking I might have offended her. The door opened and a nurse, twice the girl's age, came in carrying a covered tray, which rattled with metallic objects as she moved.

"There's a detective outside, Dr Lynes; you want me to show him in?"

Lynes – no wonder I thought I recognized her; I saw elements of Matthew in her features. She shook her head at the nurse.

"Don't let him in, Ada, not until Dr Matthew says. Put the tray there, will you, please?" She indicated the trolley next to the bed with her elbow, as she swapped the near-empty bag of fluid for a full one. The tray clattered noisily as the nurse put it down.

"Are you related to Matthew?" My head began to swim as the twinge started to polarize and intensify. I shut my eyes and concentrated on the sounds outside – anything rather than the spear in my side.

"Yes, ma'am; I'm Ellie Lynes – Dr Lynes is my uncle. You can have some more meds if you need them?" she offered.

"No – thanks, I'll wait until Matthew gets back; I want to keep a clear head." Breathing slowly, I could keep it at bay for longer, but the ache soon swarmed again. She watched me through narrowed eyes, probably wondering how long I could hold out. I jerked nervously as the double doors were flung open and a gurney was pushed in with two medical staff crowding the head of the trolley. Ellie leaned forward and drew the side-curtain of my cubicle.

"What happened last night? I don't remember much."

She surveyed me with dark-blue eyes, judging how much to tell me.

"You lost a lot of blood. My uncle had to stop the bleeding and replace the fluids fast." She hesitated. "He didn't know if he could save you."

That close! I pondered for a moment, remembering the shutters closing down on my life.

"But he did," I said out loud.

"Yes, he did." I heard an element of pride in the way she said it and I wondered what she left out. "You'd better ask Matthew if you want more details," she continued, reading my mind. That was almost funny.

"You think he would tell me?"

Ellie didn't answer. A violent cough followed by a gurgling choke from the adjacent cubicle announced the resuscitation of its occupant, accompanied by an exclamation as projectile vomit narrowly missed the nurse.

"Alcohol poisoning," Ellie muttered and began to say something but the doors opened again, and the police officer from earlier in the day came in, speaking to a couple of men over his shoulder.

"... through here. Don't know if you can talk to her, though. If she ain't up to it the Doc won't let you." He turned to look at me as he finished his sentence, then saw Ellie and did a double take.

"Who're you? Where's Dr Lynes?" he demanded, hardly civil at all.

Ellie visibly bristled at his tone. "*I'm* Dr Lynes, but if you mean Dr *Matthew* Lynes, my uncle will be back any minute now."

He eyed her up and down and dismissed her with a shrug. "You can leave now, Doc; we have some questions for the lady."

One of the men behind him – the one with a bent nose – pushed forward.

"That's all right, Joe, we'll take it from here."

An instantaneous scowl appeared on his brow and Joe – evidently not happy at being sidelined – moved out of the way and hovered in the background. Ellie's slender frame barely blocked them from view as she stepped between us.

"Dr Lynes won't allow Dr D'Eresby to be questioned at the moment." Despite her youth, she displayed an authority the men recognized in the noticeable shift in her tone. The man with the ill-tempered face and poorly aligned nose squared his shoulders.

"We have an investigation to conduct, Miss Lynes; we're not interested in what you or anybody else wants; step aside."

Ellie didn't move but the atmosphere changed subtly and I didn't want her getting into trouble over something as trivial as me answering some questions.

"Please, Dr Lynes, it's all right, I'll answer their questions, please..."

She looked at me, considering whether to argue the point. The sound of retching came from a few feet away and voices conferred quietly from behind the curtain. The detectives cringed and exchanged glances. One of them came up to the side of the bed and spoke; he had a deeper, more pleasant timbre to his voice, with none of the aggression inherent in the other man.

"I'm Detective Slater, ma'am, and this won't take long; we just want to get a few facts straight while they're still fresh in your mind... ma'am?"

I realized I had shut my eyes; I opened them again and the detective's face swam into focus closer than expected. He was the older of the two men – perhaps nearing retirement age. The grey pushing through on his unshaven face and the deep bags under his eyes spoke of a sleepless night.

"Yes, I'll try."

Slater pulled up a chair and sat down, the vinyl surface wheezing. He pulled out a battered notebook and flipped through several of the pages.

"You received a phone call from England at about..." he checked his notes, "... nine-fifty, and you..."

"No."

"You didn't receive a call, or not at the time stated?"

"It wasn't a call from England – it was a trick to get me away from the dinner, to get me alone." I swallowed painfully.

"OK, so you're saying there was no one on the line, is that right?"

"Yes."

Slater scribbled something in his notebook and then looked up at me expectantly.

"What happened when you realized there was no one on the phone?"

"There was a noise. He... Staahl... was there. I tried to run but I couldn't, the floor – it was too slippery. He grabbed me... he... he pulled me back into the room..." I stalled, fear sliding through me as it had when he cornered me, the memory still sharp and fresh. Ellie moved noiselessly towards the bed but the other detective put his arm between us. "He said things... I couldn't get away... he... had a knife... his arm was around my throat... I couldn't breathe. I tried to get away but he broke my arm... he was going to kill me... he... he..." And suddenly I wasn't in the med centre any more, but in the porters' lodge and Staahl was choking me, bleeding me, images crowding thick and fast as I drowned in the memory of dread and pain, my heart tearing inside my chest, my breathing harsh and erratic.

"That's enough!" Matthew stood inside the doors, his eyes

blazing. Both detectives swivelled around as he strode towards the bed, forcing Slater to shift out of the way. His fingers now lightly against my neck, my pulse hammered beneath them but I couldn't control it, I couldn't control the wave upon wave of terror breaking over me.

"He wouldn't let me go... he... my cross – where's my cross?" My eyes stared wildly, my vision filled with Staahl's dead eyes, his mouth drawn back revealing small, narrow teeth like a grill, like a skull; a death's head with demon's eyes intent on tearing out my soul. Matthew said something under his breath too low for me to hear and I felt his hands around my face, cold enough against my flaming skin to make me gasp. He looked through the porthole of my eyes, reaching inside me, pulling me back towards the light.

"Emma, he's gone – he can't hurt you; it's over. Your cross is here; I have it safe."

His certainty staunched the spiralling panic and I saw Matthew again, not Staahl, and his eyes were not grey, but blue, driving away the colourless fear that sought to devour me. I wanted to reach out and touch his mouth and high cheekbones and corn-coloured hair; I wanted to reach out and touch him to make sure he was *real*.

"Matthew?"

"I'm here, Emma, there's nothing to worry about – everything's going to be fine." His voice wrapped around me – soothing, reassuring – and so hard to resist, but although he was right in front of me, his hands cradling my face, Staahl still leered from my memory.

"He won't go away," I whispered. Matthew flashed a look at his niece and soon numbness spread inexorably, anaesthetizing my dread.

Slater had retreated to the end of the bed, but he now came forward again. Matthew turned slowly to look at him and the man paused.

"Dr Lynes?"

"I specifically stated that Dr D'Eresby is *not* to be questioned until I said it is appropriate to do so."

"Is she OK?" Slater asked.

"She's suffering from shock and is in a great deal of discomfort. No, she is not 'OK' and your questions didn't help."

"So grey," I moaned groggily and he put a comforting hand on my shoulder.

"I guess we have to do our job, Dr Lynes," Slater said, defensively apologetic.

Neither defensive nor apologetic, Matthew replied, "And I do mine."

"If it's OK, can we ask you some questions – it'll save time later and might clear things up a little?"

Matthew nodded briefly and led the two men over to the other side of the room. I could still hear them but the morphine had taken effect and I no longer cared what they said. In the adjoining cubicle, the retching ceased and metallic sounds of mop in bucket replaced it, along with the astringent smell of disinfectant. Ellie had gone. I tried to focus on the conversations, but they kept fading in and out of my consciousness.

"We'll need photos of the injuries." The nameless detective said it as if he expected Matthew to refuse permission.

"Of course," he responded.

I heard the crack of paper turning as Slater consulted his notebook. "You were at the same All Saints dinner as Professor D'Eresby, is that right? But you left halfway through?" They had obviously been doing their homework.

"That's correct. I had an emergency call to answer."

"So you didn't know about the phone call to Professor D'Eresby?"

Remorse edged his tone. "No."

"But you were passing by when she was attacked? That was lucky – for the lady." The second detective made it sound as if luck had nothing to do with it. "How did you happen to be in that area?"

They were digging for something. I wanted to tell them to leave him alone but my mouth wouldn't engage with my brain.

"I was returning to the dinner when I heard a noise. It didn't sound like any of the student revels and came from an area which should have been empty at that time of night, so..."

"You decided to go have a look. You must have good hearing, Dr Lynes." It was the broken-nosed man again; he spoke with a sneer.

"I do."

"And what did you find when you 'had a look'?"

Matthew outlined a clinical description of what he had seen. Even through the morphine-induced mist, I recognized an edited story; yet I remembered every word exchanged that night and somehow knew he did too.

"Did you say anything to Professor Staahl?"

"I told him to let go of her."

"And he didn't?"

Matthew's voice sounded flat and expressionless. "No."

"And then...?" Slater prompted.

"He cut her, severing her radial artery, and I had to get him away from her."

Bash-face sneered. "That was brave – I mean, he had a knife, you could have been hurt." I hated the insinuation behind the man's voice and would have punched him if I could, but Matthew continued, unruffled.

"There was no time to think – I had to act; I had no choice."

"So you would say Professor D'Eresby was attacked, then; there's no possibility that she went there voluntarily to meet Professor Staahl? That these 'injuries' were not just some tragic accident? Or a game?"

Matthew's reaction was immediate and definitive. He walked rapidly to my side. "I'm sorry," he murmured to me, and then gently but swiftly unwrapped the bandages from my left wrist and removed the dressing before looking over to the two detectives still standing by the window.

"Does this look *consensual*?" he demanded, "or a *game*?" The two men came over and stood on the opposite side of the bed. There was a quick intake of breath from Slater and the second man glanced down at me, nostrils flaring in surprise. I wondered dopily what they saw. "Staahl held her wrist here – this is where his nails dug in, breaking her skin – and this..."

Matthew indicated an area by the crease in my wrist, "is where he pushed in the tip of the knife before drawing it like this..." and he imitated the action, "down and across her arm." Matthew carefully turned my head so they could see my throat in the light of the overhead lamp, "And this... this is where he used the point of the knife to pierce her throat."

"Sweet mother...!" Slater exclaimed.

"And this..." Matthew went over to the computer and brought up the digital images of my broken arm and the X-ray before it was set. "He used the edge of the door to break it – you can see the finger marks where he gripped her arm – here, and the point of impact – here." He showed them the X-ray on the screen. "Those are purposefully inflicted wounds – not a *game*, and there was no *consent*, and they do not include the injuries that occurred afterwards as a result of the attack – extensive bruising and the massive loss of blood which nearly resulted in Dr D'Eresby's death." He paused. "And I suspect further injuries in addition to these."

The men remained silent for a moment, taking it in; I wanted to know what they saw. I couldn't lift my unbandaged arm to look.

"Can I see?" I croaked woozily. Matthew hesitated. "Please?"

Reluctantly he lifted my arm within my line of sight. An angry crimson line razored through my skin for about seven inches, the edges drawn together in fine stitches, the flesh inflamed and gaudy. Distinct finger-shaped bruises in red and plum were developing and spreading from crescent nail marks on one side of my wrist and a single thumb bruise on the other. I felt sick and looked away.

"That's enough, gentlemen; I need to get this re-dressed." Matthew recovered his composure but, from his tone, would brook no argument.

"I need to take copies of the photos as evidence, and it'd sure be helpful if I can take a few more?" Slater asked, obviously unsure about the reaction. He already held a small digital camera in his hand, but the shutter remained closed.

Matthew prepared replacement dressings. "You must ask Dr D'Eresby."

Slater looked at me and I nodded as much as my head would allow. He took a series of photos from a variety of angles more self-consciously than I was able to feel in my soporific state.

"We will still need to ask Professor D'Eresby some questions," Slater said, apologetically.

"Not now." His mouth hard, Matthew didn't look up as he answered.

"Sure, later will do."

Matthew closed his eyes, exhaling audibly as the door shut behind the two men.

"That was unconscionable – I'm so sorry."

I couldn't see why he needed to feel guilty, but then nothing seemed to matter at the moment.

"Please don't say that; there's nothing to forgive."

"Yes, there is – more than you can know." He sounded bitter and I wanted so much to tell him I would forgive him anything. "Tel-lme?" I said, words slurring drunkenly. He glanced at the cubicle next to mine, where intermittent groans indicated that the occupant still lived, and shook his head. At that moment the double doors slammed open and I jolted at the sudden noise, the morphine not able to dull the arrow in my side. Matthew looked closely at me.

"Does your chest hurt?"

"Yes," I forced out.

Another trolley appeared ahead of two more staff and one of the nurses grinned in Matthew's direction.

"Found this one in the lake this morning. Kids tried to dry him out themselves – didn't think to call us first. Heaven only knows what he's been drinking." The trolley wheeled past, a bedraggled figure draped untidily on the bed, limbs sprawling at angles off it.

"D'you need t'go?" I asked.

He didn't look up. "No, they have it covered; I want to find out what's causing you so much discomfort."

The tension in his face was unbearable. I flinched as he carefully swabbed the laceration with an orange solution that dried almost instantly; but even with the morphine the gash burned. He placed the clean dressing over it, binding it in place with fresh bandages until it disappeared under swathes of white cloth. As the ache subsided once more, I remembered what I meant to ask him.

"Please can I go back t'my apartment? I don't want to stay here; I'm just in th'way and it's so… *exposed*."

I felt totally vulnerable; although it was unreasonable, every time the door opened I expected to see Staahl walk through.

"No, Emma, you need to be looked after and I don't have the facilities over there. In any case, your pain isn't under control yet, and until I'm sure we've located all the sources of it, I want you under supervision."

He beckoned to one of the nurses hovering redundantly by the other patients nearby. She came over, straightening her uniform and looking coyly at him from under her lashes. Matthew handed her a small tray with soiled bandages and asked her to bring him something with a long name I hadn't heard of before.

"But'll be OK now, won't I?"

He frowned, picking up on the slight note of desperation I tried to hide in my voice.

"What's the matter, Emma?"

I could still taste the smell of raw flesh, of fresh blood, as it lingered in the air. The nurse glanced sideways at me, curiously; I waited until she was out of earshot.

"I don't feel *safe* here, Matthew; please take me back – don't leave me here." My eyes filled with unlooked-for tears and I silently cursed my fragility. His face softening, he leaned forwards so that only I could hear him.

"It's all right – don't be upset; I won't let anyone hurt you again."

His compassion just made it worse and tears escaped before I could stop them, trickling over my skin and down my neck. I hadn't meant to cry, I didn't mean to be so melodramatic, but my normal stoicism had been reduced to a nominal veneer that warped and cracked from the pressure of events over the past few days, and no reserves remained on which to call.

"Matthew, *please.*"

Tears tickled my skin and I tried to rub them out with my shoulder, but I couldn't move enough to reach them. He extended a finger and with infinite gentleness brushed the flow with the tip.

"Don't cry. Hush, it's all right now; I'll take you somewhere you'll feel safe."

My answering sigh was shallow and painful but one of immense relief and, a few feet away, the young nurse looked enviously at me.

Chapter 16

Into Light

H E HADN'T SAID WHERE HE WOULD TAKE ME, or when, or – for that matter – how.

I slept fitfully for what little remained of the day, dragged back to consciousness every time the door opened or someone walked past, sleeping only when my heart returned to its regular beat. Matthew did not leave the room again and, through the drug-induced waking dream that made up reality, I was vaguely aware that several times people came to see me, but he turned them away at the door.

He removed the tube from my arm when I half-slept and, at one point, he carefully examined my ribcage, running swift, experienced hands along each rib with an expression of total concentration until he found what he looked for. He bound the upper half of my body in a flexible strapping that allowed me to breathe while holding my fractured bones in place, taking immense care to move me as little as possible; but I was too far gone either to protest at the pain or to thank him when at last the strapping gave me some respite from it.

I didn't know how long I lay there – whether one day or three – because hours merged, counted only in the number of times pain expanded to fill every part of me until I thought I would explode with it, and then the relief as medication numbed it once more.

The emergency room quietened as darkness fell, and staff came on duty for the night shift. We were briefly alone and I was still barely awake when Matthew picked me up as easily as a kitten wrapped in a blanket, and carried me out of the med centre. We left the building via an internal door that led directly into the original part of the old house, exchanging the sterile cleanliness and strip lighting of the one, for the aged walls and wax-polish scent of the other.

The halls were deserted and a night hush had fallen on the old building.

"Where are we going?" I asked when I realized it wasn't to my apartment.

"Here," he said, stopping at a heavy oak door with an ornate brass handle. The light from the hall only dimly illuminated the room we entered. Matthew walked over to what appeared in the darkness to be a large day-bed with a raised scroll arm at one end. It had been made up into an improvised bed. Despite the care with which he lowered me, I ground my teeth as the infinitesimal jarring jolted me fully awake.

Concerned, he asked, "That hurt, didn't it?"

"Not really," I feinted. "Is this your office?"

"It is."

A faint draught drifted from arched windows looking out into the black night, the lamplight from a desk lamp he switched on softly reflecting in the mirrored glass. The light cast deep shadows into the large room, whose ceiling criss-crossed above me with ornate gothic plasterwork, terminating in pinnacles like icing-sugar stalactites. He reached for a blanket from a small pile neatly folded by the day-bed, shaking it out and letting it settle over me in a cloud, then repeated the process with two others until the chill of the air had been defeated. He found pillows, placing one under each arm. I closed my eyes as the soreness settled back into its normal hum, and he touched my cheek briefly.

Mahogany shelving lined two walls, and I guessed the room must originally have been the library to the big house – the same library where once Ebenezer Howard sat to transcribe the journal, a lifetime and more before my birth. And yet here I lay, part of an improbable dream – resurrecting it from obscurity, raising it to life, its saviour, its thief. I shook despite the blankets.

Matthew knelt down beside me.

"You're cold." He glanced at the pale limestone fireplace big enough to sit in, its grate already laid with logs. Although smoke-black with age, it looked unused for many years. On either side of the fireplace, new shelves were being built to match the originals – one side already nearly full of books whose spines stood regimented, gilded titles subtle in the limited light.

"Don't you freeze in here?" I asked.

"I don't feel the cold much, no." He paused thoughtfully, then strode to the fireplace and leaned forwards, peering up the length of the chimney. "I'll be back in a minute," he said, disappearing out of the room. He returned with a box of matches. The struck match flared, momentarily casting his face in a glow that grew stronger as the brittle kindling lit. He suddenly looked lost and out of his depth, and I thought then that I asked too much of him, placing him in an invidious position with the college authorities.

"Will you get in trouble for bringing me here?"

He hesitated and shot me a look as if a thought suddenly occurred to him.

"Are *you* comfortable being here, Emma? Does it – do I – worry you at all?"

I knew what he implied and it couldn't have been further from the truth.

"No, not at all; I feel totally safe here. Thank you," I remembered to say.

The fire leapt eagerly to life, filling the room with an energy of flames before generating enough heat to warm me. The room looked warmer even if it still felt cold.

"Better?" he asked hopefully.

"Much," I said. "I like fires. Is this your only room – I mean, do you have an apartment like the rest of us?"

"No, I don't need one – I go home."

He sat down on the floor next to me, resting his supple back against the day-bed, the fire playing gold and orange on his skin. I could study him legitimately from this position – his fine, angular features thrown into sharp relief by the firelight. Although he hadn't slept properly for at least twenty-four hours, he looked as he always did, strong and vigorous, as if just returned from a brisk walk in the sun.

"Yes, of course you do – I forgot. Do you live far from the campus?"

"Not really, it doesn't take me long to get back." He must have guessed my thoughts because he added, "I often stay here overnight; I'm not leaving you by yourself, in case you wondered."

He looked back at me and met my gaze. I held it for a few seconds before I flushed under its intensity and looked away, thankful for the lack of light in the room. Smiling, he settled down to watch the flames.

He read in an elegant chair behind the rosewood table that served as a desk. It was still dark outside, and the fire had developed a bed of incandescent embers on which fresh logs now burned. He closed his book and placed it on the table in front of him.

"Good morning; how are you feeling? Thirsty?"

"Yes – I think I am," I said sleepily, but he held a glass from which to drink before I confirmed that what I felt was thirst. I raised my head as far as possible and managed a few sips, but more escaped from the glass than I drank, and it dribbled icily down my chin, collecting in the crease of my neck and shocking me awake.

"I *hate* being an invalid," I exploded in guilty frustration, taking him by surprise. "I'm in the way here and you have better things to do than look after me, like a... like a Victorian *consumptive*."

Matthew disguised a smile and put the glass back to my lips, his other hand easing behind my neck to steady me.

"Well, unless you want to go back to the med centre, you'll just have to put up with being looked after by me here; it's a very simple choice."

"I'm sorry," I muttered.

"Well, I'm *not*."

And despite my injuries, I felt a fluttering in response. I

drank more this time, and without embarrassing myself. He found a clean handkerchief from somewhere and dried my neck, taking care to avoid the bruising. It felt wet like Staahl's tongue. I shrank back before I could stop myself and Matthew immediately withdrew his hand, his eyes taking on a guarded look.

"It's not you, I'm sorry. It's... it reminded me of Staahl; he licked me – my neck; it was... *disgusting*."

I shuddered, nausea seizing my gullet in an involuntary spasm that led nowhere.

Matthew's eyes flashed wide before he turned away, but not before I saw the repugnance on his face. He busied himself straightening the fleecy blankets.

"Warm enough?" he asked after a while.

"Yes, thanks."

He was quiet again for a moment.

"You know, it's ironic – this situation – considering our conversations on previous occasions." He sat carefully on the front edge of the day-bed. I thought back and referenced the discussions we'd had; our conversation about our different careers seemed so long ago – like another era.

"So, have you thought about what I asked you – about dealing with the job on a daily basis?"

He nodded.

"And...?"

It took him a few seconds before he answered. "I thought I coped – until now."

"What do you mean?"

"I was surprised by my reaction, my lack of control when you were hurt. It took me unawares. I haven't felt like that in a long time."

"I'm not sure if I understand."

He made a face. "That makes two of us."

I adjusted my legs, pulling them up as far as I could to alleviate the nagging ache in my back and chest, staring at the fairytale ceiling, trying to find the words to explain the thoughts that had gathered momentum over the past days.

"I think that being on the receiving end of someone's desire to hurt me has put my work in perspective; it's brought home the reality of what I've studied all these years. It's been too easy to be disassociated from the brutality of it by the passing of time; I'm not sure if I can go back to my particular area of research – not now, not after this." I stared out of the dark windows, the first hint of dawn beckoning, thinking it through before looking back at him. "But you have the hardest deal, Matthew, because you cope with the reality of what I went through day in, day out. Now I have experienced it first hand, I'm not sure if I would have the guts to do what you do."

He brought his face level with mine, the blue ink of the fading night reflected in his eyes as the sky lightened.

"You think you don't have courage?"

"I don't honestly know any more. I thought I did."

I straightened my legs again, the discomfort intensifying.

He regarded me thoughtfully for a moment. "Tell me, what would you do if you saw Staahl now and it was within your power to retaliate?"

I didn't hesitate. "I'd rip his throat out," I snarled, feeling my own strain with the effort, then stopped. "No – no I wouldn't, I would like to, but I wouldn't – not in reality."

"Wouldn't or couldn't?" he said, neutrally.

I had to think about it. "Wouldn't. Yes, wouldn't – because I couldn't square it with my conscience. I'm not sure if I can forgive him yet, and it's not that I think that he doesn't deserve it…" I bit my lip, "but vengeance goes against what I believe and at some point I must forgive him."

"'Even as Christ forgave you, so also do ye'?"

I looked at him appreciatively because he understood without me needing to explain.

"Something like that – and it's easier said than done – but whether that makes me a coward or not, I don't know."

I heard absolute certainty in his voice. "I do, and it doesn't."

"That's comforting, I suppose." I winced as I forgot my broken arm and tried to lift it.

"I have to put a full cast on that arm now the swelling's down." He looked at his watch. "You'll need some meds before we go any further to take the edge off it."

I pulled a face. "I would like to try to go without; it makes me feel so…" I struggled to find the right words.

"Defenceless?" he suggested.

"I was going to say 'out of my skull', actually."

He sprang to his feet.

"Now is as good a time as any – no queues and no witnesses."

"To what?"

A slow smile spread as he heard the note of alarm in my voice.

"Well, you can either go in a wheelchair or I can carry you – your choice."

The thought of being carried again definitely appealed.

"Aren't I too heavy?"

He answered by picking me up as if I were no more than an afterthought.

He was right, of course; without morphine it was excruciating. I capitulated and he waited until the medication took full effect before attempting to put a cast on my arm. The deeply embedded bruising around the area of impact had changed from red to an angry, violent purple with a blue-black heart, and I felt relief when my arm disappeared beneath the lightweight cast.

Full daylight beckoned when I awoke. Fog filled the windows like smoke, cold air seeping through the thin glass, and the world no longer existed outside the quiet, solid warmth of the old library.

"Elena has been asking to see you; do you feel up to receiving visitors?" Matthew asked, when I succeeded in drinking without spilling it this time.

"Do you mind her coming to your room?" I asked in return.

"No, not at all; why, did you think I would?"

"I thought you might prefer to keep this as your, um… inner sanctum, so to speak."

He laughed. "Thank you for that. No, it's fine; Elena's welcome. So would you like to see her?"

Actually, Elena was exactly the person I wanted to see. I remained acutely aware of wearing the same clothes I wore the night of the attack – albeit only some of them. Although still decent, I wanted to change into something more appropriate as soon as possible. Elena understood instantly I explained the situation.

"It's a good thing you were wearing matching underwear," she giggled when she thought Matthew beyond hearing.

"Cheers, Elena; I get mauled by that... that... *creature*, and all you can think about is what I wore at the time!"

She hooted with laughter. "You sound much better already. You know, we've both missed you." Suddenly serious, she sat on the end of the day-bed. "It was horrible; I... I thought you were dead, you were just lying there – in all that blood, and..." She hesitated, her waif-like face in knots as she recalled the image.

"Go on," I encouraged.

"... and Matthew was holding you and calling your name over and over, but there was so much blood – he couldn't stop you bleeding. Someone said they were calling 911, but he just picked you up and ran – he ran so *fast*." Ashen, she shook her head as if she didn't quite trust her memory. I remembered the wind beating my face so I almost couldn't breathe. "We followed you to the med centre, but Matthew wouldn't let us see you; he wouldn't let anyone in – even his own staff. We thought you were going to die," she whispered.

"So did I," I said soberly, then tried to relieve the tension; "but I didn't, so to prevent my premature death through humiliation, please, *please* help me get into some fresh clothes and clean up a bit."

"Don't you want Matthew to help you?" she suggested sneakily.

"I think he's seen enough of me already, thank you, and next time I would rather I were conscious of the fact and somewhat in control."

"Ah, so you think there will be a *next time*!"

I smiled at the thought. "I can live in hope."

"In that case, you must have some nice things to wear." She

rubbed her hands together in glee. "Leave it to me; I will see what I can do."

An unspeakable image of Elena selecting pink frilly knickers, like an old lady's lampshade, interjected before I could prevent it. Hardly an object of desire – not that I was attempting seduction – but equally, I didn't want Matthew recoiling in horror should he chance to see them.

Much to my surprise – and relief – Elena returned some time later with a small bag of clothes I would have chosen for myself, and all the necessary toiletries. It took a great deal of effort to do the very basics, but I ended up feeling more human and less like a cat-chewed corpse of a mouse. As Elena brushed my hair, and I offered up thanks for hair that didn't need frequent washing, Matthew knocked, waiting momentarily before letting himself in.

"I hope Emma's been behaving herself," he addressed Elena, appraising me approvingly as he crossed the room.

"I have had to keep her 'in order', as you say. She is not obedient enough; she is an *im*patient patient," Elena replied cheerfully, pleased with her command of the language. She tugged a little too forcefully at a knot of hair matted with dried blood and my bruised neck objected; I yelped and she peered at me in horror.

"Sorry! I'm so sorry, Emma; are you all right?"

"I'll live," I smiled ruefully.

"I have to remember that you are... you are..." she muttered something in Russian under her breath.

"Recuperating," Matthew translated for her. We both stared at him.

"You speak Russian?" Elena said delightedly, and rattled off something at machine-gun speed. Matthew replied without hesitation as he took the hairbrush from her hands before she decapitated me in her excitement. There was another knock at the door.

"I'll go," Elena chirped and bounced towards it.

Matthew stood behind the arm of the day-bed, bending close

to me, running the brush gently through my hair.

"Latin, Old Italian, Russian, Anglo-Saxon – anything else?" I murmured.

"English?"

"Don't be facetious."

He grinned down at me, and my pulse stumbled in response.

"Did you order food?" Elena called from over by the door.

"Your lunch, Matthew? Good – you never eat," I reproached him, thinking I was redressing the balance of care just a little.

"No, yours," he corrected, "and you need it more than I do, judging by what I've seen of you." I felt my face turn cerise. You know that thing doctors always say when you are down to your knickers and bra and you're desperately trying not to look acutely self-conscious – and failing: "Don't worry, I've seen it all before." Well, *hah!* He – or she – might have done but try telling yourself that when the doctor in question is all that you desire but he doesn't know it. I imagined my reddened skin clashing with my pinky-coppery hair and flushed even more. Elena said something to him in Russian that sounded like a question and Matthew answered, glancing at me. She giggled. I scowled.

"I will come and see you again," Elena said as she left the room, still beaming at their shared joke.

Matthew put the tray on the table and picked up the plate. I twigged immediately. "You're not going to feed me, are you?" I groaned.

"How else is this food going to reach your stomach if I don't?" He looked pointedly at both my arms. Only the tips of my fingers were visible and my thumbs were locked in position so I couldn't grip a fork. He pulled up a chair next to me and fed a small amount of food into my mouth. Admittedly, it was delicious, but trying to eat in an elegant and refined manner proved exhausting.

"It's not fair – you're enjoying this, aren't you?" I said between mouthfuls, the warm food settling my tummy.

"It has its moments," he said smoothly, putting everything neatly back on the tray when I finished. I laid my head back against the pillow.

"I *hate* being ill; it's such a waste of life."

He threw me a look I couldn't interpret before he answered.

"It's only for a while," he said quietly. For a horrible moment I wondered if he remembered his wife.

"Yes, I'm sorry, I'm being an ungrateful brat again." He smiled at that. "Matthew, I haven't thanked you for all you've done – are doing," I corrected myself. He frowned, but said nothing. "You saved my life," I insisted; "twice."

Standing swiftly, he fetched the glass of water from the tray.

"Here, drink this." He held it for me, avoiding my gaze while I drank.

"Matthew...?"

His eyes flicked towards mine and then away again. "You shouldn't have been put in that position in the first place," he said, his voice shaded with resentment.

"What does that mean?" I demanded.

"Nothing."

"You can't say that and expect me to accept it. I've just thanked you for saving my life and you act as if you were to blame for me nearly losing it in the first place! Why should you..."

A loud, insistent rap on the door broke through my tirade. I gritted my teeth at the interruption as Matthew left my side to answer it. He came back a few moments later, followed by Slater and the unnamed detective, and I vowed to myself that – sooner or later – I would pick up the threads of the conversation where it had been so abruptly suspended.

Chapter

17

Breaking Point

S LATER HAD SHAVED AND LOOKED much better for it.
"You gave us quite a turn there, ma'am, with you not
being in the medical centre and such, and nobody knowing
where you were." He looked at Matthew, then his gaze shifted to
my neck. "I hope you're feeling stronger." His concern seemed
genuine. I took as deep a breath as my ribcage would allow.

"Thank you, I am. What's happened to Staahl? Where is he?
Has he been charged?"

Matthew draped a rug around my shoulders, hiding my neck
from sight, and I flashed him a look of gratitude. Slater took his
notebook out of his jacket pocket and flipped it against the back
of his hand as he talked.

"Professor Staahl's in custody, ma'am. The State Prosecutor's
waiting to see whether he's to be indicted, or sent for observation
for a time to see if he's fit to stand trial."

"What do you mean – to *see* if he's fit to stand trial? Do you
mean if he's mentally competent?"

The second detective with the bent nose and mean face
laughed coarsely.

"Yeah, they want to know if he's a *crazy*."

I looked between the two of them. "Well, isn't that obvious?
Who in their right mind would behave as he did? Of course he's
mad!"

"That's as maybe, ma'am, but he's got to be sent for assessment
first."

A thought struck me, so grotesque that I quailed at the

mention of it.

"He... he won't get bail, will he?"

Slater paused long enough for alarm to spread through me like burning brushwood.

"No, he will *not!*" Matthew thumped the window-sill, making the handle rattle.

We all looked at him in surprise.

"Is that so?" I asked Slater.

"I reckon it is..." he began, but Bent Nose butted in, his heavy-lidded eyes half-closed as he watched Matthew.

"Yeah, what with the Doc here making sure he don't make bail. Got friends in high places, have you, Doc?"

Only from the tell-tale traction in the muscles of his jaw could I tell that Matthew disliked the detective as much as I did. I imagined the man's insolent disregard for authority made him difficult to promote, and his rancour for those more successful than himself stuck in his craw as much as he was sticking in mine.

Matthew declined to comment on the man's jibe; instead he reduced the tension in his voice, and said, "Emma, Staahl is a danger to the public; there is no question of him being allowed access to society until his mental state has been fully assessed, which will take a minimum of thirty days in a secure unit."

"So, no bail?" I asked, my anxiety waning.

"No bail," Matthew confirmed.

The second detective unwrapped a piece of gum and rolled it into a coil before cramming it in his mouth. He would have thrown the scrunched foil on the table but caught Slater's eye and stuffed it in his coat pocket instead.

"Yeah, like the Doc said, no bail." He chewed the gum with his mouth open, making little slopping noises as the saliva built up. If he thought his boorish behaviour might goad Matthew into reacting, he would be disappointed; with me, on the other hand, he could very well succeed. Various parts of my body were beginning to protest and the discomfort made me increasingly irascible; it wouldn't take much to push me over the edge, which the detective must have sussed.

"Do you want to ask me some questions?" I said politely to Slater so that I didn't have to look at the permanent sneer on the other man's face.

"Sure, if we can," Slater said, treading carefully, fully aware of Matthew's guarded presence. "You think we can have some time alone here, Dr Lynes?"

"I'll just be outside if Dr D'Eresby needs me," Matthew replied.

Slater waited until Matthew left the room.

"Cosy set-up you got here," Broken Nose said as if we had something to hide. He picked up one of the older books from the desk and flicked through the pages with little interest. Slater ignored him. He tossed the book back on the table like a discarded burger bun and it slid over the polished surface and fell on the floor with a *thump*. He didn't pick it up.

"Now, ma'am, the other day you began to tell us about the attack. You said Professor Staahl dragged you back in the room – the porters' lodge – and he had a knife to your throat, is that correct?"

"Yes."

"You also said that he spoke to you; can you tell me what he said?"

I tried to remember. "He said that he had wanted to speak to me for a long time. He seemed to think that I had been *sent* to him, that there was some connection between us." I couldn't keep the disgust from my voice.

Slater waved the pencil in the air. "And you're saying that there wasn't any 'connection' between you?"

"None whatsoever!"

"So you *didn't* go there to meet him – is that what you're saying?" the other detective slid in.

Aghast, I stared at them.

"Is that what Staahl says? That I went there to *meet* him?" Slater wrote something down; I strained to see but he held the notebook at such an angle as to make it impossible.

"We're just trying to get the facts straight, ma'am. So there's no possibility that Professor Staahl misunderstood your relationship and took things a bit too far?"

I replied emphatically, "No! There was no relationship. He *tricked* me; he *attacked* me." I found it increasingly difficult to breathe, my bones aching as my lungs protested.

"That's OK, Professor, take it easy. Now, at what point did Dr Lynes appear?"

The other man finished poking around the books and settled himself on the edge of the table, pushing the empty tray to one side over the delicate surface. The fragile joints audibly remonstrated under him.

"You'll damage the table!" I protested.

The man didn't move but shifted to get more comfortable; a sharp squeal like a tortured animal issued from one of the joints as it neared breaking point.

"Conte!" Slater barked at him over his shoulder.

"Sure – don't want to break the pretty table, do we?"

Slater grunted and resumed his questions. "So, Dr Lynes...?"

"Staahl had just broken my arm..."

"Against the door frame, is that right?"

"Yes, and... and he was going to cut my wrist. Dr Lynes was there – outside the room – he told Staahl to let me go, but he didn't, he cut me."

"And that's when Dr Lynes attacked, sorry – *rescued* – you?" Conte leaned towards me from the chair on which he now slouched.

"Dr Lynes *rescued* me, yes." I pulled air into my lungs, the room span briefly.

"And he did that, how...?"

"He ran at him, I think."

"You think? You're not sure?"

"I... I was losing consciousness, it wasn't clear." Confusion clouded my thoughts. "He got him away from me, I know that much."

"Did you say anything to Dr Lynes in the time between him running at Professor Staahl and him taking you to the med centre?"

I remembered it all so clearly – how could I possibly forget?

"I'm sorry – I don't remember."

Conte suddenly rose from the chair. Slater straightened and closed his notebook. "That's all we need at the moment, ma'am. Thank you for your time."

Bewildered, I stuttered; "Th... that's it?"

"Yes, thank you, ma'am." Slater moved towards the door after Conte. He halted halfway across the room and turned. "By the way, ma'am, Professor Staahl said something about Dr Lynes choking him. You wouldn't happen to know anything about that now, would you?"

Alarm bells sounded loud and clear.

"*Strangle* him?" In my shock, I mustered as scathing a tone as possible, the memory of Matthew's hand crushing Staahl's throat – unfettered fury in his eyes – crystal sharp. "Don't be *absurd*!"

Slater shrugged slightly. "Well, thanks again, Professor. We'll be in touch if we have any further questions. You get better now."

There are moments in your life when you make a decision; it might come after long deliberation, or after no more than a second's thought; but it carries the potential to change the direction your life takes and, whether conscious of the fact at the time, looking back, you are aware of the changes that decision brought. I had just such a moment. I didn't hesitate in my lie: instinctively I knew I must protect him.

Matthew closed the door on them.

"Are you OK?" he asked.

I sidestepped his query. "You heard that, didn't you?"

"Yes, I did."

"Staahl's saying I went there to meet him, Matthew."

"I doubt they really believe that."

"They're thinking it, though – that's bad enough. And why are they dragging you into it? What were those questions for?"

"I was there, they're just cross-referencing; there's nothing to worry about."

He sounded drained and I remembered that in all this mess,

his life had been as much disrupted as mine, and that what he did went far beyond what might be expected, yet he never complained, never alluded to the intrusion it must represent for him.

"I've really mucked things up for you, haven't I?" I said dully.

He surprised me by laughing mirthlessly, shaking his head in a gesture of weary resignation.

"You have no idea."

He leaned on the window-sill, looking through the fog-bound landscape, the grey light muting the colour of his hair.

"This is getting too complicated," he muttered to himself.

A cold wave of apprehension rolled through me as I heard the note of finality in his voice, as if something scarcely started had come to an end, and I realized that I must have totally misread the situation. Unwittingly I intruded on his life when in all probability he still mourned his wife. He tolerated me because I needed his medical intervention and I was a fool if I thought he wanted me for any other reason. Quite frankly, I couldn't cope knowing he considered me a *complication*; I couldn't do it for his sake – or for mine. I saw little point in staying; I couldn't stay.

I eased my legs over the side of the day-bed, my whole body protesting. My head reeled momentarily and the floor under the thick pile of the rug rocked unsteadily beneath my feet. I let them get used to the sensation before hauling myself upright. I stood shakily, time suspended while I let the room steady around me, and then I took a step forward. Instantly – hideously – the room gyrated as the ceiling turned upside-down and slid precariously towards the floor.

"What do you think you're doing?" Matthew bellowed, catching me as I collapsed. He eased me back down as I squeezed my eyes tightly shut to stop the room spinning, holding me close until the frantic caged bird of my heart accepted captivity and settled to a regular beat.

"You said I'm a 'complication'; I wanted to make your life less complicated," I protested weakly against his chest, not daring to open my eyes.

"*Life's* complicated, Emma, not you – never you."

I heard him, but I didn't believe him, and I attempted to pull away from the very arms I longed to feel around me. He didn't hold me because he wanted me, but because I needed him to, and that wasn't a good enough reason. He let me go, but instead trapped my face between his hands and made me look at him.

"Don't you ever do that again, do you hear me? Don't – no matter what happens – don't try and leave. Promise me – *say* it, Emma."

I watched the changing light in his eyes – the blue shifting between indigo and navy, the colour intensified by the dark ring that circled the irises – and I understood and accepted that he did want me and that something existed between us after all.

"I promise," I said in a small voice.

The tension dissolved and his face softened as he leaned closer, the world becoming just the two of us. "Don't ever leave me," he whispered into my hair. I heard the hidden desperation in his voice; I felt it in my soul. I turned my head, our lips almost touching.

"I can't," I confessed.

Slowly he brought his mouth to mine and kissed me.

Two things happened simultaneously. First, someone lit a thousand firecrackers, their searing heat expanding until my whole body exploded in flame. Second, I drew back in shock, my eyes wide and staring. Instantly, he withdrew.

"I apologize, I shouldn't have done that."

"No – yes... yes, you should!" I stammered. "But... but you... your lips... they're different."

He grimaced bitterly. "As I said, I shouldn't have done that."

"No, Matthew, please..." I tried to reach up to touch him, to feel his lips, but the stitches in my arm stung as they pulled and he stopped me, resting my arm back on the pillow.

"I'm sorry," he said again.

I shook my head in frustration. "There's so much about you I don't understand... your eyes look as if they're on fire sometimes, and your lips – well, they *tingle*... and I've never seen you eat, and you haven't slept in days..."

He smiled bleakly. "Would you believe me if I said I have a slow metabolic rate?"

"No."

"Can you just accept I'm a freak of nature, then?"

"If you are, then I wish there were more like you."

"Ah, Emma, *I* wish..." He laughed grimly. "No, it doesn't matter. Do I disgust you?"

Genuinely taken aback, I asked, "What sort of question is *that*? You must know you don't!"

He looked puzzled. "But... you recoiled."

"Not because I didn't like it – like *you*; it was a surprise, that's all – in more ways than one."

"So, not like anyone else who's kissed you, then?" I caught a note of jealousy in his voice, which I liked.

"No, it wasn't, but as I've only kissed one other man, there's not much with which to compare it." I looked up at him from beneath my eyelashes. "And anyway, it's difficult to judge after only one kiss."

"Does that mean you'll be willing to give it another go?" he said, his voice husky, beguiling, his mouth once again only inches from mine. I couldn't take my eyes from his.

"I think it only right – in the interests of science and a fair test... and all that."

His smile broadened and, cradling my head in his hands, he kissed me carefully, thoughtfully. My whole being reacted and I responded, feeling the energy of his lips on mine.

He pulled back suddenly, leaving me dazed. There was a knock on the door. He dropped his hands from my face and we stared at each other for a long moment, before he rose reluctantly to open it.

Ellie Lynes walked into the room with restrained grace.

"Hi, Matthew, I looked in on the med centre to see how Dr D'Eresby's doing but Ada said she was gone." We didn't miss the tad of an accusation. Bright, intelligent eyes fixed on me. "Hi, Dr D'Eresby, how are you?"

"Hello, Ellie. I'm much better, thanks."

"I came by to see if I could do anything for you."

Looking at her properly for the first time, I saw she had the same fine bone structure as her brother and uncle, and a quiet beauty, but her manner seemed uncompromising – almost hard – a coolness I found disconcerting. Very focused and direct, she lacked her uncle's bedside manner, which – given what he had been doing a minute before – was probably just as well. With Matthew's kiss still very much in the forefront of my mind, my body buzzed with the memory and I wondered if it showed.

"That's very kind... I don't think so, but thank you for asking."

"Matthew, are you coming back home any time soon? Grandad wanted to know."

It was a perfectly innocent question but one with layers of connotation attached to it, if not a smidgen of resentment.

"No, not yet." He held her gaze steadily and she looked away, but she flashed a look in my direction instead. I felt as if she dissected me in a few seconds flat, but I couldn't read what conclusions she might have come to.

"Grandad said he'll be calling you at some time," she said, making for the door. "Oh, and Harry asked if there's anything he can do."

"Tell him, 'No thanks, not at the moment.'"

She bid us goodbye perfectly politely, but as the door closed behind her, I felt as if a whirlwind had passed through, leaving a trail of unvoiced thoughts and suggestions behind in its wake. By the reflective look that passed across Matthew's face in the seconds after she departed, he thought so too.

He sat on the edge of the day-bed, his back against my hip, and I curled around him as much as I could. The aching set up again in earnest and I couldn't find a position where some part of me didn't hurt. The ache began to throb, swiftly replaced by a relentless stabbing. He placed a hand against my cheek, his thumb stroking gently upwards in soothing movements along my jaw.

"Time for some pain relief, I think," he said softly.

"How can you tell?"

He smiled, a tiny crease between his eyes as if he thought the answer obvious.

"It's my job to know."

He went over to where a bottle of fresh mineral water stood unopened, and poured me a glass. His answer was all very well, but I hadn't told him, and I had been careful not to let the discomfort show. It was yet another aspect of him that almost – but didn't quite – add up. He came back with the glass in one hand and a foil packet in the other.

I eyed it. "You'll make an addict out of me."

"I wouldn't let that happen. Your pain's at a level where these should be able to deal with it now, even if it doesn't feel like it at the moment. They're pretty powerful, but they'll make you feel drowsy."

He eased me up so I rested against him, neither of us minding the proximity.

"Tell me, are all your family like you?" I asked, suppressing a yawn.

"In what way – *like*?"

"Different."

"I've no idea – I've never kissed them like I have you."

"Matthew! You never give me a straight answer."

"Don't I? Here, take these, they'll take a few minutes to work."

But I wasn't ready to relinquish control of my thought processes just yet; but nor was I prepared to ask him all the questions I harboured in case he gave me answers I didn't want to hear.

"Don't your family need you, Matthew? You haven't been home for days… *no!*" A sudden thought struck me, and worry instantly outlined his face.

"What's the matter?"

"My grandmother!"

He frowned, not understanding, and I remembered that I hadn't told him about her since I left him in the cloister to take the telephone call from my father.

"My grandmother had a stroke a few weeks back; I need to phone my parents to see how she is."

"You won't need to," he said quietly.

I went cold. "Why? What's happened?"

"Nothing of which I'm aware, but you'll be able to ask your parents yourself soon enough."

"They're coming *here*?"

He nodded.

"How... I mean – who told them? Did you?" I looked accusingly at him.

"No, the Dean did; they are your next of kin."

"Oh no!" I groaned. "They'll think I'm worse than I am and they'll fuss. It's the last thing they need at the moment with Nanna so ill."

"Emma, they're your parents – of course they had to know."

He adopted his reasonable voice, which irritated because he was right and I knew it, but more than that, it reminded me of how close to death I had come. I huffed in annoyance and my side protested, a hot knife carving through my ribs like butter. Matthew offered me the capsules, and this time I accepted them.

"When will they get here?" I asked, as he placed the glass on the floor next to him before straightening to glance at his watch, calculating.

"Tomorrow – noon-ish. It's the first flight they can catch."

"But how'll they get here and where will they stay? They'll worry themselves sick over this."

"And you won't?" he chided me. "Stop fretting, it's taken care of." And he planted a tender kiss on my forehead, making my tummy squirm pleasantly. He stroked my cheek and I began to relax with the gentle rhythm as the medication started to take effect; I'd been holding myself tight against the pain without realizing it.

"And what do I tell them about us?" I said shyly, thinking that it was the first time either of us had used the term.

Us.

It sounded so together. You and me. Me and you. *Us.* I allowed a trickle of happiness to filter through, a feeling so alien, so remote that I had to stop and identify the sensation before I accepted it for what it was.

"What do you want to tell them?"

He drew his finger down the length of my nose, and traced my lips, distracting me.

How could I tell them, if it was still all so new to me?

"I'm not sure if I want them to know just yet; it'll be another thing for them to come to terms with. They're not very... adaptable." I shivered briefly.

"Are you cold?"

A little, but I shook for another reason. I didn't look forward to facing my parents – especially my father – at the best of times and now, even less. But Matthew didn't need to know that just yet, so I just said, "A bit."

"Your parents will think I'm not doing a very good job of looking after you."

He tucked the blanket around my shoulders, letting his hand rest by my neck. I ignored the bruising on my throat and turned my face to kiss his hand, feeling his skin beneath my lips – neither warm nor cold – igniting a thousand questions in my mind. His mouth curled gently into a smile that touched his eyes as he caressed my cheek with a finger, and all questions evaporated.

"I don't know where else I could get this level of attention," I said as I fought to keep my eyes open. His smile widened, and he bent down so close that his breath tickled my ear and I giggled sleepily.

"I doubt that what I can offer would be covered by medical insurance," he murmured in reply.

Chapter

18

Complications

LIGHT HAD FADED FROM THE WINDOW and a rising wind tested its strength against the frame. A stray leaf occasionally ghosted across the glass.

I slept a long, dreamless sleep without pain or fear to compromise its quality. I drifted into wakefulness, listening to the sounds around me before opening my eyes. No clock was visible from where I lay, and time had passed without reckoning; only the empty space inside me told me I had missed a meal.

I didn't object to being fed this time, allowing myself to enjoy the closeness between us.

"I've been thinking…"

"That sounds ominous," he interjected with a grimace.

I pulled a face at him. "Let me finish. Perhaps it would be better – more diplomatic – if I go back to my apartment before my parents arrive; it might raise fewer eyebrows." *And questions.*

He considered my proposal for a second. "It's a good idea, but only on one condition…"

"What's that?"

"That you let me stay with you – purely to keep an eye on you, of course – nothing untoward, purely professional." I must have looked disappointed because he added, "Well, fairly professional."

The proposal required little thought. "It's a deal," I said, before he changed his mind. He cleared the empty tray onto the table; I hadn't eaten so much for a long time and I had forgotten the comfort of a full stomach. He returned to sit by me, pushing an irritating piece of hair behind my ear, and I watched him as every small expression on his face mirrored his current mood. He seemed happy at the moment, the deep sadness that once shadowed him now so well veiled it might never have been there at all. I wondered how long it would be before I saw it again, and then deleted the notion before it took hold and darkened my mood.

"Tell me about your family," he said, breaking through my gloomy thoughts.

"On one condition…" I demanded in return. He continued to stroke loose strands back from my face. "As you wish," he said, more guarded now.

"That you tell me about yours."

His hand hesitated, before smoothing my hair once more.

"All right, but you first."

A log spat in the grate. "My family isn't very interesting – what do you want to know?"

"Well, let's see, do you have any brothers or sisters, for a start?"

"I have a sister – Beth; she's older than me and she wasn't at home much when I was young."

"So, were you lonely as a child?"

"Sometimes, but my mother and I were close, so it didn't matter as much as it might have done. And anyway, I've always been good at keeping myself occupied; I was never bored – I had too many interests."

My ribs had a dig at me and I moved my hips gingerly to ease them.

"Are you OK?" He shifted away a little to give me more room to move.

"Yes, thanks, just getting comfortable. Anyway, my father was in the Army and away a lot, so it was just the two of us for most of the time. I think she found it more difficult than I did in some respects; she didn't have anything to distract her." I mused briefly. "Except tennis."

"But you did have something to absorb you?"

"Yes, I had history."

Matthew's eyes creased with amusement. "You know that's quite a curious thing to say, don't you?"

"I never claimed to be normal," I told him soberly.

He laughed. "Quite. Anyway, go on. Why did you become interested in history in the first place, you strange creature?"

"Well, when I was very little, my mother's parents came to live with us. We have quite a large, old house and I think it helped my mother having them there. Anyway, my grandfather was older than my Nanna and they needed the company as well, so it worked out all round." I paused. "Is this the sort of thing you wanted to know? It's not exactly scintillating stuff."

Firelight danced through his hair as he leaned forward and kissed the tip of my nose.

"I want to know *every* detail."

I let my sprites settle again before continuing.

"Grandpa and I were always very close. He was a historian as well – from Cambridge – and I caught it from him."

"Caught what?"

"The history bug – it's very contagious, you know."

"Obviously," he smiled, the corners of his eyes crinkling, making my heart skip.

"The town where I grew up is full of history – as is our house. People often say they can feel its history in its walls – or it might be the damp."

"You surprise me," he said dryly. I nudged his back with my knee, but regretted it instantly, his back iron hard; he didn't strike me as the sort of person to work out in a gym. I would have a bruise on my kneecap by this time tomorrow. With a slightly apologetic air but no explanation, Matthew began to rub my knee through the blankets for me, since I couldn't.

"Go on – so you were brought up on a diet of old buildings, history and the elderly – all very compatible. What else?"

"Grandpa used to take me all around Stamford..."

He stopped massaging my knee suddenly; I saw a flash of recognition in his face, instantly concealed.

"Stamford – is that where you come from?"

"Yes, in Lincolnshire – why, do you know it?"

"I've heard of it; go on, you were saying about your grandfather."

He started to rub my knee again, but abstractly this time, his mind elsewhere.

"When I was very little, he taught me about my family – taking me to visit each of the houses they lived in over the centuries – some in the town and others in the country – if they hadn't been demolished or redeveloped into a housing estate. Our families have been in the same area for, oh… *hundreds* of years, you see; we go back generations. We're related to most of the families in the area; if we were cats they wouldn't allow so much inbreeding. Anyway, when I was older – about nine or ten – he smuggled me into lectures at Cambridge. I sat in on tutorials, met many academics, read what his students were reading, until it all seemed second nature. He taught me about local history and all the families with whom we were associated, then wider historical issues affecting the region, then nationally and so on… Matthew?"

Wherever his mind had wandered, it wasn't with me in this room. I kept quiet, waiting for him to come back to me. He registered my silence after a moment, his eyes refocusing.

"I'm sorry, I was miles away."

"That's OK; it isn't that interesting anyway."

"Oh, but it is – very – don't stop."

I couldn't believe it held that much interest for him, but he concentrated on my face again, so I continued.

"Well there's not much more to it, really. Grandpa died when I was in my teens and I wanted to become a historian like him; I never wanted to do anything else."

"And your grandmother – his wife – is she the one who's had a stroke?"

"Yes – Nanna," I couldn't help the note of wretchedness that crept into my voice.

His face softened. "She's your last link to your grandfather, isn't she? In a direct sense, that is."

I looked away so that he wouldn't see how close he came to the truth.

"Yes, I suppose so. They were always around when I was growing up; I always knew I could rely on them, more so than my... well, they were just *there*." I faltered, my voice becoming thin, not knowing how to explain the tensions of my childhood. A gust of wind made the window flex and I glanced at it automatically. When I looked back, Matthew hadn't taken his eyes off my face, as if he waited for some great revelation, except I had nothing spectacular to reveal.

"My grandfather led me here – figuratively speaking, of course. It was his research into a document that hooked me in the first place, and he told me that the original is here, so of course..."

"You had to come and find it," he finished for me.

"Yes, and the odd thing is, when we met, Matthew, I knew I'd heard the name *Lynes* before, I just couldn't place it." I expected him to prompt me, but instead he withdrew his hand and let it rest on the back of the day-bed, so I went on.

"The Lynes were a family local to our region – my family knew them a long time ago. I had forgotten, but then I remembered Grandpa telling me once. Strange how that happens, isn't it?"

He became very still. "Coincidences happen all the time and it's a common enough name; no doubt there are Lyneses all over the world." Something bothered him – his tone had become dismissive and he wouldn't meet my eyes. I pressed ahead, instinctively knowing I followed a vein of truth, but not sure where it led.

"Yes, it is relatively common – but not very – and I don't believe in coincidence." I watched him carefully, but he was guarded now and he drew a cloak over his face, putting him beyond my reach. "Anyway, I can't recall exactly what he said, but what reminded me is your colouring – or your hair colour, to be precise – it is very distinctive. It's also regional, and it's *exactly* the same colour as Grandpa's."

His back stiffened. "So I look like your *grandfather*?" Perhaps I should have taken note of the edge to his voice, but in true historian mode, I sensed more to his background than he admitted and, like a ferret after a rabbit in a burrow, I wouldn't give up.

"No, facially you don't, only your hair – the colour of ripe corn, Nanna would say – blond, but with pinkish-copper in it. It's thought to be from the Iceni tribe. It runs in my family as well – the pinky-coppery bit, I mean."

He ran his eyes over my hair. "So what's your theory? You *do* have a theory about me, don't you?"

He sounded level and calm – almost too calm – as if he needed to maintain control. Now definitely on the defensive, a part of me screamed *Stop!* before I pushed too far, though what I might find if I did, I couldn't guess.

"Theory? I don't have one. It's just the coincidence of your name and your colouring, that's all."

From his expression, he patently didn't believe me, his calm almost icy.

"But you don't believe in coincidence, Emma, you said as much."

A trickle of apprehension ran through me again.

"What does it matter what I think, Matthew?"

"It doesn't."

He rose abruptly and went over to the fire, stabbing at it with a piece of kindling until the embers erupted in an agony of sparks. I said nothing as I watched his shoulders flex and spring with each attack. Finally, he flung the piece of wood onto the flames and came back to sit at the end of the day-bed, his striking face smooth again. His eyes searched mine, small flecks of fire reflected in them.

"Do I worry you sometimes?"

"Sometimes."

He frowned. "Do I frighten you?"

"No, not really, but I can't fathom you – your reactions to quite ordinary things are... unpredictable." My eyes widened as I realized what he had said. "*Should* I be frightened of you?"

I couldn't decipher the glance he gave me.

"No, of course not; I wouldn't hurt you."

He looked away and a lump of iron formed deep inside me where the warmth and security had been. Like an untuned piano in an empty room, my voice sounded harsh in the silence.

"What *are* you trying to say, Matthew?"

"I'm not saying anything."

"Precisely – that's the point – you *keep* doing this; you say something loaded with inference, and you then deny it means anything at all. *Ugh*, that didn't make sense."

I wanted to put my head in my hands and knock some semblance of understanding into it, but I couldn't, which made it doubly frustrating. He stared despondently at the fire, twisting the ring on his little finger. The note of desperation crept back in again,

"Emma, I'm sorry – I don't mean to; I'm not sure how to… deal… with all this."

"Deal with *what*, Matthew? 'Complications'?"

His face twisted. "It's complicated, that's for sure."

"Can't you just *tell* me?" I pleaded.

"I wish it were that simple."

"Matthew, it's as complicated as you want to make it!"

He drew a hand across his eyes, looking in that instant more vulnerable than I had ever seen before. My heart ached for him. Instinctively I stretched out my hand to touch him, too late to stop myself from over-reaching. An agonizing spasm shot through my fractured ribcage and I squealed in pain. Matthew's hands shot out, pinning my shoulders to stop me writhing.

"I'm OK," I gasped.

"No, you're not, let me look. I need you to sit up."

In doctor mode – professional, controlled – no sign of the strain was evident from only moments before. I clenched my teeth as he helped me into a sitting position, my breathing shallow and rapid. He lifted the thin T-shirt high enough to undo the strapping holding me together. Although decent enough, I felt exposed and bit my lip.

"Would you like me to get a nurse?" he asked, with a half-smile. I shook my head, managing a smile in response.

"I trust you."

"I'm not sure if you should." I shuddered as his hands gently probed my ribs through the bruising, screwing my eyes tight as he found the fractures. "No harm done, you've just jarred them. I'll strap them more tightly – that'll keep you out of mischief."

"I'm hardly in a fit state to get up to anything, let alone mischief," I panted, trying to draw enough air into my lungs. He didn't answer, but concentrated on circling the strapping tightly, his head almost level with mine. I resisted the urge to touch his hair, so tantalizingly close.

"Am I – supposed – to be able to – breathe?"

His mouth twitched. "You're all done," he said, carefully pulling my T-shirt down and easing my legs onto the day-bed. I began to shake, a scattering of goosepimples on my bare arms down to the dressings and casts. He pulled the blankets up and folded them around me. He looked at his watch, then at my paler-than-pale face. Snapping two bi-coloured capsules out of a foil pack for me, he held the glass of water until I could swallow each in turn.

"I haven't forgotten, you know," I said quietly. He raised a speculative eyebrow, turning to secure the clasp on his bag without looking at me. "I would like... no, I *need* to understand what's going on, Matthew – and there is something, isn't there? I don't know whether I'm coming or going most of the time and it's beginning to drive me demented. Being with you is like... like riding a roller-coaster, except I don't know where it's going." Deep frown lines appeared between his eyes and the muscles in his jaw contracted sharply. "And before you say or do anything, it's not right that I can't ask you something without you reacting... oddly." My head became slightly fuzzy. He still didn't look up. "So...?" I insisted, the wooziness now distinctly there, creeping in around the edges of my brain. "Is it so unreasonable of me to ask?"

He looked at me at last, unexpectedly dejected.

"No, you're being very reasonable, very patient – far more than I deserve."

My eyes closed without me willing them to, the lids weighted. *More than he deserved. Why?*

"How are you feeling now?"

His voice flowed through me like silver water, making it

difficult to catch and hold onto his words.

"Mmm, that's not fair – don't think you've got away with it," I murmured sleepily.

"I know," he said, his voice drifting into the distance until it faded altogether.

Incoming

"**M**ORNING!" ELENA SANG OUT CHIRPILY as she stood over me, beaming. For a moment I didn't know where I was. "Matthew said it's OK for me to see you this morning and I thought you might like some tea." A large mug steamed in one hand; in the other she held a small cactus in a bright-orange ceramic pot.

"You are an angel of mercy," I muttered, still groggy after the medication. "Where's Matthew?"

She pulled up one of the antique chairs and perched on the edge, waiting patiently for me to inch myself into a position in which I could sip from the mug she held for me without risking burning myself.

"I don't know – but he said he will be back soon."

"That's suitably vague," I groused and then remembered that he had been stuck in the room with me for days and he never complained. I felt duly guilty.

"Ready…?"

Elena let me take a few scalding mouthfuls, chasing away the remnants of sleep and making me feel much better and less inclined to grumble.

"And this is also for you." She proffered the cactus for my inspection. "When I saw it at the store it reminded me of you."

"What – small, stumpy and inclined to prickle?"

"No!" she laughed. "You are not small and stumpy! You are a survivor. Would you like me to help you with changing today?"

"Yes – definitely. And thanks for Mr Fluffy, here. He'll need to be pretty tough to survive with me looking after him."

The tortuous process took less time than the day before; it helped that I could lift both arms enough without pain radiating from my ribcage. Elena lent me one of her own capacious woolly jackets, easing the sleeves over my arms. At least I could wear my favourite soft-jersey trousers without any problem. I found it frustrating to be so helpless, with only the tips of my fingers devoid of cast or bandages. I remained dependent on Matthew and Elena for most things and, as I grew stronger, it became increasingly galling to have to ask them for help.

I lay back on the day-bed, puffing like a clapped-out steam engine but definitely stronger than the day before. Elena folded my towel and put it in a bag for washing.

"You know, Elena, you are such a good friend; you put up with all my nonsense and I always know where I stand with you."

"You think that? Oh!" She glowed, evidently pleased.

"It seems pretty one-sided at times, though; you're always helping me out one way or another, like now."

"Yes, of course, you are my friend. But you do much for me, Em; who else would listen to this *cra-zy* Russian girl talk all night about Matias? And you do not boss me, like I boss you, and you do not judge me. I do not know why you put up with *me* sometimes."

"Because *you* are my friend, even if you do remind me of my mother at times."

We stuck our tongues out at each other at the same time and laughed.

"What about your friends in Britain; you have friends, no?"

"Ye-es, I do, at least I count them as friends, but... well, oh, I don't know, yes, they are friends."

"You do not seem sure of this."

"It's not them, Elena, it's me. Sometimes I don't feel I belong; I might be with my friends but it seems like I'm on the outside looking in, like looking in a... a snow-globe – a great, big snow-globe, or through a window on somebody else's life; I feel more of an observer than a participant. Does that make sense to you, or is it crazy-girl talk?"

"Yes, you are a crazy girl – definitely. It is because you are mad about history, I think. If you live always in the past, how can you be part of the present?"

I looked at her awkwardly. "I'm more comfortable there sometimes – not always, of course," I added hurriedly, in case she thought that I didn't appreciate her company. "But there are no surprises in the past – or none that can affect me now – so I feel safer there. Does *that* make sense?"

Elena shook her head and *tsked* at me. "Does Matthew know you think like this? I think he will be very worried for your... your metal health if he did."

I laughed, but only partially because of her slip of the tongue.

"*Mental* health, I think you mean. I don't know, but I do think that if anyone would understand, it would be Matthew. He seems to look right inside me sometimes; he knows without me saying anything; he understands."

"Not your parents?"

"No! Definitely not." That reminded me: "Did Matthew tell you my parents are flying over from England today?"

Elena pursed her lips. "Will they be coming here? To this room?"

"No, I'm going back to my apartment. Why?"

"Oh, you know, people talk – they say things." She shrugged, busying herself with tidying things away.

"What sort of things, Elena?"

She seemed to be having a bit of a struggle fitting all my washing into the bag. She shoved the tag-end of the towel in before looking at me, as if weighing up whether she should tell me the truth or just a version of it.

"I think they say that it is not normal for the doctor to care for his patient in his own room; they say that you should be in hospital and that Matthew has... other... motives..." She faltered as I glared at her.

My blood boiled. "Well, they can mind their own *blasted* business! Who else would have done what Matthew's done? He

saved my life, and now people are *gossiping*? Ugh, it's pathetic."
I ground my teeth in rage.

"*Da* – yes, I know it is very, very stupid, but Sam didn't mean
to…"

"Sam? I might have known he's behind it. What's he done?"

Elena chewed her lip. "The police were asking questions
about Staahl and that night and about Matthew rescuing you,
and Sam mentioned that you had seen him a few times…"

"Yes – implying *what*, exactly?" I asked crisply.

She wriggled uncomfortably on the chair. "I think he
thought… that he said… that perhaps Matthew was jealous…"

"*Matthew*, jealous? That's rich coming from Sam. What utter
nonsense; what on earth does he think he's playing at? He's
making trouble – stirring – the stupid, *stupid* idiot. I hope *you*
don't believe it," I challenged her.

She looked taken aback. "*Nyet* – of course not, but it is still
good you are going back to your own rooms. It will stop the, er,
the… the…"

"Rumours?" Matthew suggested from where he stood by
the door, making us both start. Elena looked at the floor, scarlet
flooding her fair skin as she avoided his gaze.

"I'm sorry, Matthew, I shouldn't have put you in such a
position…" I started to say.

"I'm not," he said bluntly, "not for me, anyway; I wouldn't
have it any other way, except perhaps, you not being attacked
in the first place." And to my astonishment, he grinned. "It's all
right, Elena, I know about Sam; it's hardly original." He glanced
sideways at me, his eyes gleaming mischievously. "A complication,
perhaps, but then we're used to those. Your room's ready when
you are, by the way," he said, turning back to me. "Would you
like to go back before or after breakfast?"

I still fumed. "I think the sooner the better. We can't have
anyone implying that you might be *helping* me; that really
wouldn't do."

He chuckled and I saw he had changed his clothes and shaved,
the dusky-blue jumper and plain, open-neck shirt understated
and elegant. A blue-grey scarf hung around his neck, emphasizing

his shoulders; I found it difficult to remain angry in the face of such a diversion. Elena obviously noticed as well, as she cast furtive glances at him when she thought he wasn't looking.

A heady wall of scent met us as he opened the door to my apartment.

"I hope you like flowers."

The whole centre of the low coffee table had become a tumbling mass of foliage and stems. White lilies, with throats of deepest pink, filled the air with their rich fragrance, while blousy, delicate peonies – their fresh scent cutting the sweetness – balanced the perfume. It was an exuberant, extravagant and joyful celebration of life.

"Oh!"

Behind us, I heard Elena squeak as she came into the room.

"*Oh* good, or *oh* bad?" he asked.

"Did you do this?" I demanded. He nodded, unsure of my reaction.

"I *love* flowers, thank you so much." They billowed from my desk and, through the open door to my bedroom, another arrangement filled my bedside table. Elena stood with her mouth open in imitation of a fish; she closed it hastily.

"I will tell Matias; perhaps he will do something like this for me."

I laughed. "But Mr Fluffy must have pride of place. Where would he like to be?"

She put the pocket-sized cactus on my bookshelf by the window. "It will want only a little water and no food until spring," she said, doing her best imitation of a school mistress. "Like you." She went into the kitchen to find a saucer to put it on.

"Mr *Fluffy*?" Matthew queried sceptically, eyeing the beguilingly soft-looking ginger-grey tufts on the sturdy little plant.

"Mm," I said mysteriously; "it bears a striking resemblance to someone I know."

Elena returned with the saucer for the pot and then picked up the canvas bag. "I go now and get this washing done. I will see you later." She made for the door.

"Elena – thank you – for everything," I called after her. She waved an arm in reply as she closed the door behind her.

I looked up into Matthew's face. "Thank you," I breathed. He bent his head towards me, wrapping me in his scent, at once enticing, mesmerizing. I felt the touch of his mouth on mine, gentle at first, igniting the fire in my veins. Different it might be, but I wasn't going to spoil the moment by reminding him he had some explaining to do. He suddenly pulled back.

"What's the matter?" I asked, feeling his rejection. He saw the hurt in my face and gently lowered me into one of the armchairs.

"You're so beautiful." He gave me one of his strange half-smiles, caressing my cheek with the back of his hand, before standing up.

"So…?"

"So – I don't want to lose control."

"Would that matter so much?"

He exhaled. "Yes, it would."

He turned towards the mullioned windows without further explanation, the old glass distorting his reflection so I couldn't interpret the expression he wore. Across the landscape, vibrant trees were spotted with leaves clinging tenaciously to the otherwise bare branches.

"The sun's coming out," he stated flatly. A first faint beam of light stretched across the woodland, catching colours in its rays.

"You promised you would take me into the mountains," I said, a little subdued.

He turned back towards me. "Yes, I did, didn't I? I will – when you're strong enough." He pulled himself together. "Come and have a look in your bedroom," he invited, holding out his hand. He helped me stand, and I followed him.

The room was full of flowers, and a fire burned warmly. On the bed, a forget-me-not blue rug lay invitingly soft, its luxurious fleece like cashmere.

"I thought you might need this." He picked up a knitted jacket in a delicate sage green from the back of the chair, its sleeves wide and flowing, the sculpted bodice flattering. He held it up, looking a little doubtful. "I think it will fit; I'm not used to buying such things but it'll keep you warm." He brought it over to me. "Would you like to try it on?"

"Thank you," I said, hardly audible.

He helped me take the heavy, itchy jacket off and replaced it with the sage wool, its soft, light web instantly soothing my irritated skin, creating a layer of comforting warmth. It reminded me of cuddling with my grandmother when I was very young.

"It's perfect – thank you." I sat gingerly on the edge of my bed, suddenly tired.

"Breakfast time – hungry?" he said, disappearing through to the living-room before I could answer.

"Famished," I called after him, surprising myself. I glanced at my bedside clock, its hands ticking its regular beat behind a fern frond; already mid-morning – my parents would be arriving soon and I felt instantly nervous.

He came back in a moment carrying a tray with croissants and fresh fruit.

"I'll help you," he said before I needed to say anything.

"Thanks, would you like some?" I offered, but he shook his head and sat at the end of my bed while he tore the warm, flaky pastry into manageable pieces for me. I had enough movement in my fingers to pick each piece up without accompanying torment from my injuries.

"Are you looking forward to seeing your parents?"

I finished my mouthful before answering. "Ye-es."

"You don't sound very convinced."

"It's just that I don't know how they'll react; I think my mother'll be fine, but my father can be quite…" I searched for something appropriate rather than damning to say, "… hard work. He's very protective and sometimes he can get a bit much. He means well, I'm just not looking forward to the interrogation – you know, the *who, what, which, why, when* bit. I suppose it's a habit of a lifetime for him." I ate several cubes of melon and a chunk of pineapple.

Matthew picked up an escaped crumb that had found its way

onto my duvet.

"He was in the Army, didn't you say? What regiment?"

"He was a colonel in the Royal Engineers; then he did a spell in Intelligence. He retired years ago but he'll always be a soldier, he can't help it – it's in his blood; his father was Army too."

"And did you miss him when you were growing up?"

I ate another piece of croissant, chewing and thinking.

"I think I probably did, but then my grandparents came to live with us and I don't remember missing him then. He was never around except for odd times in between postings."

Matthew lifted the glass for me. "Why didn't you live with him on the Army bases? Couldn't you have done that – it's the usual thing to do, isn't it?"

"Oh, we did, or at least my mother and my sister did before I was born; I think my mother hated life as an Army wife – the endless social stuff, coffee mornings and all that – and she wanted more stability for me as well, especially when it came to education. My sister went to three different schools before she reached ten and it didn't help her one little bit."

"So you stayed in Stamford – in your house of memories?"

"Mmm." I finished the last piece. "It's my father's family home, so it suited us, and it meant that my sister and I didn't have to change schools." I tilted my head, surveying him. "Enough information to be going on with?"

"Almost. What about your mother? You said that you get on with her."

I raised my eyebrows; I hadn't said that I didn't get on particularly well with my father, or at least, I didn't think I had.

"My mother and I are close, yes. She always... how can I put it..." I stared at the crack crossing the ceiling above my head, "she always stood up for me, even when it was difficult for her." I shifted my left arm into a more supported position where the stitches didn't pull as much.

"Uncomfortable?"

"Getting that way; it's OK at the moment, though."

"I'll need to take a look at it soon anyway; have you finished?" He indicated the tray.

"Yes, thanks."

He lifted it off me and took it through to the other room. He called back.

"What did you mean when you said she stood up for you? Why did she need to?"

I lay back against the pillows. "Oh, nothing much really, but my father made it quite clear that he didn't approve of my career choice."

He re-entered the bedroom. "Why not?"

"He said it wasn't a *proper* job. It's not so bad now that I've a doctorate and a steady income; I suppose it makes it more respectable."

The mattress gave way under his weight as he sat next to me and I rolled slightly towards him. I didn't make any attempt to move away and he shifted so he could put his arm around me – an artless movement that set my blood racing again.

"Perhaps he felt jealous," he suggested.

"Of what?" I demanded.

"Well, of your relationship with your grandfather, for one thing. He saw you growing up, you obviously adored him and then, just to rub it in, you wanted to follow in his footsteps. That must have been hard for your father, don't you think?" He squeezed my shoulder so that I knew he didn't mean it as a criticism. I leaned against him, thinking about what he said.

"I've never thought about it like that."

I brought up images of my father during one of his ranting sessions, his face twisted, his thick eyebrows pulled in an angry "V", and I realized that what I had always considered to be fury might instead have been bitter jealousy.

"You don't happen to have a degree in psychology, do you?" I asked, half-joking.

"Yes, I do, as a matter of fact, but this stands to reason; I don't need a degree for it."

"*I've* never seen it 'til now, so what does that make me?"

"Too close to see it – and a biased observer – so it's not surprising. Anyway, I could be wrong."

"Yes, you could, but you're not – it makes sense. How many

degrees do you have, by the way?"

He smiled but didn't answer, so obviously more than would be considered "normal", but then he hardly fitted into *that* category anyway. I toyed with the idea of taking up the uncomfortable conversation I had been forced to abandon the night before, questions piling up like queuing traffic. But my parents would be arriving soon, and this time was so precious – these moments of discovery and wonder at a fledgling relationship, a new-born tenderness – that my questions would wait. For the time being, I felt content to love. He leaned forwards and took the pale-blue blanket from the end of the bed and pulled it over me. I snuggled under it, feeling safe and warm, and tried to ignore the flutter of nerves.

"What about us – what are we – what do I tell them?" He looked puzzled. "I mean, are we friends, doctor/patient... what?"

"You tell me." He tipped my chin with his finger and kissed me lightly.

"That's not fair, I asked first."

"Well, 'boyfriend' sounds..."

I pulled a face. "Asinine."

He smiled. "Quite. I could be... an admirer, date, devotee, *partner*..." I looked askance, "gallant, sweetheart, lover?" he suggested.

"You sound like a thesaurus. How about we keep it simple until we know how my parents react? Doctor/patient – *friendly* doctor/patient?"

"As you wish," he said, gratifyingly reluctant. He reached into his pocket as his mobile rang, He spoke briefly. "They're here."

He withdrew his arm from around me and rose from the bed, leaving the space empty. I felt suddenly abandoned. Encumbered I might be, but I managed to get my feet onto the floor without needing to pause to let the inevitable stabbing subside. I felt pretty smug and was about to inch to my feet when Matthew stood in front of me, blocking my way.

"Whoa – and where are you going?"

I objected. "I don't want to meet them stuck in bed like an invalid!"

"No? Well, that's tough, because it's precisely what you are. You've had enough exercise for one day; give yourself another twenty-four hours and I'll let you run a marathon – until then, give your body a chance to heal and stay there."

"I *hate* being told what to do," I muttered. "And I can't even read with these… wretched things." I waved my arms as far as I could, which they didn't appreciate one little bit, and I tried not to wince. He raised an eyebrow at me, saying nothing. I relented. "Oh, all right, if you insist."

He helped me get my legs back on the bed and I lay down more gratefully than I thought I would. He went over to the fireplace and piled more fuel on the burning embers.

"Matthew?"

He looked around.

"I just wanted to say… to let you know…" I shook my head, the words stuck. "No, it doesn't matter. That colour really suits you, by the way," I finished feebly. He replied by scooping the soft, high collar around my throat, and kissing me gently.

"Me too," he said, replying to my unspoken thoughts, and smiled into my eyes, which wasn't the wisest thing to do just before my parents arrived. He straightened the duvet, blanket and pillows, brushing my hair from my face. "Ready?"

"As I'll ever be, I suppose. Aren't you nervous about meeting them?"

He laughed. "As your doctor? No." He took the scarf from around his neck and left it on the end of my bed, already part-way across the room as a sharp knock on the door told me my father stood behind it.

Balancing Act

HE LOOKED EVERY INCH THE PROFESSIONAL AS he answered it.

I heard a muffled exchange of voices, and then my mother threw her bag on the chair by the bed as she ran to embrace me. Stepping back, she searched my face, taking in the pallor.

"Darling, you're all right!" she breathed in relief, the customary deep lines between her eyes lessening a little. "We've been so worried about you. We couldn't get here any sooner – we didn't know what to expect…" She pressed her lips together as her mouth wobbled with unspent emotion. "Well, we're here at last and everything's fine," she said bravely. I couldn't bear the thought of what they must have endured over the last five days. She wore her favourite navy-blue winter coat with the pewter buttons we bought together on a shopping trip last autumn, and I felt my throat constrict in response to the memory. I swallowed the tightness away and smiled brightly.

"I'm fine, really. Did you have a good flight? How's Nanna?"

My father walked quietly to the other side of my bed, where his stocky form partially blocked the light from the windows.

"Nanna is fine, darling – she's even a bit better, and yes, the flight was no problem too, so you don't have *that* to worry about either."

Out of the corner of my eye, Matthew raised an eyebrow and Harry grinned. My father's deep, precise voice resonated next to me.

"Emma."

I turned to face him, immaculate as always in shirt and tie and the fine, herringbone-tweed jacket he favoured; he didn't look as if he'd been on a plane for hours.

"Hi, Dad."

He inspected me, his eyes lingering on my throat and I brought my hand up to it automatically, pulling the soft collar closer around it with awkward fingers; he noted my defensive movement.

"I'm glad you are safe."

He leaned over and kissed the top of my head, the scent of his aftershave an instant reminder of all the greetings and partings of my childhood. I knew the questions would start at any moment and I wanted to forestall them for as long as possible, but first, the matter of introductions.

"Mum, Dad, you've met Harry already but this is Dr Lynes; he saved my life – twice."

My parents turned around to meet him, my mother's jaw dropping slightly as she took in his assured, refined elegance properly for the first time.

"How do you do, Mrs D'Eresby, Colonel D'Eresby. I trust you had a pleasant journey?"

My father stepped forward, shaking Matthew's offered hand.

"Hugh D'Eresby. How do you do, Dr Lynes; we can't thank you enough for what you have done for our daughter."

My mother meanwhile composed herself and took his hand between both of hers. "Thank you *so* much; I can't begin to tell you how much Emma means to us; we'll always be grateful to you. And thank you for arranging to have us collected from the airport by Harry," she added, looking towards the boy. "He was most helpful and it was so very thoughtful."

She visibly relaxed under Matthew's attentive smile.

"Not at all; I'm glad we are able to help." I caught Harry's eye and it was my turn to raise eyebrows at the massive understatement. "I'll leave you to catch up; I'm afraid that I'll have to change the dressing on Emma's arm later on; and she must stay where she is and rest, so I'd be grateful if you wouldn't let her tell you otherwise."

He inclined his head briefly, darting a look towards me and then he smiled and followed Harry as he left us to our reunion.

"Golly, Emma," Mum said, staring at the door as it shut behind him. I stared with her, wondering how long it would be before he returned.

"Is he *old* enough to be a doctor?" my father asked dubiously. "Perhaps we'd better get a second medical opinion from somebody more experienced; we can't take any chances."

Here we go, I thought. "Dad, for goodness' sake!"

"He's rather gorgeous," Mum still mused. "And so is his... Harry – what is he? Are they related?"

Dad had removed his gloves and he now flapped them intermittently against his hand as he spoke. "No matter how many pieces of paper this Dr Lynes might have" – *flap* – "and the Dean seems to think very highly of him" – *flap, flap* – "there is no substitute for experience. I think it best if we talk to Mike Taylor about this and see if he can recommend a *British* surgeon." *Flap, thwack.* I sucked my cheeks in annoyance and counted to ten.

"Hugh, darling, I have his number with me; perhaps you could give him a call when Emma's having a rest. It's in here somewhere." She rustled in her bag. "Look, here it is!" She produced her little blue address book. All-too-familiar exasperation took hold, boiling out of me before I could contain it.

"Have you crossed the Atlantic to see me or to question Dr Lynes' medical opinion? Yes, Dad, he *is* old enough to be a doctor – several times over, judging by the number of degrees he has, and yes, Mum, they are related – Harry is his nephew. Do you have any more questions, or is that it for now?"

I might be tired, but it was no excuse, I shouldn't have been short with them. Regaining control, I hung my head, not able to meet their reproving eyes.

"I'm sorry, it's not fair after everything you've been through; I didn't mean it to come out like that." My mother sat next to me, her endless patience rubbing in the fact that mine lacked at the moment. She carefully patted my left shoulder reassuringly.

"Darling, you're convalescent – we understand. Did we tell

you about our rooms? *Rooms* – it's a suite and very splendid too. Did you arrange it? No, you couldn't have done – the Dean, perhaps?"

Now that *was* an irritating thought.

"No, Dr Lynes did."

"Oh! Well... that is unusually kind of him."

"Yes, he is."

I didn't miss the implication inherent in her tone, but she knew better than to say anything further, not at this juncture anyway.

Dad sat on the chair next to my bed. "You must be highly thought of here too; the Dean spoke in glowing terms about you... and all these flowers; I haven't seen this type of peony outside of the Chelsea Flower Show." He waved a hand at them. "To go to so much trouble..."

I wondered if I still had a place on the wall of Shotter's study after bringing college security into question so visibly. I really didn't want to contemplate the Dean at the minute.

"Look, please – both of you – at least have a cup of tea and a rest – we can catch up later."

Mum gave me one of her motherly we-know-best smiles.

"No, we came to see you, darling, not a suite – no matter how wonderful."

She leaned over the bed and hugged me again. I caught my breath as my chest protested at the embrace, and her blue eyes widened with dismay.

"What is it? Did I hurt you?"

I didn't know how much the Dean had told them about my injuries and I hoped to play them down. I let the stabbing subside before speaking.

"I'm just a bit sore, that's all; nothing to worry about."

"Let me get the doctor back for you, darling," she said anxiously. I shook my head, tempted though I was. "Then how about that cup of tea? You have a kitchen, don't you?"

I nodded. Gingerly she patted my plastered hand and went in search of tea as the quickest form of resuscitation and a cure for all ills.

My father pulled the chair close to the bed, sandy-grey eyebrows – stolen from a hamster – locked in their normal glowering position. "Mr Fluffy", Beth and I used to call him as children, because he was anything but. I never thought of him as ever being a young man, just old and gruff and grey. My shoulders tensed in anticipation. He lowered his voice.

"You've been in the wars a bit, haven't you? The Dean didn't tell me much; I had the impression he wasn't too happy with the attack taking place on his turf. Do you want to fill me in before your mother gets back?"

I found myself telling him an abbreviated version, emphasizing Matthew's part in it, but I didn't tell him about what Staahl had said, or the insinuations the detectives made.

Quiet when I finished, he regarded me thoughtfully. In the kitchen my mother poured boiling water into the only mugs I possessed.

"Do you know what's going to happen to this... Staahl? Is he going to trial?"

"I don't know – I don't know how the system works out here, but his mental state's being assessed at the moment and I suppose they have to wait for the results first."

"I doubt they have the death penalty in this state – more's the pity – but from what you've described, it should be a cut-and-dried case."

I remembered the detectives' questions and Sam's jealous meddling, and certainly hoped so.

Rattling mugs on a tray warned us that my mother approached hearing range. She waited until Dad cleared a space before setting them down on my bedside table.

"Have you told your father everything you don't want me to know?" she asked cheerfully. I should have known better than to underestimate her.

He *humphed*. "Yes, she has. Would you like Emma's version or mine?"

So long had it been since I'd heard his droll sense of humour, I forgot he possessed one.

"Emma's, I think – I can always tell when she's not telling the truth – and don't edit too much, darling, or I won't believe you."

I left in enough detail to make it believable while she listened intently. My father remained quiet throughout my rendition, although he would recognize the bits I left out. Neither knew how close I had come to death – I could barely believe it myself – although I think Dad probably guessed.

"Well," she said when I finished, "all I can say is that it's a good thing Dr Lynes was there."

Her face impassive, she rose and went into the kitchen. I heard the tap running, then the *clink* of a glass on metal as she filled it, and then she came back a few moments later, a wan smile in place. She changed the subject.

"Beth sends her love, by the way, and the children. They're all fine, but Archie's teething, poor little man. You should see how he's changed, darling, but I expect you'll see for yourself soon enough."

I threw her a look but she picked up her mug of tea, oblivious to my sudden pang of guilt as I acknowledged to myself that I would rather stay in the States near Matthew than see my baby nephew over Christmas. I hadn't seen much of my sister recently, and her three children must have grown since I last saw them. The twins would be getting excited about Christmas around now, making lists and dropping hints like confetti.

Mum proceeded to tell me all the gossip from home, a swirling mass of people and places I had known all my life, images flooding into my head like a snowstorm of colours and faces. All the while Dad continued to observe me as Mum chatted away. At last there was a pause in the conversation.

"Have you thought about what you are going to do over the next few weeks?" he asked.

"No, not yet," I answered truthfully.

Mum put her hot mug down. "You'll come home, won't you, darling? You need nursing."

I felt evasive. "I haven't thought about it; I might do, I'll see."

Dad's eyebrows glowered. "You need to be with your family, Emma, not here with strangers."

I heard the authoritative tone I had come to loathe creep into his voice. I took a deep breath, before answering evenly.

"I'll think about it."

A double knock on the door came as a welcome interruption.

"Good afternoon," Matthew said as he followed Dad into the room. "Emma, I need to have a look at your arm."

Although he had been gone for only a short while, it was the longest we had been apart for almost a week. He moved to my side, and I lifted my arm as far as I could without it hurting; my ribcage throbbed instead. Matthew took the weight of my arm in one hand.

"Are your ribs troubling you again?"

I nodded, quizzing him with a look because I thought I had hidden the discomfort convincingly enough.

"I'll sort that out in a minute." He turned to my parents. "You might prefer to wait in the other room," he suggested.

"We'll stay, thank you," my father stated; I felt like an exhibit in a sideshow, but I thought it more likely Dad wanted to gauge Matthew's competence first hand – not that he knew a thing about medicine.

Matthew carefully peeled back the dressing, revealing the long, livid laceration running from my wrist to half-way up my forearm. The bruising, while still distinctly recognizable as finger-marks, had evolved into a lurid, violent mass of blue and purple, black and green, turning yellow at the edges. My mother gasped, clamping a hand over her mouth, staring. She turned her head away.

"Please go into the other room, Mum, it won't help you seeing this. Dad, *please…*"

I looked at him imploringly and he rose wordlessly and guided her through to the adjoining room. Matthew swiftly kissed me, taking me by surprise before my father returned and I could react; but he was too preoccupied to notice the heightened colour in my cheeks.

"Will there be any long-term damage?" he asked tightly, a grey cast to his face.

"There shouldn't be. Emma's healing very well – better than might be expected – but I'm keeping an eye on this area here." Matthew pointed to where the wound ran close by a tendon. "There might be some loss of movement in this finger," he gently pressed my central digit, "but it's too soon to tell."

He concentrated on swabbing the area, so perhaps he didn't see my father's alarm.

Dad stared fixedly at my arm, clenched fists by his side.

"I want the best treatment there is for my daughter," he said gruffly, with barely concealed emotion.

"Of course," Matthew said quietly.

"No, I don't think you understand, Doctor; I mean I want the *best* – whatever it takes, whoever it is."

My father could be as subtle as a bus. Matthew didn't answer, but his eyes met mine briefly.

"Dad, please," I warned him. "I don't think I could have anyone better than Dr Lynes; leave it."

"But I don't want you ending up... damaged," he insisted.

"She won't be," Matthew said flatly. He redressed the wound and started to wind a fresh bandage around it.

"Can I have more of my fingers free of the bandage, please?" I asked him.

"No, not yet; I want to keep them immobilized for the time being – at least until the stitches are out."

Mum stood at the bedroom door; she had taken off her coat and her hands curled around her mug of tea to warm them. The worry lines were back again – deep ridges of anxiety worn into her brow.

"Dr Lynes, how long will that be?"

Matthew glanced up at her. "At least two – perhaps three – weeks, depending on how well Emma continues to heal."

"And what about her broken arm and her ribs; how long will they take to mend?"

"About five weeks."

"So Emma will need nursing, won't she?"

I suddenly saw where her thought processes were leading but it was too late to warn him.

"To a degree, yes – at least initially."

He didn't know my mother as well as I did and he walked right into her trap.

My father stood up. "That's settled, then; Emma will come home with us where we can look after her."

Matthew remained mute, but his eyes darkened perceptibly. In danger of being coerced into agreeing to a decision beyond my control, I felt like an animal cornered and at bay.

"*NO!*"

Surprised, they all looked at me. My words stumbled as I fought off silly, nonsensical panic.

"I can't go home – not if Ma… Dr Lynes is the best person to look after me… after my arm."

"I'm sure he isn't the only doctor who can look after you, darling, are you, Dr Lynes? We know a super doctor at home, don't we?" My mother soothed, coming over to me and putting her hand on my shoulder. Not wanting to be pacified, I shook her off more roughly than I intended, sending my ribs into spasm.

"Yes – he – *is*," I managed.

Sensing my vulnerability, Dad moved to stand by the end of my bed where he employed his favourite military tactic of a pincer-movement, with my mother forming the other line of attack.

"Emma, there's no need to get upset; I'm sure something can be worked out. The most important thing is that you get well, and I'm sure you realize that the best place for you to do so is at home where you belong."

I bolted my eyes shut against the pain and his persistence; he would keep on and on until he wore me down and I gave in. I felt Matthew's hand on the back of my neck; I opened my eyes and his face was close.

"Here, take these."

He held two of the bi-colour capsules in his other hand, and I took them from him with the tips of my shaking fingers, swallowing each in turn while he held a glass of water to my lips. He looked steadily into my eyes and I knew *exactly* what he was doing.

"Thank you," I acknowledged gratefully, then to my parents, "I've decided to stay here." Invisibly, beneath my hair, Matthew stroked the back of my neck – gentle, comforting – as Dad leaned on the foot-rail of my bed, his heavy shoulders hunched forward, emphasizing his bullish temperament.

"Don't be ludicrous, Emma, that's childish. Look at you – you can't possibly stay here in this state; who would look after you? And you certainly can't look after yourself – you've demonstrated that clearly enough. We'll book a flight for you and you *will* come back with us."

I bit my lip in frustration, adolescent ire threatening to break through the surface of my control. Mum patted my leg as she did our old cat at home when he needed a bit of love and attention.

"It *is* for the best, darling; we can look after you and then you will be fully recovered for the new term. I'm sure the Dean won't mind you finishing the term early in the circumstances. What do you think, Dr Lynes? Emma would be better off at home, wouldn't she?"

The light pressure of his finger at the base of my skull took the edge off my anger and the end of her sentence became blurry as the medication started to take effect.

"I believe that the decision should be Emma's alone, but if she wishes to stay here, I will ensure she has all the care she needs to make a full recovery."

There was something in his voice that made Mum take note because her eyes flicked between his seemingly stationary hand and my face and, through the rapidly encroaching fog, I saw realization dawn on her worn, tired face.

She sat knitting in the chair by the window when I woke some hours later. She had changed and looked rested, the dark circles under her eyes less pronounced. I watched her for a few minutes before she noticed.

"With everything that's happened, I'm so behind getting this jersey done for Archie and he's growing so quickly. What do you think, darling?" Mum held it up for me to see.

"It's lovely, Mum; I'm sure it'll fit."

"I'm making it longer, just in case; I have enough wool." She put the little jumper down and smiled reprovingly. "Emma, you should have told me."

We were alone; the clock said it was past seven and someone had drawn the curtains against the cold of the night.

"Your father's asleep and Dr Lynes said he will be back in the morning. You should have told me about him, darling," she repeated.

I inched my way into a more upright position, feeling dopey around the edges, and she came and plumped up the pillows behind me.

"There's nothing much to tell."

My mouth felt dry from the after-effects of the medication and I looked for the glass that normally sat by my bed.

"I'll get you a cup of tea; you didn't have that last one."

She touched my arm lightly and went next door; I heard the tap run, then a click as she put the kettle on. She came back in, drying her hands on a tea-towel draped over her shoulder.

"Well, darling, at least tell me what there is to know – unless you've a reason not to, of course; but *please* don't tell me it's nothing because I saw the way he looked at you, and you can't tell me that you want to stay here because of his superior surgical skills."

My neck tickled where the knife had pierced it and I used the tips of my fingers to scratch at the healing scab.

"Mum, there really isn't much to tell."

"All these beautiful flowers are from him, aren't they?" she said, stroking the pink-laced throat of a lily.

"Yes."

"Then you *do* have something to tell – before your father wakes up – unless you want him to know also."

There wasn't much point in evasion now.

"We get on well – I like him – he's different."

She gave me one of her very effective withering looks that said she was nobody's fool.

"He's very good-looking, I grant you, but you've hardly been here five minutes, and what do you know of him? Does he have children? Has he been married? Divorced?"

"Please, Mum, don't do the third degree on me; I get enough of that from Dad as it is." Contrite, she smiled, and I relented. "He's widowed and he doesn't have any children, but – apart from meeting his niece and nephew – I don't know anything more about his family."

"Well, isn't that a little odd? I mean, you want to stay here with him but you know nothing about him. I knew all about your father after our first date; I must admit that a little mystery would have been nice…" She allowed herself to be sidetracked for a moment. "However, that was then and me, and this is you and now. So where has he taken you?" I must have looked puzzled, because she clarified her question. "On a date – where have you gone?"

Never particularly forthcoming about my private life – even when so much younger and Guy was on the scene, when I could have done with some support – I found my parents' form of caring intrusive and, when it came to Matthew, I felt strangely protective.

"We haven't gone anywhere; he's been too busy saving my life and looking after me and… oooh, do you know what I fancy more than anything else right now?"

"What, darling?"

"A shower. A shower and to wash my hair, please."

I edged out of bed, gratified to find my legs not as wobbly as earlier in the day.

"All right, no more questions; you always were such a stubborn child," Mum said fondly, remaking my bed as I left it.

"I'd prefer *determined*," I said over my shoulder as I reached the bathroom.

Of course, wanting a shower and getting one were two entirely different things. Even switching the wretched thing on was nigh on impossible. I couldn't get enough purchase with the useable bits of my fingers, so I tried to use my chin instead, and managed to get a cold dribble of water down my neck. I admitted defeat and asked for help. I ended up compromising by kneeling in a few inches of warm, soapy water in the bath. Afterwards, Mum made a valiant attempt to wash my hair using the shower attachment as I knelt by the bath, with several towels wrapped around me trying to keep my dressings dry. She said nothing as she worked on the remnants of dried blood, evident as it coloured the water briefly rust-brown before it flowed away and out of sight.

"This reminds me of when you were very young," she said a little wistfully. "Do you remember breaking your leg and I had to do everything for you?"

I laughed. "Yes – but I was six years old; there's a slight difference, you know."

"Yes, I know, but I still like looking after you – it's a mother's privilege."

I understood what she was trying to say and, as she wrapped my hair in a big towel, I kissed her warm, softly creased cheek.

"Thanks for coming – especially with Nanna being ill – and I'm sorry if I've just added to what you have to deal with at the moment; but you can see I'm well looked after here. Please help me with Dad; I don't want to argue."

She smiled softly. "As long as you're all right, I think I can cope with anything – including your father. As for Nanna, I know it's part of the natural order of things, darling, but just when I think I've almost come to terms with it, I remember how we were when Grandpa died and I know it's going to be hard. But she wants to go, so I'm trying to be positive for her sake. You know," she tilted her head on one side and her smile became reflective, "Dr Lynes' hair is just the same colour as Grandpa's – the colour of..."

"Ripe corn," we intoned together and laughed.

"Yes, I know it is, but don't tell him, whatever you do – it's a sensitive subject," I warned her, remembering his reaction the last time I said something to that effect.

"Like somebody else I know," Mum said, taking the damp towel off my head and squeezing the dripping ends. "I'll get you that cup of tea first before we start drying your hair. I suppose," she considered, "he'll be doing this for you in future."

I found it a very appealing thought, which occupied several

happy minutes as the warm air blasted through my hair. It was so loud that we nearly didn't hear the door over the sound of the hairdryer.

Mum came back with a tray of food, looking baffled.

"There's another two of these – your father's bringing them in. Did you order them?"

"No, that'll be Matthew; he tries to feed me, but I keep sleeping through meals."

"It's very considerate of him." She glanced at the flowers and the cashmere blanket. "I think that it shows a certain amount of commitment, don't you?"

I didn't have to answer because my father brought in another tray, sniffing the steam rising from the covered plate appreciatively. When it came to food, he was a bit of an enthusiast; a good rest and a full stomach would restore his humour as nothing else could.

Dad replaced his empty plate on the tray and centred it with engineering precision.

"I'd quite like to have a look around the college tomorrow, Em, if the Dean wouldn't mind. What I've seen of it, it's quite splendid."

I didn't think that the Dean would care two hoots what my father did.

"I'm sure he'll be delighted, Dad."

"After that I'll phone the airline and see about an extra ticket."

I bristled but he didn't notice. Mum collected my half-empty plate and stacked it with hers.

"We'll talk about it in the morning, Hugh; it's late now, let Emma rest."

Once alone for the evening, I went into the bathroom and did my best to clean my teeth as thoroughly as I could. I caught my reflection in the mirror: two dark eyes and a speckling of freckles against my pale complexion. I needed some fresh air – preferably of the mountain variety.

The memory of Matthew's scent – of the touch of his hands on my skin, his arms around me, lifting me, kissing me – flooded my body with a heat that spread to my face and neck like summer sun after a long winter. In front of me and despite the muted light of the single bulb, my eyes came alive with a light I had not seen for many long, dull days, and I knew that whatever happened in the future, I was compelled to make him part of it.

Chapter

21

Witness

ISLEPT FITFULLY, MY NORMALLY dreamless sleep haunted by images of identical faceless shadows whose only name was fear. And, like any apparition, when I reached out to push them away, they dissolved around my outstretched hand only to rematerialize behind me, insinuating, gloating – mocking my attempts to define them.

My eyes cracked open; something moved in the room.

A log sighed and settled as it burned in the fireplace and a piece broke free and fell, sparks snapping as it rolled towards the edge of the hearth. Matthew leaned forward from where he crouched by the fire and picked it up in his fingers, tossing the glowing ember back where it belonged.

I blinked.

As if he heard my eyes, he turned his head towards me.

"I'm sorry, I didn't mean to wake you."

I wasn't sure if I dreamt it.

"You didn't... Matthew, your hand..."

He came to me and held them both out, perfect and unscorched in the firelight.

"You were dreaming." He sat on the side of my bed and stroked the hair off my face. "What were you dreaming?"

His voice acted as a salve to the nightmare that hung in suspension, waiting to reappear as soon as I closed my eyes.

"I never dream," I whispered. He looked perplexed, but now with a touch of a smile. He moved me carefully, shifting so that he could lie next to me without his body touching. I ached to move close to him, but my duvet – trapped beneath his weight – might as well have been a wall between us. He lay his head on the pillow next to mine, his face cast into a moving play of pale gold by the light of the fire behind me.

"Tell me."

The reassuring timbre to his voice became irresistible, and I found it difficult to recall what frightened me only minutes before.

"Ghosts, monsters – all grey like mist. They were there but without substance and they wouldn't leave me alone, as if connected to me somehow."

"Staahl?"

"I think so, but I couldn't see his face."

"Tell me what he said to you that night, Emma."

He didn't refer to the dream, and an echo of fear accompanied the memory of Staahl's voice in the porters' lodge.

"He said I had been sent to him – that he had been waiting for me. He said something about monsters, about how I must wish that the stories about them are true. And he said that I was alone – that God wouldn't save me. But He did," I whispered, "He sent you. And over this last week I keep coming back to *why*? Why me? Why you?"

His eyes travelled over my face, my mouth, my hair and, with an almost imperceptible shake of his head, he said, "Sometimes things happen; we don't know why and we might never know the reason but we have to trust that they happen for a purpose. 'For my thoughts are not your thoughts, neither are your ways my ways.'" He closed his eyes and his voice fell to little more than a breath. "But it isn't easy; Heaven knows – it isn't easy."

I remembered the conversation in my tutor room as we looked at the posters depicting salvation together; I sensed then an internal struggle – I sensed it now.

"Like with your wife and the crash?" I asked tentatively.

I counted the seconds it took for him to answer. He opened his eyes but I found the look he gave me indecipherable.

"Yes, among other things – like my wife."

There were issues here he hadn't dealt with and I wondered

at what point he would trust me enough to let me into his past to help him because, at the moment, he kept himself locked up so tight that I couldn't see a way through. But this was something I understood all too well because I had yet to tell him about Guy. If we contemplated a future together, we both had secrets to share and, without that level of honesty, there would be no firm basis of trust. I wanted him to tell me of his own volition; I wanted him to *trust* me. Hesitantly, I reached out a cumbersome arm to touch the frown on his face, wanting to soothe it away as I voiced a nagging doubt.

"Matthew, I know it sounds silly, but I don't know what to make of you and I want you to trust me enough to tell me, and I'm frightened that... well, sometimes I think that I only have to blink and you'll be gone."

I waited for a reaction, but it wasn't what I expected. He brought his head close to mine, his mouth curving up in a slow smile.

"And what makes you think I could ever leave you, or let *you* go?"

I could hardly hear myself over the pounding in my ears.

"I... I don't know."

He lifted his head from the pillow and bent over me, his hand on the back of my neck so that even if I wanted to, I couldn't pull away.

"Emma, I don't want to lose you and I'll do everything in my power to keep you. There is no chance I'll leave; I'm tied to you in ways I don't understand."

I breathed him in, barely able to take in anything he said. His irises reflected the changing light of the fire as he leaned down slowly and kissed me, his lips brushing mine as if to taste them, continuing along my jaw, and stopping fleetingly under my ear where my pulse struggled to break free. He drew a deep breath, stopped, then kissed my earlobe and rolled onto his back and closed his eyes, perfectly still. I watched the firelight move across the plane of his face, then reached out and touched his lips with the tips of my fingers. He didn't move and, for a moment, I thought he wasn't breathing until his smile gave him away, and then I let my fingers trace the upward crease they made. I ran them along his unyielding cheekbones, then into his hair, soft in contrast, and I wished that more of my hand were free to feel him because it seemed that, like his mouth, his skin had a strange electricity – like a positive charge – that might have been no more than my imagination. Fascinated, I mapped out the faint marks of lines between his eyes, his skin fine-textured and supple and, as I did so, I became aware of his eyes focused on my face as if waiting for something. But I said nothing, and let my fingers find his neck, imagining they were my lips instead, and followed them down his throat, pushing aside his shirt to reveal the length of his collar-bone. I stopped suddenly and his eyes flared briefly.

I didn't mean to react; I hadn't meant to let it show, but the silver scar slicing at an angle across his shoulder took me by surprise. Tentatively, I put out a finger to touch it but he drew the fabric between us, drawing my exploration to a close.

"I'm sorry…" I began.

"Don't be." His face relaxed. "It was a long time ago; it's… irrelevant." He kissed me again, lightly this time. "Now, what is it you wanted to know?"

Caught off guard and unprepared, I said the first thing that came to mind.

"I want to know what matters to you most."

"You are quite remarkable," he murmured. "Of all the things to ask me! All right, well… my family," he stated; "and my work, and my soul."

I rested my head against him, listening to the steady beat of his heart.

"Tell me about your family."

"That could take some time…" I gave him a cautioning look. "Just don't say I didn't warn you," he said, relenting, and began.

"You've met Ellie and Harry: she's the oldest and Harry's the youngest of the three children, with Joel in the middle. Then there's their father – Daniel…"

"So Daniel's your brother?"

"Mmm. He and Jeanette have been married for almost

twenty-five years now."

"So he's older than you?" I paused when I saw the humorous look on his face and did a rough calculation. "Oh, yes, he must be; maths is not one of my strongest subjects, you see."

He chortled. "Evidently. Next, there's…"

"How old is Harry?" I interrupted.

"Nineteen, and Joel is twenty-two…"

"Harry looks younger."

"Does he? Well, then there's…"

"And how old is Ellie?"

"Emma!"

"Sorry – I was just asking. I like to get my facts straight."

"Ellie is twenty-three – nearly twenty-four…" He paused and raised an eyebrow. "No comment about that? No?" I shook my head mutely and he continued. "Ellie is a doctor, as you know, and Joel is in the Army. He feels the odd one out in the family – he hasn't followed an academic route like everyone else, but he has talents he has yet to discover and refine, and when he does… anyway, he's doing well. Harry's trying to decide what to specialize in at the moment, so he is still at home; he helps me out at the lab in-between times, as does Ellie."

"Isn't she very young to be a doctor?"

It had taken me that long to work out the maths; I hoped he hadn't seen me surreptitiously using my fingertips to count. If he had, he didn't comment on it.

"Ellie's completed her medical degree and is doing her residency now. She had certain advantages over her contemporaries that gave her a head-start, and she qualified young."

I thought by what he said that he had probably helped her with her studies.

"You're very proud of them, aren't you?" I asked, and I could hear the introspective note in my voice even as I said it. He seemed astonished by my question.

"Yes, of course. Isn't it the same in your family?"

My chest aching, I moved awkwardly to get more comfortable without compromising being close to him.

"I don't know, I suppose they might be; they've never said."

"I would be so proud of you, if I were them. Perhaps they've not been able to find the words to say it, or they have but you haven't been able to hear them."

He had the uncomfortable knack of cutting through all the rubbish and getting to the heart of the matter; he meant no criticism – implied or otherwise – just a statement of fact as he saw it. It still touched a raw nerve, and I turned my head away and studied the fire while the second hand of my alarm clock ticked loudly in the silence.

"Emma..."

My throat tightened, as years of suppressed grievance ruptured my little happiness and I didn't let him finish what he had been about to say.

"You saw how my parents are, Matthew; they mean well, but... but..."

He drew my face round with his hand so I had no choice but to look at him, and his eyes were full of understanding and tenderness.

"Yes, I saw," he said softly.

"Oh."

I felt sudden tears, then sniffled back a laugh, feeling very foolish.

"Would you like to meet mine?" he asked uncertainly.

"Who? Your family?"

He chuckled. "Who else?"

As he moved his arm to pull the rug around me, a glint of gold from the ring on his little finger caught my attention. Since it was next to the plain gold wedding band that served as a constant reminder of where his heart had lain not so very long ago, I had never looked at it properly before.

"What about your parents, Matthew? Won't they mind?"

"My parents?"

A fold of the blanket fell over his hand, screening the ring from sight.

"I just thought that it might be a bit awkward if I turned up like a waif and stray or something. I was under the impression you all live together."

I pulled his hand back into the light where I could see it more clearly, feeling a slight resistance in the muscles beneath my fingers. I didn't let go, and he relaxed.

"We do live together in a way, but we each have our own home: Dan and Jeannie in theirs – a converted stable block, Pat and Henry opposite in the barn..."

"Are they your parents? Do they know about me?"

"Let me finish or I'll forget what I was saying... and I have my own home. It gives us all our own space and avoids most of the internecine complications living in such close proximity usually entails. Then there's Maggie." He stopped to gather his thoughts. "Maggie is Henry's daughter by his first wife – Dan's half-sister; she lives in town. Alone. Anyway, would you like to meet them?"

Indecision must have been clear in my hesitant reply.

"It's a big step – meeting someone's family."

"I met part of yours today," he reminded me.

"That was on different terms, though," I pointed out. I turned his hand over so that I could see the head of the ring. In the shape of a shield, it wasn't a college ring but in the dim light as the fire burned low, I couldn't make out what it might be; it seemed very worn. "Do you really want me to?"

"That *was* the idea of me asking you. Will you stay for Christmas?"

I played with his hand as I thought about his proposal and he kept quiet, perhaps hoping I would say *yes*. His hands – long and fine-boned – were perfect for a surgeon, but quite broad across the palm, and strong-looking. I twisted the ring around and squinted at it, using the firelight to cast shadows across the engraving, making the lines stand out in greater definition. It looked like three little blobs – perhaps stars – two either side of a line in the shape of an upside-down "V", one inside it. Surmounting that, a lion reared on two hind legs: a coat of arms, the gold worn so thin that the band had been patched and repaired over the years. I looked up at him. He intercepted my question, holding his hand out so that he could see the ring with me.

"My father gave it to me when I reached my majority. I haven't treated it with much respect, have I?"

I inspected it critically.

"It looks older than that – much older. It looks like an armorial ring."

He stretched his long body, putting his arms behind his head and ruffling his hair so he missed my inquisitional gaze.

"My father always liked the past, Emma; he was always delving into family history, and I imagine he liked the thought of his son wearing something like this; it gave him a sense of belonging, perhaps."

"Does it help you to feel as if you belong, Matthew?"

He brought his arms down slowly, his eyes suddenly veiled.

"What is it about me that makes you think that I *don't* belong?"

I held his stare, aware he had tensed again.

"If truth be told, I don't know what to think but, if I had to stake my life on it, I would say that there's something... unfathomable about you. Whatever you tell me, I still don't feel I really know who you are. Maybe 'obscure' is a better word."

He gave a short laugh but it lacked humour. "'Obscure', that's a good one! This from the woman who lives in the past and is too afraid to look at her future!"

"Matthew, that's not fair!"

"Then tell me what you want, Emma, where you see your life going."

I didn't hesitate. "Oh, I know exactly what I want."

"What's that?"

"I want *you*."

He looked stunned. It wasn't the response I'd expected, although I hadn't thought that far ahead – it had just sort of popped out of my mouth.

"But Emma, you don't *know* me."

I smiled encouragingly. "I thought we were fixing that." He continued to stare at me, amazed. I puffed in frustration.

"I don't understand, Matthew; you've just invited me for Christmas; what do you expect?" He leaned forwards so I could no longer see his face; I didn't need to, the set of his shoulders said it all.

"Complications," he said under his breath at last.

"For goodness' sake! You're not making sense again; don't you *want* me to want you?"

Real torment lined his face, seeping through into his voice, and he could barely look at me.

"Yes – but Emma, I want you to *know* what it is you wish for; and you might not like what you find," he muttered as an afterthought.

"You see what I mean? Obscure. We're back to all those unanswered questions again, Matthew. All I can go on is what I know of you now – I can't second-guess the unknown and, if you won't tell me, what choice do I have? What *can* I do?"

He shook his head from side to side, trying to shake some sense into it.

"I'm asking too much of you…"

I had been on the crest of the roller-coaster, but now faced the steep descent on the other side and I wasn't ready for it. I knelt next to him.

"You expect me to accept you at face value and I'm telling you that perhaps I am happy enough to do that because, quite frankly, if it's all I can get of you, I'll be content with that – for the moment, at least."

His eyes flashed open, challenging. "And when you decide you want to know more?"

"Perhaps I won't – perhaps you're right, I'm just too scared to look any further in case what I find stops me from… from…" I glanced at him, his eyes intent on my face.

"Stops you from… *what?*" he prompted.

Bother, he might as well know. "From loving you."

There, I'd said it – something I began to think I would never say.

"You *love* me?"

Did I detect hope in his voice, or did I merely try to convince myself because it was what I wanted to hear?

"Do you really think I'd let you kiss me if I didn't? What sort of girl do you think I am!"

"No, of course not, but..."

"Can't you tell, Matthew? Is it so unlikely?"

Speaking slowly, carefully, he asked, "You love me even though you know I'm *different*?"

"Yes, ridiculous, isn't it? It goes against everything I've ever believed or done, or set out to do in the States. Talk about complications – I wasn't looking for thi..."

Without warning he reached out and caught me by my waist, his mouth seeking mine with an urgency that spoke of loneliness and longing, so no element of doubt remained between us. I lifted my clumsy arms around his neck and pressed against him, all caution gone. Pain broke through my consciousness and I gasped out loud.

"Matthew – my – ribs."

He immediately released me, his eyes wide with remorse.

"I'm sorry, I'm so sorry – are you all right? Have I hurt you?"

I clamped my lips together, waiting for the pain to subside.

"I'm fine – give me a minute."

I inhaled carefully, evenly. He raised his hands to support me, then dropped them to his side, fists bunched as if they alone were to blame, watching my face for every tell-tale sign of discomfort.

"Perhaps it'd be better if we weren't alone together," he said, almost to himself.

I managed to garner enough breath to force an objection.

"Don't you *dare* say that, Matthew Lynes; it's as much my fault as yours, and I won't be *broken* forever."

"Forever," he repeated. "Forever is a very long time." He put his arms around me again – this time hardly touching – and I leaned against him as I waited for the twinge to pass. He buried his face in my hair.

"I can't bear to hurt you in any way; you give me hope, Emma. It might not seem like much, but I've lived so long without it, I can't tell you what it feels like."

"You don't need to tell me," I whispered back; "it's mutual. You can make it up to me, if you want to."

His voice came back muffled. "What? How?"

"Take me into the mountains soon; can we, please?"

He drew back to look at me. "Is that all you want from me?"

I nodded, smiling bashfully. "For now."

He smiled faintly in return. "All right, it seems a safe enough scenario, all things considered. I have things to do tomorrow, so I won't see you as much but…" he put his finger on my lips as I started to object, "we'll go the day after, as long as you behave yourself and get plenty of rest over the next twenty-four hours. Yes?"

I wrinkled my nose at the thought of not seeing him.

"Fat chance I'll get to misbehave if you're not around…"

He looked serious. "Emma, is that a deal?"

Compliance seemed the only way he would agree to terms.

"OK, it's a deal."

"Then it starts now. Sleep time. Do you need any pain relief after your manhandling?"

I shook my head, blushing slightly. "Not if they knock me out like the last lot. You are staying, aren't you? You did say you would."

"I will – but over there." He indicated with his head to the chair in the corner.

He stoked the sleeping fire with new wood, sending a shower of sparks spiralling up the chimney before settling in the chair. Holding his scarf close to me, I lay down facing him, so that the last thing I remembered before I slept was his quiet face, still and palely watching.

Chapter

22

Lines of Engagement

J UST OVER A WEEK HAD PASSED since the attack.
Sunlight streaked across the lawns, colliding with the
college windows and breaking into shattered rays of light.
Frost lined every branch of the trees – every twig and blade
of grass rimed with transient crystals that shone in the new
sun. I yearned to walk on the lawns – to feel the stiff, yielding
blades under my feet, and sharp air clean in my lungs; but I had
promised to rest and behave.

Matthew obviously didn't consider me a suicide risk because
he'd left me a bottle of painkillers and a box of the bi-coloured
knock-out capsules next to my clock. Most of the discomfort now
was tedious background aching that nagged away, but by mid-
morning I needed something to take the edge off it.

Breakfast had been delivered and consumed and I craved
to get up. Infuriatingly dependent on others, I waited for Mum
so I could bathe and then change into something with buttons.
She appeared delighted to help, partly because she could mother
me – which I hadn't allowed for a decade – but also because it
reinforced her assertion that I couldn't care for myself.

The mobile phone Matthew had given me sat wordlessly on
the bedside table next to the medication and I toyed briefly with
phoning him. Mum saw me.

"Is Dr Lynes seeing you today?" she asked artlessly, my father
just behind her.

My skin warmed as I remembered the night before, and I

fiddled about trying to get my foot into a shoe, not meeting her gaze.

"No, he's busy today, but he's taking me out tomorrow."

Dad finished rotating each shoulder in turn, feeling the effects of the previous day's journey on his joints.

"Surely you shouldn't be going anywhere in your condition. Where is he taking you and why? Is it a medical appointment?"

I didn't rise to his confrontational manner; there seemed no point. I reflected that some of Matthew's tolerance had rubbed off on me, although how long it lasted would be anybody's guess. Long enough to see us through the next couple of days, then perhaps – with Matthew's help – I could begin to work out where the relationship with my father went wrong in the first place, and start to put it right.

"He's the doctor, Dad; he wouldn't take me if he thought I couldn't cope. I'm not sure where we're going – he didn't say – but I'm off for a walk around the college today; would you like to come?"

Mum picked up on the cue. "That sounds very nice. It will do you good to get out for a bit, darling – build your strength – and we would love to see the college, wouldn't we, Hugh?"

She helped me put on my sage jacket, trying not to see the yellowing bruising around my windpipe or the healing wound on the side of my throat.

"What a *lovely* top, such a delicate colour on you; I don't remember seeing this before; is it new?" She buttoned the collar so that it stood softly around my throat. "You do look a little peaky, though; are you sure you're up to it today?"

"I won't go far, Mum; I've promised to behave and rest."

Mum could cock an eyebrow that spoke more eloquently than a thousand words, and she did so without Dad catching on. My father shrugged into his tweed coat and picked up his leather gloves; all he needed was a swagger stick to complete the picture.

I took it slowly, but I wouldn't have drawn attention to myself had it not been for my father tailing every step as if I were a toddler just learning to walk. By the time we reached the cloister, the area teemed with students heading for lunch. Passing the door to the atrium, my mother stopped, peering through the glass panels.

"Where's this, Emma? We haven't been in here yet."

Reluctantly I stopped and turned around.

"No, we haven't – it's the atrium; you go in if you want to, but I think I'll find somewhere to sit down." My pulse thumped uncomfortably, and I turned my back on the doors, not able to look at what lay beyond.

"Darling, you're as white as a sheet! We'd better get you back to your room; you remember what Dr Lynes said?"

She squeezed my shoulder, concern lining her face; she looked ten years older than when I saw her last, standing in the doorway of our home, and I felt a huge weight of responsibility for the already considerable burden she carried. I turned my back on the atrium and shook myself free of the fear.

"I'm hungry," I fibbed. "Let's get something to eat. We can go to the staff dining-room for lunch; how about it?" I smiled cheerfully, hoping it would carry the lie.

As usual, it wasn't very busy, but I instantly recognized a couple at one of the tables.

"Hi, you two!"

Matias was up and giving me a hug before Elena could warn him.

"Ow!" I protested feebly. "Not a good idea, Matias, but thanks anyway."

He grinned apologetically; I had missed him over the last week.

"Let me introduce you – Mum, Dad, this is Professor Elena Smalova and Professor Matias Lidström, two very good friends whom I don't deserve but I can't seem to get rid of anyway. Like fleas."

Matias chortled and Elena laughed. My father looked disapprovingly at me, but held out his hand in greeting to them both, formality never far away where he was concerned. My mother shook their hands warmly.

"Thank you so much for looking after Emma; she's told me all about everything you've done for her, and I know she can be a handful..."

"Mum!" I remonstrated.

Elena beamed. "Ah yes, you know it is true, Em; you are *so* stubborn sometimes; I do not know how Matthew..."

I shook my head at her, hoping my father hadn't recognized the warning for what it was; her eyes widened in acknowledgment. "How Dr Lynes puts up with you," she finished.

Dad looked at me severely. "I'm sorry to hear that. I hope you haven't been giving the medical staff any truc, Emma; they are only doing their job and it's bad form to make it harder for them."

Behind him, Matias raised his eyebrows at me in sympathy, but Elena gawped at my father until her boyfriend tugged at her sleeve and she remembered to close her mouth.

"I need to sit down," I said weakly.

"Come and join us," Matias indicated an empty chair at the circular table, and I sat down appreciatively, all too aware that it meant inflicting my father on them, but eternally hopeful that he would be more interested in the food than in ritual humiliation.

Elena lowered her voice. "Where's Matthew?"

"Busy," I whispered back.

She cast a furtive glance at my father, who had taken off his coat, and now investigated the menu with an enthusiasm he reserved for such occasions.

"That *is* a shame."

"Oh, yes," I agreed, and we both giggled like schoolgirls because that was precisely how Dad made us feel. Matias passed the breadsticks and I cast my eyes over the menu, but the medication suppressed my appetite and even the lightest dish looked unappetizing. A figure passed close behind us, bringing a gust of chilly air.

"Is there room for one more?" said Sam in a jaunty tone, already pulling out a chair next to my father opposite me and giving Matias little option but to invite him to join us. Elena looked at me nervously as I stared fixedly at my table setting. "I'm

Sam, by the way," he said, as if we were all the best of friends. I could feel my father waiting expectantly to be introduced; Matias came to my rescue.

"This is Distinguished Professor Sam Wiesner."

My head shot up – *Distinguished* Professor – when did that happen? Sam grinned his old grin at me as if nothing had happened between us and, for a brief moment, I almost believed we could be friends. Matias continued as much for my benefit as my parents': "Sam's been awarded the Endowed Chair of Metamathematics, the youngest ever to hold the position; isn't that right, Sam?"

That explained the suit and tie, then. Sam looked smug, and Dad duly impressed.

"Congratulations, young man; so you are a friend of my daughter?"

There were times when patricide would have been too good for my father; I could see *exactly* where his thought processes were going. Unfortunately, so could Sam. He eyed me from across the table, and turned towards Dad with his smoothest tone – the one he used when after something.

"Yeah, sure, I'm a good friend of Emma's; we met very early on, didn't we, Freckles?" I shot him a stony look. "We've seen quite a bit of each other over the semester; perhaps she's told you about our date? How are you, by the way, Em? Now you're on your feet, we can get together again."

His words held a challenge and I ground my teeth, feeling anger and resentment swim dangerously close to the surface. Bristling beside me, Mum sensed it too, but Dad remained oblivious, liking everything he'd seen so far. Matias cleared his throat.

"I think we better order before it gets any later – Mrs D'Eresby, girls?"

I couldn't just sit there and listen to all this drivel; whatever the relationship between my father and me, I wasn't going to let him become a sap for Sam's entertainment, or his way of getting back at me. I pushed my chair abruptly back from the table.

"I'm sorry, I've lost my appetite; you stay, I'm going back."

I started to get up, but Sam was on his feet, leaning across the table.

"Don't go, Ginger; I'll bet *Dr Lynes* wouldn't want you to miss a meal."

I met his mocking eyes and suddenly realized that Sam was playing a game, and I couldn't leave him to play it out with Matthew as the pawn in the middle. Sam hadn't forgiven either of us and he meant to make life as difficult as he could. I sat down again and he looked as if he'd just scored a point.

Food was ordered, general conversation resumed, but I couldn't join in. I racked my brain for anything Sam could use against Matthew other than suggestion and gossip; but I knew all too well that rumour became a powerful weapon, bringing down governments in the past. All it took were a few well-chosen words in the right places and, on fertile ground, the seeds of doubt would germinate and strangle the truth out of existence. Sam had almost succeeded in duping me before I realized that his insinuation was borne of jealousy of Matthew, not concern for my welfare. This was a complication I hadn't anticipated.

Sam reached out and took a breadstick from the tall jar in the centre of the table. Biting off the end, he looked at me with an exploratory expression as if weighing up the odds.

"Well, Freckles, how about it – shall we make a date?"

My mother came to my rescue unexpectedly.

"Emma needs to rest as much as possible; her injuries were very extensive and they are still causing problems, aren't they, darling?"

Before I could answer, my father interjected, "That's not insurmountable, though, is it, Penny? After all, Dr Lynes is taking Emma out tomorrow, and he wouldn't do that if she wasn't up to it, now would he?"

My mother and I glared at him.

With eyes narrowed, Sam whistled through his teeth, a smirk the size of Westminster Bridge on his face as he leaned back in his chair, tapping the breadstick into the palm of his hand like a conductor's baton.

"Well, well, Lynes sure is a fast worker, I'll grant him that.

Think he's got your best interests at heart, Em? I'm not sure if the police department think so; I mean, why *was* he in the atrium that night? And why was he so keen to get you out of the med centre all alone, when..."

I rose to my feet before I knew what I did, blind with fury, my temper erupting before I could control it.

"You're *despicable!*" I snarled at him, enunciating each syllable with venom. "You're bitter, twisted, jealous and so intent on destroying others that you can't see what it's doing to you. You... you're... *pathetic!*"

Silence fell on the room, the only sound my harsh breathing as the voices of the other diners stilled. I didn't care; he had pushed me to my limits and, whereas I could cope with a certain amount of personal abuse, when it came to insulting Matthew, my tolerance was just about non-existent. I turned my back on the stunned faces of my parents and friends and tried to push my chair away from the table with my knee, but its feet dragged on the thick pile carpet and it fell over with a resounding *thud*. I gave it a vicious kick to get it out of my way, my chest complaining at the sudden movement. Matias pulled it away from me before I could fall over it.

"Emma, sit down; you can't behav..." Dad started to say, employing his military authority to bring me back in line.

I whirled on him. "Don't say another *word*," I hissed. He blanched and I finally escaped from the confines of the table and made for the door, accompanied by the whispered stares of the other diners.

I didn't care whether anyone followed me or not and I reached the end of the cloister out of breath and near to tears. Any residual energy kept in reserve was spent, and I stopped, leaning against a stone arch, and held Matthew's scarf to my mouth, recalling his face in the faintly lingering scent that clung to it.

"Emma... darling?"

My mother put her thin arms around me and I buried my head in her shoulder. She rubbed my back and I became a child again. Behind her, my father hovered.

"Sorry," I snuffled, aware now of the semi-detached interest of people passing by.

"You're never too old to cry, darling; that's what mothers are for – you'll find out one day." She gave me an encouraging smile and I gave her a watery one back. "Anyway," she added, "that man deserved what he got; he reminded me of Guy – pushy."

In any other circumstance I might have laughed at the expression on her face, but I just nodded. By the time I climbed the stairs to my apartment, I needed to lie down, feeling as washed out as I no doubt looked.

I lay back carefully on my bed and closed my eyes, blaming Sam for everything. If someone told me he was solely responsible for global warming, I would have believed them at that moment. The last thing I wanted was for us to become enemies, but he left me no choice and, if forced to take sides, it would never be his. In the idle moments between waking and sleeping, I ruminated that in those few minutes, Mum saw what I had failed to appreciate: the similarities between Guy and Sam. The all-consuming ego – the need to control.

A low rumble reminded me that I hadn't eaten lunch. I heaved out of bed, irritated beyond belief, and went in search of my parents and something to eat. They were sitting – one in an armchair, the other on the sofa – reading a newspaper divided between themselves and drinking cups of tea; a normal, domestic scene witnessed so many times before at home. Mum looked up.

"I've made you a cup of tea, Emma, and you must have something to eat; what can I get you?"

Two plates on the coffee table bore the remains of cheese on toast; Dad must have been disappointed not to sample the best menu the college could offer.

"Some toast, please, Mum."

I sat down in the spare armchair, rested my head against the high back and closed my eyes again. The newspaper rustled as my father folded it and put it on the arm of the sofa.

"*Hummuph.*"

I opened my eyes and he glanced back towards the kitchen, making sure my mother couldn't hear us.

"I don't know what that was all about at luncheon but I didn't like what the Professor insinuated. Did you have a… relationship… with this man?"

The word sounded uncomfortably modern coming from my father's mouth.

So there would be no room for misinterpretation, I replied emphatically; "No, I did *not*. Sam hoped there would be and he's not very good at taking 'No' for an answer. He's jealous and he's making trouble – that's all, Dad; there's nothing more to it."

"Jealous of whom?" my father said, quietly.

I mentally thumped myself – tiredness left me prone to making mistakes; I would have to be more careful. I rolled my head on the back of the armchair and looked out of the window; the frost had begun to melt, threatening to turn the world dull greens and browns again.

"Sam's jealous of anybody and anything. He's had his nose put out of joint just because I wouldn't go out with him, and you can see why I didn't, can't you?"

He eyed me speculatively. "You didn't lead him on, did you?"

I jerked my head upright, glaring at him, feeling my temper beginning to flare.

"Whose side are you on?"

He looked at me calmly. "Yours – you are my daughter but that doesn't always make you right. I'm trying to get a brief on one or two things and I didn't like what he said, or how he said it. What was all that about Dr Lynes and the police?"

"Arrant nonsense. Rubbish. Tripe. He's playing games and making trouble."

"Then I have to ask again – for whom? It seems that he doesn't like Dr Lynes; why?"

I fixed my father with as steady a look as I could manage and drew a deep breath. "Because Sam recognizes that when it comes to a choice between him and Matthew Lynes, there is no contest."

I waited for the inevitable consequence of such an admission – the questions, possibly the accusations that I'd withheld information.

"I see."

He said nothing more, eyeing me for a minute from beneath his shrubby eyebrows before picking up the paper again and disappearing behind it as Mum came in carrying a cup of tea in one hand and a plate of toast-and-cheese soldiers in the other.

"Elena's a lovely girl, isn't she?"

She put them on the low coffee table in front of me, steam curling like smoke from a chimney on a still day. I agreed wholeheartedly.

"Yes, she is."

"I had to cut the mouldy bits off the cheese. You're not looking after yourself – there's barely any food in the fridge; no wonder you've lost weight."

"Have I?" I looked down again as a growl of thunder rolled from inside me as if to confirm it. "Well, I haven't been able to shop for the last week, so it's not surprising, and I don't think Matthew's used the fridge; he orders things in for me."

I trapped a piece of toast unsteadily between my fingers and nibbled down its warm, savoury length. The action made the fracture ache a bit, but I was too hungry to take much notice. I started on the next piece and almost missed the exchange of looks between my parents. "Now what?" I chewed, swallowed and reached for the third.

"Don't be angry, darling, but we booked a ticket for a seat home on the plane for you." She held up a hand as I began to speak. "I know you have certain ties here but you have to admit, you can't look after yourself and it's not right to expect others who are not your family to do so, even if they say they are willing."

Putting the piece of toast back down on the plate, I carefully wiped my fingers on the paper towel that stood in place of a napkin. I spoke slowly and deliberately, making each word count.

"I'm very sorry that you have incurred additional expense on my behalf and I will, of course, reimburse you, but I am *not* leaving. I have no intention of leaving either now, or at Christmas. Matthew has asked me to stay with his family over the holiday and, as for looking after myself until then, he's done a pretty good job of it so far and I don't think he intends me to starve. I am staying. End of discussion."

I sat back in my chair feeling like my stubborn teenage self, but it clarified one thing: I would accept Matthew's invitation, despite my doubts about my welcome from his family; I would stay and cement the relationship we had begun, one way or the other.

"But darling, Nanna..." my mother began.

"But *nothing*, Mum."

Her face fell, and she looked at my father for support but, unusually, he remained silent. I leaned forward and picked up the abandoned toast and started eating again, a casual action meant to disguise my thudding heart. They had never appreciated how hard I always found it to oppose them – especially my mother. Dad made it easier with his head-on and bellicose approach, but Mum had long understood that the only way to get me to do what she wanted was to appeal to my sense of fair play and, failing that, guilt. It hadn't worked this time because I fought someone else's corner and not just my own. Last night, Matthew said I made him happy – no, more than that – I gave him *hope*, and I needed no further inducement to stand my ground. More to the point, with Sam playing little games around the edges, I wanted to be close at hand to field any sticky questions the police might throw up.

My father leaned forwards and swapped the main newspaper for the gardening section and started to read as if nothing had happened. I picked up the scalding mug of tea, balancing it between my two sets of fingers, and sipped it – making a point.

Outside, the sun settled below the horizon, its orange fire throwing the world into hot pinks and salmon, reminding me that we were now in the second week of November. Although the frost had lifted from the morning, the clear sky promised a repeat performance if the weather held. My eyes fell on the long window seat and, with a sudden jolt, I remembered that, concealed within the innocuous velvet, lay the evidence of my theft. I would have to return it as soon as possible before its loss was discovered, or rue the consequences and my conscience.

Once it was back in place and I was recovered and back to work – probably not for another couple of weeks – I would seek out the little black journal in the library where it belonged, and pick apart its history. Then, perhaps at last, I would be able to place it on a shelf of my life and get on with the rest of it.

Time to move on – new world, new story.

Chapter

23

Beyond Reason

In this last kiss I here surrender thee
Back to thyself, so thou again art free.

HENRY KING (1592–1669)

B Y THE TIME MY PARENTS ARRIVED, I was up, washed and dressed – determined to declare my independence. I didn't tell them how long it had taken, nor how much discomfort I had endured to get to that state of readiness.

Awkwardly brushing my teeth after breakfast, I knew of Matthew's arrival by the sudden silence that fell between my parents, followed by polite but restrained conversation. I finished my ablutions, all the while listening to the tone of the dialogue. By the time I left the bathroom, I had collected my thoughts and readied myself to greet him. He smiled when he saw me, his eyes reacting slightly in surprise when I stretched up to kiss him in front of my parents, all pretence gone.

"Well, good morning! Are you ready?"

"Uh huh – where are we going?"

"You'll all just have to wait and see." He imparted an unvoiced message in the steady look he gave me.

"All?"

He saw my disappointment as my parents picked up their coats and put them on.

"Let's get your coat."

He led me through to my bedroom, his lips stilling my

protestations as soon as we were beyond their line of sight.

"It's politic, my love, let it go – we'll have other days together."

In my wardrobe he found a quilted coat I didn't recognize and helped me put it on over my mummified arms. The soft fabric belied its warmth and quality. He smiled at my bewilderment.

"It's nearly winter and you'll need something warm to wear," he said as he ran the zip up to just under my chin, before guiding me back to where my parents waited by the door.

He took us down and across the quad, where the hoarfrost lay thick on the grass, an anonymous whitening of the world under the overcast sky. The ice gave way under my first footstep in a delicious reminiscence of childhood winters on the Lincolnshire fens.

"Do you like the frost?" he asked and I nodded, feeling free of the confines of the centrally heated world from which I had emerged like a grub from the soil in spring.

Only a few vehicles waited in the staff car park at this early hour. To one side, a dark-red car – the colour of metallic mulled wine – sat low to the ground, fast and dangerous-looking. I remembered seeing it before, drawn up behind the police car at the site of the crash. Ahead of us by a dozen yards, Dad admired it from the top of the steps, running his eyes appreciatively along its sleek lines.

"Yours?" I asked Matthew.

"Mm."

"It looks fast; now, why doesn't that surprise me? And you have me tagging along and holding you up; a snail would move quicker than I can."

"True," he admitted, grinning sideways at me, "but snails are poor conversationalists at the best of times, and I have an aversion to slime."

Cars held little interest for me but even I admitted this looked impressive. My father already peered through the windows.

"Isn't this an Aston Martin DB9? Is it yours?" he said, turning as we approached, hardly containing his excitement like a ten-year-old and looking years younger than his seventy-odd.

The car unlocked in answer.

"Mrs D'Eresby, please..." Matthew opened the passenger door and pulled the front seat forward so that my mother could climb in. He held out his hand to help her and she went to take it, but then paused, looking up at him with a little smile. She called to my father as he admired the high-tech fascia behind the steering wheel.

"Hugh, darling, I believe I'm really too tired for an outing today; I think I'll give it a miss. It was so kind of you to invite us, Dr Lynes; I'm sure a day out will do Emma the world of good."

Matthew bowed his head slightly in acknowledgment of her sacrifice, and she smiled sweetly in return.

"I don't know, Penny..." Dad began to bluster, looking longingly at the leather seats and the glossy instrument panel.

"Yes, but I *do*, darling. Help me up these steps, will you; everything is so slippery."

I put my arms around her the best I could and hugged her.

"Thank you," I whispered. She held me as close as she dared, rubbed noses Eskimo-fashion as we had always done, and sealed it with a kiss on my forehead.

"Enjoy yourself," she instructed, taking a step away from me with a smile.

Matthew put the low seat back in position and eased me into it before leaning across to do my seat-belt up. For a second, as he tugged at it lightly to make sure it was secure, I had a horrible image of his wife's body in the mangled wreck of her car, her life torn from her by metal and speed. I wondered if he thought the same thing every time he drove this beautiful, lethal machine. If he did so this morning, he didn't let it show. He went around to the other side.

"Colonel?"

My father still admired the controls from the driver's side.

"Yes, sorry, of course."

I couldn't remember the last time I heard Dad apologize for anything. He stood back and Matthew slid into the driver's seat in a movement as alluring as his car. Mum watched from the bottom of the steps with the same look she wore on the day I left home for university, almost wistful, as if releasing a bird she had nursed back to liberty.

The sense of freedom when we reached the main road was immense.

"How fast does this thing go?" I asked.

He glanced at a panel glowing demurely on the dashboard, the speed creeping rapidly upwards.

"Does speed worry you?"

The surge of adrenaline as the car accelerated, pulling me back against the seat, felt as physically exhilarating as that of our family's small yacht sailing before a summer storm, splitting the waves on Rutland Water, or of a bullet hitting its mark. I revelled in it, I lapped it up, I savoured every skin-tingling second of it until he took his foot off the accelerator and the car slowed.

"No, I love it."

He raised both eyebrows in a gratifying show of surprise. The car had reached the State limit without effort, and I settled back into leather upholstery still smelling brand new, with not a hint of a crisp or a crumb in sight and certainly no chocolate.

"Are you warm enough?" he asked me.

"Yes, thanks."

I managed to unzip my coat and loosen the scarf around my neck.

"That was very gracious of your mother," he remarked.

I remembered Dad's face. "My father was gutted."

"Since we're being politic, I think I'd better take him out to make up for the disappointment."

He tried to control a smile but I burst out laughing and he grinned, his eyes dancing a vivid, exuberant blue. He took my hand and kissed my bandage-swathed palm, holding it to his face.

"It's good to hear you laugh, Emma," he said softly. "I've missed the radiance you bring." He continued to hold my hand and I let myself bathe in the warmth of the moment – in this peace we had both found – each content in the other's company.

The road wound on a steady incline towards the mountain

range I saw on my taxi journey to the college that first dripping day and which had been a constant companion to me through the weeks since. As we climbed, frost was joined by pockets of snow lingering in the shadow of rocky outcrops and along the side of the road where trees whipped past the windows. He broke the silence first.

"Is that always how it's been with you and your parents?"

"Yes, pretty much. Do you get on with yours?"

He considered my question.

"My father was always very supportive when I was growing up; I don't remember having the conflict you seem to have with yours; it must make it difficult for all of you."

A surreal mist clung to the branches of the frost-laden trees, drooping boughs hanging heavy. I stared glumly out of the window; I couldn't remember a time when we weren't at loggerheads.

"Matthew, why do you always speak of your father in the past tense?"

"Do I? My mistake." He accelerated out of a bend and slowed down again before I could comment. "It must be force of habit; I referred to my youth."

"Mmm, so *very* long ago," I said, probably more sardonically than I meant because Matthew opened his mouth to reply, thought better of it, then said simply, "Indeed," and left it at that.

We drove for a little over an hour before crossing a bridge over the river and the road branched left into a narrow track bordered by trees. Tips of branches crowded, almost touching the car, thinning as we emerged into a flat expanse of ground. Spreading beyond a parking area interspersed with trees, mist hung suspended above the cold, grey waters of a lake. Roots reached out towards the water's edge, gnarled like snakes, branches inches from the eerily tranquil plane. The car drew to a standstill by a series of picnic benches a hundred yards from the shore. Nearer than I had ever seen them, the mountains rose steeply, summits obscured by low cloud.

The engine stilled and the silence of the waters reached inside the car until Matthew opened the door for me, and I intruded upon it. Cold air bit my nose and throat, sharp and clean with not a taint of humanity in the air. He helped me out of the car, zipped me up again snugly, and pulled the lined and quilted hood over my head.

"What do you think – do you like it?"

"It's wonderful," I breathed, lost for words, and he relaxed into a broad smile.

"It's the furthest I can take you today by car; it's usually busy in the summer – families and hikers use it a lot – but not so much in the winter, and not on a day like today."

"Do you come up here often?" I asked.

"Mostly in the winter and, even so, we prefer to go up there if we have the time." He looked up at the mountains with a voice full of a hunger I had sensed before. "And that's where I'll take you, when you're better, as I promised."

The mountains seemed a very long way away.

"We'll walk?" I asked, doubtfully.

"Probably not, no, although it's not as far as it looks – if you take a direct route."

It looked bleak, cold and inhospitable.

"What's up there?" I asked.

"Nothing – just rocks and snow, trees... wildlife. Nothing. Everything."

I gazed at the mountains; the thought of just the two of us alone in the wilderness was another world I could only dream of.

"It sounds *perfect*."

He searched my face but found nothing but sincerity there, and smiled quizzically.

"You strange girl." He leaned forward and kissed me gently. He must have thought the resulting tremor the fault of the glacial air because – taking my hands between his – he rubbed the tips of my fingers lightly.

"You're cold; I should have brought you big fur mittens." His hands were neither warm nor cold, but sort of tepid. He turned back to the car. "But instead I've brought tea."

He went to the boot, coming back with a heavy-looking woven

basket which he put on one of the picnic tables, unpacking a flask and some cups. I laughed.

"You brought a picnic!"

"I thought you might get hungry and thirsty," he explained, looking a little awkward.

"It's a brilliant idea; we always used to have picnics at home when Grandpa was alive," I said with genuine enthusiasm. I felt a smidgen hypocritical as I tried not to remember the last picnic I'd been invited on; after Sam's performance yesterday, he didn't deserve my sympathy.

"There should be everything you need in there." Matthew's fair head gleamed in the low winter light as he peered in and reached for a flask.

"Do you get bears up here?" I asked, reading a sign by the table depicting a bear, with items of food scored through with a line.

"In spring and summer mostly – sometimes early fall – but food's been abundant recently so they're not a problem now; they'll be in their dens."

He twisted the lid off the flask and poured a half-mug of tea, waiting until I held it securely before taking his hand away. I perched on the edge of the table, sipping the hot liquid, studying the lake with the mountains and trees behind.

"This is beautiful – Maine is so beautiful – what I've seen of it," I began tentatively. He waited, the line of his mouth tight, sensing a "but". "Matthew, my parents have booked a flight home for me."

He looked pensive. "And?"

"And I would very much like to come and spend Christmas with you – and your family – if the offer's still open."

A wide grin replaced the frown. "Do your parents know?"

I nodded. "I told them. The only thing is, I'm not convinced I will be entirely welcomed by everybody in your family, and I don't want to be the cause of any friction between you – especially at Christmas – but not ever."

My tea cooled rapidly in the open air, and I drank it before it lost its heat.

"My family, Emma..." he seemed to be choosing his words with care. "My family will accept my decision."

I suppose that at the end of the day, it *was* his decision; in the same way that I was free to choose what I did with my life; but he knew as well as I did, that none of us has an entirely free choice where family is concerned.

"That's not quite what I'm saying. Will they be *happy* for me to be there?"

"Is their happiness important to you?"

I considered for a moment, then slowly, as I thought it through, said, "Yes, I think that it must be, because they are important to *you*."

He looked out over the lake and part of him seemed to be as distant as the mountains, and as unreal. Eventually, he looked down at me.

"They will be happy. We all have to move on; at some point things have to change."

I wanted him to go on, to tell me more, but instead he evaded further questions and leaned sideways and brought out a plate and napkin from the basket for me, followed by a selection of tantalizing foods I could easily eat with my fingers. I felt hungry again, despite breakfast.

"These are lovely, Matthew, thank you. Are you having anything to eat?" I asked, sounding fearfully like my mother.

"Yes, of course."

He picked up a finely cut sandwich, and the corners of his mouth flexed into that peculiar tightness they assumed whenever he hid something from me. My eyes widened and he saw that I had seen.

"I had a large breakfast – I'm not that hungry," he said in explanation.

"Really." My tone clearly showed I didn't believe him. He bit the edge off the sandwich and chewed, but it seemed an awkward action, as if unfamiliar. I continued to stare at him and he avoided my gaze, the sandwich abandoned in his hand.

"Tea, Matthew?" I offered, already knowing what the answer would be.

He skimmed a look at me.

"No, thank you." He edged off the table. "Perhaps this wasn't such a good idea..."

"Why?" I demanded. I put the plate on the table and waited but he didn't clarify his remark. "Why won't you eat or drink in front of me? What are you *hiding*, Matthew? *Why won't you tell me?*"

He remained standing with his back to me, and something inside me snapped. Simmering frustration, borne of weeks of suppressed emotion, erupted. I threw my napkin on the table, not caring that the sudden movement hurt, and slid off it without looking at him again. I began to march stiffly towards the edge of the lake, my mind in turmoil.

The air static, not a whisper moved the still waters. Sandy gravel lay frozen in uneven ridges under my feet where the lake had swollen in late-summer rains. A flash of memory interposed, so at odds with my current situation that I would have cried had I not been so bewildered. It reminded me of seaside holidays in Devon, when the rising and falling of the long tide left a desert of sand in intricate patterns along the beach, the evening sun casting dune-like shadows we destroyed with our toes. But this wasn't Devon, and I was no longer a child, and the man I loved lied to me.

I had known it for some time, of course, but had chosen not to acknowledge it, so I didn't have to face the inevitable questions such knowledge brings. And while I kept lying to myself, I could continue blindly believing that everything would be all right. But everything had changed because he knew that I knew, and that made all the difference. We could no longer maintain this pretence, this charade of normality; either he told me or...

... or what?

The obvious conclusion to my own question was one I dared not voice. My love for him ran through every cell of my body and I no longer doubted his feelings for me; but it wasn't enough. I had lived another man's lie before, and I had sworn then that it was a mistake I would never repeat.

The shore of the lake stretched in an arc, the water's edge encrusted with a frozen foam that collapsed crisply as I crushed it underfoot, my hooded head bent, the silence filled with splintering ice – so I didn't hear anything until Matthew shattered the calm.

"*Emma!*" he bellowed in fear from where I had left him. I turned in his direction but at the same time a low rumble sounded behind me. I whirled around to face a swaying mound of teeth and claws as a bear the height of a tall man rose above me. Brown-black fur matted its bulky frame, its small coal eyes malicious in hunger. It raised a massive paw, its claws dark, flesh-stripping crescents. Rigid with dread, I was too close to escape, too slow to run. I closed my eyes as the bear moved in to strike.

I heard feet pounding across the frozen ground and a hard moving object struck me from the side, knocking the breath from my lungs. Encasing my body, an iron cage flung me around and out of the reach of the bear like a damp rag. The wooded slopes reverberated to the bear's roar and from the corner of my eye, I saw the sweep of claws, then the sound of tearing fabric, and my body vibrated from the impact of the blow. I fought wildly, lashing out irrespective of the pain, and the cage materialized into arms that abruptly released me, and I nearly collapsed. Finding my feet, I turned unsteadily to face the animal.

"Stay still!" Matthew ordered.

I froze.

On all fours, the bear smelt the air as it swayed this way and that, looking for an opportunity to strike again, and Matthew stood between, the ragged remains of his coat hanging from his shoulders, his own body taut and waiting. The animal stopped for a moment, and then a deep, penetrating growl rolled out, filling the air with rage. Matthew shifted position, closing the gap between him and the bear, and it swayed back, surprise in its small, black eyes. At that distance, it had only to take a swipe with its paw and Matthew would be killed in an instant.

"Matthew...!"

Without moving or turning his head, he called out.

"Stay back, Emma."

The animal moaned, switching its attention to me, indecisive.

"Here," Matthew clapped his hands with a sharp report and drew its focus back to him, and the bear rumbled, confused.

"Get back to the car," he commanded me. I began to back off slowly, torn by my instinct to stay and protect him, no matter the futility of it, and the overwhelming authority in his voice. "*Now*, Emma."

The animal rose once more onto its hind legs, hunger fuelling its obstinacy. Mesmerized, my heart pounding, I saw it ready itself for the kill. Matthew stood his ground, mere feet between him and the animal; he didn't stand a chance.

"Leave him *alone!*" I screamed at the animal, dashing out from behind Matthew's protecting back towards the bear, all sense gone in my fear. Matthew swore violently, at the same time catching me in one quick movement and hauling me behind him. Turning on the animal again, he moved forwards, his shoulders hunched, his arms outstretched. The bear landed heavily on all paws, blowing in short snorts and swatting the ground with its paws. Its huge head rocked back and forth as if viewing its options and then it turned, and lumbered back towards the safety of the trees. Matthew continued to watch it until it was beyond sight, before turning back to me.

"What do you think you were doing?" he raged, coming towards me with his fists still clenched and his eyes black with fury. I shrank back and he stopped, visibly controlling his anger. He breathed deeply, flexing his fingers. I could raise no more than a whisper.

"It was going to kill you."

Exasperation creased his brow.

"No, it was not; I wasn't in any danger; it was after *you*, Emma."

I didn't believe him. "But your back, Matthew – look at your *back* – your coat!"

He twisted round, pulling his coat at the same time so that he could see more of the back. Shredded, the thick fabric hung in loose strands where the bear's claws had rent it from shoulder to waist, his shirt pale blue against the dark, like the slashed sleeves of a medieval doublet. I waited for the blood to seep through, red against blue, for him to realize his injury and collapse, his hot life staining the freezing ground around him.

"Mm, that's a shame, I liked this coat."

My voice quaked as shock set in and I began to tremble uncontrollably.

"*Matthew!*"

"I'm fine, Emma; I'm not hurt – it didn't touch me – but what about you? Did I hurt you...?"

He took a few steps towards me, concern replacing the wrath as he took in my state. I backed away from him, trusting what I had heard and seen, incredulous that he wasn't taking his injuries seriously.

"But it struck you – I felt it; I know it did, Matthew – I *heard* it."

He came closer, his eyes locking mine. "You can see I'm all right; it's just wrecked my coat, that's all."

I shook my head. "I don't believe you."

"Emma, please..." he begged; close enough to touch me, he held his arms by his sides. I closed my eyes and swallowed as the landscape rocked beneath me.

"I thought it was going to kill you."

I felt his hand on my shoulder then around my back as he drew close to me, human again.

"I know – it's all right; let's get you back."

I let him fold me in his arms, but then pulled away roughly, trying very hard to control the shaking that rolled through my body as I spoke clearly and deliberately, my jaw aching with the effort.

"I don't understand what just happened – why you aren't hurt or dead – and I don't know how you did what you did, but I will find out one way or another. So if you don't mind, I would rather you just got on with it and... and... told... and told me..."

I couldn't go on. My mouth opened and shut but my brain refused to supply it with any more words. I hid my face behind my arms.

"Emma..."

He put his arms around me again; this time I didn't pull away and instead let him walk me slowly back towards the car, every step painful because the strapping had slipped and my chest jarred. His blank expression told me there would be no point in asking any more questions; another incongruity in the long list I had been compiling that I could no longer accept at face value.

"That didn't go quite as planned," he said conversationally, as the car drew smoothly across the grit and slid between the trees, leaving the car-park empty and devoid of life. "The mild spell we've had must have delayed hibernation."

The bear could have been a tiger for all I cared at that moment.

"How did you get to me so quickly?"

Even to my own ears, my voice sounded flat and featureless – almost disinterested – as I watched for his reaction: he glanced sharply at me, although his reply was seamless.

"I used to compete in athletics – it was instinctive."

I hadn't seen him sprint towards me, but I often had an overwhelming feeling that he restrained an impulse to run – but so fast?

"You said it should have been hibernating – the bear – it shouldn't have been there, Matthew."

For a split second I thought he would defend himself.

"Yes, I should have known," he acceded.

"I know it struck you, it's no good telling me otherwise. I know what I saw – what I felt."

He put his hand on mine.

"I'm so sorry. I should have been more careful – in lots of ways; I shouldn't have let my guard down."

We walked to my apartment in silence. Matthew unlocked the door and stood aside to let me in. With clumsy fingers I started to unzip my coat, but it stuck halfway and I tugged it to get it to move. It remained stubbornly jammed and I yanked at it.

"Blast this *wretched* thing!"

I stamped my foot in frustration; I felt his breath on my neck.

"Here, let me undo it for you."

The zip moved like silk under his fingers, and he slid my coat off my shoulders, his calm infuriatingly reasonable when I felt nothing but uncertainty and turmoil. Something shattered inside me.

"And damn *you!*" I spat venomously. I could have stabbed him and hurt him less, as pain and rejection flashed across his face. He turned his back abruptly, his shoulders hunched. "No," I wailed, "I'm sorry Matthew, I didn't mean that."

His voice became ice; I had never heard him so cold, so distant.

"Then what *did* you mean?"

"I don't know. I don't know what to make of you. You… *lie* to me; in fact, the only consistent thing about you is that you never tell me the truth."

He wheeled around to face me, his eyes flint.

"Is that how you think of me – as a *liar?*"

"No." I sat down, my anger slipping into misery. "That's part of the problem – that's what I don't understand; you have complete integrity, but you don't tell me the truth. Everything about you is a contradiction."

We stared at each other, stranded in separate worlds of desolation, an insurmountable chasm between us.

"What do you want to know?"

I stood up again and this time I was ready for him, my heart thumping haphazardly.

"I know I said that I would accept you without asking questions, but things are different now – things have changed. I want to know why you find it necessary to lie to me about things that shouldn't matter. I want to know why you are so different from other people; and I want to know where I stand with you."

"I don't mean – or want – to lie to you, Emma, it's…"

"Complicated. Yes, I know, you've said before. But that isn't an explanation, and frankly I feel like a fool every time you lie to me. You are so full of secrets and you won't let me in, so what am I to think? What's so important that I can't know about it? Or…" and an appalling thought struck me, "… or is it that *I'm* not important enough for you to tell me?"

His face twisted into a bitter smile. "Not important? *You* – not important?" He stepped towards me, menacingly intense, and I stumbled back. "*Everything* I have done over these past weeks is because of you. Every *lie*, every *half-truth* has been because of you – to *protect* you, Emma, not to *hurt* you. How could I have been so stupid to think that I could hide anything from *you*!"

He slammed his fist into the coffee table and it splintered, the air filling with the sound of shattered wood and broken dreams. Flowers, glass and water spread like pooled blood. I stared at the remains of the table and then at his handsome face, so at odds with the scalding anger in his eyes, and blinked.

"What are you saying, Matthew? That you lied to protect me? From what, or... who?"

He bowed his head, closing his eyes.

"From me – from what I could do, or have failed to do."

My voice began to rise in an agony of frustration. "You're talking in riddles again!"

I kicked out at the remains of the table, fragments scattering across the polished floor, sliding under the sofa and knocking against the foot of the window-seat.

Recrimination, not self-pity, haunted him.

"From me, Emma, because I allowed you to be put in danger again and I can't forgive myself that degree of stupidity."

"I don't understand; you've saved me *three* times – how can that be so wrong?"

He began pacing the room with short, violent movements.

"Staahl got to you because I wasn't watching – I should have prevented that, Emma, I should have stopped him."

"But you did..."

"*No* – he shouldn't have got that close. And then today... I should have anticipated the animal might be there."

"What are you talking about? It's not your responsibility to watch over me..."

"Oh, but it is," he snarled.

"Why?"

"Because..." He faltered.

"That's not an answer, Matthew; you've got to do better than *that*."

He stopped pacing, canting his head to face me.

"Because it's what you're supposed to do when you love someone."

My heart somersaulted and my jaw dropped. I snapped it shut, still staring at him. *He loved me.* He started pacing again.

"Because I love you and should be able to protect you. And because I knew Staahl was a threat to you but still couldn't prevent him from nearly killing you. Because being with me, puts you at risk. Because I want you more than this life and yet I can't ask you to be with me without compromising your faith. And I can't do that – I won't do that."

Rising desperation flooded my voice.

"You're still not making any sense! Can't you trust me enough to tell me? For goodness' sake – you asked me to stay for Christmas! What was that all about?"

He bent his head. "I shouldn't have asked you; it was wrong." He raised it again, and the haunted, hunted look was back. "I can't let you know my real nature without risking losing you, and I'm too selfish to let you go; yet accepting me places you in danger every moment we are together. I can't... I *won't* lose you, Emma; I don't have the courage to face life without you."

I felt like screaming. "And *I* can't go on in this state of limbo – it's killing me!"

His hollow laughter grated, devoid of all humour. We stared at each other.

"Impasse?" I whispered.

He agreed reluctantly. "It would appear so."

I sank back on the chair and examined the floor so that he wouldn't see my tears; but he knelt amid the vestiges of the table and raised my chin so that he could look into my face, and his eyes were unfathomable depths into which I fell without hesitation. He brushed a tear with the back of his hand, then another with his lips. Then his mouth found mine, and all the agony of doubt that had held us apart evaporated as mist under the morning sun.

Hope and need, and relentless, uncompromising love combined in each breathless kiss, the tips of my fingers fighting the shredded sheets of fabric that were all that remained of his coat and shirt, through to his supple, unyielding skin, where no mark, nor rip, nor tear broke the perfection of its surface. His lips found my jaw-edge, and softly at first, then with increasing intensity, the line of my neck, until he discovered the hollow at the base of my throat. I kissed his hair, pulling his scent in shallow breaths into my lungs as his mouth travelled across my collar-bone and down, his lips hard now, and bruising. I gasped.

"Matthew... ow!"

He sprang back as if I had electrocuted him, his eyes wild, his arm across his mouth, looking at me in abject horror.

"What have I done?" he whispered.

"What is it? Don't stop – Matthew, please, what is it?"

I struggled to stand up, but my ribs wouldn't play ball. I tried again, closing my eyes against the sudden pain. When I opened them seconds later, he was gone.

Hush hung in the empty room, the only sound my heart beating frantically against my chest. My voice faltered.

"Matthew?"

I searched the deepening shadows, a persistent and growing dread settling heavy and without compassion. Pulling my jacket around my shoulders, I tiptoed towards the bedroom, as if he might be there.

"Matthew?"

A rising note of hysteria filled the barren space and, as realization hit me, I collapsed onto the cold floor, letting out a long howl of pain, ending in harsh, stifled sobs.

"No, don't do this to me, I can't do this any more..." And in the ensuing silence, I implored of Heaven, "Where do I go from here?"

My anguished whispers echoed around the room and came back empty. I knelt there, cramped and freezing and oblivious to the protestations of my body until darkness covered the room in a shroud and I faded into its obscurity.

I don't know how long I lay there; long enough for my limbs to numb and set in the cold, and for the last of my tears to die away and dry on my face. Long enough for the moon to rise and shine in arrogant stripes across the floor; long enough to have raised my head, an answer – as clear as if spoken – showing the way.

I struggled to my feet and lurched like a drunk across my bedroom, forcing blood back into my legs. Slashing on the light-switch, I grabbed my mobile off the bedside table, fumbling the keys.

"Elena, please, I need your help. No, *listen* – don't ask, please – just come."

I didn't pause to hear her worried voice as she began to ply me with questions but instead cut her off, holding back the tears that threatened to choke me again. I picked up the phone once more, punching another number into it.

Elena was with me in minutes, by which time I had dragged my flight bag out of the wardrobe, and frantically stuffed it with the minimal clothes I would need for travelling. Her sharp eyes assessed the state of the sitting-room floor and my ashen face; then her eyes dropped and she stared, horrified, at my neck and chest. I craned my head, but couldn't see what she saw. I went into the bathroom, dazzling myself briefly before my vision adjusted to the stronger light, and peered in the mirror. Small, purplish bruises were appearing, speckled like smallpox across my skin. Elena stood in the doorway, her hand over her mouth, her eyes wide and fearful as she already came to the wrong conclusion.

"What happened, Emma; what did he do?"

I swivelled on her, taking the tops of her arms in my hands and forcing her to look me in the face.

"Elena, I want you to listen to me *very* carefully. Matthew has done nothing wrong; whatever else you might think, you *must* believe me."

Her gaze flickered back to the bruises and I drew my jacket tight about my throat, cutting off the source of fascination; she looked back at my face.

"He's done *nothing* wrong – understand?" I said, more fiercely.

She frowned and then nodded slowly, doubt still clearly at the forefront of her mind. "In a minute, my parents will be here and I will go with them back to England." Her face fell, and her frown deepened. "But – and this is the bit I want you to remember – *I am not leaving*; I *will* come back. Tell him... *please*, Elena, tell Matthew that I have to get some things straight in my head; he'll understand. Do *you* understand?"

"No, I do not." She shook her head from side to side. "Must you go? If he has done nothing wrong as you say, why do you have to leave? It makes no sense."

"Yes, I *must*. I can't work this out here – I need some distance to think. Please help me pack; I haven't much time if I'm to catch the flight."

She pulled herself together, helping me make some sense of the jumbled mess. I snatched the tablets off my bedside table and, as a second thought, took the capsules as well, shoving them all in my handbag.

There was a loud, desperate knock at the door. Elena looked up, alarmed.

"It's my father," I reassured her. As she went to answer it, I scooped up the journal and Matthew's translation, which I had hurriedly hidden in the folds of his scarf, placing them carefully in the bottom of my flight-bag among the jumper and socks. I managed to close the zip as my father came in, worry and tension close companions in his face. I anticipated his first inevitable question, but let him ask it anyway.

"What has he done to you? Where is he – what the blazes...?" He saw the remains of the table. "I'll give him a good thrashing if he's hurt you!"

He glared furiously around the room as if Matthew would be waiting there in the shadows.

"He hasn't done anything, Dad, but I have. This is nothing to do with Matthew."

I hoped it would be enough. My mother stood behind him and she firmly pushed him to one side as he began to argue.

"Leave Emma alone now, Hugh; we have a flight to catch and there'll be plenty of time for questions – and explanations – later."

She put both of her warm, soft hands around my face, searching out the truth. I bit my lip, controlling tears, and she nodded briefly, smiling sadly, before letting me go. I looked once around the room, memorizing it, the fading flowers less vibrant in the artificial light, an air of decay and abandon in the tangle of cushions and splintered wood on the floor.

"Wait," I said, as we reached the door. I hurried back into my bedroom, gathering the blanket he had bought for me into my arms, and joined my friend and parents where they waited on the landing.

The journey to the airport was a blur, partly because by the time we left, cloud covered the blank face of the moon, but more because my mind began to retreat into darker recesses where it might find some semblance of comfort. My mother sat next to me in the car, not attempting to engage in conversation, her hand wrapped lightly around my fingers. I wouldn't have been able to find the words I needed to say how I felt anyway. As we drove further and further from the college, the more clearly I saw the implications of what I did – and the more intense the pain of separation until it enveloped me, and all I wanted to do was turn back. But I wouldn't, I couldn't, not like this – not without answers, not now, not yet. And if Matthew wouldn't supply them, I felt compelled to hunt them down myself.

Multiple sharp points of light indicated we were close to the airport, the traffic increasing as we neared, slowing our progress. Dad kept looking at his watch, fretting over the time. I rested my head against the cold glass and barely watched as the lights merged into one long line drawn out by the speed of the car. Several times, I thought I saw the sleek outline of a sports car, slung fast and low against the hugging ground and my heart sped with it, only to falter and stall as it passed us by.

We entered the airport under the interrogating glare of synthetic light. For once I let my father shepherd me through the crowded concourse, shielding me from the questions of officials and the curious faces of the flight-attendants on the plane. I sat by the window, oblivious to everything but the pain in my broken arm and chest that I had ignored until now, and the growing vacuum in my heart. A flight-attendant leaned over my mother towards me.

"Ma'am, you need to secure your seat-belt."

I looked blankly at her and my mother wrestled with the buckle, pulling it tight around my waist, but the woman still lingered by us instead of moving on.

"Your bag, ma'am?" Her hand hovered near my bag.

"Don't touch it!" I snapped, hearing someone else's voice coming from my mouth. The startled woman stood back, ready to assert her authority, but I already looked away, staring blindly through the black glass into the night, not hearing what she said. I clutched my bag to my chest, pressing the edges of the hidden books against the bruises – his bruises, my bruises – that kept him close to me, and she didn't try again.

We had reached cruising altitude when I became aware that my parents were talking in low, worried tones. I turned towards my mother, and she put her hand on my father's arm to stop him saying something, but I didn't care one way or the other; it was irrelevant what anyone thought any more.

"What is it, darling?"

"Please may I have some water?"

My father called the stewardess and she brought me a clear plastic cup of water, tiny bubbles clinging to its brittle surface. I managed to unzip my bag, but couldn't release the bi-coloured capsules from their silver coffins. My mother took them, puncturing the protective foil and handing them individually to me so that I could swallow them and await the numbing anonymity they would bring.

By the time the plane touched down in England, a grey dawn rumoured on the horizon, and the stale fug of a new day hung like a pall over the sleeping buildings of my homeland.

I dozed fitfully as my father drove us back along the familiar old Great North Road, the long stone wall of the Burghley estate heralding the town of my ancestors. I felt no relief as we passed the George Hotel, nor as we crossed the bridge over the River Welland by the Meadows where I used to play. And as we turned before the spire of St Mary's into the cobbled street where we lived and the sound of the engine died, the bell from the old church tolled. We slithered over the cobbles – slippery with the fine mizzle that fell from the clinging sky – to our blue front door. The stone-damp air of the old house was barely warm, but the ghosts of my past welcomed me in the flags of the foot-worn floors and the slow *tock, tock* of my grandfather's long-case clock as it measured out time.

I climbed the sweeping staircase, barely noticing when my mother switched on the lights, so familiar each tread, until I reached the broad landing where the stuffed pike loomed in eternal belligerence from its glass-fronted case. On and up the servants' stairs, along the dark upper hall and under the arch to the end – where the door opened to my childhood bedroom. Only then, when I shut the door behind me and felt the walls close in like a womb, did I allow myself the luxury of succumbing to the desolation that had been my constant companion since I left the States.

I did not think, I could not feel. Had I been in possession of a heart, it would have cleaved down its seam, because I left that better part of me in Maine. What I had now was but an empty shell; this was my self-imposed exile, my self-inflicted hell.

Below is Chapter 1 from *Death Be Not Proud*, the second volume in the series *The Secret of the Journal*.

Chapter

I

Abyss

I HAD GOOD DAYS AND I HAD BAD DAYS.

It wasn't as if I could blame anyone else for the condition I found myself in, so I didn't look for any sympathy. I knew that my near-vegetative state caused my parents hours of anxiety, but I couldn't face the questions that queued in my own mind, let alone answer any of theirs.

I stayed in my room. Where I lay at an angle on my bed, I could watch the winter sun cast canyons of light as it moved across the eaved ceiling. Sometimes the light was the barest remnant from a clouded sky; at others, so bright that the laths were ribs under the aged plaster, regular undulations under the chalk-white skin.

I hadn't spent so long at home for many years. Here at the top of the house, the cars droned tunelessly as they laboured up the hill beyond the sheltering walls of St Mary's Church. Below, the voices of the street were mere echoes as they rose up the stone walls, entering illicitly through the thin frame of the window. I listened to the random sounds of life; I watched it in the arc of the day. And the sounds and the light were immaterial – the days irrelevant – time did not touch me.

Sometime – days after fleeing Maine – my mother knocked softly on my door, her disembodied head appearing round it when I did not answer.

"Emma, you have twenty minutes to get yourself ready for

your hospital appointment; your father's getting the car now."

Her voice hovered in the air above my bed, and I heard every word she said, but they didn't register. I didn't move. She came into the room and stood at the end of my bed, her hands on her hips, her no-nonsense look in place. The lines creasing her forehead were deeper than I remembered, or maybe it was the way the light from the window fell across her brow.

"I know you heard me; I want you to get up and get dressed *now*. I won't keep the hospital waiting."

She hadn't used that tone with me for nearly twenty years and I found it comforting in its severity.

"Emma!"

My eyes focused and saw her shaking, her hands clutching white-knuckled at the old iron-and-brass bedstead.

"Emma, I am asking you, please..."

My poor mother; with my Nanna in hospital and her youngest daughter tottering towards the edge of reality, she was strung out just as far as she could go, eking out her emotional reserves like food in a famine. I blinked once as I surfaced from the dark pool of my refuge, my mouth dry; I half-rolled, half-sat up. Wordlessly, I climbed off the bed and went stiffly to the bathroom down the landing, my mother a few steps behind me. I shut the door quietly on her, and turned to look in the mirror above the basin. Sunken eyes stared back from my skull-like head, skin brittle over my high cheekbones. Even my freckles seemed pale under the dim, grim light from the east window. Mechanically I brushed my teeth and washed, not caring as the cast on my arm became sodden. The bruises above my breasts and below my throat stood out against my fair skin. I pressed my fingertips into them, my hands spanning the space between each smoky mark. I closed my eyes at the subdued pain and remembered why they were there.

Mum waited for me outside the door, and I aimlessly wondered if she thought I might try and escape – or something worse. I understood the effect of my behaviour on my family; I understood and cared with a remorse that should have torn the very heart from me, had I one. But my head and my heart were divorced, and I witnessed my distress in their pinched, tight faces and harried, exchanged looks as no more than a disinterested observer.

I also realized that, from a clinical point of view, I probably suffered from delayed shock – the result of two near-fatal attacks in a very short period of time with which I struggled to come to terms. But neither Staahl nor the bear seemed even remotely important when compared with what had passed between Matthew and me that precipitated my leaving the only man I had ever really loved.

I dressed in what Mum put out for me, substituting the cardigan for my sage jacket, and all the while I ached, but I couldn't tell whether the pain came from my broken body or from my heart.

The hospital wasn't far from where we lived and my father parked in a lined disabled bay, ignoring the disapproving stares of the people sitting on a nearby bench. They stopped staring and averted their heads when he helped me out of the car, all the justification he needed in my fragile frame as I leaned against him for support. The strapping still loose, my ribcage felt as if the semi-knitted bones grated with every step I took, but I welcomed the pain as relief from the indescribable emptiness that filled every waking moment.

The double doors to the reception hissed back into their recesses, releasing a gust of warm, sanitized air. I felt suddenly sick as it hit my face, and I retched pointlessly, my hollow stomach reacting to the acrid smell of disinfectant, each spasm pulling at my chest, and I felt my legs give way beneath me. A flurry of activity and hands and voices alerted me to the fact that, although I was drifting, blissful unconsciousness eluded me.

"When did she last eat?" a pleasant-voiced man asked from beside my head. He lifted my eyelid and a beam of directed light hit me; I twisted my head to escape it. He lifted the skin in the crease of my elbow and it sagged back into place like broken elastic.

"She's dehydrated as well; how long's this been going on?"

Mum sounded tense. "Five days. She refuses to eat, she barely drinks a thing and she was already too thin. We don't know what to do with her; she just won't talk to us."

Five days? Had it been so long? I counted only three. Five whole days without him.

"I'll have to admit her – get her rehydrated. These injuries need seeing to and I'll contact someone in the mental health team at the same time."

My eyes flicked open.

"No," I muttered weakly.

Humorous hazel eyes met mine. "Ah, she speaks; you're back with us, are you? Did you have something to say?"

"No – I won't be admitted," I said, strength returning along with my stubborn streak.

"Well, you haven't left yourself with much of a say in the matter – you're a right mess. However..." he continued, "if you promise to eat and drink starting from now, I could be persuaded to reconsider."

"If I must."

I wasn't far off being churlish but he didn't seem to mind, and I wondered why everyone was being so kind to me because I didn't deserve it, not after the way I treated them, not after what I had done.

The dry biscuit scraped my throat and the tea from the little cafe next to reception tasted stewed by the time I drank it, but it helped.

"Sorry about the biscuit." The young doctor eyed it, pulling a face. "The nurses ate all the decent ones; there's not a Jammy Dodger left in sight. Hey ho – at least that's better than nothing, and I suppose we must be grateful for the little we are given." He smiled cheerfully, his harmless chatter scattering brightly into the bland room. I stared at the ceiling, impassive and beyond caring.

I finished the tea under his watchful eye, his excuse being that business was a bit slow and he had nothing better to do than to sit there and watch me. He took the empty cup, chucked it in a bin and rolled up the wide sleeves of my jacket, revealing both arms.

"So, what happened here, then?"

He started to unwind the bandage on my left arm. My throat clenched uncomfortably, remembering the last time it had been dressed by Matthew as he stood so close to me – his hand on my arm, my skin running with the connectivity between us.

He misunderstood my reaction. "That hurt?"

"No."

"OK, so what did you do here... *heck*, whew!" He whistled, "That's quite something; not a case of self-harm, I'm guessing. Accident?"

The long scar had lost its lividity, and the edges of the bruising were beginning to fade.

"No."

"This is healing well; nice job – very impressive stitching, almost a shame when they have to come out." He admired the fine stitches, turning my arm to catch a better look under the glare of the overhead lamp.

"Our daughter was *attacked*." Dad sounded none too impressed by the young man's obvious enthusiasm about my injury. The doctor's tone moderated.

"Ah, I didn't know – not good. This as well?" He indicated the cast on my arm, looking only at me for an answer.

"Yes."

"And two of her ribs," my mother interjected. "I think Emma's in a lot of pain but she won't tell me."

He stood up straight, pulling at one earlobe as he contemplated his course of action, his hand barely visible beneath thick, brown hair that curled up a little over his collar.

He checked his watch. "This cast is sopping wet – you're not supposed to swim the Channel in it – it needs changing. I could send you to the main hospital in Peterborough, or you could let me have a bash at it – your choice."

"Whichever, I don't mind."

He came to a decision.

"Right then, we'd better get on with it – I need the practice anyway. Footie's on tonight and I want to get home for the kick-off." He winked at me. "Off you go, I'll manage without you," he said, ushering my surprised parents out and beckoning to a nurse at the same time. "So this happened... when? Three, four weeks ago?"

"No."

He waited and I realized that he wanted an answer with more information than that.

"Two weeks – just over two weeks."

"You're sure? This is healing well – looks nearer four weeks old, and you wouldn't believe the number of lacerations I've seen over the last few years, 'specially on a Saturday night in A and E, though none as clinical as this, I grant you. Just over two weeks; hmm, well, if you say so..."

For all his cavalier chatter, he was surprisingly gentle as he redressed my arm, and then started to remove the cast Matthew so carefully applied all those dark nights ago. I felt a pang of regret as it fell to the floor, as if he were slipping away from me along with the cast. A stifled sob came out of nowhere, catching me off-guard.

The young doctor didn't look up. "Want to tell me about it?" He must have thought I remembered the attack.

"No."

"Can sometimes help to talk," he encouraged, still focusing on the messy process in front of him, a fixed grimace on his face as he tried to get the gauze under the cast on straight.

I wiped my eyes on the back of my sleeve. "No, thanks."

He made a pretty good job of it, although the new cast felt heavier than the last one, and my arm objected to carrying the additional weight.

"Two down, one to go," he said, nodding in the direction of my chest. The nurse started to unbutton my jacket and, instinctively, I drew my arms in front of me to stop her. She looked to the doctor for back-up, and he smiled apologetically.

"The top has to come off, sorry."

Reluctantly, I let my arms drop and she continued. I felt exposed under the harsh light as he interrogated my body, and I kept my eyes fixed on the shadows of people moving across the floor, just visible in the crack at the bottom of the door where light peered under. He became suddenly businesslike and professional as he unwound the strapping and probed my ribs. I caught my breath and craned my head to look. "That sore?"

"Yes."

I tried not to react but, from what I could see, at least the intense bruising from my collision with the edge of the shelves in the porters' lodge was definitely fading and, although my ribs ached, I could tell they were on the mend.

"They're OK – just need strapping again."

He completed the task and thanked the nurse and she left. The doctor stood with one hand on his hip.

"Like to tell me how you got those?" he said, looking at the small, regular-shaped bruises across my breastbone and around my neck. "And don't tell me they were done at the same time as the rest of the damage – these are more recent."

"They don't bother me."

"That wasn't what I asked; has someone been hurting you?"

I laughed hoarsely, the irony not lost on me. "Not in the way you think; this is *entirely* self-inflicted."

He lifted an eyebrow, obviously not happy with my reply. I dragged my soft jacket back on and, although my hands were more free, my stiff fingers struggled to do up the buttons again. He leaned forwards to help.

"So, there's nothing more you want to say; I can't contact anyone for you?"

His brown-green eyes were kind and concerned; he had a sweet face.

"No – thanks."

"OK, you've got your reasons, no doubt, but if you were a dog, I'd be calling the RSPCA right now. You're all done. I'll fetch your parents, but remember, I don't want to see you in here again in your emaciated state. Drink plenty, eat lots and I won't report you."

He chucked the remains of my old cast in the pedal-bin, the lid clanging shut long before I took my eyes off it.

"Report me? For what?" I asked dully.

"Oh, I don't know, causing unnecessary suffering to the NHS budget, or some such; doctors like me don't come cheap, you know."

No, I knew that.

He left the room, taking my notes with him, and took longer than I expected to return. Minutes later, when I joined my parents in the seating area, the expressions on their faces were ambiguous. He must have said something. I sighed internally, dreading what conclusions they might have drawn between them and deciding I needed to make a bigger effort to appear more normal to prevent a repeat of the earlier farce. When we reached the reception area I did something I had longed to do for the last month or so.

My grandmother resided in a side ward in a part of the hospital to which I had never been. Single-storey and purpose-built, its windows overlooked a paved courtyard with raised stone beds filled with semi-naked plants waiting for spring, now shivering under the overcast sky. Although made as pleasant as possible, even the brightly coloured curtains and cheerful prints that decorated the windows and walls of the assessment unit could not disguise the sense of imminent death that accompanied the living corpses inhabiting the beds.

Mum went over to talk to the nurses, and I was left to gaze at my grandmother from where I stood. Better than expected, she looked well, her face full and her skin still softly coloured, not sallow and drawn. She lay with her eyes closed. I went over to her and tentatively reached out to touch her hand as it rested on the peach-coloured cotton cover, to find it warm.

"Nanna?"

She did not respond. I pulled the high-backed chair close to her bed. The card I sent from Maine weeks ago sat on the bedside cabinet along with the regulated clutter of my family's gifts, a few personal items and a photo of my grandfather in its over-polished frame.

"How are you, Nanna?" I asked softly. "I'm so sorry I haven't been to see you; I've been away but... but I'm back now."

Her breathing came as a rhythmic pattern of in and out. I held her small hand between my newly liberated fingers, stiffly stroking them in time to her breaths.

"I've been working. I went to America, do you remember? I went to where the journal came from – as I said I would – and I've found it, Nanna; I've found Grandpa's journal."

Perhaps I hoped that she could hear me or would somehow respond. I laid my head on the bed, the movement of her chest so slight that it barely lifted the bedclothes. I watched as it rose and fell.

"I haven't read it yet, but I will; we've waited so long, haven't we? Will you wait a little longer – until I've read it – then you can tell Grandpa for me, because he'll want to know, won't he? He'll want to know all about it, like the last chapter of a book." Her breathing halted for a second, and I lifted my head to look at her anxiously, but she seemed peaceful and the pattern of her breaths returned to their slow, shallow beat. I laid my head down on my arm by her hand and closed my eyes.

"I met someone when I was out there. I think you would like him – he reminded me of Grandpa; his hair is the *exact* same colour – the colour of ripe corn." I smiled to myself despite the bitter, wretched ache somewhere in the middle of my chest.

"But I left him there, I had to. He's different... I can't explain it, there's so much about him that I don't understand and, until I do – until I've worked it out – I can't be with him, I can't go back..."

A soundless tear heralded an unlooked-for stream and I let them flow, glad that Nanna remained unaware of my sorrow.

"Sorry, Nanna," I managed after a few minutes, the top layers of bandage on my wrist already soaked. "That wasn't supposed to happen. You're stuck in here and I'm blubbing all over the place; what would Grandpa make of the pair of us?"

The faintest touch on the crown of my head startled me and I lifted my face. My grandmother's eyes were open, their faded blue alert. The corner of one side of her mouth lifted in a weak but discernible smile.

"Nanna? *Nanna!* You can hear me? Oh – you heard me," I said as I realized that she might have heard my ramblings. "I'm sorry," I said again. "I didn't mean you to hear *all* of that. I'll get Mum for you." I turned my head and saw that my mother still talked to one of the nurses. I felt a slight touch against my fingers and I looked down. My grandmother had moved her hand towards mine.

"What is it? Don't you want me to get her?"

Her fingers lifted and tapped against mine again, a slight question in her eyes.

"Oh this – it's nothing; I had an accident, that's all."

I looked away from her, hating lying. She tapped again, a persistent glare in her eyes. "All right, I was attacked, but I'm fine now; I had someone to look after me."

I couldn't hide the shake in my voice. Nanna made a guttural sound in her throat made of frustration that she could not speak.

"I bet if Matthew were here he could help you – he's like that – full of surprises."

Raw pain twisted inside me, but it was worth it just to be able to speak his name. Her fingers fluttered again, accompanied by the smile, and I smiled back. I heard a noise behind me.

"Hello, Mummy, you're looking *much* better," my mother said over my shoulder.

"You didn't tell me Nanna's awake, Mum!"

"I did tell you she is much better, but you weren't listening, darling."

She leaned over from the other side of the bed and kissed her mother tenderly on her forehead. Nanna smiled her half-smile in response, then swivelled her eyes to look at me, then back to her daughter again, questioning.

"Emma's fine; nothing time won't heal." She looked at me. "Darling, I need to talk to Nanna for a minute…"

I nodded and kissed my grandmother's warm, soft cheek. "Thank you," I whispered in her ear; "I will come and see you again soon." She grunted in her throat, her blue eyes watching my face.

That evening, I sat in the dining-room and ate for the first time in days. It felt cold by the great floor-to-ceiling windows that let in a steady stream of air through the insubstantial frames, and I remembered that I needed layers of jumpers to survive the raw winter here. I moved around to the other side of the table, closer to the electric fire that did its best to make inroads on the chill. Dad pushed the kitchen door open with his foot, carrying several plates and bringing with him a waft of cooking-scented air. He laid a plate of hot food in front of me, spirals of steam rising.

"Your mother said not to wait and tuck in while it's hot. It'll do you good – put some colour in your cheeks," he said in an attempt at being positive. I regarded the food with a singular lack of enthusiasm. "Come along now," he chivvied; "step to it. Chop, chop. Remember what the doctor said. We don't want you ending up in hospital now, do we? And it'll take a load off your mother's mind," he added, as the door began to open and she came in.

The increased mobility of my hands made eating much easier, although my right arm ached with the effort and my left hand could barely grasp a fork. My parents said nothing but the questions were not far away. I sensed they waited for me to eat something before they started. I was right.

"What a very pleasant young doctor you saw today," my mother ventured. I put my fork down and waited. Dad had almost finished his food and he eyed my near-full plate.

"Eat up, Emma; don't let it go to waste."

Mum shot him a glance and he shut up; she continued.

"He said that you're healing very well and your stitches can come out in a week's time; that's good, isn't it?"

I loathed being humoured.

"The thing is, darling, he is a little concerned…"

Here it comes, I thought.

"He mentioned that you have some bruises that weren't caused by… well, by the attack, and that you said that they were self-inflicted. He thinks that you might benefit from a little help."

My dearest mother – always trying to be diplomatic – but she might as well have just come straight out with it and said: "The doctor thinks you're off your rocker, darling, and he thinks you should be committed."

I had to laugh. Dad looked shocked.

"It's not a laughing matter, Emma. What your mother is trying to say..."

"I know what's being implied, Dad," I cut in, "but they weren't self-inflicted, not in the way he means, so I don't need any *help* – of any kind."

I pushed my plate away from the edge of the table, ready to rise, the silver fork sliding to one side, the remnants of my fragile hunger gone.

Dad frowned at the food on my plate. "And that's another thing – you're not eating; it can be a sign of emotional difficulties. It's nothing to be ashamed of; it can happen to anyone."

I stared at him and then at Mum in disbelief.

"I don't need any help because there's nothing emotionally wrong with me. I've told you, I need time to get my head straight about... things... but I don't need anyone to do it for me. I just want to be left alone to get on with it."

I pushed my chair back, the legs scraping painfully across the stone floor as they left the quietening pile of the rug. I picked up my plate to take it through to the scullery.

"So if *you* didn't make those bruises, darling, who did?"

The subtle approach, direct but always when I'd dropped my guard; Mum knew me well. She saw me falter and stood up, taking the plate from me and putting her arm around my shoulders. I looked straight into the depths of her eyes, inflicting as much sincerity as I could pile into a few words.

"*Nobody* has hurt me, Mum." I ducked out from under her arm, reclaiming the plate, and into the steamy kitchen scullery. I washed my plate under a stream of hot water, the steam condensing almost immediately on the uneven stone walls. There were sounds of subdued whispers, then the door opened behind me and the heavier tread of my father's footsteps, but I didn't turn around.

"Emma, did that *man* do this to you?"

For a moment I didn't know to whom he referred, then anger flashed through me, blood rushing to my face.

"Matthew has *never* hurt me. How can you accuse him, after all he's done?"

Disgusted, I flung down the tea-towel I had just picked up to dry my plate; it missed the draining-board and sank below the bubbles left in the washing-up bowl. I went to push past my parents as they stood blocking the doorway.

"Don't be angry, darling, but you did leave the States in a hurry – what else were we to think? That broken table in your room... and you had been out with him all day; I mean, what else..."

"Not *that*, Mum."

Guilt twisted my voice. I was angry all right – angry at them for even suggesting that Matthew would have purposefully hurt me – but furious with myself for all the doubt and fear I put them through – and tormented by what Matthew himself might be feeling right now. They let me pass and I slammed out of the kitchen, through the panelled sitting-room and up the stairs. In the fading light, the watchful eyes of my ancestors followed me, the only points of light in portraits blackened with age.

I reached the sanctuary of my room. I seemed to make a habit of wrecking people's lives. Guy had deserved it and I felt little guilt in that respect. But my parents? If I were in their place and I saw my child behave in the way I acted, and witnessed the damage I bore, would I not also have come to the conclusion they had logically reached? And Matthew? I turned and buried my face in my pillow.

Matthew – what have I done to you? Would you ever believe me if I said that I loved you beyond boundaries, and that the only limits to that love were those defined within the mess in my head?

I made certain to be seen eating and drinking regularly, and my parents watched me, never leaving me in the house alone. Despite the size of the building, I felt confined and couldn't clear my head enough to think. Flashes of thoughts and images lingered on the edge of dreams I wasn't sure I had, words and faces tugging at my memory but always just out of reach.

I woke early several mornings later and lay under the thick duvet listening as the first birds began to stretch their voices; but the world sounded remote. Climbing out of bed, I drew the curtains to one side, letting in the feeble dawn. A dense fog shrouded the windows. I washed and pulled on my clothes, and found my quilted coat that I hadn't worn since the fight with the bear. From under my bed I dragged the bag that had lain there since my return home. Through the soft wool of his scarf, the hard edges of the two books made their presence known, but I dared not look at them, placing them instead on my little desk and, doubling the long scarf around my neck, I went quietly downstairs.

My parents still slept as I let myself out of the house and made my way past the Town Hall, crossing the road to the Norman arch where the entrance to the ancient passage made a black mouth in the golden stone. I entered it as I had always done as a child – with a sense of crossing a threshold into the past.

Beyond the passage, the Meadows were silent except for the soft rush of the river running through them and away under the bridge. Shaggy tufts of grass, decorated with beads of glass, left my shoes saturated within minutes of wading through them. Out here I found a sense of freedom I hadn't felt for days. Out here, in my solitude, thoughts and ideas began to coalesce and from the disorder in my mind, take shape.

By the time I returned to the house, traffic piled up the hill, filling the air with heavy fumes and protesting engines. The front door opened before I could turn my key in the lock, Dad's face instantly relieved when he saw me.

"I just went out for a walk," I explained a bit defensively as I went into the hall. Mum came out of the sitting-room, cup in hand. Her brow cleared when she saw me and I started to unzip my coat.

"We have a visitor, darling," she said brightly. I bristled, because what she meant was "*You* have a visitor", but I didn't let it show. She went back into the sitting-room where I heard her say something, and a man's voice answered. My father helped me out of my coat.

"Do this for your mother, Em," he said quietly; "she's finding all this a little tough."

I looked at him with a degree of surprise at his uncustomary sensitivity, but he didn't elaborate and instead indicated the open door.

The wiry, white-haired man stood up when I entered.

"Hello, Emma – it's been a long time."

He held out his hand and I shook it automatically; he was careful not to squeeze too hard. I remembered him as a friend of my parents.

"Mr... Taylor."

"Mike, please – it must be at least eighteen years since I last saw you."

"At least," Dad said, balancing on the edge of the sofa arm, adjusting his position as it creaked under him. "Emma had just won the inter-house tennis tournament at school and developed sunstroke."

I was surprised he remembered that; I'd been forced to spend the rest of the blazing summer day in bed with the curtains drawn and a cold flannel on my head. I knew Mike Taylor as a doctor of some kind, and he had ruffled my hair and tugged my thick rope of a plait when last we met, congratulating me on my win before I succumbed to the effects of the sun. Easy-going with an open, approachable manner then, nothing seemed to have changed. I sat in one of the old armchairs, the high arms and padded wings supporting my back and arms which ached from the unaccustomed exercise. He sat on the sofa, stretching his arms across the back and crossing his legs, revealing lively red socks. I eyed him guardedly. My mother called from the dining-room, and my father went to help with the tea.

"You've been busy since I last saw you," Mike said cheerfully. Ah, so this wasn't a social call; I thought as much. "You've been in the States, Hugh said. What did you make of it?"

I cut straight to the point. "What did they tell you?"

He cocked his head on one side and eyed me speculatively beneath thick eyebrows, the colour long gone.

"They're worried about your emotional state."

I blinked at his bluntness.

"Oh – yes."

"Do they have any reason to be worried?"

"No."

"You've had a bit of a rough time out there, I believe – the attack nearly killed you; is that right?"

I kept my tone quite even.

"Yes."

"And then something else happened, your mother said?" He stroked his top lip, waiting, but I said nothing; he didn't need to know about the bear, or anything else that followed. "Not bad going for one term, all things considered. How are you feeling about that, then?"

"Oh *please!*" I rolled my eyes.

"That's too obvious a tack, is it? I'm out of practice," he said ruefully, running his hands through his shock of white hair, his scalp bright pink where the dense thatch thinned. "Well, I said to your parents I'd give it a try." He grinned. He must be in his sixties, his good looks grizzled by time.

"You must have had a good doctor to get you back on your feet so quickly," he went on. I viewed him suspiciously.

"Did my parents say that?"

"Well, no," he admitted, "but they did describe your injuries in some detail, so it doesn't take a brain surgeon to work it out – which is a good thing, because that's not my line; stands to reason. A *Dr Lynes*, I think Penny said."

I recoiled at the mention of his name.

"Yes."

I looked away. A newly lit fire snapped and hissed greedily as the damp wood began to catch. The vigour of the flames made me feel tired.

"He must be good. Does he work at the university?"

I knew what he was doing in trying to engage me in conversation, drawing me out until he could delve deeper, penetrating the darker recesses of my mind; but it took less effort to go along with the pretence than to oppose it.

"Yes, Matthew heads up the medical faculty there." I felt a swell of pride for him but I tried not to let it show in my voice in case it spilled onto my face, and then goodness only knew where it would end, and I didn't want to cry – not in front of this near-stranger.

"Matthew... *Matthew* Lynes?" he said sharply. "Matthew Lynes treated your injuries?"

I sat up, my eyes directly on him now, alert to the changed tone.

"Yes. Why, have you heard of him?"

"It can't be, it was *years* ago, but... the name," he said, almost to himself. He looked at me. "What is he like – describe him."

I struggled to find words to capture him. "He's quite tall, slim, blond, reserved and quietly spoken... he has very blue eyes..."

"Very good-looking? Or, he was," he interrupted.

"Yes, he still is – very." I blushed, wondering why he shouldn't be.

He stared at me curiously. "How old is he, roughly?"

I frowned, "Early thirties, I think."

He dismissed the notion with a wave of his hand. "Hah, well, obviously not the same person, then. That would've been quite a coincidence, though," he mused.

"So you knew someone by the same name?" I probed.

He sat forward on the sofa, the old feather seat squishing under the pressure.

"Yes, some thirty years ago, it must be. I had a difficult op to perform – still the early days of some forms of cardiothoracic surgery, you see. We'd run into difficulty, and the only person who'd performed this particular procedure – pioneered it, actually – was in the States. Well, I had the patient on the slab – chest open – you're not squeamish, are you?" I shook my head. "Heart failing as we watched, and we had nowhere else to turn. So we called this young chap up on a sort of improvised video link – very grainy picture, but it worked. It was the middle of the night there and he talked us through it – didn't bat an eyelid, very self-possessed, very calm for his age. Remarkable man. Only in his late twenties, early thirties, I'd say, but years ahead of the rest of us. Wonder what's happened to him?"

My heart leapt erratically and I stared at the man sitting in front of me. Even with my dodgy maths I could work out that Matthew would have been a young child at the time Mike referred to, yet I had never believed in coincidence.

"Remarkable chap," he said again, shaking his head. "What a coincidence – that name. Still..."

I made an attempt to appear politely indifferent, but really my mind was in turmoil. It made no sense whatsoever, yet that made it all the more plausible. Matthew never added up, and here – in this chance meeting – I had the first indication other than my own observations, that my growing suspicions might be right after all.

My face cracked into a smile. "Yes – *what* a coincidence," I said brightly. "Gosh, I'm hungry – it must be breakfast time; would you like a cup of tea?" I stood up. "So, what are you going to report to my parents?" I asked, blithely, showing him the way.

He beamed. "Oh, that you're a basket case quite definitely, young lady; no doubt about it," he replied, genially. *He had no idea...*

I smiled at his joke. "And that's the medical term for it, is it?"

"From a cardiothoracic surgeon's point of view? Quite probably!"

I couldn't wait to leave them all drinking tea and chatting. I knew that as soon as I left my parents would press him for a medical diagnosis, and I felt confident now that he would give them what I wanted. I made my excuses, grabbing toast and a mug of tea for appearances' sake and retreated to the sanity of my own room where I could filter out the information I had gleaned.

How many blond, unusually attractive and highly skilled American surgeons with his particular name could there be? And thirty years apart? That would make him in his sixties now and that would hardly describe the man *I* knew – not by a long stretch of the imagination. I thrummed my fingers on my desk as I thought, pleased that at last I had the flexibility in my hand to do so. Matthew's translation of the Italian medical treatise lay on top of the journal, and I opened it halfway through. His beautiful script – so unlike a typical doctor's scrawl – antique in style, and quite different to anything I had seen outside historic manuscripts. I closed the book, tapping its front cover, and thinking while my tea cooled enough to drink.

A thought struck me and I seized my handbag, emptying it of trivia onto my bed. I found my bank-card and stuffed it in my back pocket. I gulped the hot tea, sending it scalding down my throat, before hurrying downstairs and through the front door without stopping to say goodbye.

The fog had partially lifted by the time I tracked down a computer shop, but the day remained grey and lowering, the damp sky clinging stubbornly to the rooftops. It didn't take long – I knew what I wanted – my eyes glazing as the salesman started to point out all the irrelevant details of the laptop in front of me. Exasperated, I pushed the bank-card towards the dazed man, thanking him and leaving the shop before he could tell me about its superior memory. As long as it was better than mine, I really didn't care.

I took it straight back upstairs to my room, grinding my teeth in frustration every second it took to load, drawing Matthew's scarf around my neck and feeling him closer to me now than I had dared for the last week. Only a vague idea presented itself but, in terms of regaining my sanity, whatever I did must be better than the indeterminate state in which I remained suspended.

Using my mobile to connect the laptop to the internet, a search of his surname brought an overwhelming number of results, none of which looked promising. I thought for a second and then typed in his first name as well. There were innumerable references to "Matthew" and various ones to "Lynes" – some in other languages – but the two names did not occur meaningfully together until the mention of his appointment to the college in Maine issued by the Dean some six years ago. I continued to scroll down until – on the eleventh page – I stopped. On impulse, I clicked a link to a site specializing in archival material – sports memorabilia and its ilk – mostly from the USA. I typed in a search and watched as a photograph of a yellowed newspaper sheet appeared, the foggy picture inserted in the tight type of a previous century. The headline seemed clear enough – "Triumph for Top Team". I smiled at the use of the well-worn alliterative title, then peered at the article more closely, wondering how on earth anybody could be expected to read it. I tapped the "Magnify" icon in one corner, and the page enlarged. I read the caption under the photograph:

Squad celebrate athletic title in record time.

I pulled the cursor over the photograph and right-clicked "Magnify" again… and choked. Behind four other young men and looking as if he didn't want to be there – stood Matthew. A little taller by perhaps an inch or two, his fair hair and distinctive good looks set him apart. Even the sepia photograph aged by time and corroded in quality, could not disguise the attraction that exuded from him, nor extinguish the fire that he set ablaze within me.

"*What on earth…!*" I exclaimed out loud, then breathed deeply to calm my scratchy nerves, and searched for a date on the paper: 1932.

I began to laugh and then found I couldn't stop, hysterical tears blurring the image in front of me. Confused by intermittent sobs and barks of renewed laughter, I wiped my eyes and blew my nose, carefully checking the article, the date and the photograph once more, noting in the text that he had been given an age of twenty-four, and the accolade: "an outstanding sprinter and athlete of our time".

"And the rest," I thought – and *all* the rest. If this was indeed Matthew – and I saw no reason to disbelieve it other than the date – he must be around a hundred years old now.

"Yeah, *right*." I started to describe the boundary of my room in short steps, shaking my head periodically to clear it, like a dog with ear mites. "This is so weird," I said to the mice in the walls to whom I had habitually talked as a child. "Oh, come *on*; he's an anomaly, sure, but a *hundred-year-old* anomaly? Is that rational? Is it *reasonable*?" As usual, the mice remained passive. "Fat lot of good you lot are." A thought struck me. "He's not a ghost, is he?

No – no, he can't be; he's too *alive*. Who are you, Matthew? *What* are you? Come on – talk to me, for goodness' sake – this will drive me insane!"

A rattling on the door made me jump.

"Emma, who are you talking to? Can I come in?" The door-handle turned impotently in my father's impatient hand. "Emma – let me in; *now*."

I minimized the page on the screen, at the same time calling out to him, "I'm fine – hold on a mo, I'm just changing."

I grabbed the big auburn knitted jacket and pulled it over my top, hoping he wouldn't notice the minimal change in attire, and turned the key in the lock. He pushed the door open, and looked around the room as if expecting to find someone else sitting there, then at my face, which burned. He peered suspiciously at me.

"Who were you talking to?"

I picked up my hairbrush and ran it through my hair, hoping the action would lend a semblance of normality.

"Only the mice, Dad – you know – they're great listeners."

He grunted; I had spent many hours in angst-ridden solitary conversation with the mice before leaving home for university, and it was something of a family joke.

"As long as you are all right. Your mother wanted you to know that lunch is ready; we'll expect you in five minutes."

"Great – I'll be down in a moment."

Taken aback by my enthusiasm, he paused before leaving the room, checking it out once more, his thick eyebrows drawn together. My heart galloping, I saved the link as a bookmark and shut the screen of my laptop, before joining him on the stairs.

I ate lunch with them around the family table with more gusto than I had shown for a long time. My mother couldn't disguise her relief.

"Darling, you're looking much better. Did your chat with Mike help at all?"

I thought about our exchange and answered with absolute honesty.

"It was a revelation – thank you so much for inviting him

over." I felt a smile come from nowhere, and she smiled back.

"Are you *sure* you're all right? You seem a little flustered, and Mike did say that the effects of shock can last for some time; 'acute stress', I think he called it." She exchanged glances with my father at the other end of the table.

"Quite sure," I said firmly. "I'm starting work again – you know how it gets under my skin."

"Oh, Emma, that's wonderful." She rose from the table and came over and kissed me on the forehead, her hands around my glowing face. I felt the slow creep of guilt but pushed it away before it could get a hold; she didn't need to know anything that would destroy her happiness at this moment.

"But I might spend an awful lot of time on research; you won't worry, will you?"

"Darling, no, of course not." She seemed genuinely pleased and I hugged her.

Dad still regarded my sudden zeal with caution; he hadn't yet told my mother about my conversation with the mice, and I hoped that he wouldn't feel the need to any time soon. "What are you researching?" he asked.

"The journal."

"Ah, that." He looked both relieved and gloomy at the same time. The journal had been a constant in our family since long before my birth, and he viewed it almost as a rival. I picked up my empty plate and glass.

"Leave that, darling; we'll clear up. You go and get on with your work." Mum took them from me as I began to argue, and pushed me gently towards the door of the room. "Just don't overdo it; you know what you're like. And Mike said you need to rest," she called after me as I disappeared around the curve of the staircase. "He said you're not as strong as you think and that you should…"

But I passed beyond earshot and into another life.